BLEAK SPRING

Jon Cleary, an Australian whose books are read throughout the world, is the author of many novels, including such famous bestsellers as *The Sundowners* and *The High Commissioner*.

Born in 1917, Jon Cleary left school at fifteen to become a commercial artist and film cartoonist – even a laundryman and bushworker. Then his first novel won second prize in Australia's biggest literary contest and launched him on his successful career.

Seven of his books have been filmed, and his novel, *Peter's Pence*, was awarded the American Edgar Allan Poe Prize as the best crime novel of 1974.

Jon Cleary's most recent novels have been *The City of Fading Light, Dragons at the Party, Now and Then, Amen, Babylon South, Murder Song, Pride's Harvest* and *Dark Summer*.

Acclaim for *Bleak Spring*:

'A steadily absorbing plot with some untraditional facets, a clutch of well-drawn characters and a detective who continues to be warm, intelligent and unsmug make *Bleak Spring* one of Cleary's best'   *Kirkus Reviews*

'Mr Cleary is never less than highly readable'
                                        Western Morning News

'Moves swiftly and expertly on to a reasoned conclusion . . . his touch is still firm and expressive'   *Oxford Times*

JON CLEARY

Bleak Spring

HarperCollins*Publishers*

HarperCollins*Publishers*
77–85 Fulham Palace Road,
Hammersmith, London W6 8JB

Special overseas edition 1994
This paperback edition 1994
1 3 5 7 9 8 6 4 2

First published in Great Britain by
HarperCollins*Publishers* 1993

Copyright © Sundowner Publications Pty Ltd 1993

ISBN 0 00 647624 4

Set in Sabon

Printed in Great Britain by
HarperCollinsManufacturing Glasgow

For Vivienne Schuster and Jane Gelfman

Chapter One

1

'An auction is a dangerous place to be,' said Malone. 'There's a terrible risk you'll end up buying something.'

'It's for charity, for heaven's sake,' said Lisa. 'Otherwise, why are we here?'

'Alan Bond started going broke at an auction. He paid millions he couldn't afford for that Van Gogh painting, *Dahlias*.'

'*Irises*,' said Lisa and turned to the Rocknes. 'The last time Scobie put his hand up, he was at school. He wanted to leave the room. Is Will mean with money, Olive?'

Olive Rockne looked at her husband. 'Are you, darling?'

Will Rockne spread his hands, as if he thought that was a philanthropic gesture in itself. 'You'd know that better than I would, love.'

Malone listened with only half an ear to the Rocknes. They were not friends of the Malones nor did he want them to be. He and Lisa had had dinner once at the Rockne home, the result of an unguarded moment of sociability at a meeting of the parents' association of Holy Spirit Convent; he had been bored stiff with Will Rockne and he had asked Lisa not to reciprocate with a return invitation. Tonight, at this arts and crafts festival to raise money for the school, the Rocknes had attached themselves to the Malones like long-time friends.

Malone hated these school affairs; at the same time he wondered if he were growing into a social misfit. He had never been one for parties or a night out with the boys, but at least he had been sociable. Now he found himself more and more reluctant to sound agreeable when Lisa told him there were certain functions they were expected to attend. He knew he was being selfish and did his best to hide the fact, but the other fact was that he had lost almost all his patience with bores. And Will Rockne was a bore.

Holy Spirit was a Catholic school, with the usual school's catholic collection of parents. There was the author who lived on literary grants and was known in the trade as Cary the Grant; there was his wife, who wore fringed shawls summer and winter and made macramé maps of some country she called Terra Australis. There were the tiny jockey and his towering blonde wife who, it was said, had taken out a trainer's licence the day they were married and had been exercising the licence ever since. There were the stockbroker who was being charged with insider trading and his wife who was terrified of becoming a social outsider. And there were the low-income parents, blue-collar and white-collar, whose children were at the school on scholarships and who, to the nuns' and lay staff's credit, were treated as no different. The Malone children's fees were paid by Lisa's parents, a generosity that Malone both resented and was glad of. He was becoming a bad-tempered old bastard in his early middle age.

'Will counts the pennies,' Olive Rockne told Lisa. 'But he does throw the dollars around. Especially with the kids.'

'But not with her, she means.' Rockne gave Malone a man-to-man smile.

Malone had been idly aware all through the evening of something in the air between the Rocknes. He was no expert on marital atmosphere; as a Homicide detective he usually arrived at the scene of a domestic dispute after

8

either the husband or the wife, or both, were dead; whatever had gone before between the couple was only hearsay. There was no visible argument between the Rocknes, but there was a tension that twanged against Malone's ear.

The Rocknes lived half a mile down the road from Holy Spirit and half a mile up from the beach at Coogee. Will Rockne practised as a solicitor, with an office down on the beachfront. Malone had had no dealings with him and had no idea how successful he was; all he knew about the Rocknes was that they had a solid, comfortable home, owned a Volvo and a Honda Civic and were able to send their two children, a boy and a girl, to private schools. He knew that most suburban solicitors did not make the money that partners in the big city law firms did; he also knew that they made more than detective inspectors did, though that didn't disturb him in the least. He was rare in that he was almost incapable of envy.

Will Rockne was capable of it; he was expressing it now: 'Look at that Joe Gulley, will you! The horses he rides have got more brains than he has, yet he makes two or three hundred thousand a year – and that's counting only what he declares! He'd make as much again betting on the nags he rides.'

'Aren't jockeys forbidden to bet?' Malone sounded pious, even in his own ears.

'Are you kidding?'

Rockne had a wet sort of voice, as if the roof of his mouth leaked; whatever he said sounded as if it came out through a mouthful of bubbles. He was as tall as Malone, but much bonier, with a long face that somehow stopped short of being good-looking, even though none of his features was misplaced or unshapely. His casual clothes were always the sort with the designer logo prominently displayed; Malone was sometimes tempted to ask him if

9

he was sponsored, but Rockne had little sense of humour. He was the sort of man who physically made no lasting impression, the face in the crowd that was always just a blur. As if to compensate he waved opinions like flags, was as dogmatic as St Paul, though, being a lawyer, he always left room for hedging. Right now he was being dogmatic:

'If you knew what I know about the racing game . . .'

'Tell them, darling.' His wife was sweetly, too sweetly, encouraging.

Olive Rockne was small and blonde, a girlish woman who, as Lisa had said, looked as if she were trying to catch up with her birthdays. She was in her late thirties, but in a poor light might have passed for eighteen. She always wore frilly clothes, giving the impression that she was on her way to or from a party. On the one occasion the Malones had gone to her home for dinner she had played old LPs of the Grateful Dead and Pink Floyd; which, though it dated her, made her more contemporary than Malone, who still listened to Benny Goodman. She was intelligent and even shrewd, Malone guessed, but she hid her light under the bushel of her husband's opinions. Though not this evening: tonight she was showing some signs of independence, though Rockne himself seemed unaware of it.

'It just bugs me,' Rockne said, 'that people with no education can make so much money. Some of us sweat our guts out studying . . . I've got a rock band as clients, they can't say "G'day" without saying "y'know" before and after it, and they make five times the money I do – *each* of them. When you arrest crims, Scobie, don't you resent those of them who make more money than you do?'

'I don't know why,' said Malone, 'but in Homicide we rarely get to bring in rich murderers, really rich. If money is involved, it's usually the victims who have it.'

The four of them were sitting at a table, apart from the makeshift stalls in the school assembly hall. They were sipping cask wine from plastic cups and munching on potato crisps; Malone mused that if the Last Supper had been staged at Holy Spirit it would have been a pretty frugal affair. He was thirsty, but the cask wine was doing nothing for him. He had played tennis this afternoon, four hard sets of doubles, and he was tired and stiff, as he usually was on a Saturday night, and all he wanted to do was go home to bed. He looked up as Claire, his eldest, approached with the Rockne boy.

'Dad,' said Claire, 'are you going to bid in the auction?'

Malone shut his eyes in pain and Lisa said, 'Don't spoil his night. Do you want us to bid for something?'

'There's a macramé portrait of Madonna –'

Malone opened his eyes. 'Are you into holy pictures now?'

'Don't be dumb, Dad. *Madonna.*'

'Oh, the underwear salesgirl.' He looked at Olive Rockne. 'That's the sort of taste they teach here at Holy Spirit. I'll tell you what, Claire, if they put your English teacher, what's-her-name, the one with red hair and the legs, if they put her up for auction, I'll bid for her.'

Lisa hit him without looking at him, a wifely trick. 'I'll bid for the portrait, Claire.'

'Are you going to bid for anything?' Jason Rockne looked at his parents. He was taller than his father, at least six foot four, even though he was still only seventeen, bonily handsome and with flesh and muscle still to grow on his broad-shouldered frame. He had a sober air, as if he had already seen the years ahead and he was not impressed.

'We're looking at a painting,' said his father. 'Your mother doesn't like it, but I think we'll bid for it.'

'That makes up my mind for me,' said Olive and gave everyone a smile to show she was sweet-tempered about being put down by her husband.

Claire and Jason went back across the room; Malone leaned close to Lisa and said, 'Why's she holding his hand?'

'She's escorting him across the traffic. What's the matter with you? She's fifteen years old and she's discovered boys. I was having my hand held when I was eight. She's backward.'

Malone had no hard feelings towards any boy who wanted to hold hands with his daughter, though he was having difficulty in accepting that Claire was now old enough to want to do more than just hold hands. He did not, however, want relations with the Rocknes cemented because their son was going out with his daughter.

The macramé portrait of Madonna was bought by the jockey's wife. 'What is she going to do with it?' said Olive. 'Use it as a horse rug?'

'Maybe she's going to wrap her husband in it,' said Malone and was annoyed when Rockne let out a hee-haw of a laugh.

The evening wound down quickly after the auction and Malone, eager to escape, grabbed Lisa's hand and told the Rocknes they had to be going – 'I'm on call, in case something turns up.'

'You get many murders Saturday night?' said Rockne.

'More than other nights. Party night, grogging-on night – murders happen. Most of them unpremeditated.'

'Let's hope you have a quiet night,' said Olive. 'We'll be in touch when we get back.'

'Where are you going?' said Lisa.

'Oh, we're having seven days up on the Reef. A second honeymoon, right, darling?'

'Twenty years married next week,' said Rockne. 'That's

record-breaking, these days. She's paying — I paid the first time.' He winked at Malone, who did his best to look amused.

'Have a good time,' said Lisa, and Malone dragged her away before she committed them to a future meeting.

Mother Brendan, the principal, stood at the front door of the assembly hall, small but formidable, her place already booked in Heaven, where she expected to be treated with proper respect by those who ran admissions. 'Enjoy yourselves, Mr and Mrs Malone?'

Straight-faced, Lisa said, 'My husband in particular, Mother.'

'I didn't see you raising your hand for anything in the auction, Mr Malone.'

'I have a sore shoulder.'

'Both of them,' said Lisa. 'Have you seen Claire?'

'She's out there on the front steps with the Rockne boy. I've been keeping an eye on them.'

'Thanks, Mother,' said Malone. 'If ever you'd like to work undercover for the Police Department, let me know.'

Mother Brendan looked at Lisa. 'Is he a joker?'

'All the time. Goodnight, Mother. I hope the school made lots of money this evening.'

'No thanks to men with sore shoulders. I'll pray for your recovery, Mr Malone.'

The Malones went out, collecting Claire from the front steps, where she stood holding hands (*both* hands, Malone noted) with Jason Rockne. 'I'll see you tomorrow, Jay. Call me about ten, okay?'

Jason, sober-faced, said goodnight to the Malones and turned back into the assembly hall.

'He's a bucket of fun, isn't he?' said Malone.

'He's *nice*,' said Claire.

Malone took the car down the slope of the school's driveway, came out opposite Randwick police station, where he had begun his first tour of duty twenty-four years ago, apprehensive and unsure of himself, still to learn that the scales of justice rarely tilted according to the laws of physics. He turned left and headed for home.

'What's happening tomorrow?' Lisa said over her shoulder to Claire.

'Jason wants me to meet him down on the beach.'

'The water's going to be too cold,' said Malone. 'I once went swimming the first week in September — '

He stopped and Lisa said, 'Yes?'

'Nothing.' You didn't tell your fifteen-year-old daughter about having your balls frozen to the size of peas.

'I'm not even *thinking* of going in the water. You don't go to the beach just to *swim*.'

'Do you like Jason?' said Lisa.

'Come on, Mum, don't get that tone of voice. I'm not *serious* about him. He's nice . . .'

'You said that. But?'

'I dunno. He's *nice, but* . . . He's always holding something back, you don't know what. Like Dad.'

'I'm an open book.'

'You are to me.' Lisa patted his shoulder. 'But you're not to everyone. I know what Claire means. Jason's not weird, is he?'

'Oh Mum, no! Nothing like that. He's just — well, I think it would take *ages* to know him.'

'Does he like his parents?' Malone kept his eyes on the road, threw the question casually over his shoulder.

'Funny — ' Claire had been leaning forward against her seat-belt, but now she sat back. She was twisting her blonde hair into a curl, a habit of hers when she was studying or thinking hard. 'He won't talk about them, either of them.'

'Well, take your time with him,' said Lisa.

14

'Would you rather I didn't see him? You don't like his parents, do you?'

'Not particularly,' said Malone, getting in first. 'But how did you guess?'

'You had your policeman's look.' He glanced in the driving mirror and in the lights of a passing car saw her turn her young, beautiful face into a stiff mask. Crumbs, he thought, is that how my kids sometimes see me? A policeman's face, whatever that was? But he wasn't game to ask her.

They reached home, the Federation house in north Randwick with its gables and turn-of-the-century solidness. By the time he had put the Commodore away, Claire was in the bathroom on her way to bed and Lisa was in the kitchen preparing tea and toast. Tom and Maureen, the other children, were staying the night with Lisa's parents at Vaucluse.

Malone sipped his tea. 'Where did they get that wine we had tonight? Was it left over from the marriage at Cana?'

'You didn't have to drink it.' Lisa spread some of her home-made marmalade on toast.

'There was nothing else except watered-down orange juice. No wonder the Vatican is so rich. Who picks up Tom and Maureen tomorrow? You or me?'

'You. I'm baking cakes all day, for the freezer. It's Tom's birthday next Saturday or had you forgotten?'

'No.' But he had. He stood up, stretched his arms high. 'Look, I can raise my hand!'

'A miracle. What a pity an auctioneer isn't here to see it.' She raised her face and he leaned down and kissed her. 'Why can't all wives love their husbands like I love mine?'

'Meaning who?'

'Meaning Olive. But who could love Will anyway?'

An hour later they were sound asleep in the queen-sized

15

bed, their limbs entwined like those of loving octopi, when the phone rang. Malone switched on the bedside lamp. His first thought was that it was Jan or Elisabeth Pretorious calling to say that something had happened to Maureen or Tom. He could forget birthdays but he could never forget how protective he was of his children.

'Inspector Malone? Scobie, it's Phil Truach – I'm the duty bunny tonight. There's a homicide out at Maroubra, in the parking lot of the surf club. We've just had a phone call from the locals at Maroubra.'

'Who else is on call?'

'You and Russ. There've been three other homicides today and tonight, everyone else is out on those. I can round up Andy Graham, but he's not on call this weekend – '

'Never mind, I'll take it. Leave Russ alone.'

He rolled reluctantly out of bed, looked over his shoulder at Lisa, now wide awake. She said, 'Why can't people keep their murders between Monday and Friday?'

He leaned across and kissed her. 'I'll be back as soon as I can. Keep this space vacant.'

2

As soon as he saw the silver Volvo Malone knew it was the Rocknes', even though he could not remember seeing it more than two or three times before. The Celt in him never let him deny intuition; it was never admissible in court, but he knew from experience that it had started many a trail to justice. He got out of his Commodore and walked across the well-lit car park. A wind was blowing from the south-west, but it had been a long dry winter and the wind held no promise of rain. Even the salt air smelt dry.

'It's a couple named Rockne.' The detective in charge from Maroubra was Carl Ellsworth, a good-looking red-head who smiled without showing his teeth, as if he found no humour in what people did to each other.

'Both of them, or just the wife?'

Ellsworth looked at him curiously. 'Why the wife? It's the husband who's dead, shot in the face. A real mess.'

Why had he expected Olive Rockne to be the victim? And why did he feel no shock that something terrible had happened to the Rocknes out here on this windswept car park four or five miles from their home? 'Where's Mrs Rockne? I'd better explain. I know them, we saw them tonight at our kids' school.'

'She's over in the caretaker's office at the surf club. She's pretty shocked.'

'You questioned her yet?'

'Not yet, other than the basics. What happened, that sorta thing. I thought we'd give her time to get her nerves together.'

The Physical Evidence team had arrived and the crime scene had been cordoned off by blue and white tapes. There were still forty or fifty cars parked in the big lot despite the late hour, the overflow from the car park of the big social club across the road, where the usual Saturday night dance and entertainment had finished half an hour ago. People stood about in groups, the night's revelry oozing out of them like air out of a pinpricked balloon. From the darkness beyond the surf club there came the dull boom of the waves, a barrage that threw up no frightening glare.

As Malone and Ellsworth walked across towards the surf club, the younger man said, 'We haven't dug up a witness yet. If anyone saw what happened, they haven't come forward.'

Malone paused and looked around. 'I used to come here

17

when I was younger, to surf. At night, too. They used to hold dances at the surf club in those days. You'd take a girl outside, along the beach or out here in one of the cars . . . Don't the kids today go in for nooky in the back seat or out in the sandhills?'

Ellsworth's grin showed no teeth. 'Not tonight, evidently. I think the girls object to getting sand in it.'

The surf club's pavilion stretched across the eastern end of the car park, separating it from the beach. It was built in the newly popular Australian style, with curved corrugated-iron roofs over its two wings and a similar roof, like an arch, over the breezeway that separated the two wings. Atop one of the wings was a look-out tower, glass-enclosed, a major improvement on the wooden ladder stuck in the sands of Malone's youth.

The caretaker's small office smelt of salt air and wet sand, even though its door faced away from the sea. Its corners were cluttered with cleaning equipment; a wet-suit hung like a black suicide from a hook on one wall; the other walls were papered with posters on how to save lives in every situation from drowning to snakebite. There was none on what to do in the case of a gunshot wound.

Olive Rockne sat stiffly on a stiff-backed chair, spine straight, knees together, hands tightly clasped; if she was in shock, she was decorously so, not like some Malone had seen. 'You all right, Olive?'

She looked at him as if she did not recognize him; then she blinked, wet her lips and nodded. 'I can't believe it's happened . . . Are you here as a friend or a detective?'

'Both, I guess.' It was a question he had never been asked before. 'You feel up to telling me what happened?'

'I've already told him.' She nodded at Ellsworth, who stood against a wall, the wet-suit hanging in a macabre fashion behind him.

18

'I know, Olive. But I'm in charge now and I like to do things my way.'

He sat down opposite her, behind the caretaker's desk. There was a scrawl pad on the desk; scrawled on it in rough script was: *Monday — Sack Jack*. He didn't know where the caretaker was nor was he interested; the fewer bystanders at an interview like this the better. There were just himself, Ellsworth and the uniformed constable standing outside the open door. Olive Rockne was entitled to as much privacy as he could give her.

'What happened?'

Olive was regaining her composure, reefing it in inch by inch; only the raised knuckles of her tightly clenched hands showed the effort. 'I got out of the car — '

'First, Olive — why were you out here?'

She frowned, as if she didn't quite understand the reason herself: 'Sentiment. Does that sound silly or stupid?'

'No, not if you explain it.'

'It was out here on the beach that Will — ' her voice choked for a moment ' — that he proposed to me. When we came out of the school, he suggested we drive out here before going home. We were going to go for a walk along the beach.'

'Where were you when Will was shot?'

She took her time, trying to get everything straight in her mind: 'I don't know — maybe twenty or thirty yards from the car, I'm not sure. I got out and so did Will. But then he went back — he'd forgotten to turn the lights off. Then I heard the shot — '

'Were the lights still on when you heard the shot?'

'No.'

'Did you see anyone running away from the car? That car park out there is pretty well lit.'

'I don't know, I'm not sure . . .' She was reliving the first

19

moments of her husband's death; Malone knew they were always the hardest to erase, whether the death was gentle or violent. 'I think I saw a shadow, but I can't be sure. There were other cars between me and ours . . . Then I got to the car and saw Will . . . I screamed – '

She shuddered, opened her mouth as if she were about to vomit, and Malone said, 'Take it easy for a while. Would you like a cup of tea or something?' An electric kettle and some cups and saucers stood on a narrow table against a wall. 'It might help.'

'No.' She shook her head determinedly. 'All I want to do is go home, Scobie. There are Jason and Shelley – '

'Where was Jason? Did you drop him off at home?'

'No, he'd already gone by the time we left the school – he said he'd walk. I should go home, tell 'em what's happened – Oh, my God!' She put a hand to her eyes, hit by the enormity of what she had to do.

'We'd better get in touch with someone to look after them. What about your parents?'

'There's just my mother. And I have a married sister – she lives at Cronulla. Her name's Rose Cadogan – ' She gave a phone number without having to search her memory for it. Malone noticed that she was having alternate moments of calm control and nervous tension; but that was not unusual. It had struck him on their first meeting some months ago that there was a certain preciseness to her; and habit, whether acquired or natural, was hard to lose.

'What about Will's family?'

'Just his father, he lives out at Carlingford with Will's stepmother. I suppose we'd better call him.'

She sounded callous, but Malone kept his reaction to himself. Out of the corner of his eye he saw Ellsworth purse his lips, making him suddenly look prim. 'Didn't Will and his father get on?'

'They haven't spoken for, I dunno, three or four years. His father is George Rockne. You *know* – '

'The ex-communist union boss?'

'Ex-union boss. He's still a communist.'

'Will was so – *right-wing*. Was that why they didn't get on?'

She nodded. 'I'll ring him. May I go?' She stood up, wavered a moment, then was steady.

Malone looked at Ellsworth. 'Do you have a woman PC?'

'Constable Rojeski is outside somewhere. She can take Mrs Rockne home.'

Malone took Olive's arm as they went out of the caretaker's office. 'I'll have to come and see you tomorrow morning.'

She looked sideways at him; she looked her age now, she had caught up with her birthdays, gone past them. 'This is just the start, isn't it?'

'The start of the investigation? Yes.'

'No, I didn't mean that.' But she didn't explain what she had meant.

She left him, let herself be led away by the young policewoman. 'What's Rojeski like?' he asked Ellsworth. 'Can she handle something like this?'

'She's okay, sir. I've used her a coupla times before in a situation like this. Females come in handy.'

'Yes, don't they?' But Ellsworth missed the dry note. 'Let's see if Physical Evidence have come up with anything.'

The car park now was as busy as a shopping mall on Thursday night. It was bathed in light, police cars stood about, blue and red lights spinning on their roofs; revellers from the social club across the road were collecting their cars, and knots of spectators, those ubiquitous watchers-on-the-fringe that appear at the scene of every urban crime, as if called up by computer, were in place. The silver Volvo stood roped off by blue and white tape like the latest model at a motor show.

Romy Keller, the government medical officer, was examining the body, still in the car, when Malone approached. She straightened up and turned round, her dark coat swinging open to reveal a low-cut green dinner dress underneath.

'All dressed up?'

She drew the coat around her. 'Russ and I were at a medical dinner. I'm on call.'

'Like me. Where's Russ?'

'Over there in his car. He didn't get out, he's in black tie. He thought one of us in fancy dress was enough . . . It looks like just the one shot, through the right eye and out the top of the cranium. Death would have been instantaneous, I'd say.'

He looked past her at the dead Will Rockne. The body was slumped backwards and sideways, one hand in its lap, the other resting on the dislodged car phone, as if he had made a last desperate call for help, from God knew whom. The car keys were in the ignition and the steering wheel was twisted to the left, as if Rockne might have tried to drive away before he died. The dead man's face and the front of his shirt and jacket were a bloody mess.

'We've got the bullet, Inspector.' That was Chris Gooch, of the Physical Evidence team, a bulky young man with more muscles than he knew what to do with; he was forever strenuously denying he was on steroids, but no one believed him. 'Looks like a Twenty-two. It was in the roof. Looks like the killer shoved the gun upwards at the victim, maybe at his throat, but missed and shot him in the eye.'

'You done with the body?' Malone asked Romy.

She nodded towards the government contractors who had now arrived. 'They can take it away.'

22

She drew the high collar of her coat up round her throat against the wind; her dark hair ruffled about her face. She looked glamorous, ice-cool, she whose own father had been a four-times murderer and a suicide. Malone did not understand why she had stayed on as a GMO at the city morgue, but he had never asked Russ Clements if *he* knew the reason. She still worked with cool efficiency and a detachment that Malone, when he saw it, found troubling. But she was Clements's problem, not his. It was Russ who was in love with her.

He walked across to the green Toyota where Clements, in dinner jacket, black tie unloosened, sat behind the wheel like a moulting king penguin. 'They tell me it's a guy named Rockne. You know someone with that name, don't you?'

'It's the same one. We were with them at Holy Spirit tonight. They've just taken the wife home. Are you on call tomorrow?'

'Yes.' Clements looked at Romy, who had got into the car beside him. 'It looks like he's gunna spoil our Sunday.'

She smiled at him, then at Malone. They were the men who had caught her father, who had been there when he had committed suicide; yet she loved one and almost loved the other. They, and Lisa, were the ones who had reconstructed the floor of her life when everything had fallen apart around her. 'Why don't the three of us open a post office or something? Five days a week and no overtime.'

Clements smiled at her. He had had countless women friends, but Malone had never seen him so openly in love as with Romy. 'With our luck, there'd be a body in the parcel post.'

'I'll see you tomorrow morning,' Malone told him. 'You're on this one with me. Don't bother to come dressed up.'

The Toyota pulled out of the car park and Malone

turned as Ellsworth stepped up beside him. 'Do I work with you on this, sir?'

'I guess so — Carl, isn't it? I'll see Mrs Rockne in the morning, but I'd rather do it on my own. I know her, slightly anyway, and I think she'll talk more freely to me if no one else is there. You do the legwork on what the Crime Scene fellers give you.' He still sometimes slipped into the old name for the Physical Evidence team. In recent years the New South Wales Police Service had undergone so many reorganizations and name changes that some joker had fed it into the police computer system as the AKA Force. 'Mrs Rockne may give us a lead. In the meantime set up a van here, see if anyone comes forward with any information.'

'She's a bit odd, don't you think? Mrs Rockne.'

'Most wives are a bit odd when their husbands get blasted. You married?'

'Divorced.'

'How long were you married?'

'Eighteen months.'

'Not long enough. You'll learn, Carl. About wives, I mean.'

He left Ellsworth and walked across to his car. He leant on the roof, cold as ice under the wind, and looked at the scene, at the silver Volvo at the centre of it. For the next few days, maybe weeks, this was where his attention and effort would be focused. As the officer in charge of Homicide, Regional Crime Squad, South Region, he would be supervising other murders, but this one would be his major concern. On the other side of the world an empire was falling apart; putty-faced old men had attempted to turn the clock back in a last-minute coup, only to find the clock had no works; hundreds of thousands of people were filling the squares of Moscow and Leningrad and Kiev, filling the world's television screens: the century was going out as it had begun, in turmoil. The murder of Will Rockne would not be marked as history, but it had to be witnessed, recorded, and, maybe, solved.

He got into the Commodore and drove towards home, where the effects of history were peripheral.

3

He went to early Mass, dragged there by Claire, who didn't want her day delayed by late church-going. On the way home he told her of Will Rockne's murder – 'Oh no, Dad! Jason's *father*?'

On the way to Mass he had debated with himself when he should tell her; he had put it off because, he had told himself, she was not yet wide awake enough to take in the dreadful news. She took it in now, slumping sideways in the seat. 'Oh God, poor Jay and Shelley!'

'Poor Mrs Rockne.'

'Yes, her too. Are you on the case?' He nodded. 'Can't you let someone else do it? Uncle Russ, for instance?'

'Why?'

'I dunno, it's just – well, you're going to bring it *home* every night.'

'I've never done that before. You know I never discuss a case in front of you kids.'

'I know that. But . . . will you tell me how it's going if I ask you?'

'No.'

She looked at him with Lisa's eyes. 'Does being a Homicide detective wear you down?'

They had pulled up at an intersection; he looked at the red traffic light, a warning sign. But he had to tell her the truth: 'Yes.'

'Then why do you keep on with it?'

25

'I ask myself that at least a dozen times a year.' The light turned green. 'I think it's because I feel I'd be deserting the victim if I walked away from it. Do you understand that?'

'Of course,' she said, and he realized his elder daughter had grown up, almost.

When he reached home Lisa was up, getting ready to go over and collect Tom and Maureen. Claire went out to make breakfast for herself and her father, while Malone leaned in the bedroom door and watched his wife dress. After seventeen years of marriage he still got delight watching her first thing in the morning, it was the proper start to a day. She still had her figure, a little fuller now than when they had first married, and, as with some women, the beauty of her face had increased as she had got older. She was forty now and he hoped her beauty would last till the grave, an end that didn't bear thinking about. For her, not for himself: he was not afraid of death, though he would not welcome it, not if it meant leaving her and the children alone.

'I wonder if Will Rockne looked at Olive every morning like I look at you?'

'I doubt it.' She pulled on her skirt, a tan twill. 'He wasn't the sort to appreciate what he had.'

She had been shocked when he came home last night and told her who had been murdered. But this morning she seemed to have accepted the fact. A certain callousness was necessary for a Homicide detective, but he hoped none of his was beginning to rub off on her.

She slipped a yellow sweater over her head, then fluffed out her blonde hair. 'Do you think I should call Olive?'

'No, I'll do the sympathy bit for both of us. Tell Claire not to call Jason, not till I've got the police bit sorted out down at their place. I'll be home for lunch, I hope.'

She came round the bed and kissed him. 'Don't be too hard on Olive.'

'Why should I be?'

It was 9.30 when he knocked on the door of the Rockne home in Coogee Bay Road. It was a solid bluebrick and sandstone house, built with the wide verandahs of the nineteen-twenties, when sunlight in a house was as welcome as white ants. It stood on a wide block, thirty metres at least, behind a garden where early spring petunias, marigolds and azaleas mocked the gloom he knew must be in the house itself.

The door was opened by a middle-aged woman instantly recognizable as Olive's sister, though she was plumper and had kept pace with her birthdays. 'I'm Rose Cadogan. We've been expecting you.' She looked past him, seemed surprised. 'You're on your own?'

'I thought Olive would prefer it that way.'

'Oh, sure. Come in. But what one sees on TV, police are always swarming over everything . . . This is our mother, Mrs Carss. And this is Angela Bodalle, a friend of Olive's. I'll get Olive, she's with the kids. They're taking it pretty bad.'

'We all are,' said the mother, the mould from which her daughters had been struck. Ruby Carss was in her sixties, had henna hair worn thin by too much dye and too many perms, was thin and full of nervous energy and looked as if she had suddenly been faced with the prospect of her own death.

Malone sat down, looked at Angela Bodalle. 'I didn't expect to see you, Mrs Bodalle.'

'I'm here as a friend of the family, Inspector, that's all.'

She was, Malone thought, the most decorative, if not the best-looking, of the barristers who fronted the Bar in the State's courts. There were only five female silks in New South Wales and she was the most successful of them. She was in her late thirties or early forties, he guessed, a widow whose husband had already made his name as a Queen's

Counsel when he had been killed in a car accident some years ago. She had then gone to the Bar herself and last year had been named a QC. She specialized in criminal cases and had already gained a reputation for a certain flamboyance. The joke was that she wore designer wigs and gowns in court, her arguments were as florid as the roses that decorated her chambers, she castrated hostile witnesses with sarcasm sharper than a scalpel. Even the more misogynistic judges tolerated her as she stirred blood in desiccated loins.

'Do you want to sit in while I talk to Mrs Rockne?'

'We all do,' said Mrs Carss, settling herself for a long stay.

Malone looked at her. 'I think it'd be better if you didn't. I'm going to have to ask her to run through everything that happened last night.'

'Then she'll want us to be there, to support her –'

'I think what Inspector Malone is suggesting is best,' said Angela Bodalle.

'Everyone's taking over – ' Mrs Carss was resentful, outsiders were taking away her role as mother.

Olive Rockne came into the room with her sister. She was dressed in a light blue sweater and dark blue slacks; the frilly look had gone, she was fined down, this morning the girlish woman had vanished. Her hair was pulled back by a black velvet band and her face was devoid of make-up. Malone wondered if, for the first time, he was about to see the real Olive Rockne.

'Let's go outside,' she said in a calm firm voice and led him and Angela Bodalle out to a glassed-in back verandah that had been converted into a pleasant garden room. It looked out on a pool in a garden bright with camellias and azaleas. The room was carpeted and furnished with cushioned cane furniture; the whole house, Malone had noted with his quick eye for furnishings, was comfortable. But

28

there was little, if any, comfort in this house this morning.

Rose Cadogan brought coffee and biscuits. 'I'll leave you alone,' she said with more diplomacy than her mother had shown and went back to the front of the house.

'Olive, I won't go over what you told me last night,' said Malone, taking the coffee Angela Bodalle had poured for him. 'But I'd like you to tell me – did Will have time to argue with whoever shot him?'

Olive, refusing coffee, said, 'I don't think so. It was all so *quick*.'

'I'm trying to establish if it was someone attempting a robbery, shoving the gun at Will and demanding money and then panicking when Will tried to push him away. Was there time for that?'

Olive looked at Angela, who sat down on the cane couch beside her, then she looked back at Malone. 'No, I'm sure there wasn't. I – '

'Yes?'

'I – I've been wondering – could he have been waiting for someone else, he made a mistake and shot Will instead?'

'He could have been. But yours was the only silver Volvo in the car park. There might've been other Volvos, but yours was the only silver one.'

'Then who could it have been?' said Angela. 'Some psychopath, out to kill *anyone*, the first person who presented himself? There seems to be a plague of them at the moment.'

Malone nodded, but made no comment. Yesterday afternoon, out at Haberfield, an armed robber, holding up a liquor store, had paused, unprovoked, to put his gun at the head of a customer lying as commanded on the floor and had blown his brains out. The previous Saturday a man had run amok in Strathfield, a middle-class suburb, with a semi-automatic rifle and killed seven people in a

29

shopping mall before shooting himself. All the past week the air had been thick with the clamour for stricter gun laws, a demand Malone totally supported, but the politicians, more afraid of losing votes in the rural electorates than of being hit by a bullet in the cities (who would waste bullets on a politician?) were shilly-shallying about what should be done. The incidence of killing by guns in Australia was infinitesimal compared with that in the United States, but that was like saying a house siege was not a war. Someone still died, one life was no less valuable than a hundred.

'Olive, had Will received any threats from anyone? A client or someone?'

'I don't think so. He would have told me — well, maybe not. He didn't tell me much about his practice, what he did, who he acted for.'

'Did he ever refer any clients to you?' Malone looked at Angela Bodalle.

'A couple. One civil suit, I took that as a favour to him, and a criminal charge.'

Malone waited and, when she did not go on, said, 'A murder charge?'

'It was an assault with intent, a guy named Kelpie Dunne.' She seemed to give the name with some reluctance. 'I got him off.'

'I remember him. He tried to kill a security guard down at Randwick racecourse. He's a bad bugger. Some day he's going to kill a cop. I hope you won't try to get him off then.'

Her gaze was steady. She was not strictly beautiful, her face was too broad to have classical lines, the jaw too square, but the eyes, large and almost black, would always hold a man, would turn him inside out if he were not careful. She raised a hand, large for a woman's but elegant, and pushed back a loose strand of her thick dark brown hair. Malone felt that, with that look, she would make an imposing, if biased, judge. If ever she made it to the Bench, he was sure her sentences on the convicted would be more than just slaps on the wrist.

'If I believe a client is innocent, I'll always try to get him off.'

'Did Will have any other clients like Kelpie? Innocent but violent?'

Angela smiled: she didn't think much of men's wit; or anyway, policemen's. 'I wouldn't know, Inspector. Will hadn't passed a client on to me for, oh, twelve months or more.'

Malone turned back to Olive. She had been watching this exchange with wary, almost resentful eyes, as if she felt excluded from what was her own tragedy. 'Olive, Will made a mention last night of what he knew about the racing game. Did he have any clients from the game, jockeys, trainers, bookmakers – people like that?'

'I told you he never mentioned his clients to me.' Her voice had a certain sharpness.

'No, but you did say last night – as I remember it, Will said, if I knew, meaning me, what he knew about the racing game, and you said, Tell them, darling, or something like that . . .'

'You have a good memory.'

He hadn't expected to be complimented, not at a time like this. 'You learn to have one, as a cop. You sounded last night as if you knew something about racing that Will had told you.'

She shook her head; last night the frilly curls would have bounced, but this morning not a hair moved. 'It was nothing, I was just taking the mickey out of him. You know what Will was like, he knew everything about everything.' She said it without malice, but it wasn't something he expected from a grieving widow.

31

'Dad had one client, a bookmaker.' Jason stood in the doorway, all arms and legs and lugubrious expression. But his voice was steady, if the rest of him wasn't.

Malone, seated in a low chair, had to turn and look up at him. From that angle the boy looked even taller than he was: Malone had the incongruous image of a basketballer who didn't know where the basket was. 'Did your dad talk about the client with you?'

'No. But I was with Dad one day, about, I dunno, about a month ago, he was taking me to basketball practice — ' So the image wasn't so far off, after all. 'We called in at this bookie's house and when he came out, he was there only about ten minutes, he was ropeable, really angry. He didn't tell me what it was all about, all he said was never trust a bookie.'

'You know who the man was?'

'Sure. It was Bernie Bezrow, he lives up in that weirdo house in Georgia Street. Syphilis Hall.'

'What?'

'That's what we call it, the guys, I mean. Tiflis Hall.'

Angela Bodalle said, 'I don't think you should get involved in this, Jason.'

'Is that legal advice or friendly advice?' said the boy.

'That's enough!' For a moment Malone thought Olive was going to jump up and slap her son's face; but she would have had to jump a fair height. 'Don't talk to Angela like that! She's only trying to help.'

The boy didn't apologize, only looked sullenly at Angela; then abruptly he was gone from the doorway, folding himself out of sight. Olive put out a hand and took Angela's. 'I'm sorry.'

'It's all right, darling.' Angela squeezed the hand in hers, then gave it back to Olive as if it were something that embarrassed her, like a gift of money. 'Inspector, let's cut this short for this morning. Give Olive time to get over

32

what happened last night, then perhaps she'll be able to give you more help.'

Malone stood up. 'Righto, we'll give it a rest for today. But there will have to be more questions, Olive. In the meantime I'd like to go down and have a look through Will's office. Did he have any staff?'

'Just a secretary. She called me this morning, she's terribly upset. Her name's Jill Weigall.'

'Could you get her for me? I'd like to speak to her.'

He followed Olive in to a phone in the front hallway. She dialled a number, introduced him, then handed him the phone. 'Treat her gently.' Then she left him, a little coldly, he thought, as if he had suddenly turned into some sort of enemy.

As soon as he spoke to Jill Weigall he knew that she was a girl on the edge of hysteria. 'I was going to ask you to meet me at Mr Rockne's office – '

'No, no, I'll be all right. I'll meet you there – it's something to do – '

He wondered if she lived alone, but it was none of his business. When he hung up Angela Bodalle was standing beside him. He could smell her perfume, a subtle bouquet, and he wondered why anyone, coming to console a friend on the loss of her husband by murder, would bother to apply perfume. 'If you are thinking of going through Will's files, forget it. You can't get an open warrant. You'll have to name something specific you want.'

'Is that free legal advice?'

She looked at him appraisingly. 'Inspector, are you looking to fight with me? I'd have thought we were both friends of Olive, that we'd be on the same side.'

He backed down; he didn't know why she irritated him. Perhaps it was no more than that she was a lawyer. 'Righto. In the meantime I have to get some helpers . . .'
He called the Maroubra station, spoke to Carl Ellsworth.

'Have you come up with anything since last night?'

'We set up a van near the surf club. We've been trying to trace everyone who had their cars in the car park. There were four hundred people in the social club last night. Not counting the staff and the entertainers.' Ellsworth sounded peeved, as if everyone should have spent Saturday night at home watching television. Preferably *The Bill*, the British series that showed how tough life was for cops. 'Oh, Sergeant Clements is here, he wants to speak to you.'

Good old Russ: on the job, starting at the starting point. 'I think the boys here have got everything under control, Scobie. It's gonna be the usual slog, unless they come up with a witness who saw everything. Where d'you want me to meet you?'

'I'm going down to Rockne's office – ' He turned to Angela Bodalle, who was still shadowing him. 'What's the address?'

She gave it to him. 'I'll come with you.'

Malone gave the address to Clements. 'If Carl Ellsworth has anything for me, bring it with you.'

He hung up, gestured for Angela to go ahead of him and followed her into the living room, where the family was now congregated. It was a large room, but had the narrow windows of the period when the house had been built; Olive had attempted to lighten it with a pale green carpet, green and yellow upholstery on the chairs and couch, and yellow drapes. The only dark note in it this morning was the family. They all looked at him, the intruder, and not for the first time he wondered why the voters bothered to call the police, why they didn't clear up their own messes.

'Will you let me know if you find anything?' Olive sat between Shelley, her thirteen-year-old daughter, and Mrs Carss. The tableau suggested the three ages of a Carss woman: the resemblance between them all was remarkable. They had another common feature: shock.

34

'I'll come with you,' said Jason, unwinding himself like a jeans-clad insect from a chair.

'There's no need,' said his mother. 'Angela has said she'll go down with Mr Malone – '

'Mother – ' The boy was treating his mother almost formally, as if to mask his defiance. 'Now Dad is dead, I'm the man of the house. I better get used to whatever I've gotta do.'

His sister frowned and screwed up her pretty face. 'Oh God, Jay, don't start that Big Brother crap – '

Her grandmother reached across a generation to slap her arm. 'Watch your language, young lady!'

'Let's go, Mr Malone.' The boy spun round and went out of the room.

Malone looked at the assembled women. Rose Cadogan was gathering up the coffee cups to take them out to the kitchen. Malone noticed for the first time how remarkably neat the whole house was; it might be full of emotional debris, but the carpet would be swept, the corners dusted, the cushions plumped up and arranged. He wondered who the housekeeper was, then guessed it could have been any one of Olive, Rose or Mrs Carss. There was a neatness about them that would always be with them, they would *die* neatly if they had anything to do with it.

'For what it's worth, I think Jason is right. He's got to start learning to be the man of the house. Don't worry, Olive, I'll teach him gently.'

He went out of the house, followed by Angela Bodalle and Jason. 'Can I ride with you, Mr Malone?' said the boy, not looking at the lawyer.

She seemed to take no offence; she had built up a defence against all males, from schoolboys to senior judges. She walked away to her car: a red Ferrari, Malone noted.

'I thought you'd have preferred to ride in a car like that,' he said to Jason as they got into the seven-year-old Commodore. 'She wouldn't need to get out of second gear to outrun this bomb.'

'It's not the car. I just don't like flash women.'

'I wish I was as much a connoisseur as you. What do I call you, Jay or Jason?'

'Fred.' A slight grin slipped sideways across the thin, good-looking face. He had thick blond hair which, Malone guessed, would be even fairer in the summer, and the sort of complexion that would always need a thick coating of sunblock to protect it from sun cancers. 'Bloody Jason, I hate it. Call me Jay, I guess. Everybody else does, except my mother and my grandmother. And Dad.'

'How did you get on with him? Did you confide in each other?'

'Is that what fathers and sons are supposed to do?'

'Tom and I do.'

'He's, what, nine years old, Mr Malone. He confides in you, but you don't tell him everything, right?'

This boy, unlike his mother, was years ahead of his birthdays. 'So you and your father didn't talk much, is that it?'

'Not as much as I'd have liked. This is it, next to the milk bar.'

There was council work going on at the northern end of the beach promenade; at long last it seemed that someone had decided to give Coogee a face-lift. Malone had come down here as a boy and youth to surf, but it had never been a popular beach with real off-the-wall surfers. For the big, toe-curling waves you went south, to Maroubra.

He pulled the Commodore into a No Parking zone. Last night's wind had dropped and today promised to be an early, if very early, spring day. Out of the car he paused a moment and looked away from the beach. Over there, in its shallow hollow, was Coogee Oval, where he had begun his cricketing career; but if he closed his eyes, all he would see would be the darkness of his lids, nothing of the small glories of his youth. He doubted that he would ever confide any of those memories to Tom. He had never been a headline hero, even though he had gone on to play for the State. That would make life easier for Tom; he had never regretted that Tom was not the son of a famous father. He wondered what Will Rockne had thought of this gangling boy beside him, what he had tried to protect him from.

A row of shops, their paint worn by the salt air, stood at this northern end, some with offices above them. There had once been an indoor swimming baths on this site; one winter it had been closed to swimmers and used to exhibit a grey nurse shark caught by the local fishermen. The shark had spewed up a tattooed human arm and the resultant murder case had become famous; police had caught the murderers but had also dredged up connections that stank as high as a dead shark. Malone was grateful that the Rockne case promised no such connections.

The Ferrari, exhaust gurgling like an expensive drain, pulled in behind the Commodore and Angela Bodalle got out, exposing a nice length of leg as she did so. Malone, a connoisseur of limbs if not of flash women, remarked that she had very good legs. Some surf kids were standing in a group outside a milk bar and one of them whistled, but he was whistling at the car, not its owner.

Angela looked up at the No Parking sign. 'Do we worry about tickets?'

'You can defend me if we cop any. Who has a key to the office?'

'I do. Olive gave it to me.' She handed it to Jason, as if it were a peace offering.

The boy just nodded, unlocked the door to the flight of stairs that led up to the offices of William A. Rockne, Solicitor. There was a reception room with a secretary's

37

desk and chair; some flowers drooped in a vase on the desk. Four leather-seated chairs lined one wall, fronted by a coffee table neatly stacked with old copies of the *National Geographic* and *Vogue*; there was also a single copy of *Bikies' Bulletin*, but that could have been left by a client who had departed in a hurry, presumably on a Harley-Davidson or a Kawasaki. The inner office was larger than Malone had expected, with a bank of steel filing cabinets along one wall, an old-fashioned Chubb safe in a corner and a studded leather couch, that looked too expensive for its surroundings, against another wall. Facing the door was a wide leather-topped desk and a green leather chair to match the couch; in front of the desk were two clients' chairs, also in green leather. Will Rockne's degree was framed and hung behind his chair; below it was a wall-length shelf of legal books. The windows on either side of the framed degree looked out on to the beach and the sea, where gulls hung in the air like chips of ice.

'Dad always liked his office,' said Jason. 'He did it up, all new, about six months ago. He never wanted to move from here.'

'Did anyone ever suggest he should?'

'My mother did. I think she wanted him to be in the city. You know, a little more class.' He looked sideways at Angela, who just smiled.

'Did he rent this office or did he own it?'

'He rented it,' said Jason. 'I dunno who from. Jill will be able to tell you that.'

Jill Weigall and Russ Clements arrived together. Malone introduced Clements, then looked at the secretary. She was young, perhaps twenty or twenty-one, her attractive face smeared this morning with shock. She came in ahead of Clements, stood for a moment looking lost, like a girl on her first morning in a new office; or her last. Clements had paused behind her, waiting for her to find herself.

'I'm still trying to make myself believe this – ' She spoke to Jason rather than to the two detectives and Angela Bodalle. She had a light, flutey voice that threatened to crack at any moment, a schoolgirl's voice. Then she made a visible effort to settle herself; she sat down behind her desk as if ready for business. She looked up at Malone: 'Yes?'

Malone had to restrain himself from smiling; instead he admired the girl's attempt to fit herself back into what he guessed was her usual efficient self. 'First, we're checking if Mr Rockne ever received any threats here at the office. Did he?'

She shook her head. Her dark hair was cut short in what Malone, always a decade or more behind in fashion, somehow thought of as the French style; the front of it fell down over her forehead and she pushed it back. More settled now, the shock absorbed, her looks had improved; it struck Malone that she was a very attractive girl. 'Mr Rockne didn't have the sort of clients that would *threaten* him.'

'Did he handle Family Court cases?' He knew of solicitors and judges who had been threatened by men, most of them immigrants from male-dominated societies, who had blamed the law and its practitioners for taking away their wives from them. In Homicide's computer there was still the unsolved murder of a judge's wife who had been killed by a bomb.

'Of course. But we never had any trouble with any of them.'

'It's not as bad as it used to be,' said Angela Bodalle. 'The men seem to be learning.' She made it sound as if all men, not just the immigrants, had been taking lessons.

'I'm glad to hear it,' said Malone. 'Righto, Miss Weigall. Mrs Bodalle tells me, quite rightly, that we can't touch

39

the files. But maybe we can open the safe?' He looked enquiringly at Angela, who shrugged, then nodded.

'I can't do that, Inspector. Mr Rockne always kept the key himself.'

Malone raised an eyebrow. 'How long have you worked for him, Jill?'

'Two years.'

'And he never trusted you to open the safe?' Out of the side of his eye he saw Jason frown resentfully. Whatever the boy's relationship with his father, he obviously didn't want him criticized.

Jill Weigall, too, didn't like the implied criticism. 'It wasn't that he didn't trust me. It was just, well . . .' But her voice trailed off.

'Scobie – ' Clements had been silent up till now, his bulk against the closed front door of the office. He took a plastic envelope out of his pocket. He was in sports jacket, slacks and a rollneck cotton sweater this morning and looked his usual rumpled self, nothing like the dude he must have looked at last night's medical dinner. Malone wondered what he would have talked about with the diner on the opposite side of him from Romy: the relative effects of a bullet or a blunt instrument on one's health? 'They cleaned out Mr Rockne's pockets last night, Maroubra asked me to bring them back to Mrs Rockne. There's a key-ring – '

He held up a key-ring with five keys on it and Jill Weigall said, 'It's that big one. He always carried it with him.'

Malone took the key, held it out in front of Jason. 'You're the family rep, Jay. I'm going to open the safe, okay?'

'Go ahead, Mr Malone.' The boy was building blocks of maturity by the minute.

'Okay, Mrs Bodalle?'

'Let's see what's in the safe first. If there are any clients' confidential files in there, I'll have to advise you against looking at them.'

Malone went into the inner office, unlocked the safe and swung back its heavy door. It was stuffed with papers: files, wills in envelopes, legal documents tied with ribbons, a cash box and a flat metal box, the sort that Malone had seen in bank and hotel safety-deposit vaults. The keys to both boxes were lying on the shelf beside them.

Again he looked at Jason. 'Okay to open the boxes?'

For a moment the boy looked uncertain; he glanced at Angela. 'Is it okay, Mrs Bodalle?'

'You're on thin ice, Mr Malone, but so far I think you might be able to convince a judge that you haven't invaded any client's privacy.'

Malone opened both boxes. The cash box was stuffed with money, all one-hundred-dollar notes. He handed the box to Clements. 'Count it, Russ.' He saw the expression on Jill Weigall's face. 'You're surprised to see so much?'

'I had no idea – ' She shook her head in wonder, the hair fell down, she pushed it back again. 'During office hours that cash box was out in my desk. We never carried more than a hundred dollars, maybe a bit more, in it. And stamps, things like that.'

'There's ten thousand here.' Clements's big fingers had handled the notes like those of a flash bank teller; but then he had served time on the Fraud Squad. 'All of them brand-new and genuine.'

'Shit,' said Jason bitterly, 'did you expect my dad to be into forgery or something?'

Clements gave the boy a look like a back-hander, but Malone got in before the big man could say anything: 'No, we're not thinking that, Jay. Relax. At the moment all we're intent on is finding out who shot him.'

'Sorry.' The boy stood awkwardly in the inner doorway,

41

shifting from one foot to the other. He looked suddenly afraid, as if he had just realized that doors were going to be opened that might best be left shut.

Jill Weigall stood up, took his arm. 'Come on, Jay, let's make some coffee. We need it, I think.'

The two of them went into the outer office and Malone sat down in Rockne's leather chair and looked at Clements and Angela Bodalle. 'The money could mean nothing, he could've been holding it for a client. What's your opinion on that, Mrs Bodalle?'

'Could be. Before I went to the Bar, when I was a solicitor, I'd hold money for clients. But never as much as that, not in actual cash. Solicitors hold money for clients all the time, but usually in trust accounts.' She was sitting in one of the chairs across the desk from Malone, her legs crossed, showing a lovely curve of instep. She was wearing a pink wool dress that moulded her figure; a navy-blue cardigan with brass buttons was thrown over her shoulders. It was early in the day, but she looked as if she was already dressed for lunch. 'Are you going to open the other box?'

'You're the witness. If it's clients' stuff, I won't touch it.'

There were no clients' papers: just Will Rockne's passport, a bank statement, a chequebook and a small flat gun. 'A Beretta Twenty-two. A lady's special.'

'I must remember that,' said the lady opposite.

'Very effective at close range,' said Clements. 'We had a woman do her husband in with one of those about six months ago.'

'Is that supposed to mean something?' She looked up at Clements, her gaze as sharp as a knife.

'No,' said Clements blandly. 'Nothing at all.'

Malone sniffed the barrel of the gun. 'I doubt if it's ever been fired. We'll ask Jill about it.'

Then he looked at the chequebook. It was for a joint

account in the names of William A. Rockne and Olive B. Rockne, held in the Commonwealth Bank, Coogee. The last stub showed a balance of $9478.33, the last amount drawn $5000 in cash. Then he looked at the bank statement, which was in Rockne's name only.

'What would you think of a suburban solicitor, a one-man band, who has a bank account with five million, two hundred and twenty-one thousand dollars in it?'

'I'd nominate him for Solicitor of the Year,' said Clements and looked around the office. 'This is okay, but it ain't a rich practice, would you say?'

Malone was studying Angela Bodalle's reaction; there had been none. 'You aren't surprised?'

'Yes.' But if she was, she was disguising it well.

'What's the bank?' asked Clements.

'A merchant bank, I'd say — I've never heard of it. The Shahriver Credit International.' He hadn't looked at Clements, but at Angela.

'Are you asking me if I've heard of it? No.'

'Where is it?' said Clements. 'Here in Sydney?'

'Sydney, Hong Kong, Manila, Kuwait — *Kuwait*? They wouldn't be doing much business there right now. Oh, and Beirut. Some nice-smelling places on that letterhead.'

'Remember the days when all banks smelled like roses — or like the Mint?' Clements moved around and sat down next to Angela in the other client's chair. 'Mrs Bodalle, why aren't you surprised to learn that Will Rockne had that much money in a bank?'

It was an old ploy between Malone and Clements: switch the bowling without telling the umpire or the batsman. She looked first at Malone, as if expecting him to put Clements in his place, then she looked at the big man. 'I told you I was surprised.'

Clements shook his head. 'Mrs Bodalle, I think I've spent as much time in court as you have. You've learned

43

how to read reactions. So have I. You weren't surprised.'

'Does it matter whether I was or not?' She was not going to let a mere cop get the better of her in cross-examination. 'Mrs Rockne will be the one who'll be surprised.'

Jill Weigall came in with three cups of coffee on a tray. 'It's only instant. Mr Rockne never drank coffee – he'd become a bit of a fitness freak lately – '

Mr Rockne appeared to have changed quite a bit lately. 'How's Jason?'

'He's okay. He's a very intelligent boy, but I guess that doesn't help much when a situation like this happens, right?'

Malone had seen the stupid and the wise equally devastated by grief; it didn't require much intelligence to remark that. He looked at Angela Bodalle. 'Would you leave us alone with Miss Weigall for a few moments?'

'I think I should remain here – '

'Only if Miss Weigall insists?' He looked at the girl.

She hesitated, then said, 'I'll be okay, Mrs Bodalle. If I need you, I'll – '

Angela stood up abruptly and went out of the room; she did it in such a way that Malone had a mental image of her swirling her barrister's gown as she exited; she left behind a strong smell of her perfume, as if she had generated some sudden heat. Both Clements and Jill Weigall were impressed. The girl said, 'Now I've upset her – '

'Don't worry, Jill. Sit down. Did Mr Rockne hold trust accounts for clients, money held in escrow, stuff like that?'

'Of course. All solicitors do.'

'With what bank?'

'The Commonwealth, the one here in Coogee.'

Not a bank with branches in Kuwait or Beirut. 'What about Shahriver Credit International?'

She shook her head, the hair fell down, was pushed back up again; Malone began to wonder if the gesture was part

44

of the fashion. 'We never did any business with them – wait a minute!' She had thick, unplucked eyebrows; they came down in a frown. 'They called a coupla times. I put them through to Mr Rockne, but then he'd hang up and call them back on his private line. He had that put in about four or five months ago, the private line.'

'Did you think that was strange?'

'Well, yes, a bit. He used to be always so open with me. And then about six months ago, maybe a bit more, he just sort of, well, played things close to his chest. Just with one or two clients.'

'You remember who they are?'

'Inspector, I dunno I should be telling you all this . . .' She glanced towards the still open door. 'I mean, there's client confidentiality – '

'That's true. Do you have a law degree?'

'No, why?'

He kept one eye on the doorway, wondering how much Angela Bodalle could hear in the outer office. 'Well then, there's no client confidentiality, is there? You were Mr Rockne's secretary, not his law partner.' He knew he was drawing a fine line, but the law, after all, was a mass, or mess, of fine lines. He had suffered more than once from judges who had had their own reading of the law. 'We're not here to probe clients' secrets, pry into their affairs. We're just trying to find out if there is something in this office that might lead us to whoever killed Mr Rockne.'

All at once she broke down, leaned forward as if she were about to fall off her chair. Clements leaned across from his own chair and eased her back; the two men waited while she wept silently. Then Jason said from the doorway, 'Leave her alone, Mr Malone. She was in love with my dad. They were having an affair.'

The words had been blurted out. Then suddenly he looked embarrassed and angry at himself; he had opened a door and was hurt by what he had exposed to the police. But it was obvious that he had sympathy for Jill Weigall, that he did not feel she was to blame for the affair. He appeared more puzzled by her than angry at her.

Angela Bodalle appeared in the doorway behind the boy. 'I wouldn't say any more, Jay, not right now.'

Malone ignored her, looked at the girl. 'Jill?'

'It wasn't an *affair* – it was just one weekend – ' She dried her eyes, pushed back the hair that had fallen down over her brow again; it was beginning to annoy Malone and he felt like offering her one of the paperclips on the desk in front of him. 'I knew it was never going to get anywhere – '

He had long ago given up wondering what attraction women felt for certain men. What had this very good-looking girl seen in the opinionated, chauvinistic, bony-faced man twenty years her senior? But no detective, from Homicide or even the Fraud Squad, will ever solve a woman's emotions. He looked up at Jason, still hanging like a bag of bones in the doorway. 'Did your mother know?'

'I don't think you should be asking the boy those sort of questions,' said Angela Bodalle.

'Why not?'

'It's a question you should ask her, not her son.'

'How did *you* know, Jay?' That was Jill, turned questioner.

'Just luck. *Bad* luck.' A sardonic air coated him at odd moments, like something borrowed from an older gener-ation. 'You went to that place at Terrigal, Peppers, and one of my mates from school, he was there with his parents, he saw you and Dad.'

'Did he tell all the school?'

'No. I'd of belted him if he had, he knew that.'

46

'Thank you, Jay.' For a moment she looked as young as he.

Malone nodded to Clements. 'Russ, take Jay and Mrs Bodalle back outside. I want a moment alone with Miss Weigall.'

The girl suddenly looked apprehensive, but it was Angela who caught Malone's attention. 'Are you going to question her, Inspector?'

'Yes.' His voice was sharp; he was growing tired of her interference.

'Would you like me to stay with you, Jill?'

Again the girl hesitated; then again she came down on Malone's side, if reluctantly. 'I'll be okay. I'll call you if Inspector Malone gets too tough with me.'

'You're not going to do that, are you, Inspector?'

Malone's smile was more like a grimace. 'I'm a gentleman, Mrs Bodalle.'

Her smile was wide, one of disbelief; but she went out, closing the door behind her. Then Jill looked at Malone, all at once seeming to gain some confidence. 'What are you expecting me to tell you you didn't want them to hear?'

'It's not that I don't want them to hear, it's that I think you'll talk to me easier if they're not in the room with us. Did *you* kill Will Rockne?'

He hadn't altered his tone, but the question was like a rock thrown at her head; she seemed to duck, then looked up at him from under the fallen hair. 'How can you say something like that? Jesus!' She pushed the hair back, sat up. She looked towards the door, as if she meant to call for Angela Bodalle, then she turned back to Malone. 'No, I didn't! What makes you think I'd want to kill him?'

'Righto, forget I asked. Have you seen that before?' He had put the Beretta in a side drawer of the desk; now he

47

took it out and laid it in front of her.

'No.' She stared at it, her fear genuine. 'Where was it — in the desk?'

'No, in the safe. Did Mr Rockne ever talk about wanting to defend himself?'

'Never.'

'How long ago did you have the af — did you have that weekend with him?'

'Two months ago, the last weekend in June.'

'And what happened? I mean afterwards, when you came back here on the Monday?'

She picked up a paperweight from the desk. It was a brass lion on a marble base; there was a Lions Club emblem on the base. Malone hoped she was not going to throw it at him. 'Nothing happened. That was it — the one weekend, and just *nothing*. I thought I was in love with him, but it only took that weekend to find out I wasn't.'

'What about him?'

She put the paperweight back on the desk. 'He couldn't have cared less. I was just someone who'd given him a good weekend, a bit of young stuff. I don't mean Mrs Rockne is *old*, but you know what I mean. Do we really have to go on with all this?' She said it almost with boredom; she was a mixture of gaucheness and sophistication. But it was disco sophistication, a veneer as skimpy as the clothes they wore to the clubs. 'To tell you the truth, I would've gone looking for another job. Only they're so scarce, the recession and that.'

Malone put the gun in a manila envelope. 'I'm taking the gun with me, okay? Now let's get back to what I asked you before. You said there were one or two clients he kept to himself, played things close to his chest. Who were they?'

She gazed at him a moment, but she appeared to trust

48

him now. 'Mr Bezrow was one, Bernie Bezrow the bookmaker. He was our landlord, too.'

Even Malone, who hadn't the slightest interest in horse-racing, who hadn't known Phar Lap was dead till he'd seen the movie, knew Bernie Bezrow. 'Who was the other one?'

'He just called himself Mr Jones, but I never believed that was his real name. I asked Will about him once and he just smiled and said not to worry my pretty head about it. He actually said that, *my pretty head*. He could be bloody annoying at times.' She was beginning to sound as if she was not regretting Rockne's death after all. 'Mr Jones came here twice, I think. He was tall and well-dressed and, I suppose, not bad-looking. He had an accent, but I couldn't tell you what it was.'

'Was he dark? Fair? Bald?'

'He had dark hair, but I think it was thin on top. I remember thinking, I dunno why, he was like an expensive car salesman, you know, Rolls-Royces, cars like that.'

'I've never been in a Rolls-Royce saleroom.'

Somehow she managed a weak smile. 'Neither have I. But you know what I mean.'

'What about Mr Bezrow?'

'Oh, he never came up here to the office, he couldn't get up the stairs. He's so fat – he's *huge*. He came here once in his car, *he* has a Rolls-Royce, he had someone driving it, and I had to go downstairs and give him an envelope. Will wasn't here.'

'Are there any letters to him in the files?'

'None. That's what I meant by Will playing things close to his chest.'

'You didn't suspect there was something fishy going on with Mr Bezrow and Mr Jones?'

She looked down at her lap; her hair fell down again.

She was dressed in grey slacks and a black sweater, the casual style for a death; the slacks were tucked into black suede boots. She was very still for a while, then she sat back in the chair, seeming to go limp. She tossed her head back, the hair flopping away from her brow. She was giving up, but Malone was not sure what: her job, her love or infatuation for Rockne.

She said quietly, 'Of course I did. But everything's fishy now, isn't it? Men get away with murder — well, no, that's the wrong word this morning, isn't it? They get away with shonky schemes, or they did, and everyone thought they were heroes, the government gave them decorations. My mother and father are old-fashioned, they believe in morality and honesty and all that, and I was brought up that way. But out in the real world . . .' She looked past him out at the sky above the sea; but there was no evidence written there of the real world. Then she looked back at him, pausing as if wondering whether she was wasting her words on him. 'I knew Will was up to something fishy, as you call it. But I didn't know what and I didn't want to know. I just wanted to hold on to my job.'

He stood up. 'That'll be enough for today, Jill. I'm taking the cash box, the safety-deposit box and the gun with me — I don't think they should be left here, not even in the safe. I'll get you to sign a release. Either I or Sergeant Clements will be back tomorrow or the next day. You'll be opening the office?' She nodded, the hair falling down again over her brow. He was standing beside her now and he reached down and pushed back the hair. 'That's been annoying me.'

She looked up at him, suddenly smiled, a full-toothed effort. 'It annoys my father, too.'

'Thanks,' he said with a grin. 'That puts me in my place.'

They went out to the outer office where Clements sat

with two people who didn't want to speak to him or to each other. Jason stood up at once. 'You okay, Jill?'

'Sure. How about you?'

'I'm fine. Can you give me a lift back home?'

'You can come with me, Jay,' said Angela Bodalle. 'I'm going back there – '

'Thanks, Mrs Bodalle, but I want to go with Jill.' It was rude, a slap across the face, but Angela showed no expression.

The boy waited while Jill signed the release form she had typed out for Malone; the silence in the office was so heavy it made even the tapping of the word-processor keys sound like that of an old iron-frame portable. Angela Bodalle said nothing till the two young people had departed. Then:

'Will you be coming back to talk to Olive?'

'Not this morning. I'm sure you'll tell her everything we've found here.'

'Of course. If you should want me again, call me at my chambers. My home number is unlisted.'

'Oh, we never phone,' said Malone amiably. 'We just knock on the door.'

She appeared to be looking for the last word, but couldn't find it; she gave up and went clack-clacking down the stairs in her high heels. Clements let out a deep breath. 'I been sitting here doing my damnedest to be polite – '

'I wouldn't worry, Russ. Not with her. Get on to Randwick, ask them to send someone down here and put a seal on the downstairs door and that front door there. We don't want someone busting in here tonight looking for that cash and that bank statement. Ask them to keep the place under surveillance, at least till I talk to them tomorrow. Tell them the secretary will be coming in here tomorrow. When you've done that, you can tell me what you know about Bernie Bezrow.'

Clements was, or had been, Homicide's expert on the racing game. His luck at punting had been legendary; it was said that the horses ran with one eye on him on those days he was at the races. Then, some years ago, he had switched to punting on the stock market, a switch that Malone, an idiot when it came to punting on anything at all, had failed to understand. Clements had patiently explained to him that it had to be either shares or property; property meant possessions and he was not a man for such things. At least that had been his philosophy till he had met Romy Keller last summer and since then Malone had had no idea what was Clements's attitude towards punting or possessions. He, Malone, was an old-fashioned man who did not believe you asked another man what lay in his secret heart.

When they stood beside their cars in the street outside, Clements said, 'To begin with, Bezrow is Sydney's biggest bookie, weight-wise and betting-wise. But on-course punting isn't as big as it used to be — the TAB has taken a lot away from them, the crowds don't go to the races like they used to, so Bernie wouldn't rake in what he used to. But that doesn't mean he's on the breadline.'

'If he's so loaded, why would he use a small-time solicitor? Why wouldn't he use a big firm, the sort of lawyers who know all the tax lurks? Let's go and talk to him.'

Clements got into his Toyota and Malone walked along to his own car. He paused for a moment and looked across towards the Oval. Some cricketers were at one end of it, wearing baseball mitts and playing catch, testing their arms in preparation for the coming season. He had had a good arm in his day, able to put the ball right over the stumps from anywhere on the boundary; he felt the urge that all old players feel, to go over there and show the youngsters how good he had once been. But, of course, the arm wasn't there any more, not the way it used to be.

He got into the Commodore and drove up to see Bernie Bezrow, someone else for whom, it seemed, the good old days had gone.

Chapter Two

1

Tiflis Hall was a Coogee landmark. It stood just below the crest of the ridge that was the southern rim of the valley that ran down from Randwick to the beach. It stood in about an acre of terraced gardens, a small mansion with two towers, topped by copper cupolas, like bookends holding up the wing of the house that faced the street. Balconies bulged in the upper storey, inviting fantasies of fairy-tale princesses imprisoned behind the grey stone walls and the barred windows. Four Chinese rain trees, bare but for a sprinkling of early spring green, stood beneath the balconies like the skeletons of lovers who had forgotten their ladders. A high iron-spiked fence surrounded the property and two white bull terriers roamed through the blaze of azaleas and marigolds like two red-eyed demons in the wrong fairy-tale illustration. Coogee, in its day, had had its share of eccentricities but most of them had been human. This house had outlasted them all, was well over a hundred years old.

Malone announced himself and Clements through the intercom beside the big front gate. A moment later there was a piercing whistle over a hidden sound system and at once the dogs came at full gallop out of the azaleas and went up and round the side of the house. Then the gate-release buzzed.

As they walked up the long flight of stone steps Malone

said, 'They don't build 'em like this any more.'

'Who'd want to?' said Clements, for once showing some aesthetic taste.

The front door, thick enough to have withstood a tank attack, was opened by a Filipino maid, who turned pale and looked ready to flee when the two tall men said they were Inspector Malone and Sergeant Clements. But Malone smiled and told her they were not from Immigration and she stepped back and gestured for them to enter. Then she led them into a big room off the wood-panelled hall.

Bernie Bezrow looked like a half-acre of fashion-plate. He was no more than five nine, Malone guessed, but he weighed at least three hundred pounds. He wore a cream silk shirt, a caramel-coloured alpaca cardigan, beige trousers, yellow socks and brown loafers, polished till they looked as if they had been cut from glass. He was sixty years old, but looked at least ten years younger; his unblemished skin was stretched tightly across the good bones beneath it. His dark eyes, unlike many fat men's, were not trapped in rolls of fat; he had a well-shaped nose and a wide mouth in which the slightly turned-out lips sat one on the other like steps. Only his chins did not assert themselves; there the fat, firm as it was, had taken charge. The steps parted in a bookmaker's smile, the cousin of a politician's.

'A Sunday morning visit from the police?' He had a light voice, too light for his size; Malone had expected a bass. 'Inspector Malone, I've heard of you. How is it we've never met?'

'I'm with Homicide.'

'Ah, that explains it.' Bezrow was quick; he would never be slow to calculate the odds. 'I hope this hasn't something to do with a homicide?'

'I'm afraid it has.' Malone told him about the murder of Will Rockne. 'I thought you might have heard about it on the morning news.'

'Inspector, I don't own a radio.' Malone raised an eyebrow and Bezrow smiled and went on: 'I hate being chattered at. There is enough pollution in the air without all those voices. How was Mr Rockne – *murdered*?'

'Gunshot, in the face.'

Bezrow shook his head just a little; none of the fat wobbled. 'The world is becoming too violent. But why have you come to see me?'

'We understand you were a client of his.'

'No, no. Not a *client* . . . I see you are taking notes, Sergeant. Is this going to be held in evidence against me?' He smiled again. 'Only kidding. But I shouldn't be, should I? This is serious.'

Malone nodded, unsure of how he felt towards the bookmaker, whether he liked or disliked him. 'I'm afraid it is. If you weren't a client, what were you, Mr Bezrow? We understand Mr Rockne had some sort of dealings with you.'

Bezrow folded small, well-shaped hands across the slope of his belly. 'Dealings? I am – was his landlord. And he would occasionally come to me for advice, that was all. But no dealings.'

'Advice on horses?' said Clements.

'No, no. I don't think he had the slightest interest in racing. No, I met him some years ago, he ran for alderman on the local council. We had a terrible lot in the town hall in those days – you may remember it, the newspapers had a field day. The council's motto was an honest day's work for an honest week's pay. They used to boast none of them was afraid of work – they'd go to sleep beside it every Monday to Friday. I organized the campaign to throw them out. Surprises you, eh? A bookmaker involved in

56

local politics? Why not? Politics is just another question of the odds, everything's a gamble, isn't it?'

'Sergeant Clements doesn't think so.'

Bezrow winked at Clements. 'I didn't mention it before, Sergeant, but I've heard of *you*. You are, or should I say were, on every bookmaker's poison-ivy list. We were always thankful you never betted hugely like some of those who shall be nameless.'

The room in which they sat was a combination drawing room and library. Two walls were stacked to the high ceiling with books, many of them leather-bound. Bezrow spoke in a slightly literary way, as if whatever time he spent in this room had its influence on him. It was not a room for betting sheets, form guides and computers.

'Back to Mr Rockne?' Malone suggested.

'Oh yes. As I say, he ran for alderman. He didn't make it, but I was impressed by him.'

'In what way?'

'For one thing, he had a very analytical mind.'

Argumentative would have been Malone's judgement, not analytical. 'So why did he keep coming to you for advice?'

Bezrow ran a hand over his head. He had dark wavy hair that lay flat on his flat-topped head; there were streaks of grey along his temples. His hand rested a moment on top of his head, like a child's nervous gesture, then he took it back to rejoin its mate on his lap. 'Advice on local politics. Solicitors come up against local politics all the time. Is this conversation going to go on for long? Perhaps you'd like some coffee?'

Clements, who would have stopped for coffee in the middle of a hanging, nodded; but Malone said, 'No, thanks. Are you telling us you are some sort of political boss?'

'No, no!' Bezrow held up a modest hand. 'I'm *interested*

in politics, not just at the local level, but all levels. People know that. Look at the books on those shelves, most of them political history or biographies, the good and the bad.'

Clements, denied coffee, got up and scanned the shelves. 'He's right,' he told Malone. 'There's a lot here on Russia, Mr Bezrow. You're not a communist, are you?' The thought of a communist bookmaker amused him and he sat down laughing. 'That'd be one for the books.'

Bezrow also laughed, a gurgling sound coming from within his huge frame. 'I'm of Georgian descent. My great-grandfather came out here from Tbilisi in Georgia in eighteen-fifty-four — Tbilisi has sometimes been called Tiflis, hence the name of this house. Our name then was Bezroff, he was a count — though the joke used to be that anyone who owned three sheep in Georgia had a title of some sort. Could you imagine if I called myself Count Bezrow in the betting ring? The eastern suburbs ladies would be flocking back to the races. It was my great-grandfather who built the house. His son, my grandfather, became a horse breeder, thoroughbreds and remounts — he supplied a lot of the horses for the Australian Light Horse in World War One and for years he supplied horses to the Indian Army. My father took the interest in horses one step further — he became a trainer. He trained two Melbourne Cup winners. The next step — downwards, I suppose some might call it — was for me to have been a jockey. But you see — ' The hands spread like upturned starfish on the beach of his stomach and thighs. 'Bookies are not numskulls, Sergeant. Some of us know there is another world outside the racing game.'

For a moment the affability had disappeared; there was sharp venom in the light voice. Clements showed no sign of resentment at being ticked off; but Malone, who had been reading his partner's signs for a decade or more, recognized what lay behind the blank stare on the big man's face. He took up the action again himself: 'Did he ever come to you for financial advice?'

Bezrow quickly regained his good humour. 'What makes you think bookmakers are financial experts? That's a myth, Inspector. There are as many bankrupt bookies as there are in any other business, especially in these times.'

Malone grinned. 'I don't think you'd find too many punters who'd believe that.' Then he bowled a bumper, straight at the wavy-haired head. 'Did he ever ask you about a bank called Shahriver Credit International?'

The dark eyes clouded for just a moment. 'Shahriver? No.'

'We guess it's a merchant bank. Neither Sergeant Clements nor I have ever heard of it, but then we keep our money under the mattress. Banks don't have a very good reputation these days. Shahriver has branches in places like Kuwait and Beirut.'

'An Arab bank?'

'We don't know. We'll check on it tomorrow. But we thought Mr Rockne might've mentioned it to you, especially since you say he came to you for financial advice – '

'I didn't say that, Inspector. You said it.' The smile was not quite a smirk.

'So I did. Well, anyway, he had a sizeable deposit with Shahriver. We don't think he would have put it there without advice from someone.'

'How much?'

Malone's smile was also almost a smirk. 'Mr Bezrow, do you tell the other bookies how much you have in your bag?'

Bezrow's smile widened. 'Of course not. Sorry. I'm just surprised Mr Rockne would have bothered with such an obscure bank.'

'I'm surprised you're surprised,' said Malone and bowled another bumper, two in an over, the allowable limit in cricket these days; but this wasn't cricket: 'You didn't show any surprise when we told you Mr Rockne had been murdered.'

Bezrow said nothing. He shifted slightly in the wide chair, a small couch, on which he sat; the springs beneath the green velvet upholstery sighed metallically. The hands were very still on his thighs; the fat of his face seemed to have turned to stone, or anyway hard putty. Then he said very quietly, 'Nobody's death surprises me, Inspector. I'm a fatalist.'

'Is that the Russian in you?'

'It could be, except that no Georgian would ever call himself a Russian. Not these days, nor in my great-grandfather's day.'

'Stalin was a Georgian, wasn't he?' said Clements, not highly educated but a barrel of inconsequential data.

Bezrow ignored that and Malone said, 'Did Will Rockne ever mention to you that he'd received a death threat?'

'Never. Why should he? We were not confidential friends, Inspector.'

'Did you ever have any falling-out with him?'

Bezrow's gaze was steady. 'No. If you are implying did I threaten him . . .'

'No, Mr Bezrow. Have you yourself ever received any threats?'

'Death threats? Yes, three or four times.'

'Did you report them to the police?'

'What would be the point? They were phone threats, I had no idea who they were.'

'Dissatisfied punters?' suggested Clements.

'You would understand their frame of mind better than I would, Sergeant. I've never been a punter, not on horses, just in politics.'

60

'Did you arrange for any protection?' said Malone. 'A bodyguard?'

Bezrow shook his head. 'I told you, Inspector, I'm a fatalist. You really are trying to connect me in some way with Mr Rockne's death.'

Malone stood up. 'No, Mr Bezrow. But nothing any of us ever does is unconnected to anyone else. I read that somewhere. I'm working on the meaning of it.'

Clements rose, too, but Bezrow remained seated, as if the mere act of getting to his feet was something he avoided as much as possible. 'Never send to know for whom the bell tolls, it tolls for thee . . . I don't think Mr Rockne's bell is going to toll for me, Inspector.'

Malone could think of no literary answer, settled instead for, 'We'll be in touch, Mr Bezrow.'

'Just a moment till I call off the dogs.' He picked up a small microphone from the table beside him, put two fingers in his mouth and uttered an earsplitting whistle. A few moments, then Malone heard the two dogs, barking excitedly, go round the side of the house. 'You have about two minutes before they'll be out front again.'

'Have they ever attacked anyone?'

'Only punters,' said Bezrow and smiled at Clements.

As soon as the Filipino maid had closed the front door behind them, Malone and Clements went briskly down the steps, ears cocked for the rush of the bull terriers behind them. Once outside the front gate the two detectives stood beside the Commodore. Clements's green Toyota standing behind it shone as it hadn't shone since it had first come out of the showroom; Romy was either polishing the car for him or she was holding a gun at his head. 'What do you reckon?' said Malone.

'Despite all his fat, he's got a bigger sidestep than David Campese,' said Clements.

'I thought so, too. He missed his step once, though. He

61

said that Will Rockne wasn't the slightest bit interested in racing. Last night Will said, I quote, "If you knew what I know about the racing game . . ." Will was a bullshit artist, but I don't think he was playing that game last night.'

'I just wonder . . .' Clements was staring back up at Tiflis Hall. 'I wonder if that five-and-a-bit million in Shahriver belongs to Bernie? He doesn't just field on the courses – legitimately, that is. He has a big SP business – the Gaming Squad have tried to close it down a coupla times, but have never been able to nail him. That'd all be cash he wouldn't want to declare for tax.'

'Get what you can out of the Gaming Squad on him. In the meantime we'll stay off his back for a while.'

Inside the house Bezrow was making a phone call: 'You better get over here quick smart. We're in deep-shit trouble.'

Which is not a literary term.

2

'You're joking!' said Olive Rockne. 'How could you, Jason? This is no time for joking!'

'I tell you it's true, Mum. There was ten thousand dollars in the safe and a bank statement saying Dad was holding five-and-something million dollars in an account at some bank. In his own name.'

'Did you see the statement?'

'No, I was outside in Jill's office by then, but I heard them through the door, it was open and I could hear everything.'

Olive looked at Angela Bodalle. 'Is it true?'

'I'm afraid it is.'

'Afraid? Why are you afraid?'

The three of them were in the living room at the front of the house; Mrs Carss, Rose and Shelley were out in the kitchen getting lunch. As Mrs Carss, light-headed but with her feet on the ground, had said, the dead might die but the living had to go on eating. She had said it with the best of intentions, trying to make everyone feel better.

Jason lay slouched in a deep chair, his long limbs piled about him like sticks stacked on a sack of shit; which was the way he felt, he told himself. He looked at his mother and Mrs Bodalle and wondered what his mother saw in the other woman. He was no expert on what made a friendship, Christ knows; he had no close friends of his own, unless you counted Claire Malone and she wasn't really that close. He got on okay with the guys in the basketball team, but that was only on the court; they threw him the ball but nothing else, nothing like friendship. Angela, he had decided after meeting her only twice, was the most self-contained bag he'd ever met. Not that she was exactly a *bag*: she was sexy-looking, if you went for older women, though he could never imagine himself having a wet dream about her. He'd been reading in one of his mother's women's magazines about older women and their toy-boys, but Angela, it seemed to him, didn't seem to like even *men*. She hadn't liked his father and Dad certainly hadn't liked her. Maybe it had something to do with her being in the legal profession, which was chock-a-block with men.

Angela said, 'Inspector Malone seems very interested in it. He's probably going to ask you questions.'

'I know nothing about – how much did you say it was? *Five million!*'

'Five and a bit.' Jason was doing his best to look laid-back, but inside he could feel himself beginning to bubble. *Five-and-a-bit million dollars, for Chrissake!* He knew now how Charlie Sheen had felt in *Wall Street*. He had seen the video of that movie only six months ago, for the first time, and he had been disgusted at the greed in it; he had also been disgusted at the way his father had nodded approvingly all through the goddamn film. But now . . . Five-and-a-bit million, all in his father's name! 'Plus the ten thousand. Chicken feed.'

'Don't be so laid-back, Jay,' said Angela; he could have hit her. 'It's a lot, a lot of money.'

'You still haven't told me what's to be afraid of?' said Olive.

'Darling, it complicates things. It adds more mystery to why Will was killed.'

'Of course it does,' said Olive peevishly. 'But if it's in Will's name, who does it belong to now?'

'Us,' said Jason and frowned, trying to imagine what all that money was actually *worth*.

'I don't think you should lay claim to it,' said Angela. 'Not yet.'

'Why not?' Olive, unlike her son, was not laid-back, never had been. She had always been nervy, her emotions always on springs. Now she was holding tightly on to herself, but the effort was plain, bones and muscles showing through her thinness. 'Why not?'

'Let's wait till we see if someone else, a client or somebody, claims it. At this stage I don't think you should run the risk of looking *greedy*.'

'Oh, for Chrissake!' Jason stood up, all of him falling into place.

Olive looked at him as if she meant to reprove him; then she changed her mind and looked back at Angela. 'Yes, for Chrissake! What are you getting at, Angie? God, *greedy*? Is that how you think it's going to look?'

Jason sat watching the two women. He had never understood their relationship; it was different from those his mother had with other women. He could not tell you

64

what the difference was, except that Angela always seemed to be the one in charge. Of course, Mum was weak: Dad had had her under his thumb ever since he could remember. Lately, though, since Angela had come along, she had started to stand up to Dad. Not in any up-you-Jack sort of way; just a sort of taking the mickey out of him. He had begun to admire Mum, even if the influence had come from the wrong direction.

Angela said, 'Jay, would you leave your mother and me alone for a moment?'

'Do I have to?' He looked at his mother.

'Just for a few minutes, Jason.' He knew she would give in to Angela.

He climbed out of the chair, trying to be adult. 'Okay. But if any big decisions are gunna be made, Mum, I wanna be in on them, okay?'

'Yes, Jason.'

He wasn't sure, but his mother seemed to look at him with a new eye, as if she had just realized he *was* the new man of the house. But then she turned away to look at Angela and he felt his grasp on her slipping. Maturity was being thrust on him, though he did not recognize it; it felt uncomfortable, whatever it was, like a school guernsey that belonged to an older, more talented guy. He had been impatient to grow up, which is natural, since the real world is made up of bloody adults. But now he was not so sure.

'Don't let the money go,' he said, which is what Charlie Sheen would have said.

3

Sunday evening Sergeant Ellsworth rang from Maroubra. 'Scobie? We've come up with someone who was in the car park last night. He says there was no shot, none that could be heard.'

'Where was he last night when we were looking for him?'

'He did a bunk as soon as he heard Mrs Rockne scream. He was out there in the car park with some piece who wasn't his wife.'

'And he didn't bother to find out why Mrs Rockne screamed?'

'No.'

'Nice feller. So what's he told you?'

'He says he was about thirty or forty yards from the Rockne Volvo. He saw it come into the car park, but didn't take any notice of who was in it. He saw Mrs Rockne walk towards the surf pavilion, stand waiting for, he doesn't know, maybe a minute, maybe less, then she walked back to the Volvo and the next thing he heard her scream.'

'He didn't see Will Rockne get out of the car?'

'He swears not.'

'Did he hear the shot?'

'He swears blind there was no shot. He says he'd wound down his car window to throw out his cigarette.'

'If there was no shot, then it looks as if there was a silencer on the gun. That makes it a professional job. Were the Volvo's lights on? She says her husband had left them on and went back to turn them off.'

'This guy says no, that Rockne didn't get out of the car.'

'He sounds pretty sharp-eyed.'

'He's a tax agent,' said Ellsworth, adding another scout to the lynx-eyed of the world.

'Righto, put his statement on the running sheet, I'll read it tomorrow when it comes through on the computer. Have Physical Evidence come up with anything?'

'Nothing exciting so far. There's a lot of fine sand on

the car park, but there are dozens, more, shoe-prints. There are some fingerprints on the car, but those could be anybody's. They're checking. I think we should question Mrs Rockne again, Scobie.'

'I'm going to do that, Carl.' Any inspector loves being told by a sergeant what he should do. 'She's not going to run away, not with two kids to anchor her.'

'I dunno, you never know with women. Have you got something to follow up?'

Malone told him about the money Rockne had mysteriously accumulated. 'I'll have someone check that first thing tomorrow morning. Then there's Bernie Bezrow, Russ Clements and I are keeping an eye on him. He was closer to Rockne than he's prepared to admit.'

'I know Bezrow, he doesn't have a record, though in the racing game he knows some characters you wouldn't take home to meet your mother. I don't think he's the sort of guy who sends out stand-over men to break punters' kneecaps. Or shoot 'em in the face.'

Malone hung up and went back into the living room where Lisa and Claire were watching the latest in a series on SBS devoted to women in the world: it was a programme that would have had Ellsworth hit the Off button at once. Maureen was in her room, earphones on, listening to a rock programme, and Tom was in bed reading, halfway between sleep and the world of Roald Dahl. Malone sat down in his favourite chair across from his wife and daughter; they were leaning against each other, feet up, on the couch. Two women on the screen, no external bruises showing but with bruises behind their eyes and in their very being, were telling in quiet voices what life was like for a battered wife.

'Do you get much of that, Dad?' Claire said, taking her eyes away from the screen for a moment. She had a lot to learn about married life and, the protective father, he wondered if she was learning too much too early.

'By the time we get there, the wife is dead. Or the husband,' he added.

Lisa switched off the set. 'Anything on Will Rockne's death?'

'I don't think we want to spend Sunday night talking about murder, do we?'

'You mean, not in front of the child, right?' said Claire. 'Come *on*, Dad. If you want to be a cop, what d'you want us to do? Think of you as a bus driver or a schoolteacher like Mr Cayburn next door? For God's sake, I *knew* Mr Rockne! Why can't I be interested?'

Malone sighed, nodded. 'Have you spoken to Jason?'

'I called him this afternoon, he sounded really low. God, just imagine when he goes back to school tomorrow!'

'He probably won't be going to school tomorrow,' said Lisa. 'When's the funeral?'

'I dunno. That'll depend on when the coroner releases the body. Romy's handling it.' He looked at Claire, who had suddenly stiffened. 'That's what murder is all about, love, at least after the event. Mr Rockne is now just a body, a name and a number on a computer print-out – you still want to discuss it?'

'That's enough!' said Lisa.

Tiredness had brought cruelty. 'I'm sorry, Claire. Maybe I'll talk to you about it when it's all over, when we've caught whoever killed him – if we ever do. But right now . . .'

Claire stood up, crossed to him and kissed the top of his head. 'Why couldn't you have been a lawyer or a doctor?'

'Tom once asked me why I couldn't have been the Pope. I think he saw us there on that balcony at St Peter's every Sunday morning, waving to the mob. The Holy Family, Part Two.'

She kissed him again, this time on the forehead. 'Mother Brendan thinks you're a heretic.'

'I've had the Commissioner call me that, too. I must look it up. Goodnight, love. Tell your sister to get her ears out of that rock concert and go to sleep. And put Tom's light out.'

Claire went in to prepare for bed and Malone went out to the kitchen to make himself some tea and toast; he had not eaten much during the day and now suddenly he felt hungry. Lisa followed him. 'So how *is* it going?'

'The Rockne case? We're stumbling. Olive told me a few things last night that don't jell with some of the evidence we've dug up today.'

'Are you saying *she* might have killed Will?' She showed no surprise, but that was because over the years she had learned not to.

'I don't know.' He dropped two slices of multigrain into the toaster. 'Do you know Angela Bodalle?'

It took her a moment to identify the name. 'The QC? Is she representing Olive? *Already?*'

'No, not officially, not yet. She's a friend of the family. Didn't Olive ever mention her to you?'

'Darling, I've never been close to Olive. You warned me against getting too involved with them, remember?'

'Just as well I did. Where's the leatherwood honey?'

Lisa reached into a cupboard for a jar, put it on the table. This morning the honey had been in the plastic container in which he had bought it yesterday; now it was in the decorated jar with the silver spoon beside it. Lisa's table was always properly set, none of your slapdash cartons and plastic containers cluttering it. Her Dutch neatness was legendary with him and the children, though sometimes he wondered if neatness was a myth back home in Holland. It struck him that Olive Rockne probably ran

69

her own house with the same style, though he suspected there would be a fussiness to her neatness.

'I can't believe you might suspect Olive of – you know. She always struck me as being a bit wimpy. I mean Will trod all over her.'

'That sort get tired of being trodden on, though usually they kill their husbands on the spur of the moment, not cold-bloodedly. What would you do as a wife if you found out your husband had five and a quarter million dollars tucked away in a bank account?'

'You've probably got that much salted away somewhere, you never spend anything.'

'Be serious.' He told her what he had found in the Rockne safe. 'Would you claim it or would you turn your back on it because it might have blood on it?'

She thought about it while she made the tea: tea leaves, not tea bags, in a crockery pot. 'I honestly don't know. What are you expecting Olive to do?'

'I'm expecting Olive to claim it. I don't think she is as much of a wimp as we thought.'

4

Monday morning Clarrie Binyan, the sergeant in charge of Ballistics, came into Malone's small office in Homicide. Binyan was part-Aborigine, the recognized expert on white men's weapons; he often joked he couldn't tell the difference between a boomerang and a didgeridoo, but he could tell you whether a bullet had been fired from a Webley or a Walther. 'There you are, Scobie, the Maroubra bullet. Fired from a Ruger, I'd say.'

'Through a silencer?'

'Could be. Silencers usually have no effect on a bullet.

But if it was a Ruger fitted with a silencer, then I'd say it was a professional hit job.'

'How many hitmen do we know who use a Ruger?' But it was a useless question and he knew it. Crime in Australia had become organized over the past few years, coinciding with the national greed of the Eighties. But professional killings were still just casual work, often done crudely. 'We don't have much in the way of clues on this one, Clarrie.'

'I can't help you there, mate. You gimme something more than one bullet to go on and I'll try and build you a case. Or gimme a particular gun. But one slug . . .' He shook his dark head, rolled a black eye that showed a lot of white. 'Some day you're gunna bring in a spear and ask me to name it. I'm looking forward to that. I might run it right through you.'

'Get out of here, you black bastard.'

Binyan grinned and left: the two of them respected each other's ability and there had never been a moment's friction between them. The big room outside began to fill up with detectives; Malone had seventeen men under him in Homicide. There had been a spate of murders since the Strathfield massacre, but that was often the case, as if a damn had burst and murder had escaped. All the detectives were assigned. He looked out at them through the glass wall of his office and, not for the first time, remarked how few of them had come out of the same mould. Some of them were straight down the line, as if they worked under the eye of some stern judge; others bent the rules because, they argued, life itself didn't run according to the rules. There was Andy Graham, all tiring enthusiasm; chain-smoking Phil Truach, so laconic he seemed bored by whatever he had to investigate; John Kagal, young and ambitious, his eye already on Malone's chair, a fact that

Malone had noticed without letting Kagal know; and Mike Mesic, the Croat whose attention for the past month had been home in Yugoslavia where his hometown was being blasted by the Serbs. There were twelve others and there was Russ Clements, who came into the room as he sat staring out through the glass.

'What's the matter? You counting the bodies or something?'

The men outside had begun to disappear, going off on their enquiries. 'I was looking in at a show the other night. *Cops*, on Channel Ten. The Yanks seem to have a bloody *army* of cops. And *hardware*! When their helicopters take off, it's like that scene in *Apocalypse Now*, you remember? I sat there and I lost heart.'

Clements dropped into a chair that threatened to break under his bulk. 'Let me cheer you up. I've done a trace, through a mate of mine in a stockbroker's office, on Shahriver Credit International. It's as gen-u-ine as those Reeboks they sell you off the back of a truck.'

'It's not a bank?'

'Oh, it's a bank all right, properly registered here, with its headquarters in Abadan.'

'Abadan? That wasn't mentioned on the letterhead. Where's that?'

'In Iran, just over the border from Iraq. My contact tells me nobody worthwhile here in Sydney does any business with it.'

'It sounds like the O'Brien Cossack Bank.' He and Clements had worked on that case. 'Or Nugan Hand.'

'Worse. It's nowhere near as big as that other one that's in the news right now, the Bank of Credit and Commerce International, the BCCI – '

'I love the way these banks just roll off your tongue.'

Clements went on as if he hadn't been interrupted: 'Shahriver is the same shonky set-up, I gather.'

'Is it being investigated?'

'Not yet, but it's on the cards, according to my mate. They took forever to get into BCCI and that's twenty times bigger than this outfit.'

'Who deals with it if no one here in town does?'

'That's something we've got to track down.'

'You come up with anything else?'

'Yeah, I got in touch with the Commonwealth, out at Coogee. There was a withdrawal last week from that joint account – five thousand in cash.'

Malone pondered that a moment, then: 'Where does Shahriver hang out?'

'Down in The Rocks.'

'That's not bank territory.' He stood up, reached for his hat. 'Let's go down and see if they offer us anything. We might get a cheap pair of Reeboks.'

The area known as The Rocks is a narrow strip crouched between Circular Quay, where the harbour ferries dock, and the hill that carries the southern approach to the Harbour Bridge. For the last half of the nineteenth century it held its own as one of the roughest, toughest enclaves in the world; its gangs, or 'pushes', with their eye-gouging, elbows to the jaw and knees in the kidneys had set the example for footballers of the future. For a brief while it was Sydney's Chinatown; the smell of opium was only slightly less than that of the sewage that ran down the hill. A prostitute did not cost much more than a meal, except that, when the exercise was finished, her pimp stood over the client and, with a knife or a razor, extorted his own value-added tax. Nowadays The Rocks is a tourist area, the old shops dolled up, the warehouses turned into museums, the Chinese opium dens now Japanese *sushi* restaurants. The occasional prostitute can be seen propositioning male tourists, but she is tolerated by the police as reducing the country's external debt. The Rocks is chicly historical, but at least it is where it was born and happened and has not been transplanted.

Shahriver Credit International was housed in a restored colonial mansion in what was known as the High Rocks. Driving up through the Argyle Cut, the 80-foot-wide and 120-foot-deep cut hacked out by convicts using only picks and shovels, Malone said, 'When they first moved me in from the suburbs, I was posted down here.'

'You want to come back?' said Clements. 'You'd look good in uniform. A nice cap with silver braid on it instead of that bloody awful pork-pie you're wearing.'

'I'll stay where I am. One thing about Homicide, the public isn't always on your back.'

Here in the High Rocks one caught a glimpse of what life, for the colonial middle class, had been like. They had built homes that reminded them of Home; from the rear windows of their houses they could look down on the ships bringing them their wealth, for most of those who had lived here on the ridge had been shipowners or importers. Devon House, headquarters of Shahriver Credit International, was the largest house in the street, an English Georgian residence given a colonnaded verandah across its front as a concession to the southern sun. A spiked railing fence separated it from the street; a discreet brass plate beside the big oak door was the only hint that business was conducted inside the mansion. It was not a bank that invited small-time depositors or offered charge-free cheque accounts.

Malone and Clements, having taken the receptionist by surprise, were shown into the office of the managing director. The receptionist, a Chinese girl whose English was as affected and precise as that of a bad elocution teacher, said, 'We have two police officers here, Mr Palady. They had no appointment.'

74

'That's all right, Kim.'

Palady rose from behind his big desk. He was short and thin, black-haired and sallow-skinned, further monotoned in banker's grey. It was impossible to tell his nationality; the roots of his family tree could have stretched from Constantinople to Cathay. He had a soft silky handshake and a voice to match. He would not have had a clue how to run a suburban bank branch, but one had the feeling he could rip off a million or two in added fees from even the smartest entrepreneur. Still, his smile was practised enough to make the two detectives feel not unwelcome, though Malone doubted they would be asked to stay to lunch in the boardroom.

'Mr Palady, we're investigating the murder of one of your depositors, Mr Will Rockne.'

'The name doesn't ring a bell, Inspector.'

'He had five and a quarter million dollars deposited here. I don't want to sound a smart-arse, Mr Palady, but how much do you have to have in your bank before a name rings a bell?'

Palady smiled; he had been offended by the best, so a smart-arse Sydney cop could be suffered. 'I am new here, Inspector, only a few weeks in your country. I still have to acquaint myself with all our depositors. At the moment, like all banks, we are concerned only with those clients going bankrupt or reneging on loans.'

'You have your share of those?' said Clements, making notes.

'Not as many as other banks.' He smiled again, smugly.

'Where did you come from, Mr Palady?' said Malone. 'You said you've just arrived here.'

'From Kuwait. I was there all through the Iraqi occupation. Our board thought I needed a rest cure.'

'Where are your board?'

'In Curaçao, the Netherlands Antilles.'

'Your board's in Curaçao,' said Clements, 'but your head office is in Abadan?'

Palady seemed to look with new respect at Clements; up till now he had hardly glanced at the big man, as if treating him as Malone's office boy. 'Our board is international. Curaçao is safer at the moment than Abadan.'

'I'm sure you'll feel safe here in Sydney,' said Malone. 'Now, could we see someone who would know of Mr Rockne?'

'Certainly.' Palady spoke into his intercom. 'Kim, would you ask Mr Junor to come in? . . . You say Mr – Rockne? – was murdered, Inspector?'

'It's in the morning papers.'

'Ah, I never read such items. By the time I have read and understood what your politicians are doing, I have no stamina for matters such as murder and rape. I saw enough of that in Kuwait, performed by experts. Ah, Harold, come in.'

Harold Junor was English, an ex-rugby forward, ruddy-faced and flustered, who looked as if he had just come out of a ruck without the ball; the Chinese scrum-half had told him there were two police breakaways waiting to tackle him, with or without the ball. Told why the police were here he said in a loud voice, 'Ghastly! I read about it this morning – I knew it was our Mr Rockne, it's not a common name. Ghastly! Do you want me to take the gentlemen out to my office, Walter?'

'There's no need, Harold. I should like to acquaint myself with our Mr Rockne, dead though he may be.'

Malone could hear echoes in his head; but Palady's phrasing was not literary, as Bezrow's had been, but hinted of the pedantry of someone whose English was not his native tongue. Palady was stroking his grey silk tie, which was no softer than his hands. It struck Malone that he was feline, a description he had never applied to a man before.

'Where did we acquire him, Harold?'

Junor seemed to wince: he was a rugby forward, blunt and head-on, but he would never have *acquired* a client. 'I think he was recommended by another client.'

'Would you know who the other client was?' said Malone.

'Oh, I don't think we could tell you that,' said Junor, and Palady nodded appreciatively. 'Not without the client's permission.'

'Would you ask him?' said Malone.

Junor looked at Palady, who left him in no-man's-land. 'Well, yes, if you insist. Yes, we'll do that.'

'Now.'

'*Now?*'

'I don't know what merchant banking is like, Mr Junor, but murder is handled better if you can beat it from going cold on you. The murderer has about thirty-six hours' start on us at the moment and I'd rather he didn't get any further ahead.'

'But why do you need to talk to our client?' said Palady.

'Because, Mr Palady, the starting point for any murder case is the victim. The next step is who knew him and why.'

'Of course. Elementary. Go ahead, Harold, call your client, see if he wishes his name to be used.'

Junor went out of the room and the two detectives and Palady sat watching and smiling at each other. The room showed its colonial heritage. The metal ceiling pictured cream Aborigines hiding among cream English trees; the half-panelled walls were of cedar no longer available. Colonial prints hung on the regency-striped upper halves of the walls: ships at anchor in Sydney Cove, St Philip's

77

Church, the original still standing just up the street from this house. There were no prints of Kuwait or Abadan or Curaçao.

Junor came back, smiling apologetically. 'I'm afraid I could not raise him. No answer.'

'Keep trying, Mr Junor. I'll leave you my card. In the meantime we want Mr Rockne's account frozen.'

'Oh, no trouble at all there. Frozen it is, as of now. But we'll need a piece of paper, a court order or something. Will there be any claimants?'

'I'm sure there will be. If not his family, then someone else. Five and a quarter million isn't usually left in limbo, is it?'

'There is no limbo in a bank,' said Palady, the smile still at work. A feline smile, Malone thought, and wondered if he had ever seen a Persian cat smile. Cheshire cats were said to smile, but Palady came from further east than there.

'We'll get a court order and I'll send someone here to look at the account. I take it that the five and a quarter million wasn't all in one deposit? And you'll be able to trace where the cheques came from?'

Neither Junor nor Palady looked at each other; but the current that passed between them was palpable. Palady said, 'That may be something that Mr Rockne wouldn't have wanted.'

'I'm afraid it's too late to ask him. In the meantime keep trying with the man who recommended him to you. It was a man?'

Junor's smile was the sort he would have given a referee who had just awarded a penalty against him, right in front of the goalposts. 'Yes. Yes, it was a man. We don't deal very much with the ladies. They don't appear to have the money, not in this country.'

'They're working on it,' said Malone, whose wife was continually working on him.

Outside in the bright sunshine the two detectives exchanged glances that said they had both arrived at the same conclusion: Shahriver Credit International, for all the dignified façade behind which it hid, had darker secrets than most banks. Clements said, 'I don't think I'd deposit pocket money with them.'

The Harbour Bridge towered above them like a grey rainbow; Malone waited till a train had rumbled across it, taking its sound with it. 'Do you think their client who recommended Rockne could be Bernie Bezrow?'

'I'd put money on it.'

'Take John Kagal off whatever he's on and put him on this. He's thorough and he's quick. Get him to check on that joint account withdrawal.'

Clements nodded. 'Where do we go from here?'

'We go back and see Olive. We'll see what she has to say about no sound of a shot. And we'll see how she reacts when we tell her we've frozen that five and a quarter million.'

Chapter Three

1

Jason opened the front door. 'Hello, Pa. We wondered if you'd come.'

'Sugar and I thought we'd better.'

Though George Rockne was a good six inches shorter than his son had been, the resemblance was clear: he had the same bony face, though it was more weatherbeaten and the lines were deeper, the same aggressive eyes, the same shaped head, though his was entirely bald. The woman beside him was as tall as he, blonde and buxom, full of life but not aggressive about it. Jason had a lot of time for his step-grandmother, Sugar Bundy, the Kings Cross stripper who, against all the odds, had married his commo grandfather and made the old man happy.

'Anyone else here?' George Rockne sounded wary.

'Just Grandma Carss.'

Rockne wrinkled his nose, though the wrinkling was barely discernible amidst all the other lines on his face. 'Well, she's the least of our worries. Forget I said that, Jay.'

The boy grinned. 'I know what you mean, Pa. Hello, Sugar.' He kissed her on her well-powdered cheek. 'Was that you I saw on Saturday night on *That's Dancing*?'

She dug him in the ribs. 'None of your cheek, kid. How are you?'

'Pretty down. So's Mum and Shelley.'

He led them out to the back room, the garden room as

his mother called it. Olive and Shelley kissed George's cheek and did the same with Sugar; they were funeral kisses, when dislike and disagreement were buried for the day along with the corpse. Mrs Carss, unforgiving, offered neither kiss nor cheek, but did offer coffee.

'Tea?' said Sugar. 'I'm off coffee.'

Mrs Carss nodded sourly, as if she would have to go all the way to Sri Lanka for the tea, and went out into the kitchen. Jason remained standing, leaning against the door jamb, but the other four sat down. There was silence for a long moment, that of strangers: they had nothing in common but a dead man. Jason, embarrassed by the silence, wondering why adults always had to be so bloody uptight with each other, looked out at the back garden and the pool, where a magpie strutted like a developer marking out his territory. In another month the bird would be dive-bombing them in the pool, coming out of the big camphor laurel where he and his mate had already built their nest. He thought of going out and grabbing the maggie, bringing it in here and letting it loose just to shake up his mother, his grandfather and Sugar. Shelley, sitting there like the doll she thought she was, was no bloody use.

At last George Rockne said, 'Did Will tell you him and I've been talking to each other the last few months?'

'No.' Olive was in all black this morning, sweater, slacks and hairband. She frowned, as if she did not like the thought of Will and his father having been on good terms again. 'Why?'

'Why?' The lines on George's face seemed to increase. 'Olive, we were father and son! Fathers and sons, they sometimes become reconciled.'

'He didn't mention it to me. Did he make the first move?'

'No-o. I suppose I did that. I rang him up about some legal advice and it just sorta went on from there. Just three or four times, no more than that, but at least we weren't arguing any more.'

'It did George the world of good,' said Sugar. 'He would come home looking real pleased, you know what I mean?'

'He didn't come to the house?' said Olive and looked real pleased when Sugar said no.

Jesus, Mum, Jason thought, relax for Chrissake. They've come offering an olive branch or whatever it is they offer and all you can goddamn do is spit in their face. He had never tried to fathom his father or mother, there really hadn't been any desperate need; but now, ever since Saturday night, he was understanding less and less of her. She was turning into someone he had never recognized before.

Mrs Carss came back with coffee and tea; Jason noticed she had got out the Spode cups and saucers, another of his mother's treasures. Who was she trying to impress, for Chrissake? Sugar, who, he guessed, would bustle, maybe even bump and grind, her way through life unimpressed by anyone but God? He'd heard she had found religion, which couldn't have impressed Pa, the old commo atheist.

Shelley, pretty but bloody stupid, a real pain, said, 'Did you know we're going to be rich, Pa?'

'I don't think this is the time to talk about that,' said Olive.

'No, I didn't know that, Shelley.' George Rockne seemed to be taking care to balance his cup on its saucer, as if he recognized he and Sugar had been favoured with the Spode. Then he looked up at his grandson. 'Did you know that, Jay?'

'Yeah, sure.' Jason saw the look of disapproval, almost anger, on his mother's face. His grandfather had side-stepped her, was going to pump him instead of her. Feeling some anger of his own, he thought, Why not? 'Yeah, Dad's

82

supposed to have five-and-a-bit million in some private bank.'

Sugar coughed into her tea, almost dropping the Spode-ware. But George Rockne's face remained impassive, didn't take on a single extra furrow. 'Your father told me about some money in a private account. I didn't know he had left it to the family.'

'He hasn't,' said Olive, 'Not officially, I mean. We haven't seen any will. But how did you know about it?'

'It just came up in conversation.'

'Some conversation you must've had,' said Mrs Carss, down-to-earth as usual. 'Your tea all right, Sugar? I forgot to ask if you took sugar.'

Sugar gave her a big smile, peeled off her jacket; Jason wanted to laugh, seeing his step-grandmother peeling off her feathers or balloons or whatever she had worn in her stripper days. 'No, I've never taken sugar, even though I come from Bundaberg. Up there in the sugarcane country, if you don't take sugar they run you outa town.'

'I often meant to ask,' said Mrs Carss, 'so your real name's not Bundy? Short for Bundaberg?'

'My real name's Rockne,' said Sugar. 'Now.'

A goal to you, thought Jason, a two-handed slam-dunk right into the basket.

George looked back at Olive. 'Are you gunna claim the money?'

'Of course, if it's legitimately Will's. Otherwise, where would it go?'

'I wouldn't start spending it till you get it, Olive. It'll probably have to go before the courts and you can never trust them.'

'That's because you're a communist,' said Mrs Carss.

George's wrinkles increased; he had decided to humour the old bat. She was actually six years younger than he,

83

but he knew an old bat when he met one. 'I'm retired, Ruby. Didn't you know communism is dead? It's in the papers every day.' His face was smiling, but his eyes were not. You couldn't laugh at the end of the world. 'Take my word, Olive. Don't trust the courts. Wait till you've got your hands on the money before you spend it.'

When Jason had opened the front door to his grandfather he had experienced the sudden sad, mad hope that all the enmity and bitterness would be forgotten, though he had never been told or understood what had caused all the ill-feeling. He had just had the hope that as a family they would be *together*, as he had dreamed they might be. He had never confessed it to anyone, never could, never would, but he had always wanted the sort of extended family that he had read about in some books. He knew that family life on TV was all crap, but he had wished for something like it, to have a grandfather, even if he was a commo, who would tell him what life had been like when *he* had been a kid, who would tell him where his roots were. He had never known what his father and grandfather had fought about, though he guessed it was politics; there had been something more, though, something to do with ethics and example, something that had gone beyond politics: his mother and his grandmother had had something to do with it. He knew that his grandfather hated what he called 'yuppy greed', and he hated it himself; but surely that wasn't enough to have caused all the bitterness. If that was all it was, then half the families in the whole bloody country were in the same boat as the Rocknes.

For a few moments Jason had drifted off into a fog of resentment at the way things were going. He came back to hear his mother say, 'George, do you have any interest in the money?'

The front doorbell rang. Jason waited for his grandfather's answer, but the old man just smiled at Olive, then looked up at his grandson. 'You gunna answer the door, Jay?'

2

Malone said, 'G'day, Jay. Your mother home?'

'Sure, Mr Malone. But we've got visitors, my grand-father and his wife.'

'Good.'

'Good?'

'You're too young to start questioning how a policeman thinks. May we come in?'

Jason led the two detectives through the house and out to the garden room. The two tall men and the even taller boy crowded the entrance. Olive, Mrs Carss and Shelley looked up, startled; Shelley grabbed her mother's hand. Sugar gave the newcomers a wide smile; she had been smiling at men all her life, stripped in the crib. Only George Rockne showed no expression; he smelt *copper*. All his life there had been police who had hounded him, fascist bastards who had never acknowledged that he was fighting for them as well as for himself.

'We'd like another word, Olive,' said Malone. 'It's George Rockne, isn't it? I'm Inspector Malone, this is Sergeant Clements. I don't think we've ever met.' There was no politics in Homicide, at least none that concerned outsiders.

'Pleased to meet you,' said George, who wasn't. He rose, jerking his chin at Sugar. 'Time we were going, love. We'll be at the funeral, Olive.'

'If you could just spare a minute?' said Malone. 'Is that all right, Olive? Then we'll talk to you.'

'You got a hide,' said Mrs Carss, 'coming here, taking over like it was the police station.'

'Would you rather go up to the station?' Malone asked Olive.

'No. No, it's okay. Make some more coffee, Mum.'

'That's all I'm good for! Bloody tea lady!' Mrs Carss headed for the kitchen again.

'I'll give you a hand,' said Sugar.

'Never mind! I can do it m'self!'

Olive smiled wanly at her mother's rudeness; then she, Shelley and Sugar went out into the garden. At the back door she paused. 'Jason?'

'I was gunna stay, Mum.'

'I think it'd be better if you went with your mother, Jay,' said Malone.

The boy looked hurt, as if he had expected Malone to be on his side. He looked at his grandfather. 'What do *you* say, Pa? If you want any back-up – '

'I'll be jake, son.' Malone's ears pricked: George Rockne sounded like Con Malone, old slang on his lips like old sun cancers. 'Keep your mum and Sugar company.'

When the women and Jason were gone, he gestured for Malone and Clements to sit down. 'I don't think this is gunna take long, is it?'

'Probably not – mind if I call you George? I feel I know you, I've been reading about you for years.'

'On charge-sheets?' But George Rockne smiled. 'Not much of that, not for years, not since I got out of union politics.'

'There was a piece about you the other day in the *Herald*,' said Clements.

The old communist nodded, the smile gone. 'A snotty-nosed girl reporter, you knew she'd been educated at one of them private schools. She wanted to know what I thought of the death of communism, did I regret all the years I was deceived. *Deceived!* Christ – ah, you don't wanna talk about that, do you?'

'I don't,' said Clements, who had seen enough dreams die; not his own, but other people's. 'I don't think the inspector does, either.'

'No,' said Malone. 'George, I understand you and Will didn't get on?'

'We got on better over the last few months.' Rockne sounded cautious; but then, over the years, he had been subjected to a lot of interrogation, had had his words taken out of context. 'I guess Will didn't tell his missus about it. We don't get on well, Olive and me, I mean.'

'Did Will ever talk to you about enemies, threats, things like that?'

Rockne shook his head. 'Inspector, Will was nothing more than a suburban solicitor, he wasn't a big-time criminal lawyer, he never got himself into any business with gamblers or crims like – '

'Like who?'

Rockne shook his head again. 'No names, no pack drill.'

'Will must've got himself involved with *someone*. He has over five million bucks squirrelled away in a small bank in his own name.'

Rockne said nothing for a moment; the lines on his face deepened, like eroded earth falling in on itself. 'In his own name? You sure?'

'We're sure, George.' Malone was watching him carefully.

'Jesus! How'd he make that much? All he was ever interested in was making a dollar, that was one of the things we used to argue about. You'd ask him what someone was like and he'd tell you how much he was worth, that was his yardstick, how much anyone was worth. I used to call him the Eighth Dwarf, Yuppy. I never thought to ask him how much *he* was worth. Where'd he get it?'

'He could of stole it,' said Clements from the sideline.

Rockne jerked his head quickly towards him. 'Shit, no! I wouldn't wanna think that of him!' It was hard to tell whether he spoke as a father or as a communist; it was bad enough having a greedy materialist as a son, but a *thieving* one? 'Nah, I think you're making a mistake there.' But he sounded neither convinced nor convincing. 'Are you looking into that?'

'Yes,' said Malone. 'If he did steal the money from some client, it could've been the client who murdered him.'

'This has floored me, I don't mind telling you. What'll it do to Olive and the kids?'

'I hate to think. I mean that, especially to the kids.'

'But not so much to Olive?' Rockne lowered his head, looked at the detective from under sandy brows.

'Olive is bearing up better than I expected. What do you think?'

'Women are tougher than we give 'em credit for.'

'Is that why you never let 'em get far in the Party?' said Clements, but smiled.

The bony face creased again. 'Give 'em an inch and they take a mile. It's a man's world. That's the only thing God got right.' Then he added, 'If you admit there's a God.'

Malone stood up. 'Righto, George. Could you give Sergeant Clements your address and phone number, just in case we want to talk to you further?'

'You think you will?'

'It's on the cards, George.'

Rockne called in Sugar and they both left, their farewells abrupt except to Jason, who escorted them to the front door. Malone and Clements went out to the garden, took coffee from Mrs Carss and sat with Olive on fold-up chairs beside the pool. Shelley had gone into the house and the two detectives sat facing Olive; a neighbour, peering over one of the side fences, might have mistakenly remarked that Olive was questioning the two men. The house was built on a double-block and the three of them were far enough away from the next-door gardens not to be overheard.

'Olive – ' Malone sipped his coffee; Mrs Carss made a poor cup, too weak. Or maybe it was some sort of revenge for being kept on the outer. 'Something you told me Saturday night doesn't fit with something we've heard since.'

'Oh?' Olive, like the coffee in the cup she had been holding when the two detectives came out to her, was cold. She put down the cup and saucer on the tiles surrounding the pool, then sat with her knees together and her hands folded in her lap. Like an old-fashioned convent girl, one educated by nuns cloaked in old habits. 'In what way? What did I say?'

'You said you heard the shot that killed Will. We have a witness who swears there was no shot, we think a silencer was used on the gun. He also swears that Will never got out of the car.'

'Who is this *witness*?'

'I'll give you his name at the proper time.'

'He's lying or he's mistaken. There *was* a shot.'

'We're not saying there wasn't. I've told you, we think a silencer was used and in that case you wouldn't have heard any shot. You also said that Will had left the car lights on and he went back to turn them off while you waited for him. The witness says that's not the way it was. He saw you, but there was no sign of Will and the car lights were switched off as soon as you drove into the car park. When I looked at the car on Saturday night the keys were still in the ignition.'

Olive looked at the pool, where camphor laurel leaves floated like dead green fish. She was young middle-aged this morning; or anyway, no longer girlish. Then she glanced at Clements, taking notes, then back at Malone.

89

'Are you accusing me of something, Scobie?'

'Not yet. Did Jason tell you about the money we've found in Will's name in a private bank?'

'Yes. I find it hard to believe . . .'

'Oh, it's true enough. We've been to the bank this morning and checked it. Do you have a bank account of your own?'

She hesitated. 'No-o. Will and I always had a joint account. He – he always said I couldn't handle money.'

Malone could imagine Will Rockne's arrogance there. 'We also found ten thousand dollars in a cash box in his safe. I checked with the joint bank account book we found in the safe – he hadn't drawn that much money from the account. He would've had an office account and probably several clients' trust accounts – we're having those checked. But there was a withdrawal of five thousand from your joint account last week. Did he mention that to you?'

'No-o. God, the things I didn't know about him!' She looked accusing, as if she blamed Malone for keeping this information from her. 'Ours was an account where both signatures were necessary. But sometimes he'd get me to sign a blank cheque or two.'

Clements said, 'Did you know he had an affair with his secretary, Miss Weigall?'

Her thin face was suddenly pinched; she was hurt, badly. She said nothing, just shook her head. A magpie flew down out of the camphor laurel, perched on the pool fence and sharpened its beak for future use. Malone said gently, 'She told us, Olive, that it was only for one weekend. I don't think she meant anything to him. Did Will, er, play around?'

'Never.' She was recovering. 'He wasn't perfect, by a long shot, but no, he was never like that, chasing other women. He wasn't exactly a ladies' man.'

Lisa had thought that too, had once said that, like most Australian men, present company excepted, Will had as much charm as an empty beer bottle. But then she was European; Malone had been tempted to ask her how charming Dutch men were on their home turf, but hadn't been game. Jan Pretorious, her father, had charm, though Con Malone, the true blue Aussie, had called it smarm.

'Olive, could Will have withdrawn that five thousand? It might be part of the ten thousand.'

'He might have. I sometimes wouldn't see the cheque-book for a couple of weeks.'

Clements, the bachelor, said, 'You mean he kept tabs on everything you spent? I thought women these days had their own money?'

Malone got in before Olive could bite Clements's head off; she actually bared her teeth. 'You said on Saturday night you were planning a trip to the Barrier Reef. Would Will have drawn the money to pay for that?'

'That was probably it – ' Her reply was a little too quick.

'Five thousand for a week on the Reef? With all the bargain rates I've seen advertised?' Lisa had brought the advertisements to his notice only a couple of weeks ago, but he hadn't taken the hints she had thrown at him like rocks.

'We were going to Lizard Island. It's exclusive, it's not cheap . . . And I was going to buy myself a new outfit . . .'

'What about the other five thousand? Where d'you think that came from?'

'I have no idea. I told you yesterday morning, Will never discussed his practice with me. Scobie, why are you grilling me like this?'

'Grilling? That wasn't the intention, Olive. Russ here will quote you some examples of what *grilling* is like. But

91

if you feel that's what we've been doing, maybe next time you'd like to have your lawyer with you. Maybe Mrs Bodalle?'

'You're coming back, to question me again?'

'I think you can bet on it, Olive. So far you know more about Will than anyone else we've talked to.'

3

Detective Constable John Kagal always looked smug, as if he had just won the State lottery or been invited to dinner by Michelle Pfeiffer. He was always dressed as if he expected a call from La Pfeiffer; Malone, whose ideal tailor was St Vincent de Paul, wondered if Kagal's entire salary went on his wardrobe.

He was a good-looking young man with bright, intelligent brown eyes and custom-cut dark hair; he was slim, of medium height, and he moved with a certain grace that was natural. He was the only university-educated man in Homicide and he did not intend wasting that advantage. He was damned near perfect, a fact he modestly acknowledged if pressed.

'Righto, John, what've you got?'

It was late afternoon and Malone was tired. The Rockne case was still tops on his pad, but four other murder cases, which he was supervising, had begun to turn sour; evidence that had looked rock-solid had begun to crumble, willing witnesses had suddenly become deaf, dumb and blind. The natives voted for law and order every time, but too often they wanted their vote kept secret.

'Okay, here it is.' Kagal had a brisk voice; he would sound exactly right when he became Police Commissioner twenty-five or thirty years down the track. 'I went out to the Commonwealth Bank's branch at Coogee, where the Rocknes hold their joint account. That five grand withdrawal – it was drawn, in cash, by *Mrs* Rockne.'

'They're sure of that?'

'One of the tellers remembered giving it to her – that's a large withdrawal in cash by an individual. The usual withdrawals were for four or five hundred weekly – I guess they were for housekeeping. There were cheques made out to stores, electricity accounts, things like that.'

'Mrs Rockne told me she knew nothing about that five thousand.' He did not ask why the bank had been so co-operative in revealing the details of the Rockne account. He never queried how his men worked, unless there was a complaint from outside; he knew that Kagal was not bent nor was he a stand-over man. Kagal, like every cop, knew that the proper channels too often led to a delta of silt. So if you had to detour round the rules or crash through them, you did so. 'That's a couple of lies she's put to me. Why?'

'Is she the killer?' Kagal was always direct, a real arrow always on target. It was one of his few handicaps, if he wanted to make Commissioner. He was sitting opposite a man who had fired too many direct hits for his own good. The politicians swore with their hands on their hearts that the State would have no more corrupt Commissioners; they kept their hands on their breasts so that no straight-arrow appointee might pierce them with too much honesty. 'If she knew of that other money, the five-and-a-bit million . . . ?'

Malone nodded. 'She's starting to look more and more like Number One suspect. But it's a bit early yet . . . You know Bernie Bezrow, the bookie? Find out what you can about him.'

'Scobie, I don't know anyone at all in the racing game,

93

it's not my scene.' It obviously hurt Kagal to confess that he did not know everyone and everything. 'Russ would do better than me there.'

Malone had known that all along; he wondered at the mean streak in himself that had made him show Kagal to be less than perfect. Had he started to protect his own back, was he like some old lion (well, a young middle-aged one) intent on holding his own against the young one? He had never really been competitive, or ambitious, but now it struck him that he was going to suffer no competition from Kagal, not if he could prevent it.

'Righto, I'll let Russ handle it. In the meantime – '

Then his phone rang. 'Scobie? It's Don Cheshire.'

Sergeant Cheshire ran the Fingerprints Section out at Parramatta. He was one of the old school, suggesting he was more of a knuckle-man than a specialist in finger-prints, but there was no one in his job better than he. He had started thirty years ago when there had been two basic powders used to develop a fingerprint; now there were over a hundred chemicals that could do the job. He had first used a bellows camera; now there were a computer and the latest high-definition camera. Gruff and lumbering, he resembled a bull in a laboratory, but he had built and kept his reputation as the best.

'We been all over the Volvo in the Rockne case. Prints everywhere on it, but they'd be the family's, too many of 'em and some of 'em are old. But we come up with a single print on the door, the door on the driver's side, same side's the body was. Nice and clear, couldn't have been better if I'd ordered it. We know who it belongs to, too, I've checked. A villain named Garry Dunne, got a record from here back to the First Fleet.'

'Garry Dunne? *Kelpie* Dunne?'

'That's him. I tried to get an address on him, but all the computer shows is the Gold Coast, but that was back in

94

eighty-nine. He'd just been acquitted of doing a security guard. He must of pissed off up north soon's they let him outa court.'

'Thanks, Don.' Malone hung up, looking across his desk at Kagal. 'As I was saying, in the meantime you can try and find a crim named Garry Dunne, Kelpie Dunne. You heard of him?'

'Vaguely.' Kagal had been in Homicide only six months, had come from the detective squad in one of the southern stations.

'He used to be a bouncer for a gambling club out in Rozelle, the Lay Down Misère, I think it was called. I dunno if it's still going, but try it. If there's no luck there, try all the other gambling joints around the suburbs, just leave out the Asian ones. They don't employ whitey bouncers.'

'What about the Cross?'

'He never hung around the Cross. He was *persona non grata* up there, I dunno why.'

'*Persona non grata*? I've never heard that about a crim before.' Kagal made the mistake of letting his smile slip into a smirk.

'You will when you get to inspector,' said Malone and felt better: a little malice occasionally flavours the soul. 'Ring me at home if you come up with something on him.'

Kagal looked at his watch. 'You want me to start looking *now*?'

'Gambling clubs do most of their business at night. Have an early dinner and then get to work. Good luck.'

Kagal straightened his Macquarie University tie; he would have preferred it to be a Sydney Uni tie, but one couldn't have everything. 'Does it matter what time I ring you?'

'Any time. There's a phone right beside my bed. On my wife's side.'

Kagal smiled; he wasn't all smugness. 'You win, Inspector.'

Malone, too, smiled; the young lion had had pointed out to him his place in the pride. 'Good luck, John. Don't try to bring Kelpie in on your own. He's a bad bugger.'

Half an hour later he went home, driving through rain, the first good downpour for weeks. By the time he reached home, however, the rain had stopped and the clouds had climbed high again and were disappearing. A weather expert on the car radio told him that the dry spell was expected to continue, that the rain had been an aberration, a leak in the sky. Malone put the Commodore into the garage, noting that there was a leak in the rubber round one of the windows of the car; perhaps it was time to start thinking of a new car. He closed the garage door and stood for a moment smelling the moisture on the flowers and shrubs in the front garden. The world, occasionally, smelt fresh.

He went into the house, kissed Lisa, then kissed the children, something that, though he never made a big thing of it, gave him more pleasure than the children knew. Brigid, his mother, had never kissed him again after he had made his First Communion; Con, his father, would have looked at him queerly if he had put up his cheek to be pecked. Claire, Maureen and Tom, when they kissed their father in return, made his day.

'I think I'll have a swim,' he told Lisa.

'The water's still freezing, it'll make you impotent.'

'I'll leave my balls in the bedroom.'

'Did you say you're gunna leave your balls in the bedroom?' Tom, the nine-year-old, stood in the kitchen doorway.

'You want to clean the wax out of your ears.'

'What did you say then?'

Kids weren't always kissable. 'Never mind. You want to come for a swim with me?'

'Not if I gotta leave my balls in the bedroom.'

Malone looked at his wife. 'You've raised one of those cute kids out of TV.'

'Blame me. Hurry up and have your swim. Russ and Romy will be here at seven thirty. You know that she sees they're always on time.'

'I'd forgotten they were coming.'

He had his swim, not diving in but going carefully into the water; his genitals went up into his belly and his breath disappeared altogether. But gradually he became adjusted to the chill and after a few minutes he was stroking slowly up and down the pool and the stiffness of the day slid out of him. As he dried himself he was glad to find everything returning to normal, all things in their proper place.

Russ Clements and Romy Keller arrived on time. The children swarmed all over Clements; he was their favourite and only uncle, adopted. They were as affectionate towards Romy, if a little inhibited; they were still getting used to the idea that, if all went well and Lisa the matchmaker's prayer were answered, she could be their one and only aunt. As the children, already having eaten, went off to their rooms and Lisa went out to begin serving dinner, Romy said to Malone, 'We finished the autopsy on Will Rockne today. The cause of death was straightforward, you'll get my report tomorrow. The irony is, he was going to die anyway.'

Malone, leading the way into the dining room, looked at Clements, who shrugged, then back at Romy. 'Going to die, anyway?'

'He had a brain tumour. He'd have had six months at the most to live, maybe less. I'd say it was totally inoperable.'

97

'You never know, do you?' said Clements, sounding enigmatic.

'The killer certainly couldn't have,' said Malone, pouring the wine. It was a 1975 Grange Hermitage, the last bottle of Lisa's parents' Christmas present last year; even after seventeen years of marriage, it still prickled when Jan and Elisabeth Pretorious gave him and Lisa presents that cost so much. But it didn't sour the wine; his palate was less sensitive than his pride. 'But if his wife knew . . .'

'Yes?' said Clements.

'If anyone knew, it would be her. In which case, why would she want to have him killed?'

Romy widened her heavy-lidded eyes. 'You suspect the wife?'

'I was beginning to. But now . . . Unless, of course, she didn't know and neither did Will Rockne. Can someone be unaware of having a brain tumour?'

'Yes. There'd be symptoms, headaches, maybe some vomiting, but too often people ignore those sort of things till it's too late.'

Clements tasted the wine Malone had poured for him. 'Don't let's spoil this. Grange Hermitage?' He whistled. 'Did it fall off the back of a truck?'

'I wish it had,' said Malone, being enigmatic, and went out to help Lisa bring in the first course.

They had reached the coffee and florentines stage when the phone rang. Malone went out into the hall to take the call; it was Kagal. 'Scobie? I've traced Kelpie Dunne. He's here in Sydney, though I can't get a home address on him. But he works as a mechanic for a garage workshop out in Newtown, a place called Hamill's, in Brumby Street. I can be there first thing in the morning.'

'No, leave him to me, John.' He wasn't sure that Kagal was the right man to send after a thug like Dunne. 'Russ and I'll handle him.'

He went back to the dinner table, all at once feeling pessimistic, though not sure why. The Grange Hermitage tasted like something that actually had fallen off the back of a truck, been scooped up and rebottled.

Chapter Four

1

'Course there'd be my prints on the car! I serviced the fucking thing, didn't I? You checked the engine block? My dabs would be all over that. Jesus, you guys gimme the shits!'

Kelpie Dunne had no respect for the law or those who tried to enforce it. For a thug, he was a small man; but he was an artist at fighting dirty. He was thin-featured, with a widow's peak to his reddish-brown hair; there was a resemblance to the dog after which he was nicknamed. Though short and lean, he was muscular and had hands that looked more comfortable, or anyway natural, as fists. His voice had the right rasp to it; he had a *de facto* wife, but nothing sweet had ever been poured into her ear. At the moment he wore overalls and a T-shirt and was covered in grease stains, like tribal marks. But Malone knew he belonged to no tribe, he was a loner.

'How long had Mr Rockne been bringing his car here for service?'

'Just the once, about a month ago. He said he wasn't happy about who'd been doing it before.'

'This is a bit out of the way, isn't it, for someone who lived at Coogee?'

'Easy seen you ain't a car man. This place's got a reputation. Look around you, all quality cars, no shit.'

Hamill's workshop itself had no look of quality. In a

100

back street of Newtown, it was a plain one-storeyed brick building with a corrugated-iron roof and a front wall covered with graffiti, not the artistic kind; pigs, nigs and wogs were told to Fuck Off! and there was a large swastika that someone had tried to scrub out. The workshop was long and narrow, running from the street through to a back lane. The street had two rows of narrow-fronted cottages facing each other, drab as the banks of a dry gully; gentrification had not yet washed into this part of Newtown. But within the long clangorous tunnel of Hamill's there were a dozen or more of the gentry's carriages: Jaguars, BMWs, Porsches, a Ferrari.

'Who recommended that Rockne come here?' said Clements.

Dunne cleaned his big teeth with the inside of his lips. 'I was a client of his, once.'

'That was several years ago,' said Malone. 'Did he come looking for you, all the way out here? Come on, Kelpie, don't bullshit us.'

He cleaned his teeth again. 'Then I dunno who recommended him.'

'Would your boss know?'

'He might. Why don't you ask him?'

'Okay, we'll do that. Where is he?'

'He's on holiday, up at Kakadu.'

Three thousand kilometres away, Crocodile Dundee country. 'You're a real smart-arse, Kelpie,' said Clements. 'Where did you learn to be a mechanic? I thought you went in for other ways of earning a crust.'

'I did a course while I was in Bathurst. I was doing three years.'

'What were you in for?'

'A guy got in me way. I didn't see him till he was unconscious.' The big teeth made an ugly smile, like a

101

dog's. 'But they rehabilitated me in Bathurst. Made me into a mechanical engineer, I'm part of the Clever Country.'

The Clever Country had been one of the catch-cries out of Canberra, another piece of rhetoric aimed at solving the nation's problems. 'I don't think the government had you in mind to show us the way, Kelpie. You've been up before the beak twice since Bathurst. I looked up your record. Did Mrs Bodalle recommend Rockne to bring his car in here?'

'Mrs Bodalle?' Dunne's look of innocent puzzlement was as ugly as his smile.

'That's her Ferrari over there, isn't it?' Clements pointed to the red car standing in a corner, its bonnet raised. 'I saw it Sunday morning. I made a note of the number plate. QC-LAW. Bit fancy, isn't it?'

'Oh, *that* Mrs Bodalle!' He made it sound as if Sydney were a Bodalle breeding ground. 'That come in yesterday morning. Beautiful bit of machinery. Yeah, she could of recommended him. Like I said, you'd have to ask the boss. I don't do none of the booking in.'

'Who's the foreman?' said Malone. He had seen the Ferrari without recognizing it; good old Russ had come good again. 'Or is he up at Kakadu, too?'

'He's off with the flu. You're outa luck, looks like.'

'Could we have your home address?'

'You can always find me here.'

'I know, but we'd like to know where you live. Put you on our mailing list for police Christmas cards.'

'You're a real card, ain't you? Okay, it's – ' He gave an address in Penrith, one of the outer western suburbs. 'But you're wasting your time, you gunna get nothing on me. I'm clean.' He held out his grease-stained hands, then grinned. 'Well, almost.'

'Yeah,' said Malone. 'Almost.'

Malone and Clements went out to the unmarked police Commodore, which Clements had had to park on the footpath. Two women, surrounded by a shoal of toddlers, stood beside the car. 'Are you two coppers? Don't you know it's against the law to park on the footpath? One law for the law and another for us mugs, right? We oughta report you, only we dunno who'd take any notice, you're all up each other's jack.'

'Is that any way to talk in front of the children,' said Clements.

The woman who had spoken, in her thirties, worn thin with battling, looked at her companion, a plumper, younger woman who looked as if she could be happy, given the opportunity. 'You hear that, Cheryl? I was wrong. He ain't a cop, he's a parson.'

'Does that workshop park cars on the footpath?' said Malone.

'All the time.' She broke off for a moment to snap at the toddlers, who were relieving their boredom by punching each other. 'We're always complaining, but they just give us the middle finger, you know? My hubby complained once and they just give him a hiding. They're all crims in there, every one of 'em. But then you know that, right?'

'That's why we're here. Just checking. Would you notice if the cars come and go pretty quickly?'

'I wouldn't know. Would you, Cheryl?'

Cheryl shrugged, leaning sideways against the weight of the baby on her hip. 'I wouldn't know, either. But most nights of the week, they work right through the night. They shut the doors, but you can still hear 'em banging away, especially if you live next door, like I do.'

'Thanks, ladies. And we apologize for leaving our car on the footpath. It won't happen again. If you have any more trouble with Hamill's, if they beat up your husband again, let the local police know. They'll straighten 'em out.'

'Are you kidding? The cops come down here, everything would be quiet for a day or two, right, Cheryl? Then one day we'd come home to find our house had been burned down. They're real bad buggers, I tell you. Stop it!' She swept her hands round, clipping the fighting toddlers, not missing a head. 'You wouldn't like to run this lot in, would you?'

'Hardened crims like them? No way.'

The two detectives got into their car, drove along the footpath to the corner and bumped down over the kerb into the road. As they waited at a traffic light Malone said, 'I'd say Hamill's run a stolen car racket. They do some servicing, a few legitimate clients as a front, but I'd bet half those cars we saw in there were stolen.'

'Do we mention them to the Motor Squad?'

'Not yet, but we will. Give us a day or two, we want to keep tabs on Kelpie. So long as he doesn't pinch my car, he's more use to us where he is. I don't think he's going to disappear, he's too shrewd to give us any suspicions.'

'There's a lot today who have Ferraris and Porsches who'd be glad to have them pinched, have 'em written off for the insurance.'

'Not Mrs Bodalle, though. I'd say she and Will Rockne were two of the legitimate clients.'

Clements looked sideways. 'But?'

Malone looked sideways in return. 'Like you say. But . . .'

2

Jason and Claire sat in a booth in Brick's milk bar and coffee lounge, the meeting place before and after school for the boys from Marcellin College and the girls from Holy Spirit. Jason wore jeans and a blue and white striped shirt and Reeboks. Claire was in her school uniform: green and blue plaid skirt, blue shirt and blue blazer with the school emblem on the breast pocket; her felt hat, to be replaced for summer with a straw one, was on top of her schoolbag on the seat beside her. Holy Spirit did not believe in self-expression, at least not in wardrobe.

Brick, who owned the place, was an overweight ex-rock musician in his late thirties who wore his dark, oiled hair in a ducktail and had an array of T-shirts all with the same message: Elvis Lives! The walls of the coffee lounge were hung with framed blow-ups of record covers of Presley, Bill Haley, Buddy Holly and other kings of the ancient past. Brick (no one knew if he had another name) knew he was an anachronism, at least to most of his customers, but he also knew where his dreams were, still back there in the past. Something he would never have confessed to any of the kids who came in here every day of the week.

He brought Jason and Claire two caramel malteds. 'There, build you up for the day. Sorry about your dad, Jay. I dunno what the world's coming to. When's the funeral? I'd like to send some flowers or something.'

'The end of the week, I think. They haven't released his – his body yet from the morgue.'

'You going to school today?'

'I'm taking the week off.'

Brick went back behind his counter. He ran a well-ordered place and the police and those parents who knew their kids came here never bothered him; he had two kids of his own and was said to be a stern father. It was not his usual practice to bring orders to the kids in the booths or at the tables; but life wasn't all rock'n'roll and the shouted lyric, there were moments when you offered to send flowers to a funeral and you didn't want the world to know. He turned down the taped music, wished he had put on something else but the Beatles doing 'Roll Over Beethoven'. He had never liked them, anyway.

In the booth Claire said, 'You sleeping okay?'

'You sound just like my mum.' He grinned and put his hand on hers. 'No, I'm okay, hon.'

'Hon? I'm your honey?'

'That slipped out. No. No, it didn't. I guess I really like you, Claire. You know how a guy really feels when something like this happens. I've really looked forward to you calling me every day.'

'You'd do the same for me.' Then the horror of what she had said struck her; her eyes opened wide and she shook her head. 'Oh God, why did I say that?'

'I guess because your dad's in danger every day, practically. Cops are, it's part of the job, I guess. It wasn't for my dad,' he said wonderingly. 'Jesus, I still can't get it through my head the way he died!'

'How's your mother?'

He sucked on the straw in the caramel malted. 'She's taking it much better'n I expected. Or anyway, she's hiding it better. She's in, you know, *control*. You think you know someone and then – '

'Then what?'

'Do you know your mother and father? Really know 'em?'

Claire pushed the malted aside. 'I'm dieting . . . Jay, I don't think I know *anyone*, not really. Oh, I know Maureen and Tom, but they're only *kids*. I don't know *you*. When it comes to Mum and Dad and *adults . . .*' She shook her blonde head at the unknown tribe of an unknown country, one the map of which she had been allowed only to peek at. 'I think school should make it a compulsory subject for the HSC, the study of adults.'

He smiled, really enjoying her company. 'Do you have to go to school?'

She sighed, pressed his hand. 'I wish I didn't have to . . .' She wanted to kiss him, he looked so lonely, but if the word ever got back to Holy Spirit that she had been seen kissing a boy in public, and she in her school uniform for God's sake, Mother Brendan would kill her. 'I'll see you here this afternoon.'

'I'll miss you, hon.'

He watched her go out of the coffee lounge, the only good thing in his life right now. He got out of the booth, paid for the malteds, said goodbye to Brick, a good guy, and headed for home. He passed Randwick police station, wondered if soon they would have a poster in there asking for information on the murder of William Rockne. There had been half a column in yesterday's papers, but nothing this morning; he wondered if it would be worthwhile starting a scrapbook, just in case. But that, he decided at once, would be really bloody ghoulish.

He stopped halfway down the hill of Coogee Bay Road and looked ahead to the ocean stretching out to the horizon and beyond, to Tahiti and South America, to places he would see some day when they collected his father's five-and-a-bit million. He suddenly felt better, though ashamed by the reason for it.

When he turned in the front gate at home his mother was backing her Civic down the driveway. 'Where are you going, Mum?'

'To aerobics.'

Aerobics, for Chrissake!

'What's the matter? You don't think I should be going? Jason, I'm trying to take my mind off what's *happened*! I can't just sit inside the house and *think* all the time!'

'Okay, Mum. I didn't mean anything – '

But he turned away from her and went into the house, wondering what she expected him to do to stop thinking about what had happened. Shelley had gone to stay for a couple of days with Gran Carss and, as he walked in, he all of a sudden felt how goddamn lonely and empty the house was, like a bloody mausoleum, though he'd never been in one of those. As he walked into the kitchen to get a Coke from the fridge, the phone rang.

It was Jill Weigall. 'Jay? I just wanted to speak to your mother – '

'She's out, Jill. She – she's gone shopping.'

'How're you feeling?'

'Pretty lousy.'

'Me, too. You're not going to school, right? How'd you like to come and have lunch with me here at the office? I can't leave it, just in case. We can get some hamburgers – '

'Great! I'd like that.' Suddenly she was as clear in his mind as if she were standing next to him; he wanted to see her. 'How about twelve thirty? I'll bring the hamburgers, okay?'

He hung up, wondered at the excitement rippling through him. She couldn't be *interested* in him, surely? Sure, she was an older woman, but . . . The phone rang again and he grabbed it, wanting to hear her voice again.

'Jason? It's Angela Bodalle.'

It was a let-down, a drop right from the rooftop. 'Oh, hello, Mrs Bodalle.'

'Jay, why don't you call me Angela? I'm a friend of the family, all of you. I'll be seeing a lot of you from now on.'

He ignored that, said, 'You want Mum? She's out. She's gone to her aerobics class.'

'*Where?* Aerobics?' He said nothing, there was silence on the line, then she said, 'You don't approve, do you?'

'You don't, either, do you?' He had stepped into adult territory, talking as man to woman, an older woman.

Again there was silence; then: 'I don't think it's my place, Jay, to approve or disapprove.'

'You're a friend of the family, you said.'

'Are you cross-examining me, Jay?' He could imagine that goddamn smile of hers. 'All right, I disapprove. But only because of what other people will think. Most of them don't understand how your mother feels.'

'Do *you* understand?'

'Yes, of course I do. You are forgetting, Jay – I deal with people almost every day of the week in situations like your mother's.'

She actually sounded sympathetic, somehow softer, dammit, than the way he usually saw her. 'Well, yeah, I guess so. It's just – well, never mind.'

'I'd like you to talk to me, Jay. We have to help your mother.'

'Yeah, well . . . I'll tell Mum you called. You at your chambers?'

'Yes, I'm not in court this morning. I'll be here till noon.'

He hung up, went into the family room and turned on the TV and got, you wouldn't bloody believe it, a programme called *Aerobics Oz Style*. He lay slumped on a couch, sipping Coke, and watching the sweating bodies gyrate, arses out, boobs bouncing, and thought of his mother doing the same thing at that very moment, trying, she had said, to stop thinking. He closed his eyes to stop the tears.

He was still lying on the couch, still watching TV, this

time an American soapie, when his mother came home. She came into the family room, looking young and slim and so bloody *healthy* he felt angry. 'Mrs Bodalle called,' he said and looked back at the television screen.

'Why don't you call her Angela? She's asked you to. Where is she, at her chambers?'

She went out to the kitchen. As soon as she disappeared he turned the sound right down on the TV and sat up, ears strained. He felt ashamed and embarrassed, just like the time he had lain in bed and listened to his mother and father making love. But, like then, he kept his ears wide open.

'Angela, don't tell me what I can and cannot do! I had to get out of the house, can't you understand that? It's all right for you, you're not surrounded by things that remind me of him. It's as if he's still *here*!'

Jason looked at the screen: two women were arguing, their mouths wide open in silent abuse. He wondered what Angela was saying that had his mother so much on edge.

'Yes, of course I'm going to claim it! . . . How can it harm me? We're entitled to claim it, it's in Will's name . . . Oh, for God's sake! Angela, are you losing your nerve? I'm the one who's under pressure . . . Okay. All right, darling, I know how you feel . . . No, I'll wait. It's just that it's such a temptation . . . Yes, you know I do . . .'

Jason heard her replace the phone and at once he turned up the TV sound again. He slumped back on the couch, but his limbs were as stiff as poles and his head abruptly began to ache. He looked up as his mother came and stood in the doorway.

He forced himself to ask, 'What did she want?'

'She just wanted to know how we're coping. She's a *friend*, Jason, I wish you'd accept that. What are you doing, watching something like that? You should be studying.'

'I can't concentrate. Maybe I should've gone to school.'

'It's up to you. I still don't know when we can have the funeral. Angela is trying to find out when they're going to release Dad's – Dad's body.'

'Why is she doing that? Why didn't you ask me to do it?' He stood up, every inch of him aching, as if his goddamn bones had turned to iron.

She looked up at him, a slight look of puzzlement on her face, as if she were wondering whether she had lost all touch with him. 'I just didn't think of it . . . Could you have done it? I mean, faced up to something like that?'

'Who's organizing the funeral?'

'Angela.'

'Jesus!'

Then the front doorbell rang. He pushed past her, almost roughly, and went down the hall and opened the front door. Inspector Malone and the other one, the sergeant, stood there. He was suddenly glad to see them: at least they were an interruption.

'Your mother home, Jay?'

He led them back through the house, out to the garden room, where his mother had retreated, where she stood in her electric-blue gym outfit, her hair tied back with an electric-blue ribbon, looking so young and healthy it was gross. He caught a glimpse of himself in the small mirror above the drinks cabinet and he winced, he looked so goddamn *old*.

'I said we'd be back, Olive. A few more questions.'

'More?' She sat down, arranging herself in her convent-girl pose again. 'Would you like some coffee? Jason, would you make some? The kettle's on.'

Jason went into the kitchen and Malone and Clements sat down apart from each other, so that Olive would have to keep turning her head from one to the other to watch them and their reaction to her answers to their questions.

111

It was an old ploy, but still a good one.

Malone, as a fast bowler, had never believed in a few warm-up balls; he had always bowled the first ball as fast as he could, hoping to surprise the batsman by bowling him or at least hitting him somewhere vulnerable. 'Olive, when we mentioned the five thousand dollars that was withdrawn from your joint account last week, you let us believe Will had drawn it.'

'Did I?' She had ducked under the bean-ball. 'It wasn't intentional. I can't remember anything I told you – when was it? – Sunday morning?'

'No, it was yesterday morning.'

She shook her head; but she was totally composed. 'I've lost track of all time, Scobie.' She ran her hands up her lycra-clad thighs, not sensually but as if testing that her muscles had benefited from her work-out. 'I went to aerobics this morning – I thought if I had a really good work-out, I could put my mind back into gear . . . Yes, I withdrew the money. It was to pay for our holiday on the Reef.'

Clements looked at his notebook; Olive turned her head to watch him. 'Mrs Rockne, that's definitely not what you said yesterday morning. You said then that your husband must've withdrawn the money. You were going to Lizard Island, which you said is pretty expensive – *exclusive* is the word you used – and you had to get new outfits. I don't know what Inspector Malone thinks, Mrs Rockne, but I think you're lying. Are you?'

Olive stared at him, then slowly turned her gaze on Malone. 'Do you let him talk to everyone like that?'

'I never try to stop him, Olive. More often than not he gets us the answer we want.'

'And what sort of answer do you want? You're grilling me again, Scobie. Or should I call you Inspector?'

112

'Please yourself. What's your answer to what Sergeant Clements just asked you?'

Then Jason came back with four coffees and a plate of biscuits. 'These are Mum's home-made, you'll like 'em, Mr Malone. Claire told me you had a sweet tooth.'

Malone smiled at the boy as he sank down, all arms and legs again, into a low chair beside his mother. 'Do you two swap gossip about your respective parents?'

'Jesus — sorry. No, geez, no. I dunno what made me say that — about your sweet tooth, I mean.'

'Jason, I think it'd be an idea if you went in and did some study. He's missing school and he's got the HSC trials coming up. He wants to go to university and do law, like his father.'

He didn't; he wanted his share of the five-and-a-bit million and to take off for the other side of the world. 'No, I'll stay, Mum . . . I keep trying to tell her, Mr Malone, she has to accept I'm man of the house now, right?'

'Yes, I think you could say that, Jay. Let him stay, Olive. Unless you have something to say that you don't want to say in front of him.'

'No, no. It's just that — I suppose I'm trying to protect him and Shelley. I can't get used to the idea that Jason's suddenly grown up, over a weekend.'

The boy wiggled his big hands at the two detectives; the gesture was too awkward for supplication, it suggested helplessness. Clements nodded sympathetically, but said nothing. The boy was under siege, but didn't know whom to strike out at.

Malone, not pausing to indulge his sweet tooth, passed up the plate of biscuits, bowled another fast ball at Olive. 'Did you know Will had a brain tumour?'

She did not play that one at all well; she had prepared herself for a certain line of attack and he had flung one at her out of the dark. 'Where did you get *that*?'

'The GMO, the government medical officer who did the autopsy. It'll be in the official report for the coroner. She, the GMO, says it looks to her as if it would have been inoperable. You didn't know? He'd never complained of headaches or anything?'

'Once or twice he complained of a headache in the morning, but when I'd ask him at night he'd say it had gone during the day.'

'That's one of the symptoms,' said Clements, who had talked to Romy. 'Unlike a migraine, which gets worse as the day goes on. Did he vomit at all?'

'Once, I think. But he said it was probably something he'd ate.' She looked genuinely shocked, her face pale and stiff; the gym outfit now seemed a mockery, fancy wrapping on a lifeless mannequin. Jason put out a tentative hand, but she seemed unaware of it, and he dropped it back on his own knee. Then she said, 'I wonder if he knew?'

'There might be something in his papers – we'll have to get permission to go through all of those. What about insurance?'

'He was insured – I don't know how much for.'

'We can check that. At the same time we can check if he increased the insurance recently.'

'Why would he do that?' said Jason, trying to be adult.

'People do that sometimes when they know they have something incurable. They try to dupe the insurance company, but they rarely get away with it. Of course, with all that money in the secret account, why would he worry about trying to dupe the insurance company?'

Olive had her eye on the ball again; she was once more composed, the stiffness gone from her face. 'You're starting to hint that you suspect Will of something. I don't think I want you to talk about him like that in front of Jason.'

'I'm not suspecting Will of anything – yet. So far all we're trying to do is establish a motive for his murder. We've had the five and a quarter million dollars frozen, by the way.'

'Can you do that?' Her composure cracked a little. 'Isn't it ours? Mine and the children's?'

'Not till we've been through all of Will's papers. Then there'll be probate. I wouldn't start spending it yet, Olive.'

Exactly what Pa Rockne had said, thought Jason; and suddenly wondered if the money would ever be theirs. And, strangely, all at once didn't care.

Malone stood up and Clements followed suit. 'Olive, could I see you alone a moment?'

Without a word she got up and followed him out of the house, to stand behind the gate that led into the pool enclosure. Jason got to his feet and looked at Clements. 'Is my mother in trouble, Sarge?'

'I don't know, Jay.' Clements played a dead bat. 'The inspector doesn't always let me know what he's thinking.'

Out by the pool Malone was saying, 'You're not telling the truth, Olive. Or your memory is falling apart. Either way, I think you'd better start talking to your friend Mrs Bodalle or some other lawyer.'

'You do suspect me of having something to do with Will's murder, don't you?' There was no note of anger or shock in her voice; he could have been an inspector from the Randwick council, telling her she was behind in her rates. 'That's really shitty, Scobie.'

'Unfortunately, that's how my job is most of the time. I think you'd better talk to Mrs Bodalle. In the meantime, Olive, don't do anything foolish, like trying to disappear.'

In the house Jason was staring out at his mother. 'Sarge, why do people commit murder?'

115

Clements almost said, *Ask your mother*, instead he said, 'Jay, I've worked on a hundred homicides. For every one there was a different reason.'

He knew that countless juries had asked the same question as Jason had. But now was not the time to talk of juries while Malone was outside there pointing the finger at the boy's mother.

3

Malone had always liked elegant women; her elegance had been what had first attracted him to Lisa. The attraction lay, perhaps, in the fact that as a boy, his contact with such women had been nil; Erskineville, where he had grown up, and later the Police Department, had never been metaphors for refined taste. Angela Bodalle, he had to admit, was good to look at, even if her manner could rub him raw.

'I've been half expecting you, Inspector, after what you said on Sunday morning.'

'What did I say?'

'That you never phoned, you just knocked on the door. What did my clerk say when you announced yourself?'

'He knows me, I've been here before to these chambers.'

Clements had dropped him off outside Temple Chambers in Phillip Street and had then driven back to Homicide. Phillip Street, named after the colony's first governor, is flanked for the most part by unprepossessing buildings. It is, however, the main breeding ground for the city's lawyers; the air is thick with smug professional superiority, most of it male. Round the southern corner is the State Supreme Court, twenty-two layers of even greater smug superiority, again most of it male. Barristers, in wigs and gowns, stalk the street between their chambers and the courts like black peacocks; the occasional peahen can be seen, but she knows her place and walks some steps behind. Tradition rules here, though it runs close to snobbery. The grey horsehair wigs come from the same makers in London who supply English Queen's Counsels. QCs once wore robes that dazzled the eye, but in 1714, on the death of Queen Anne, they donned black and had worn it ever since, though half the local silks would have had trouble placing Anne in the British royal succession. Tradition rules, at up to seven thousand dollars a day. Angela Bodalle, Malone had heard, commanded about half that price but was working her way up the scale.

She was dressed this morning in a cream silk blouse and a discreetly patterned blue and black skirt; the jacket of the suit was hanging on a coat-tree in one corner. The room was large and airy, unlike some of the nooks Malone had been in in older chambers. A royal-blue carpet gave the room an added lift. There were two large prints by American artists on facing walls and a third wall held an original by Frank Hodgkinson; Malone knew none of the artists, but remarked the difference between them and some of the prints and paintings he had seen in other barristers' rooms. The furniture was light oak, the up-holstery a paler blue than the carpet. The law might have a gloomy rather than a bright side, but Angela was obviously determined to lighten her own mood, if not her clients'. Four large bowls of early roses stood on small tables against the walls. Even the shelves of legal books looked as if their bindings had been retouched.

She gestured at the papers on her desk. 'You're fortunate to catch me in. I have a case tomorrow, it'll probably be a long one. The Filbert murder — not your turf, was it? No, of course not, it was in North Region.'

'I read a bit about it. You're defending the husband?'

'No, I'm prosecuting this time.'

117

'That's a turn-up, isn't it? I mean, for you.'

'My first time. I thought I should show a little public spirit, so I put my name to the DPP. He agreed. I think it amused him to have a woman prosecuting a man for killing his wife. We lawyers like to be amused, we pride ourselves on our wit. Or the males among us do. How's Olive?'

'You mean she hasn't rung you? I thought she'd have been on to you by now.'

She smiled, but showed very little of her teeth. 'She has, Inspector. You have been leaning on her pretty heavily. You shouldn't do that, not without her lawyer present.'

'Meaning you?'

She nodded. 'I think I'll have to insist that if you want to talk to her in future, I be there.'

'That may not be easy, Mrs Bodalle. Not if you're going to be in court for the next six or seven weeks. I try not to work at night, if I can avoid it.'

She smiled again, showing more teeth this time; she looked almost friendly. 'I'd like meeting you in court, you and I could have quite a time jousting, as my more pompous male colleagues call it.' Then she shuffled the papers in front of her. 'But I'm busy now, Inspector. Why have you come?'

He liked direct women; there were more of them around than many men, including Clements, were prepared to admit. He was equally direct: 'Why did you recommend that Will Rockne take his car to Hamill's to be serviced?'

'They told you I recommended him?'

'No. I met your client Kelpie Dunne there and I put two and two together. It's an old police habit.'

The almost-friendly look had abruptly gone from her eyes; she was prepared to joust, seriously. 'I recommended Hamill's because they are so damned good.'

'Not because Kelpie works there?'

118

'It was Mr Dunne who told me how good they were.'

'He got in touch with you especially to tell you that?'

'No, I bumped into him one day in the street — he saw me getting out of my car.'

'Does Olive know Kelpie?'

Her gaze was direct. 'I wouldn't know.'

'Where do you live, Mrs Bodalle?'

'I don't know that's any of your business, but you'll find out anyway, I'm sure. I live at McMahon's Point. Why?'

McMahon's Point lay in the western shadow of the Harbour Bridge, a narrow finger shoved into the waters of the harbour. 'I just wonder why you go all the way out to Newtown to have your car serviced. There must be good workshops on your side of the water.'

'I told you, I go to Hamill's because they are so good. I'm very careful of my car. I'm what I suppose they call a car woman. If I were a man you'd be claiming there was some sexual symbolism in what I drive.'

'Not me. If you saw what I drive, you'd class me as impotent. So you would never drive a Volvo?'

'No. They are just for safety-minded drivers. Not that I'm reckless. But when you've driven a Morgan or an Alfa or a Ferrari . . . What do you drive?'

'A Commodore, nearly eight years old. You'd leave me standing at any traffic light. If Hamill's are so good at servicing high-priced sports cars, why did you recommend that Will take his Volvo there? Wouldn't the mechanics have turned up their noses at it?'

'They might have, but not when I asked them.'

'Are they sweet on you or your Ferrari?'

She smiled again. 'Both, maybe.'

'Would any of the mechanics, besides Kelpie, have been clients of yours?'

'No.' The smile had gone again.

'Where does Olive take her Honda Civic?'

'I haven't the faintest idea. Not to Hamill's — they'd draw the line there.'

Malone had never understood the snobbery about cars, but he wouldn't dare voice that to someone who had called herself a car woman. 'Mrs Bodalle, you've been a friend of the family how long?'

'A year, maybe a little less.'

'Oh? Somehow I'd got the idea that you'd been a friend a long time, that you and Olive were *old* friends.'

'We're *close* friends. How long we've known each other doesn't really matter, does it? How many old friends do you have?'

Come to think of it, and he had not thought much about it at all because it did not worry him, he had no old friends or even close ones. Except, of course, Russ Clements, and (wrongly, he admitted now) he had always thought of Russ as a workmate. He was not an authority on friendship, so she had him there.

'How did you meet?'

She considered the question, as if debating whether she had to answer or not; then she said, 'We went to the same school, I was a couple of years ahead of Olive. Then we bumped into each other again at a legal convention, she was there with Will . . .'

'Were you a close friend of Will's?'

The thought amused her; she shook her head. 'Are you hinting I might have had an affair with him? Forget it, Inspector. Neither of us ever really liked the other.'

'Did you dislike him enough to want to kill him?'

She was far from amused now; her look could have killed. 'That's a stupid question! If you're going to continue that line, your time's up.' She shuffled her papers together.

He grinned. 'Mrs Bodalle, you're not on the Bench, not yet. Only judges tell a cop when his time's up. I'm not

120

accusing you of killing Will Rockne, I just asked you if you disliked him enough to *want* to kill him. You're a lawyer, you should know the difference.'

She didn't relent. 'I think you'd better go.'

He stood up, not made awkward by his dismissal. Police are always being dismissed or told to get lost or to fuck off, depending on the manners of those being bothered by the police. He had been dismissed by women with tongues like spiked leather: at least Angela Bodalle was coldly polite.

'If you didn't get on with Will, I don't suppose he ever confided to you that he had a brain tumour?'

That stopped her shuffling her papers; her hands were as still as dead birds. 'Does Olive know?'

'She does now. I don't think she knew till I told her. The autopsy showed it was inoperable. He'd have been dead in six months or less. The killer could've waited if he'd known. Good luck with your prosecution. How's Filbert pleading?'

'Not guilty. You men usually do, don't you?' Then she said quickly, 'Sorry, I didn't mean that.'

'Why don't you like men, Angela?'

He went out without giving her time to reply. Outside in the street he stood and watched as four barristers, gowns aflutter in the wind that had sprung up, heads bent to keep their wigs anchored (why, he wondered, did they wear their wigs in the street; how many white horses had given up their hides to supply this conceit?), made their way round the corner to the courts, where more wind would blow at thousands of dollars a day. Like most cops, he had little time for lawyers, even those on the police side, the prosecutors; he could not imagine his being enthused at working with Angela Bodalle as the prosecutor. He wondered what her fee would be if she had to defend Olive Rockne against a charge of murdering her husband.

It had been a bad day for bookmakers at the Randwick midweek meeting. There had been seven races on the card and in six of them the favourites, heavily backed, had romped home; the horses, as they passed the post, had been laughing and even those most lugubrious of characters, the jockeys, had been smiling. Bernie Bezrow sighed, a hissing sound, and looked at his clerk.

'Charlie, this has got to stop. The punters have stopped coming to the course and those who do have an unearthly anticipation of what's going to win. How did the TAB do today?'

Charlie Lawson, thin as a slide-rule and as old-fashioned, thirty years a bookie's clerk, an old-timer who never used a calculator but still persisted with his pencil and his nimble mind that could tell you the square root of the national debt in ten seconds flat, pushed back his straw hat and nodded in agreement with his boss. 'Things are crook, Bernie. The TAB was down twelve per cent today.'

That was the only satisfactory note in the day, that the government betting agency was also feeling the pinch of the recession. 'I hate to break the law,' Bernie said piously, 'but it looks as if we'll be forced to concentrate on the footy.'

'We been doing that since the start of the season.' Charlie Lawson was a matter-of-fact man, as a good penciller should be.

'Don't flourish the obvious, Charlie. I'm trying to ease my conscience, if I can find it. I had one, once, but it got lost somewhere in all this fat. What's the money now on Penrith for the grand final?'

'Too much. If Penrith wins, we might have to retire.'

Bezrow sighed again. 'The thought doesn't frighten me, Charlie. The good old days have gone.'

He looked round the betting ring, at the now empty stands, the litter, the backs of the departing small crowd. He was one of the privileged, the rails bookmakers, the last of those who had been household names, or anyway stables names, in the racing game, Jack Shaw and Ken Ranger and Terry Page and now himself, the last identity. Punters such as Hollywood George and Melbourne Mick and Kerry Packer had bet hundreds of thousands of dollars with him; he had taken them and they had taken him and there had never been any ill-feeling; it was a game that no one but true gamblers understood. Now, it seemed, it was all coming to an end; maybe only a temporary end, but he would be dead before it revived. He sighed once more, struggled out of his chair, took Charlie Lawson's hand to help him as he stepped down off his stand.

His private security man, whom he employed only on race days, came across the paper-strewn lawn. 'Not much to worry about today, Matt. Charlie has it all there in the bags.'

The Australian Jockey Club didn't allow security guards other than their own to wear uniform; Matt, a big blunt-faced man, wore slacks and a jacket, but carried a gun in a shoulder holster. There had been several attacks on bookmakers over the past twelve months, not on the racecourses but, mostly, as they were about to enter their homes. Bezrow had never been attacked, but, like most of the top bookmakers, he had been tested with threats of extortion. He had lied to Malone and Clements when he had claimed to be a fatalist. He was a long way from being a cowardly man, but when it came to personal safety, of his own and of Charlie Lawson, he didn't believe in long odds.

'You want us to drop you off first, Mr Bezrow?' The

security guard took his job seriously, especially now in the recession. Young punks, amateurs, were moving into areas where previously only professional stand-over men had operated.

'No, just escort Charlie. I have someone waiting for me in my car. I'll see you tomorrow morning, Charlie. We'll talk about the odds on Penrith.'

He walked out of the betting ring towards the car park. Despite his huge bulk he didn't waddle; he walked almost daintily, as some fat people do. Cars were still easing their way out of the racecourse and he dodged them with some grace. Then he came to the peacock-blue Rolls-Royce. His chauffeur, a thin dapper Vietnamese, held open the rear door for him.

'The gentleman is waiting for you, sir.'

'Leave us for fifteen minutes, Trang. I'll signal you when we're ready to go.'

He got into the car with some difficulty, sank back beside the slim body already in the rear seat. 'Hello, Walter. Thank you for coming. You have enough room?'

Walter Palady was pressed hard up against the leather trim, making room for his host. 'Yes, Bernard. Did you have a good day?'

'Not a good day at all. But that's the least of my worries. Have the police been back to you again?'

Palady shook his head. 'No. But that is not to say they have forgotten us.'

'Did my name come up at all?'

'No. The two officers asked who had recommended Mr Rockne to our bank, but my manager had a convenient lapse of memory. It is an advantage that banks have a reputation for not thinking fast on their feet – when did a bank manager ever give a snap decision?' He smiled and Bezrow smiled in return as a fee. 'Some clients, *most* clients, complain, but they are the stupid little depositors

124

in ordinary banks.' He smiled again at the big, and not stupid, depositor beside him. 'No, Bernard, you are safe. So far.'

'So far? That's what worries me. How long does it take you, Walter, to move my money through your branch here to the Caymans?'

'We can do it overnight, if we have to. But it looks better if we send it out in parcels. It goes a roundabout route, through places not as obvious as the Caymans.'

Bezrow chewed his thick lips. 'I'll be depositing a lot of money with you in the next couple of weeks, a lot. The rugby league grand final,' he explained when he saw the polite puzzlement on Palady's face. 'You haven't been here long enough, Walter, but you'll find that Australians' main cultural pursuit is sport,' he said, sitting there in his Rolls-Royce in the car park of the State's biggest racecourse. 'Nobody ever made money in this country betting on the arts. Of course some pop stars have made a fortune or two, but one can't say they are part of the arts.' He smiled at Palady; the latter smiled back, though he was musically deaf and wouldn't have known Beethoven from boogie-woogie, whatever that was. 'This year the rugby league, and remember it is played in only two States, will pull in fifty million dollars in bets. All of it illegal, except up in Darwin, where, it seems, anything goes.' He spoke with the bitterness of a man who hated unfair competition. 'My SP network – '

'SP?'

'Starting price betting. It's illegal, but it's like Prohibition was in the US in the Twenties – nobody sees anything wrong with it, except the wowsers. Don't ask me to explain wowsers to you, Walter, or we'll be here till dark. They are sort of civilian ayatollahs. What I'm telling you is that in the next couple of weeks I shall be depositing several million dollars and I don't want anyone coming to you and asking awkward questions. Have you moved any of the money Will Rockne deposited with you?'

'Not yet. I don't think he had any intention of doing so.'

'It wasn't Rockne's money, you know that? He came to me and said he had a client who wanted to bury some money, bury where no questions would be asked. I met the client and recommended your bank. That was before you arrived out here.'

'Harold Junor tells me it was originally deposited in a trust account, with Mr Rockne as the trustee. Then two weeks ago it was transferred to an account in Mr Rockne's name only.'

'Junor didn't query it?'

Palady shifted awkwardly in his confined space. 'Bernard, how would you feel if we queried what you did with your money? We're not that sort of bank. If we were, what use would we be to our clients?'

Bezrow nodded. 'Point taken. So what's happening to the money?'

'The police told us to freeze it till further notice, which we've done. After that . . .' He shrugged, the only movement he could make without fighting the heavyweight beside him for space. Other people's money never worried him, once they had paid their commission and fees.

'When the police come back, Walter, keep my name out of it. Understand?'

'That may not be so easy, Bernard.'

'Harold Junor will think of something, he's been here long enough to know the ropes. This country has some of the most incompetent and dilatory investigators one could ask for – you have only to read the accounts of the royal commissions and other investigations going on all over the country at the moment.'

'Inspector Malone didn't strike me as either incompetent or dilatory.'

126

'He's a Homicide detective, Walter. Throw him into the money field and I'm sure you and Harold Junor can bamboozle him. After all, your bank has fooled some of the best financial brains in bigger countries than this backwater.'

Palady looked hurt, but did his best to smile in agreement. It was taking him some time to become accustomed to Australians, even those with Russian blood in them. Their rudeness was not as civilized as that of the English and the French. He admired those two, aspired to be a blend of them, perhaps because in his polyglot blood there was a pint or two of those nationals.

Chapter Five

1

'What do you want for lunch tomorrow? Or are you going to disappear again without telling me?'

'Mum, I did tell you – you just weren't listening. I told you Jill had called, she wanted you, and then she asked me if I wanted to go down and have a hamburger with her.'

'What did she want me for?'

Jason and Olive were making their slow way down the aisles of the supermarket here in the Randwick shopping centre, he pushing the trolley and she choosing what she wanted from the shelves. Olive had always done her grocery shopping here at Franklins at Will's insistence; Franklins was cheaper than the other chains and Will had been a compulsive comparison shopper. Olive, on the other hand, was an impulse buyer; the true species, not the lovers, who made the real world go round. Jason had grown tired of hearing the constant arguments over her spending. Today, he guessed, they had come here to Franklins out of habit.

'I'll tell you when we get back to the car.'

She looked at him curiously. 'Something important?'

'I dunno, it could be. Not here, wait till we're out in the car.'

A well-dressed man said, 'Excuse me,' and went by, pushing a trolley containing a box of cornflakes. He did not look like the usual shopper here in Franklins, but Jason took little notice of him.

He followed his mother on automatic pilot, thinking about Jill and what she had told him and what he now felt. When he had arrived at his father's office with the hamburgers, the chips and the cakes he had bought as an afterthought, she had got up from her desk and closed and locked the front door. 'So's we can eat in peace . . . You look tired, Jay.'

'Yeah, I haven't been sleeping too well. You look okay, though. No, you look better than that. Great.'

She was dressed in a khaki skirt and a yellow blouse that showed off her breasts; he had noticed them before and sometimes had wondered if his father had. Dad obviously had: hence the weekend at Peppers. 'Thanks. I don't *feel* great. I'm sort of up in the air – what's going to happen here?' She gestured around her. 'Will your mother sell the practice?'

'I haven't a clue. Mum seems to be stumbling around in the dark at the moment. Here.' He gave her a hamburger, sat down opposite her. Her skirt was short and it slid up well over her knees. He had never been a leg man, that was something older guys seemed to appreciate, but now all at once he saw what good sexy legs she had. 'Great.'

'What?'

'Nothing. Are you worried about your job?'

'Of course. They're hard to get. I've got two girlfriends who've been out of work for six months, nine months, one of them. If I lost my job I'd have to move back home and I don't want that – it's nice being free.'

'Yeah, I guess so.' He wondered for the first time if she had a boyfriend, if she lived with some guy.

'Jay?' She was looking at him carefully, a slight frown between her brows.

'Yeah?'

'I'm worried. And scared, too.'

He paused in his eating, the hamburger halfway to his mouth. 'What's been happening?'

'Nothing, really. Except — ' She pushed her hair back from her forehead; he liked the way it fell down to cover one eyebrow. 'The police told me on Sunday, that Inspector Malone, that nothing in here was to be touched. Then the police from Maroubra came here on Monday and told me they were sealing the filing cabinets — they're coming back this afternoon to go through everything.'

'So what are you scared of — the police?'

'No. No, they've been pretty decent — they're young guys — '

He'd be pretty decent, too, if he had to deal with someone as pretty as Jill. He'd taken notice of her before, what guy with balls wouldn't, but today, somehow, he was looking at her with different eyes.

'This morning, just as I got in, a Mr Lawson came in. He said he'd been sent by Mr Bezrow and he wanted all Mr Bezrow's files. I said I couldn't give them to him because all the cabinets were sealed. He didn't seem too upset, he just sorta shrugged and left. But then not long after, Mr Jones came — '

'Mr Jones? Who's he?'

'He's the guy you heard me telling Inspector Malone about — no, you didn't, I think you were out here then, while I was inside with the inspector. He's the foreign guy who came a coupla times to see your father, a real smoothie. He asked for his files, too. But then he got pretty — agitated? You know, worked up — when I told him the same as I'd told Mr Bezrow's man. He asked if there were any files of his in the cabinets and I told him I couldn't say without checking. Then he snapped something at me, I dunno what the language was, and he stormed out, pretty angry and het up.'

'Did you ring the police?'

130

'No-o. I thought I'd talk to your mother first.'

'Did this guy Jones threaten you?'

'No, not in so many words ... Jay, I hate to say this, but I think your father was into something fishy before he was – was murdered. And I don't want to be any part of it.'

He leaned across with a comforting hand; without design, it fell on her knee. He left it there when her own hand came down on his. 'Jill, I think you'd better tell the cops when they come this afternoon.'

'Jay, I don't want to make things complicated for you and your mother. And for your father, even though he's dead now.'

'Jill, you don't owe me and Mum – and Dad – anything, not if it's gunna cause you any trouble. Jesus, I'd hate anything to happen to you!'

She squeezed his hand; under the pressure his hand tightened on her knee. 'You're sweet.'

'Sweeter than Dad?' He couldn't help that: he could have bitten off his goddamn tongue.

She looked at him, her hair down over her brow again. 'Yes, I think so. But you should never ask a girl a question like that. You'll learn.'

He grinned, pressed her knee. 'Yeah, I guess so. You want coffee?'

He stood up, feeling her fingers press his hand again as he took it from her knee. He stood above her, looking down at her from his full height. She looked up at him from under the fall of hair, her lips slightly open. They were a woman's lips, fuller than a young girl's like Claire's. He could feel the discomfort growing in his jeans and he hoped to God it wasn't going to show. In the shower after basketball he was both proud of and embarrassed by his dong; the guys, knowing his father was a lawyer, used to ask him if he was what was known as a well-hung jury.

He didn't want Jill to think that all he felt about her was randiness. He bent, slowly, waiting for her to turn her face away, but she didn't; he kissed her, feeling her lips open wider under his. Then, abruptly grown-up, knowing when not to push it too far, he straightened.

'Thanks,' he said quietly. 'That was nice.'

She nodded, still gazing up at him; he hadn't noticed before how beautiful her eyes were, dark blue and slightly slanted, as if maybe her great-grandmother or someone had gone to bed with a Chinaman. 'You've all of a sudden got older, haven't you?'

'I guess so . . . Have you got a boyfriend?'

'No one special. I go out with several.'

'Would you go out with me some time? A disco or something?'

She hesitated, still looking up at him. 'I'll think about it, Jay. In the meantime . . .'

'Sure. In the meantime . . .' He tried to sound – suave? – but he knew she had gently brushed him off. He had, after all, rushed things. 'In the meantime, I think you'd better tell the cops about that Mr Jones.'

'Are you going to tell your mother about him?'

'No, I don't think so. She's got enough on her mind right now.'

And now, as he pushed the supermarket trolley down the aisle behind his mother, he wondered how much he should tell her when they got out to the car. Though she was doing her best to keep to her regular routine, he could see that she was barely holding herself together. He had loved his mother and father, in a way that he could never put down in a letter to them. If he couldn't actually tell his mother he loved her, he could show it by protecting her. He made up his mind to lie to her, to tell her he didn't know why Jill had called her. If Jill had told the cops, as she had said she would, let the cops come and tell his mother.

When they got to the Honda Civic in the covered car park, a man was standing beside it with something under his arm. It was the well-dressed man who had passed them in the aisle inside the supermarket; the something under his arm was the packet of cornflakes. He straightened up, dipped his head in a little bow.

'Mrs Rockne? May I have a word with you?' His English was good, but he had an accent. Jason, who had a good ear and was a good mimic, thought there was a trace of American in the accent, as if the man might have learned to speak English in the States. But he was foreign, all right. 'I should like to speak to you alone, if I may?'

'Who are you?' said Olive, key in the door of the Civic. 'Why do you want to talk to me?'

'Just a little business talk, Mrs Rockne.' He was tall, almost as tall as Jason, with a broad-cheeked face, thick eyebrows and thick dark hair combed straight back. He wore what Jason thought might be an Italian suit, though he really wasn't into suits, and a dark blue tie with tiny red shields on it, like a university tie. He looked professional and successful and Jason wondered where his father had managed to snare a client like this. If he was a client. 'Alone, I said.'

'No,' said Jason. 'I'm staying. If you wanna speak to my mother, then you'll have to say it in front of me. Okay?'

Olive looked at him and for a moment he thought she was going to send him away; then she looked back at the stranger. 'Whatever you have to say, say it in front of my son. Who *are* you?'

'A client of your dead husband's. I don't think my name matters.'

'It wouldn't be Jones, would it?' said Jason.

Both his mother and the stranger turned their heads sharply; then the stranger said, 'It will do. You've heard of me?'

'The police mentioned your name the other day.' Leave Jill out of it.

That seemed to trouble the stranger; for a moment he seemed as if he might turn and walk away. Olive was still looking at Jason, almost as if he were as much a stranger as this tall man confronting her. Then she turned back to Jones. 'Say what you have to, Mr Jones.'

He gazed at the two of them a moment, as if debating whether he had anything to gain by saying anything at all. Then: 'Your husband stole five million two hundred and twenty-one thousand dollars from us.'

'Stole?'

'Yes, *stole*.'

'Who is *us*?' Jason had to admire his mother: she was cool, her mind clicking over in the right gear, like a lawyer's. Like Angela's, goddamn it.

'I don't think you need to know that, Mrs Rockne.'

'I think we'd need to know if we had to make out a cheque to hand it back to you.' Jason was surprised at how well his own mind was working. He was scared, sure, but he was almost *enjoying* standing up to this stranger. 'You wouldn't want it in cash, would you? Five-and-a-bit million?'

Jones glanced at him, almost smiled, then looked back at Olive. 'You have a smart son, Mrs Rockne. Smarter than his father was.'

Cars were coming and going, their noise accentuated in the low-roofed cavern. There was a crash of metal as someone drove in out of the bright sunshine to the comparative gloom of the car park. Jason turned his head and saw an elderly man get stiffly out of a small Ford and look at its dented fender; the car he had hit suddenly began to complain as its alarm went off. Jones looked irritably over his shoulder at the noise, then turned back to the two Rocknes.

'We want that money, Mrs Rockne, let there be no mistake about that.' He spoke precisely; there *was* a slight American intonation. 'Your husband did steal it, let there be no mistake about that, either.'

'Then why don't you go to the police?' Olive had opened the door of her car and was putting the groceries on the back seat. Jason, one eye on Jones, the other on his mother, wondered at this coolness he had never seen in her before. 'They'll check your story.'

'Then they will check your husband and the way he ran his business. You wouldn't want him branded a thief, would you, not now he is dead and can't defend himself? Or explain why he took our money.'

'You keep saying *us* and *our*,' said Jason, helping his mother with the groceries; their matter-of-factness was having an effect on Jones. 'Tell us who you represent.'

'Are you going to be a lawyer, son? Like your father? Or an honest one? Don't!' He raised a hand as Jason bunched a fist; they stared at each other, their gaze well above Olive's head. 'Don't be stupid, son, you'll only get hurt. Are you going to be stupid, too, Mrs Rockne?'

Olive looked down at the tin of tomato soup in her hand; her arm was bent for throwing. The burglar alarm of the car in the next row suddenly stopped; the big car park was abruptly, almost strangely silent. Olive looked again at the tin of soup, then she dropped it on the back seat of the Civic. 'No, Mr Jones, I won't be stupid that way. But I'd be stupid if I handed over all that money without knowing who you are. Do as I suggest, go and tell the police.'

'You don't care if your husband is labelled a thief?'

'No,' said Olive, avoiding Jason's eye.

'You're a strange one, Mrs Rockne.'

'I would be if I handed over all that money without knowing who you are.'

Jesus, thought Jason, what's got into her? He was suddenly afraid that his mother was pitching them into something that might have no bottom to it. Yet he heard himself say, 'Did you kill my father?'

'Don't ask questions like that, son.'

Jason had never belonged to any gang, had never in any way been dangerously threatened. But he could feel the menace in this stranger, knew the man *could* kill, and he felt suddenly cold.

If his mother recognized the menace, she didn't show it. She put the last of the groceries in the car. 'Put the trolley over there, Jason.'

He took it across to the line of trolleys against a wall. He stood there a moment looking back at his mother and the stranger; with cars coming and going, he couldn't hear what was being said. But they were both obviously angry with each other. Again he was abruptly afraid: *For God's sake, Mum, tell him they can have the money!*

He went back towards the Civic, jumping out of the way of some dumb young woman driver who reversed her Range Rover out of a row of cars without looking behind her. He glared at her, but she just gave him a smile as if apologizing for missing him. He hated these young mums with their four-wheel-drives and their bull-bars; he reckoned they could have won the bloody Gulf War, given their heads, in much less than three days. Then the mad thought dropped into his head that, if he had been behind the wheel of the Range Rover, instead of the dumb young mum, he could have driven it right over Mr Jones. The thought frightened him: he was thinking *murder*.

When he got back to the Civic he heard his mother say, 'Write a letter to my lawyer, Mr Jones. Her name is Angela

136

Bodalle, B-O-D-A-L-L-E. You'll find her office address in the phone book.'

Jones said nothing, just looked at her, then at Jason. Then he shoved the box of cornflakes at Jason. 'You have this. It's the sort of mush that should be brain food for you and your mother.'

Then he was gone, striding quickly off among the cars, moving arrogantly into their paths, ignoring the tooting of horns and the screech of brakes. Jason looked at his mother. 'He'll be back, Mum. Who is he, did he tell you?'

She was staring after the disappearing Jones, now just a silhouette against the bright light of the exit. 'No. But we're not going to give him the money.' Then she looked at him across the roof of the Civic. 'You want us to keep it, don't you? I think Dad meant for us to have it.'

'Why?'

'Because I think he knew he was going to die.' She ducked her head, slid into the driver's seat. His own door was still closed, the window up, and he barely heard her: 'I think he paid someone to shoot him.'

2

There had not been one cheerful headline on the main pages of the morning's newspapers. Malone remembered a line from the old Don McLean song, 'American Pie': bad news on the doorstep. Yugoslavia was reviving the old meaning of Balkanization, though that bastard word had not been invented when that part of the world had been known as the Balkans. The US Secretary of State was on a merry-go-round in the Middle East, with the Arabs and the Israelis standing on opposite sides of the carousel watching him go round and round. There were typhoons and droughts and starvation and unemployment; bad

137

news, it seemed, was infinite, the Four Horsemen were just four runners in a crowded field. So editors filled their back pages with news of the coming rugby league grand final: good news about Alexander's ankle, Meninga's hamstring, Stuart's groin. A balance had to be kept, or what was a sports editor for?

'No homicides today,' said Greg Random, folding his *Herald* and laying it on his desk.

'There's still time,' said Malone.

He had come across to Police Centre for his weekly half-hour chat with Chief Superintendent Random, Commander, Regional Crime Squad, South Region. They were old workmates; Random had been in charge of Homicide for ten years, and there was never any awkwardness or questions of rank between them. Still, Random had others above him whom he had to answer to: Assistant Commissioners, the Deputy Commissioner, the Commissioner, the Minister. Occasionally he answered to God, but that was not obligatory under public service rules.

'Don't spoil my day, Scobie. I've looked at the weekly report. You still have five unsolved murders. How's it going on the Rockne case?'

'Round and round. Up till this morning I thought the wife might've done it. Not that she did the actual shooting, but that she paid someone else to do it.'

'Motive?' Random had been born and raised on a wheat farm out west and, outwardly at least, he suggested he still worked to the slow rhythm of the bush. His build conjured up the image of a weatherbeaten fencepost, topped by grey hair thick as wire grass. His voice was a slow-motion drawl, words kept to a minimum by the unlit pipe that was always between his teeth.

'Several motives. I knew them slightly and I don't think they got on that well. He was heavy-handed, I don't mean he belted her, but he treated her as if she was a dumb blonde. Women get tired of that treatment.'

'It's not enough to drive 'em to murder. Go on.'

'He had an affair – well, a weekend – with his secretary. There may have been other women, I don't know. But the wife could have found out about them and that, on top of the way he treated her, could've put her over the edge.'

'Is she the hysterical type?'

'Not at all. In fact, she's surprised me since the murder, she's more in control than I'd expected her to be. Finally, there's a fortune, five and a quarter million dollars in a hidden bank account that she says she knew nothing about. But maybe she did know. Add up all those factors and she'd have a reason for getting rid of him.'

'There's something else you're thinking about. What is it?'

'Well, this is just a feeling, intuition, if you like – '

'I've never knocked intuition. My dad used to stand in the middle of a paddock in a dry spell and hold up his finger and say, "Rain's coming". He couldn't feel a bloody thing with his finger, but he was right nine times out of ten. It was intuition.' He took his pipe out of his mouth and sucked in a deep breath, as if such a long speech had winded him.

'Righto, intuition. I don't feel there's any grief in her. She acts as if shock has belted the soul-case out of her, but it's bullshit. Very restrained, but still bullshit. And Russ Clements and I have caught her out a coupla times in straight lies.'

'Lying isn't a crime, otherwise we'd be locking up every politician, and bureaucrat in the country, including myself.' He no longer considered himself a working cop but a bureaucrat; he had been much happier, if less well paid, lower down the totem pole. He took his pipe out of his mouth again, looked at it as if he had removed a molar. 'You haven't much to go on for an arrest.'

Malone nodded. 'I know. There are too many loose ends at the moment. Where did Rockne get the five million from? It's obviously not his, but it's in the bank in his name, so legally it goes to the widow and the two kids. Unless the real owner comes forward, and intuition tells me that's not going to happen.'

'What about this bookie, Bezrow? Could the money be his?'

'I don't know. We can't pin anything on him, not yet. But he's in it, somehow. Then there's Kelpie Dunne. It's just too coincidental that he starts servicing Rockne's car only a month before Rockne is murdered.'

'Has he got a record for being a hitman?'

'He has a record on just about everything else, ever since he was sixteen years old. I wouldn't put it past him to knock someone off for a price. He was up not too long ago for assault with intent, but he got off because of a smart lawyer. She's another factor.'

'She? Who? You mention Angela Bodalle in the running sheet – you don't mean *her*?' He aimed his pipe at Malone like a gun. 'You're a bugger for complicating things. A leading QC mixed up in a murder case . . . Go on.'

'I don't know at this stage what her involvement is. She's a friend of the family – or anyway, of the wife.' He paused, then sighed and sank a little lower in his chair. 'There's all that, but there's something else. Two things. Rockne's secretary told Sergeant Ellsworth, from Maroubra, yesterday afternoon that Bezrow's penciller, a feller named Charlie Lawson, called at Rockne's office and asked for all of Bezrow's files. She told him we'd put a seal on the filing cabinets. He made no trouble, just went away, presumably to give Bernie Bezrow the bad news. Then this other bloke, a Mr *Jones*, a foreigner was how she described him, he puts in an appearance and asks for *his* files. When she told him the same story about sealing the filing cabinets, he got very shirty. Now maybe the five and a quarter million belongs to him and he was the one who bumped off Rockne. Except that when Ellsworth's men went through the files, there was none on Mr Jones. And none for Bernie Bezrow.'

Random nodded. 'But there's something else, right?'

'How did you know?'

Random wet his finger and held it up.

Malone grinned, wearily. 'Yeah, there's something else. Russ Clements went to see Rockne's doctor, the family GP. Rockne knew he had a brain tumour, he'd known for a month. But he asked the doctor not to tell the wife, to give him time to put his affairs in order. Two weeks after he got the bad news was when he transferred the money out of a trust account into an account in his own name. He might have stolen it for his family and then paid someone to blow his head off.'

'Who, for instance?'

'Kelpie Dunne? Kelpie was originally a client of his.'

'Why wouldn't he just commit suicide? Why pay someone, unless he was trying to collect insurance, too?'

'Maybe that was it, I dunno. Rockne was pretty tight with money, he could've been the sort who, even with five million in the bank, couldn't bring himself to turn his back on an insurance pay-out. But Russ has checked and he didn't increase the premium after he'd found out he had the brain tumour.'

'So what are you going to do?'

'Kelpie works for a place called Hamill's out in Newtown — we think they're in the stolen car racket. Could you get the Motor Squad to look into them, stir up the water a bit? That might tickle Kelpie into doing something. What, I dunno, but something. We could drop him a hint

141

about the five and a quarter million and he might be stupid enough to come back on the widow for an extra fee, assuming he did the job.'

'I'll talk to Ric Bassano about it. They've got a thing called Operation Pluto going right now. They're a whimsical lot, the Motor Squad, they like to call their ops after cartoon characters. Anything else?'

'The Fraud Squad. I want to see if they can dig up anything on that bank in the running sheet, the Shahriver Credit International.'

'Done. Nobody else you'd like to use? The Audit Branch, Vice, Community Relations?'

'Your sense of humour's turned sour, Greg. It's sitting here on your bum doing nothing.'

'I keep holding up my finger – ' he illustrated ' – hoping something exciting will turn up, but I don't have my dad's intuition. Maybe it's because you can't open a window in this bloody place. There's nothing written on the wind in here – it's all filtered out by the air-conditioning.' His office was spartan, by his own choice; as if to remind himself never to become too comfortable here in the higher ranks. 'Good luck. Don't jump off the springboard before you've made sure there's water in the pool.'

'That's original. Where'd you get it – the Police Boys Club?'

He went out of the room as Random took a bead on him with his pipe. He walked out of the fortress of Police Centre and through the bright dry day to the Hat Factory, the one-time commercial building that now housed Homicide. He and the rest of the Homicide detectives had been resentful when they had been moved out of the near-luxury of the newly built Centre into the run-down Hat Factory. But a lick of government paint, some old but unused carpet discovered in a warehouse and a relaxed atmosphere had resulted in an acceptance of the

142

new accommodation. A good deal of police detection is taken up with thinking and discussion, which are often indistinguishable from malingering. Time-and-motion consultants, a breed watered and fed by the State's new Conservative government, never found their way into the Hat Factory.

As Malone entered his office, his phone was ringing. It was Sergeant Ric Bassano, of Motor Squad: 'Scobie? Chief Super Random has been on to me. I gather you're interested in Hamill's, out at Newtown? Coincidence, mate. So are we. We've got Operation Ninja Turtle going – '

Malone held his tongue before it could ask what had happened to Operation Pluto. 'Are you going to raid them?'

'Tonight. You want anyone held?'

'There's a cove named Kelpie Dunne, a mechanic. Get his particulars, as if you're meaning to get back to him, but let him go if you can. I'd like him out of work for a few weeks, see what he does.'

'What's he done?'

'Nothing recently, nothing that we can pin on him. But I've got my suspicions.'

'Haven't we all? As Pogo said, trust in God, but tie up your alligator.'

Pogo? 'Yep, he said it all.'

He hung up, went out to the computer and ran through all the running sheets on the squad's other homicides. None of them, it seemed, was as complicated as the Rockne case. He leaned back in his chair, wondering if he could start another hare running. If, of course, Kelpie Dunne did start running; the bastard might just stay put. He looked up as Clements came in and sat with his haunches on the table beside the computer.

'Do you think we'd gain anything if we leaked to some

reporter that there is a large sum of money in the background of the Rockne case?'

Clements looked dubious. 'Who, for instance?'

'Grace Ditcham. She'd never let on where the leak came from.' Ditcham was the city's best crime reporter, a terrier bitch, in the best meaning of the term, who had dug up more bones than the entire kennel of police dogs.

Clements thought a while, biting his lip; then he shook his head. 'Better not. A good lawyer would pounce on that as prejudicial before they'd even sworn in a juror. Let's wait. But I've got something else.' He followed Malone back into the latter's office, dropped a large desk diary in front of Malone. 'Take a look at that. Open it where the ribbon marker is.'

Malone opened the diary. The first entries at the top of the page listed half a dozen appointments, none with a name that meant anything to him. The last entry was not an appointment, simply: *Dad called, wants me to call him back. Why?*

Clements said, 'Rockne and his dad hadn't spoken for God knows how long. Then the old man phones, but obviously Rockne wasn't there to take the call. So he does what the old man asks – he calls him back. Turn the page.'

Malone turned the page. The entry for two days later listed four appointments. The last one, for 5 P.M., was with Mr Jones. 'So what's the connection?'

'Who's Mr Jones? Nobody seems to have a clue. But he comes to see Rockne two days after Old Man Rockne rings up his son who he hasn't seen or spoken to in we dunno how long.'

'What's working for you? Intuition or suspicion?'

'They're the same thing with me, but maybe that's a cop's dirty thinking. I think we oughta have another talk with George Rockne.'

'Righto, first thing tomorrow. In the meantime I've

asked Ellsworth to put Olive under surveillance. If Will
Rockne didn't pay someone to bump him off, then Olive
is next on my list of suspects. You agree?'

'Either her or Mr Jones.'

3

The Motor Squad carried out their operation that night.
Next morning Sergeant Bassano called Malone. 'We did
over Hamill's last night. We got nothing out of the
Newtown set-up – that was just a legitimate front, all the
cars in there belonged to reputable clients. But they had
another workshop, no signs, nothing, out at Tempe –
when we raided it, they had fourteen stolen cars in there.
Your mate Kelpie Dunne was working there, but we let
him get away. Was that what you wanted?'

'Just so long as you frightened him.'

'Oh, I think we did that all right. He fell over the back
fence getting away and one of my men said he went
hobbling off as if he'd been kneecapped or something.'

'We'll keep an eye on him, we know where he lives.
Thanks, Ric. And thanks to the Ninja Turtles, all of them.'

'We changed the code name. It was Operation Peanuts.'

4

George and Sugar Rockne lived out in Cabramatta, one of
the far south-western suburbs. Malone and Clements
drove out through another cloudless sky, the air as dry as
that a thousand kilometres inland. They drove through the
main shopping centre, past stores that suggested they were
in the suburbs of Saigon or Phnom Penh. There were as
many signs in Indo-Chinese characters as in English; a

McDonald's stood alone, like a last outpost. Asian faces seemed to outnumber European; two elderly women in black pyjamas stood gazing into a Jeans West boutique; they looked at each other, smiled, shook their heads and walked on. As Malone and Clements turned into a side street, half a dozen Asian youths on the corner turned to look after the unmarked Commodore, their faces as impassive as plates.

'They smell cop,' said Clements. 'I'd hate to work out here. A foreigner in my own country.'

'You sound just like my dad.'

'You don't feel the same way?'

Malone shrugged. 'I might if I had to work out here. But it's the future, mate, like it or not.'

He was, indeed, glad he did not have to work out here. Local gangs had most of the Vietnamese and Cambodian citizens intimidated and more than half the crimes committed were never reported to the police by the victims. The Force, pressured by ethnic groups who complained that there was not enough ethnic representation among the police, had recruited two young Vietnamese for enrolment at the police academy; one of them had resigned on graduation and the other had lasted only two months in the Force. Malone had never heard the reasons for the resignations, but he could make an educated guess that the two young men or their families had been threatened. He sometimes felt like telling the pressure groups that they should solve the problems themselves in their communities before asking the police to do it. But to make a remark like that would only have him, and the Force, branded racist or anti-immigrant.

The Rlocknes' house was small and unpretentious, built of fibro and with a corrugated-iron roof; but it was neat and well cared for. Malone noted at once that every window was barred and there was a strong security grille on the front door; George Rockne, for all his beliefs, didn't trust the proletariat. The street was a mixture of similar small houses, some brick, some fibro, one or two very old weatherboards, and half a dozen two- and three-storeyed flats. There were also three small factories: one sign announced *Pork & Duck Roasting*. Several of the houses and flats had For Sale signs on them; Malone guessed they were enforced mortgage sales. Cars, all of them inexpensive models, some of them only an accident short of being wrecks, were parked along both sides of the street. Unemployment was high out here; only a year or two ago these cars would have been missing during the day, with their owners at wherever their owners had worked. The street was quiet, soulless in the bright glare, as if all those within the houses and flats were dead or dying.

The two detectives walked up a concrete path between beds of marigolds, yellow nuggets on stalks; the two strips of lawn on either side of the path looked more like brown rush mats. Two large metal butterflies were attached to the grille security door; a ceramic kookaburra sat on a perch to one side, not laughing, morose as a crow. Sugar Rockne opened the front door behind the grille.

'Oh, Mr Malone and Mr Clements!' Professionally she had always called men by their first names; it is difficult to be formal when wearing only a feather or two. This morning she was wearing a bright yellow track-suit, her hair fluffed up, her make-up, ready, it seemed, for any visitors who might call. Though Malone wondered how many visitors she and George would get way out here in the boondocks of Little Asia. She smiled broadly, as if delighted to see them. 'George is out in the back yard.'

She led them through the house, which appeared to be furnished with more knick-knacks than a tourist trap. George Rockne, in a neatly pressed shirt and shorts and long socks, was fitting a new nozzle to a length of plastic hose. He did not seem surprised to see Malone and Clements. His face crinkled into a wry, rather than a welcoming, smile.

'Well, you said it was on the cards. That you'd wanna ask more questions, I mean.'

'Better come inside, love.' Sugar jerked her head to the left and the right. In the neighbouring windows curtains had fluttered. 'They're all getting their ears ready.'

George Rockne smiled. 'Sugar lived up the Cross for so long, everybody up there minded their own business. She forgot what it's like to live in the suburbs. Personally, I couldn't care a bugger.' As they went into the house he said, 'Still, I think we done the wrong thing, coming way out here. It was a matter of finance, but. I bought this place for a song from a Wog, he couldn't stand the neighbours.'

'It's fulla Asiatics,' said Sugar, ushering them into the small living room.

'Every one of 'em a bloody capitalist.' Rockne grinned again. 'Them that know I'm a commo, they won't talk to me. They think I'm spying for Pol Pot.'

There was small talk till Sugar brought them coffee and home-made rock cakes; Malone wondered if the cakes were baked each day in expectation of the visitors who never called. The room was crowded with cheap furniture, all of it spotless. A bookcase stood against one wall, its shelves heavy with political volumes; the only title that Malone recognized was *Ten Days That Shook the World*, once upon a long time ago Con Malone's bible. On the opposite wall was a row of shelves crowded with plaster figurines; Malone looked for Lenin or Marx, but then recognized that the shelves were Sugar's. A tiny Mae West lounged between a fan dancer (Sugar herself?) and a bust of the Queen; half a dozen small kookaburras, more hilarious than their big brother outside, had their beaks open in

148

silent laughter. But Malone didn't laugh, not even silently. He had been in too many homes like this one to miss the significance of the security of what furnished them.

'George, do you know a Mr Jones?'

It was a brutal first delivery, but Rockne didn't blink or duck. He just frowned and amidst all those wrinkles it was impossible to tell whether the question had surprised him or frightened him. 'I suppose I've known a dozen Joneses over the years. Which one are you referring to?'

'We think he's a foreigner, he has an accent of some sort. Tall feller, well dressed, looks like he sells Rolls-Royces.'

The wrinkles turned into another smile. 'You expect me to know what a Rolls-Royce salesman looks like?'

'I knew a man owned a Rolls,' said Sugar. 'Before your time, sweetheart.'

Rockne smiled affectionately at her. 'One of her capital-ist boyfriends . . . What gives you the idea I might know a Mr Jones?'

'Just a wild guess,' said Malone. 'There was a note about him in Will's diary.'

'Mentioning me?'

'Yes.' The way to the truth is often through lying: old police proverb.

But George Rockne wasn't going to fall for that one. 'I don't think so, Inspector. I never took anyone, Mr Jones or anyone else, to see Will.'

'You could've *sent* Mr Jones to see him,' said Clements around a mouthful of rock cake.

'This is getting nasty,' said Sugar and sounded disap-pointed in the two detectives.

'We're not meaning to be,' Malone reassured her. 'We've got nothing against George. It's Mr Jones we're after.'

'What's he done?'

'Well, for one thing he's been to Will's office in the last

149

coupla days and threatened Will's secretary, a nice harmless girl, for not giving him his files. She couldn't do it because we, the police, had a warrant on them.'

'What did the files say?'

'Oh, I couldn't tell you that, George.' Which was true.

Rockne looked round the room, bouncing a cake from one hand to the other as if it were indeed a piece of rock and he might throw it at something or someone. Then he looked back at Malone, his eyes almost lost amidst the wrinkles; he looked suddenly worried and tired and old. 'Has he been to see Olive and the kids?'

'I don't know. We're going there next. Who is he, George?'

Rockne put out his hand to Sugar; it still held the rock cake. 'You wanna go outside for a while, love?'

'No,' she said, clutching his wrist as if he might run away. 'I don't. Definitely. I'm staying, sweetheart. If you're in trouble . . . Is he?'

'I don't think so, Mrs Rockne. I don't think he'd have anything to do with the murder of his own son.'

She gasped at the brutality of what he had said. In the caves of Kings Cross she had seen more than enough violence: stand-over men with knives, crazed junkies running amok with smashed bottles, pimps belting their girls. But this was her own home, this was her husband, her sweetheart, sitting beside her. She still held his wrist, her grip tightening now.

'George,' said Malone quietly, 'tell us what you know.'

Rockne said nothing for a long moment; all his life had been devoted to keeping secrets. Living in a country where Special Branch and ASIO and the CIA and even, so he had heard, a certain Prime Minister had kept files on *him*, he had learned never to trust anyone; not even some members of the Party, not since the break-up post-Stalin. Matters had eased over the past few years, with the Party dwindling away till it was only a faint, mocking shadow of what it had been in the Thirties, when he had first joined as a very young man. As a youth of seventeen he had volunteered to join the fight against fascism, to go to Spain and fight Franco; but then they had asked him to pay his own fare and that had been the end of that. He remembered his reply, an old joke: 'Mate, if it cost only a quid to go round the world, I couldn't get out of sight.' Those had been the days, when there had been something to fight for; though there had been shock and disbelief when Joe Stalin had signed the pact with Hitler. But he and the Party had weathered that, as they had weathered the invasion years later of Hungary and Czechoslovakia. He had somehow kept his idealism alive, like a fragile plant, and only in the last couple of years had he admitted, only to himself, not even to Sugar, that idealism was not enough, that human nature would always defeat it. But you couldn't give it away entirely, not even when you saw the Wall come tumbling down, Lenin pulled by a crane from his pedestal: all you could do was pray (pray? Hail Marx, full of grace . . .) that human nature would see the light. He was a communist, once, now and for ever.

'His name's Dostoyevsky.'

'Like the writer? You're kidding.'

'You ever read *Crime and Punishment*? I'd have thought it was required reading for cops.'

Malone shook his head. Lisa had tried to introduce him to nineteenth-century writers, but they had proved too turgid for him; the only ones he had liked were Jane Austen and Mark Twain, a choice that had puzzled Lisa but not himself. He liked anyone who took the mickey out of pretension.

'Igor Dostoyevsky. He used to be a Second Secretary at the Soviet embassy in Canberra. I'm not sure, but I think he was the KGB boss, what the CIA calls its station chief.'

'He used to be at the embassy?'

'Yeah, but he resigned a year ago when things started to fall apart in Moscow. The same time as I retired.'

Sugar said to the two detectives, 'I still dunno whether he's happy or not.'

Rockne smiled gently at her. 'Love, everything I believed in went down the gurgler. You can't expect me to start singing "Happy Days Are Here Again".'

'Did the commos ever sing that?' But she, too, smiled. Maybe, thought Malone, she, too, had had her dreams that had collapsed about her. He had seen enough to know the world was littered with fallen icons.

'Did our government give him permission to stay here?' said Clements.

Rockne nodded. 'They had no proof he wasn't what he said he was – a disillusioned communist who wanted to start a new life out here. Personally, I think Special Branch and ASIO are still watching him, but what else have they got to do now? I don't think it worries him.'

'What does he do for a crust?'

Rockne's face was an abstract etching of amusement. 'He sells cars. Mercedes, not Rolls-Royces.'

'Then where did he get five and a quarter million dollars?'

Rockne sighed, sat back in his deep chair. 'He'll have me killed if he finds out I've blown the whistle on him.' Sugar gasped again and he glanced at her with concern. 'I told you to go outside, love. But I've gotta tell 'em. If he's been threatening the girl who worked for Will, next thing he could be doing the same to Olive and the kids. I don't care about Olive, she can look after herself. Or let that old bat of a mother loose on him.' He tried for humour, but it fell flat, too loaded with bitterness. Malone, a father, recognized how much the older man had missed his son and his grandchildren. 'I care about the kids, but. I don't

152

want Igor going anywhere near them.'

'We'll see he doesn't know who put us on to him,' said Malone. 'And we'll see Olive and the kids are protected. But what about the money?'

Rockne hesitated again; he was pouring part of himself, his principles, down the gurgler by blowing the whistle. 'It's money the hard-liners smuggled outa Moscow. He told me they've sent money all over the world, anywhere where there's a stable currency and there's a bank willing to take the money with no questions asked. I dunno what they're gunna do with it — maybe they're hoping for Lenin to come back from the dead, I dunno. But there's millions, *hundreds* of millions, all around the world. It belongs to the Party and it should of stayed in Moscow, but the hard-liners weren't having any of that, they say they still believe in the dream, that *perestroika* and *glasnost* are bullshit.'

'Are they, George?'

He sighed once more. 'I dunno. It's all history now, anyway.'

'So what did Dostoyevsky want with you?'

'He thought the Party, our party, had money salted away out here — he was like the CIA in that regard. I hadn't the heart to tell him the truth, that if it cost a thousand bucks for a revolution, we couldn't have bought a demonstration.' He smiled, remembering his old joke of over fifty years ago. 'When I retired, there wasn't enough cash in the kitty to give me a farewell do. Last year we celebrated May Day with a BYO — bring your own grog, your own snags for the barbecue. I dunno what they did this year, maybe held a wake. He told me how much money he was dealing with, and I thought Will might be able to help. I knew he handled a bookmaker or two and I knew some of them had to bury money they didn't want the taxman to know about. He was a bit surprised when I

153

called him, we hadn't spoken in years, but he said yes, he could arrange something. After I'd sent Dostoyevsky to see him, I had nothing to do with what went on from there. When Olive and Jason told me last Monday how much was in that bank – which bank was it?'

'Shahriver Credit International. Its headquarters are in Abadan, in Iran. I don't think it takes Bankcard.'

'Five million, or whatever it is. Though I thought there was more . . .'

'Maybe there is, maybe there's another account we haven't traced yet.'

'Whatever, Dostoyevsky and the men behind him aren't gunna let it go without a fight.'

'They'll have a job proving it's theirs, legally,' said Clements. 'What will Moscow say? Gorbachev and Yeltsin and the others, whoever finishes up in charge? What'll the Party here say? Especially if Dostoyevsky spreads the word that you and your son were in cahoots?'

Sugar gasped a third time and Rockne said, 'Jesus, I never thought of that!' He pondered a moment, then looked from one detective to the other. 'Do you *have* to do anything? I mean, why have you gotta let him know you're on to him?'

'Because,' said Malone, 'he could've known that Will had stolen the money. He might've followed Will and Olive out to Maroubra last Saturday night, waited till Olive got out of the car, gone up to Will and threatened him with the gun.'

'What would he of gained by killing Will? That wasn't gunna get him back the money.'

'Maybe something went wrong, the gun went off accidentally.'

'Maybe.' But Rockne didn't sound convinced. And Malone himself, having spelt it out, was also unconvinced.

'Where do we find him, George?'

154

Rockne demurred. 'No, I'm not gunna get any more involved – '

'George, don't make it any harder for us. We want to pick him up, question him, before he starts playing the heavy with Olive and the kids. Where can we find him?'

'Tell them, sweetheart.' Sugar had grabbed Rockne's wrist again.

He glanced at her: his love was plain, not hidden at all by all the wrinkles. 'If you say so, love . . . You'll find him at – ' He gave an address closer to the city. 'It's on Canterbury Road. He's not known as Dostoyevsky or Jones there. It's Boris Collins. It's a Mercedes dealer. Just don't tell him who sent you, okay?'

'You're safe, George.' Malone looked at Sugar. 'I promise you that, Mrs Rockne.'

'We'd like to move, go up north,' she said. 'But we can't afford it. This is where we finished up, the workers' paradise.' She looked out of the window, seeing nothing; then she looked back at Rockne. 'I don't blame you, sweetheart.'

'You should've taken some commission on the five million, George,' said Clements.

'Ah, I thought I was doing it for the cause. I was living in the past.'

Malone stood up, nodded at the bookshelves. '*Ten Days That Shook the World*. That was once my father's favourite book.'

'Once? What changed his mind?'

'He was never a commo, George, just anti-boss. On top of that he's never recovered from the shame of me joining the police force. He now reads biographies of crims who get away with it.'

'So many of 'em do, don't they? Especially the white-collar ones. Ah, it could of been a different world. What went wrong, Scobie?'

'If I knew that, George, do you think I'd still be just a cop?'

Outside in the street a purple Fairlane was drawn up behind the Commodore, its bonnet up as three youths made a pretence of working on the engine. It was the sort of car that highway patrol cops referred to as night-cars: they came out mostly after dark, prowling the streets, open exhausts rumbling, their occupants looking for easy pickings among the girls outside the hotels and games parlours. The three youths' heads came out from under the car's bonnet as Malone and Clements approached the Commodore.

'You troubling our friend George?'

Malone recognized the cop-baiting; it was an old ploy. The three youths were remarkably similar, Greek or Italian or Lebanese triplets. They wore their black hair the same way, high over their foreheads and long at the back; Malone had a quick memory flash of a late-night movie, the Andrews Sisters singing 'Don't Sit Under the Apple Tree'. He waited for the three youths to burst into song, but they just glared insolently at him and Clements.

'Not at all,' he said. 'We're old Party mates of his.'

'Bullshit. You're pigs.'

Malone looked at Clements, who was champing at the bit. 'Don't, Russ. You'll only muss up their hair.'

The two detectives got into the Commodore and Clements pulled it away from the kerb. Malone clipped on his seat-belt and sat back. 'Why do we bother even taking any notice of them?'

'They give me the shits, most of 'em, but then I sometimes wonder how I'd of finished up if I had grown up out here. It's bloody barren and depressing.'

Though Clements's parents were now living in a country town, he had been born and brought up in Rockdale, a comfortable bayside suburb close to beaches. In his youth he had driven souped-up FJ Holdens and Valiant Chargers, but he had always had respect for the law and its officers and had certainly never called any of them pigs. But he had come from another time, almost another country. There had been no unemployment then, the plum tree fruited every year and all year round, everyone knew the good times would last for ever. It had been only just over twenty years ago, an ancient era.

Canterbury Road is an eighteen-kilometre main artery heading south-west out of Sydney. It passes through several suburban shopping sections and then, further out, its length is dotted with new and used car lots, all of them festooned with the trade's universal theme of pennants and banners hailing the Sale of the Century. These strips have also become the beat for the cheaper prostitutes, many of them part-timers, housewives earning a bit on the side or any position you asked for. The used cars and the used women often share the same customers, the cars glossier than the women and higher priced and guaranteed.

As the two detectives got out of their car at the kerb, two women approached them. Their looks were mostly paint-jobs, but they had good figures and they were not the stripteasers who worked the beat in the inner city.

'Hi. You gentlemen looking for some company?'

'We've got each other,' said Malone, taking Clements's hand. 'We're also police.'

'Oh shit! We thought you were a coupla Canterbury footballers, the size of you.'

'Footballers at our age? Golden oldies? Relax, girls. We're not from the Vice Squad. Just move away from our car, we don't want the Vice fellers driving along here and thinking we've moved in on them.'

Kangaroo Mercedes, a name that couldn't have brought too many cheers back in Stuttgart, was a wide lot packed with cars, a glare of glass and paintwork.

'Look at 'em,' said Clements as he and Malone walked on to the lot. 'I wonder how many bankruptcies produced this many trade-ins? My heart bleeds for all those executives who have to catch the bus now or go to work in a Hyundai.'

'Stop gloating, you sound like a real commo. You're loaded enough to buy any one of these, even a couple, one for you and one for Romy.'

'Could you see me turning up at Homicide in a Merc? Internal Affairs would be on to me before I'd turned the motor off.'

A salesman in a pink cashmere pullover and a corporate tie marked with tiny three-pointed stars fell on them out of the glare. 'Morning, gentlemen! I'm Chris Dooligan, manager here. You thinking of trading up?' He glanced out at the Commodore at the kerb, managing not to sneer. 'A good car, the Holden, but we always hope to do better, don't we? What were you looking for?'

'A model named Boris Collins,' said Malone and produced his badge.

'Oh shit.' The manager could not have been more than thirty, but he had the look of a man who had spent most of those years on a used car lot. The eyes were weary from sizing up prospects, those who could pay and those who would renege; there was the paunch from too many liquid lunches with the more promising buyers; the mouth was loose from too many forced smiles. He didn't smile now, but looked positively downcast. 'What's he been up to?'

'Does he get up to much?'

They were standing amidst the mass of metal. The manager put on dark glasses, expensive shades with gold bars, and Clements took out his, a cheaper pair, and put them on. Malone just squinted.

'Well, no-o. But – don't quote me – things are so bloody desperate in the trade, you know, some guys bend the rules

158

a bit, you know, promise things we can't deliver . . . Anyhow, he's not here. He walked out last night, said he was going back to Russia. I didn't even know he came from fucking Russia. Who'd wanna go back there, I ask you?'

'Had he talked to you about leaving?'

'No, it came just outa the fucking blue.' He was letting his thinning red hair down; he didn't talk like this to customers, not even ones who might renege. 'He hadn't made a sale in, I dunno, a month at least, but he said he was out there, following up contacts with people he said he knew. He came to us with pretty good references.'

'Like what?' said Clements. 'The Russian embassy?'

The manager's brow furrowed. 'The what? What would their references be worth in our game? You ever seen a Ziv or a Zim or whatever they call 'em? They look like something outa Detroit in the Fifties. Nah, his references were from overseas. He'd worked for Mercedes in Europe and the States – '

'Did you check the references?'

'Well, no-o. You mean they were faked? Christ, I must be getting dumb in my old age. Tell you the truth, I took him on face value. He had what I was looking for – *class*, if you want a word for it. He wasn't the sort of sales rep you'd find on a Holden lot. No offence, you know what I mean. He's been with us six months and for the first four or five months, no matter how bad things were, he outsold us all. Except myself.' Pride had to be defended.

'Do you have a home address for him?'

'Sure, come across to the office. You sure you don't wanna trade up? I'll give you five hundred for the Commodore and you can drive off today in last year's 450SEL, just the job for running down the hot-rod hoons.'

'We're in Homicide,' said Malone. 'We go slow.'

Dooligan stopped dead in the doorway of his glass-fronted office. 'Has he murdered someone? Jesus!'

159

'No. We just hope he can help us with some enquiries. His home address?'

'Darlene, could you scribble out Boris's home address for these gentlemen?'

The girl in the office had enough hair to have stuffed a sofa, was pretty, wore a tight sweater and an even tighter skirt and would have been subjected to sexual harassment every day of the week; but she looked as if she would have been able to deal with it, even better than some of the girls out on the beat. She typed out an address and gave it to Malone with a smile. 'Give my love to Boris when you see him.'

'You knew him socially?'

'I went out with him a coupla times, but I never *knew* him. Nobody did.'

'You went out with him?' The manager sounded incredulous. 'You kept that pretty quiet!'

'We have our little secrets, us girls.' She gave him a smile that cut his balls off.

On the way out of the office Dooligan said, 'I got on okay with Boris, but like Darlene said, he was always a bit of a mystery man, you know what I mean? Never went out with us to a party or dinner, never anything like that. Never mentioned any family. That was why I was surprised when Darlene said she'd been out with him.'

'Maybe she had something more to offer him than a night out with the boys,' said Clements.

'She's never offered it to any of us. Well, give him my regards when you see him, tell him business is still lousy. You win Lotto, come back and see me. I'll give you a deal that'll have you driving away from here in a top-of-the-range model. You can pass on the Commodore to the wife then.'

'Actually, it belongs to the Commissioner's wife. Good luck. We hope business picks up.'

As they approached the Commodore the two whores came strolling along. 'How's business?' said Clements.

'Lousy.'

'It's that way all round.'

'Not with cops, I'll bet.'

'No, we're still getting plenty. Take care. Use a condom.'

They smiled and walked on. Only another hour or so before going home to greet the kids coming back from school, before preparing the meal for the husband who might or might not suspect where the extra money was coming from.

The address Malone had been given for Igor Dostoyevsky, aka Boris Collins, aka Mr Jones, was in Potts Point, buttock-by-buttock with Kings Cross but less soiled.

'Drop me off in Coogee. I want to see Olive again. Pick up John Kagal and have him with you when you bring in Mr Jones.'

'What are you gunna ask Olive this time?'

'If Mr Jones has been to see her.'

As the Commodore pulled up opposite the Rockne house Malone glanced across to the nearby side street. 'There are two fellers in a white Commodore over there. Would they be Ellsworth's men?'

'Either them or they're Mr Jones and one of his mates. I'll wait.'

Malone crossed the road and walked round the corner. He approached the Commodore, leaned on the roof and bent down to speak to the burly young man on the passenger's side. 'I'm Inspector Malone. I hope you're who I think you are.'

'Detectives Tilleman and Blake, sir, from Maroubra. We're part of the Rockne surveillance team.'

Malone straightened up, waved to Clements to move off, then opened the rear door of the car and slid in. 'Has Mrs Rockne had any visitors? A man, for instance, a tall feller, well dressed?'

'No male visitors, sir.' They were both young, probably in their first year as detectives, Malone thought; one lean, the other burly, both of them eager to show they were wide awake and nothing had escaped them. 'A woman visitor arrived about half an hour ago, with a young girl. An elderly woman.'

'That's probably Mrs Rockne's mother and the daughter Shelley. Any sign of the boy, a long drink-of-water of a kid?'

'No, sir. But — ' Malone waited, and the burly detective, Tilleman, went on. 'Twice since we've been here Mrs Rockne has come out to her car, that Honda Civic parked in the driveway, and used the car phone. Why would she come out of her house to use the car phone?'

'Unless the house phone, for some reason, is out?'

'It's working, sir. Ben here went down to that phonebox down the street and called the Rockne house, they're in the book. Mrs Rockne answered, but Ben said he had the wrong number and hung up. The house phone is working all right.'

'So, as you say, why would she come out to use the car phone? I think I'll think about that one for a while. In the meantime, ring Sergeant Ellsworth, tell him I want a warrant and a request on Telecom for a full list of calls made from Mrs Rockne's car phone since Sunday. Telecom keep a record of all calls on cellular phones. Tell him I'd like it on my desk by tomorrow morning. Oh, give him my regards. And good work, you two — I'll see he gets to know about it.'

He left them, walked round the corner and across the road to the Rockne house. He did not see the brown Mercedes parked further up Coogee Bay Road nor the tall, well-dressed man seated behind its wheel.

Chapter Six

1

Jason had answered the phone when it rang. A man's voice asked, 'Can I speak to Mrs Rockne?'

His mother had come along, taken the phone and waited till he had gone down the hall into the kitchen. There, standing just inside the doorway, he had strained his ears to hear what was being said. He despised himself for eavesdropping like this, but Mum had brought it on herself. The family was in trouble, under threat even, and she was still trying to lock him out as if he were some outsider.

He heard her say, 'I'll call you back — where are you?' Then she hung up and he heard her go up the hallway and out the front door. He ran silently up the hall and into the living room. From there he could see out through the side windows to the driveway. His mother's car was parked at the front corner of the house; he could just catch a glimpse of her in the front seat, just her left shoulder and arm. Then she leaned forward, her head coming into view, and he saw she was on the car phone. What was going on with her, for Chrissake?

Then she got out of the car and he went swiftly back to the kitchen, took a milk carton out of the fridge and poured himself a glassful. It was the wrong drink for the moment; it thickened in his mouth and he could hardly swallow it. He was angry and puzzled and hurt; what the hell was going on? He waited till his mother came into the kitchen and then he blurted out, 'Who was that on the phone? Why'd you have to go out to the car to call him back?'

She pulled up sharply, her head going back as if he had slapped her. 'Have you been spying on me?'

'Yes!' He put down the glass of milk, thumping it on the kitchen table; a few drops of milk splashed on the worn oak surface. It was an old country piece, one of his mother's prides, a relic from her grandmother's farmhouse. 'Yeah, I was!'

'That's bloody despicable, Jason! It's none of your business who I talk to on the phone!'

'Nothing is my business, it seems!'

Coming back from the supermarket yesterday, she had refused to discuss the encounter with Mr Jones – 'No, Jason, forget it. I don't want you and Shelley involved in any of this. I'll work it out.'

'Who with? You and bloody Angela?'

That was the wrong thing to say; she had shut up like a bank vault. She had not spoken to him the rest of the way home and last night had been an edgy and uncomfortable three or four hours before he had finally given up and gone to bed. Claire Malone had called him, but he had found he had nothing, really, to say to her; she was sweet and friendly, but he had kept comparing her with Jill Weigall. He had even thought of calling Jill, asking her if she would like to go to a disco or something, but that would have meant going to his mother and asking for money. No way would he do that: money was not to be discussed, fifty bucks or five million.

Now, his throat thick with milk and anger, he said, 'It *is* my business, Mum! Jesus Christ, do you think Mr Jones, or whatever the hell his name is, is gunna concentrate on just you, leave Shelley and me alone?'

'Don't swear at me!'

'I'm not swearing at you, for Chrissake! You wanna hear me *really* swear?'

'No!'

She turned away from him, went to the kitchen sink, stood there as if puzzled that she had nothing to do; she looked right and left along the draining board, as if looking for meat or vegetables, anything, to be prepared. It was a big kitchen, with timbered cupboards, a double wall-oven, a microwave oven, a jumbo-sized refrigerator and enough appliances, Will had once said, to stock an Elcom showroom. But, Jason remembered, it had been the one extravagance of his mother's that his father had never harped on. Now she turned back from the sink and looked round the kitchen as if she wanted to escape from it. Or (the thought hit him with horror) from *him*.

'Jason, I have to handle this myself. It's a – a self-discipline, if you like. It's my way of holding on. Do you understand what I'm trying to say?'

He wanted to say, *You're trying to say you don't trust me*; but all he did was nod. She didn't seem to realize it, but he, too, was holding on.

'Dad's funeral is tomorrow – we have to get through that and it's not going to be easy. After that . . .'

'After that – what?'

'I don't know, Jason. I honestly don't know. Maybe we'll sell the house, move away from here . . . I just don't know. But whatever happens, don't make it any harder for me.'

She looked suddenly vulnerable, no older than Shelley, for Chrissake. He moved to her, put his arms round her, waited for her to cry on his chest; but she didn't, just stood leaning against him, her arms round him but not pressing him to her. She doesn't love me, he thought; but that couldn't be true. She had always loved him and Shelley; when he was a little kid, she had embarrassed him with

165

how clinging she could be. She couldn't have changed that much; but something had happened to her. Maybe he should look in the mirror: maybe his father's murder had changed him, too.

'We'll get through, Mum.' But he wondered where to.

Then he released her and went into his bedroom and shut the door. This was his retreat, but now he wondered how safe it would be. He looked at the posters on the walls: cricketers, American basketballers, Michael Jackson, all of them smiled at him as if he were their friend. Pretty soon it would be time to tear them down; but what would he replace them with? The future looked as if it was going to be no more than a blank wall.

He turned on his radio, put on headphones (Mum hated loud music) and listened to Two Triple J; the station was playing the old Jimmy Barnes's track, 'Working Class Man'. He'd never be one of those, not with his share of the five-million-and-a-bit. He pushed the headphones back, so that he could barely hear the music; he dozed off, another singer lulling him to sleep, and Jill Weigall walked in his dream through a mist of banknotes. Then the ringing of the phone woke him, a faint sound beyond the music. He sat up, pulling off the headphones, and heard his mother pick up the receiver in the kitchen. He could hear only the murmur of her voice, then the phone was put back on its cradle, he heard her go out the back door and down the side of the house to her car. He lifted himself off his bed, peered out of his narrowly opened window. His mother was in her car, on the phone again.

He sank back on his bed, wanting to weep. He was still lying there, still feeling absolutely bloody dreadful, when he heard her come back into the house. Then ten minutes later there was a murmur of voices coming up the side driveway; it was Shelley and Gran Carss, a gruesome twosome if you needed a pair. He put on his headphones

166

and lay back, this time with some wide-awake dreaming of Jill that made him horny. When Shelley knocked on his door, he pulled an open copy of the *Women's Weekly* over his groin.

'Come in.'

She came in, flopped on the end of his bed and reached for the magazine. 'What are you doing with that, for Pete's sake?'

He grabbed it, held it in place. 'Trying to find out what makes you weaker sex tick. How was it staying with Gran?'

She wrinkled her nose, dropping her voice. 'Drack. She's even worse than Mum about the music being too loud. She thinks Michael Jackson shouts. *Michael!*' She rolled her head and her eyes at the sacrilege, looked at his poster and rolled off the bed and genuflected. Then she got back on the bed. 'How's Mum been? She don't – *doesn't* – ' she waved a finger at him and smiled before he could pick her up on her grammar ' – doesn't look so hot. I mean she looks, you know, *worried*.'

Her own concern showed; he wanted to confide in her his own worry. 'She's got the funeral on her mind. It's gunna be rough, Shell. You reckon you're gunna be able to cope?'

'Well, we've got to, haven't we?' She sat up, all at once looking much older than thirteen. God, he thought, we're going to be geriatric before our time! 'Jay, don't you think Mum has become sorta – well, *cold*? Is that what a murder does to some people?'

There was a ring at the front door. He sat up, the *Women's Weekly* slid off his lap: everything was okay down there, flat as an hermaphrodite's. 'I'll get it,' he shouted to his mother and escaped from his room before he had to give Shelley an answer.

He groaned silently when he opened the front door.

Claire's father stood there, Mr — no, *Inspector* Malone. More trouble? 'You don't look too happy, Jay.'

He was surprised that he still had his wits about him. 'The funeral's tomorrow, Mr Malone. None of us are happy.'

'No,' said Malone. 'I suppose I could've picked a better time to call. Is your mother home? I see her car's outside.'

Jason led Malone through the house and out to the garden room, where his mother stood with his grand-mother, both staring out at the garden as if planning some replanting. The two women turned their heads to look at the detective with unwelcoming eyes. 'Hello, Scobie,' said Olive in a cold flat voice. 'More questions?'

'You might've waited,' said Mrs Carss. 'The funeral's tomorrow, you know.'

'I know,' said Malone, 'but some things can't wait. I'll make it quick, Olive.'

'And hurtful?'

Oh, for Chrissake, Mum, back off! Shelley came into the room and Jason wished she hadn't. All at once he felt protective towards his sister.

'No, I hope not,' said Malone. 'This time it's — concern, if you like. Has a Mr Jones been in contact with you? A Russian, a tall, well-dressed feller?'

'A Russian?' said Mrs Carss. 'What would she have to do with any Russians?'

Olive said nothing and Jason knew at once that she was going to deny meeting Mr Jones. He stepped forward and said, 'Yeah, he's been in touch with us. Yesterday up at the car park in Randwick Village.'

'That right, Olive?'

Olive glanced at Jason before she looked back at Malone; her look was strange, almost as if she hated him for having spoken out. 'Yes, that's right. I had no idea he was a Russian.'

'What did he want?'

Jason waited for his mother to answer that; she hesitated, then said, 'He said that money in Will's secret account was his.'

'*Theirs* was what he said, Mum.' Jason looked at Malone. 'I asked him who *they* were and he just told me to mind my own business. He looked as if he was gunna get pretty heavy.'

Malone glanced at Olive and she nodded. 'He was threatening us, yes.'

'You never told me any of this!' Mrs Carss looked affronted.

'What did you say?' said Malone. 'That he could have the money?'

'No!' Then Olive seemed to realize her tone was too emphatic; she softened it: 'I told him he would have to prove it belonged to him, to *them*, whoever they were.'

'What did he say to that?'

'We left it at that,' said Olive flatly.

'I think we're going to have to put you and the children under police protection, Olive.'

'I should damn well think so!' Mrs Carss put a protective arm round Shelley, who had stood silent during the interrogation, watching it with growing puzzlement. 'I'm not going to have my grandchildren in danger from some crazy communist!'

'I don't think he's a communist, Mrs Carss, not any longer.'

'They're always communists, they never change. Like Will's father, he'll be one till he drops dead.'

'That doesn't make Pa a thug.' Jason wanted to shout at his dumb grandmother; God, she got up his nose! 'This guy is different. Real cold,' he told Malone. 'I think it'd be a good idea if you could give us protection, Mr Malone.'

'We'll do that ... Olive, could I see you outside? No, Jay, just your mother.'

Jason stood back, rebuffed; he had thought Mr Malone was on his side by now. He watched as his mother and Malone went out to stand beside the pool. He saw his mother look up sharply as Malone said something to her. What was going on?

Malone had said, 'Olive, what have you done with the five thousand dollars you withdrew last week?'

She leaned back against the pool fence, not negligently but as if she needed its support. 'Scobie, what *is* this?'

'Just answer the question, Olive. Where's the five thousand?'

'I – I've spent it. I told you, the holiday up on the Reef, clothes. There's some left, spending money.'

'Did you book through a travel agency?'

'Yes, Kidlers, down in the Bay.'

'Would you care to show me the clothes you bought?'

'Scobie, for God's sake!' She came off the fence almost as if she were going to throw herself at him; he took a step back, not wanting any physical contact between them. 'No, I can't show them to you. I didn't collect them after what happened to Will – I'd left them to be altered – '

'Where'd you buy them?'

'God, you really have no respect for me, have you?'

'Where'd you buy the clothes, Olive?' He was cold with her: it was the only way to be when an interrogation reached this stage, when you knew she was lying.

'At several places – ' She put out a hand, grasping at the fence. There was a burst of music from the house next door as someone opened a door; then it was gone. She turned her head, as if glad of the distraction; when she looked back at Malone it seemed she had gathered her thoughts, and he noted it. 'At David Jones. At a boutique called, I can't remember, it's in Castlereagh Street. At

170

another shop over at Bondi Junction — Penthouse — ' She was grabbing places out of the air, like someone in a quiz competition racing against the clock. She stopped, drew a deep breath and almost shouted at him, 'I didn't kill my husband!'

'Righto, Olive.' His tone suggested neither acceptance nor denial of her plea. 'You'll get the police protection immediately. Has Mr Jones phoned you?'

She looked at him warily. 'No. Why, are you going to tap my phone?'

'It might be an idea,' he said. 'Take care, Olive. You're in much deeper water than you think.'

He went down the side driveway, checked there was a phone in the Civic and went on out into the street. Since he had not noticed the brown Mercedes when he had entered the Rockne house, he did not remark that it was no longer parked up the street. He went round the corner to the unmarked Commodore and the two young detective constables.

'The family doesn't know it's been under surveillance. I'm going to ask Crime Squad to put them under police protection — you fellers from Maroubra and probably Randwick will get the job. I'll be in touch with Sergeant Ellsworth and give him the details. In the meantime, if the family has any male visitors, especially a tall, well-dressed feller, intercept him and ask him his business. Hold him for me. He has an accent, he's Russian, and he has several names — Dostoyevsky, Collins, Jones.'

'Dostoyevsky?' said Tilleman, the burly one. 'The guy who wrote *Crime and Punishment*?'

'You're a well-read lot out at Maroubra. Yes, that's the one. Grab him and hold him for questioning. Ask him to autograph the running sheets.'

171

2

Malone caught a cab back to the Hat Factory, riding up front with the driver like a true-blue Aussie democrat. The driver, a young Chinese student, hadn't a clue where the Hat Factory was; indeed, he seemed to have some trouble in knowing in which direction the inner city lay. 'Don't you fellers have to do a test to get a taxi licence any more?'

'Sure.' He had a big smile; his glasses seemed to glint with humour. Life was a joke, at least outside China. 'They put a map of Australia in front of you, ask you where Sydney is and that's it.'

'Where are you from?'

'Beijing.'

'What's the test for taxi drivers in Beijing?'

'You belong to the Communist Party, that's all. Corruption the same there, like here. This is the Hat Factory?' Then he saw the three uniformed policemen going in the door. 'You the manager, you make hats for the police?'

'No, I'm a cop. Being a communist, you're not expecting a tip, are you?'

He went into the squad room, settled down to paper-work and half an hour later Clements came in and flopped down in a chair.

Malone looked up, glad of the interruption. 'Any luck with Collins or Jones or whatever he calls himself up in Potts Point?'

'He's Boris Collins up there. Or was. He moved out this morning. He lived in a one-bedroom service flat and according to the caretaker was a quiet, well-behaved tenant who always paid his rent on time. He owns a brown Merc. He came down this morning with three suitcases, the caretaker helped him, put 'em in the Merc and drove off. Told the caretaker he was going up to the Gold Coast, he had a new job up there. On the off chance, we went out to the Soviet consulate in Woollahra, but they haven't heard from him since he left the embassy. The guy there told me they've got their own problems. Said when you lose a country, losing one citizen doesn't amount to much. How'd you go with the grieving widow?'

Malone told him. 'Put John Kagal on to checking the travel agency and DJ's and the boutiques. I think Olive is lying herself blind. She's getting panicky.'

'You've gone back to thinking she did the killing? Or anyway, paid to have it done?'

'Yes,' he said and couldn't disguise the reluctance in his voice.

The phone rang; it was Ric Bassano from Motor Squad. 'Scobie, we've come up with something that might interest you. One of my guys was going through some stuff we hauled in from Hamill's last night. In a box with a lot of gear in it, old car parts and stuff, he found a length of pipe. It looked like nothing, till he took a squint through it. It's a home-made silencer, baffles in it and all. You wanna look at it?'

'Send it over, Rick, soon's you can.' He put down the phone, feeling the quiet excitement he always felt when things suddenly started to go right. He dialled Ballistics, got Clarrie Binyan. 'Clarrie, that bullet that killed Will Rockne, did it have any markings on it?'

'Just the normal lands and grooves identifying it with a particular gun. You give me the gun and I'll mate them.'

'Nothing else?'

'Just a minute – ' There was silence for a while, but Malone waited patiently; then Binyan came back on the line: 'There was a slight mark on it – I ran it through the macroscope again. It could of been done by the baffle in a

173

silencer. But you'll have to produce the silencer.'

'You're my favourite Abo, Clarrie.'

'We call ourselves Koories, mate, you know that. I'll see you keep your job when we take the country back off you whiteys.'

Malone put down the phone and looked across his desk at Clements. 'I think I'm going to get a good night's sleep.' He told Clements what he had got from the two phone calls. 'It's time we kept an eye on Kelpie Dunne. Get on to Penrith, he lives out that way, ask their Ds if they'll help out with some surveillance. We'll pick him up when Clarrie has checked out the silencer against the marking on the bullet. Then . . .'

Then he might have to pick up Olive; and he was not looking forward to that. He had looked at Jason and Shelley this morning and seen in their faces the bewilderment and fear that he would never want to see in the faces of his own children.

3

He didn't sleep at all well that night. In the morning, lying beside him, Lisa said, 'If you're going to toss and turn like that till this Rockne case is over, you'd better sleep out in the living room.'

'How do you know it had anything to do with the Rocknes? It could've been something I ate.'

'Two helpings of beef burgundy with vegies, two helpings of French rice pudding, two glasses of red — why would that keep you awake?'

'I had no lunch yesterday.' He held her to him, feeling the bed-warmth of her, the silkiness of her legs entwined in his. 'You once said something to me. Those who were never in love, never were happy.'

'Dr Samuel Johnson. But I don't know that I could ever have fallen in love with *him*. What made you think of that?'

'I don't know what Dr Johnson knew about love, but he hit the nail on the head with that one. I'm very happy.'

She kissed him. 'So am I. Now get your knee out of my crotch before I wet on it. I have to go to the bathroom.'

'Who said the Dutch weren't romantic?'

'Dr Johnson?'

Over breakfast he covertly watched his children. Or so he thought, till Maureen, who had eyes far sharper than any Aborigine's, who would have seen Captain Cook's ship when he was miles out at sea and aroused the tribe, said, 'What's the matter, Daddy? You're looking at us as if you don't know us.'

He looked along the table at Lisa. 'Where did you find these kids — at the Police Academy?' Then he said to Claire, 'Have you seen Jason this week?'

'Just the once. I – he's avoiding me, I think. I can understand it. Everyone's talking about the murder, they want to ask him about it.'

He wondered how deep were her feelings for Jason. At fifteen he had been in love with three girls, each passion lasting a month; girls, he was sure, felt more deeply. 'He's upset and worried. I think it'd be an idea to leave him alone for a while.'

'Have you got the murderer yet?' said Tom.

'Not yet.'

'Can I be there some time when you arrest a murderer?'

'I'll bring my camera,' said Maureen. 'If you bought me a video camera for Christmas, that'd be even better. We could run it when the TV programmes aren't worth watching.'

'You're raising a voyeur,' Malone told his child's mother.

175

'Voyeurs,' said the child, 'are dirty old men who perv at naked people on nudist beaches.'

'I knew that,' said Tom.

'I give up,' said Malone, rising and then kissing each of the children and Lisa. 'I'm going into Homicide, where all the fellers are angels compared to you lot.'

Lisa followed him out of the house, waited while he raised the garage door. 'What's on your mind? Olive?'

He nodded. 'She's making things worse and worse for herself every time I talk to her.'

'If she did kill Will, she did the worst thing right at the beginning. Are you going to arrest her?'

'Looks like it. It'll depend what's on my desk this morning.'

She kissed him. 'Don't be too tough on her.'

'Not even if she murdered her husband?'

'I'm not thinking about her feelings. I'm thinking of Jason's and Shelley's.'

He drove in through the peak-hour traffic, noticeably thinner than it used to be; there had been more bad unemployment news this morning. He had glanced at the headlines; they were as gloomy as the death notices in the back pages. The day was dry and cloudless, the sun brighter than a winter's sun should be: spring was letting the voters know that it was early this year. The sunshine did nothing for him; he, too, was gloomy. But when he walked into his office the faces of Clements and Clarrie Binyan were as cheerful as lottery winners'. He took off his jacket, sat down and saw the reports on his desk.

'I'll go first,' said Binyan, putting a length of pipe in a plastic envelope on the desk. 'That's the silencer Ric Bassano sent over. I come in early, checked it against the bullet that killed Rockne. The markings match – one of the baffles must of been a millimetre out of alignment. I don't think you're gunna get a fingerprint off of it, it's been handled too much. But I'll go into court and swear it silenced the gun that killed Rockne.'

'Thanks, Clarrie.'

Binyan left to go back to Police Centre and Malone looked at Clements. 'Now it's your turn.'

'It's all there in those notes. I haven't fed them into the computer yet, they're John Kagal's and my bits and pieces. Maroubra sent in that Telecom sheet. First, Olive made a booking with that travel agency in Coogee, but she never went near them to pay for it, they haven't seen her in three weeks. DJ's and the boutiques, likewise – she bought nothing from any of them, so she didn't leave anything to be altered. So, as you said yesterday, she's lying herself blind. Finally, take a look at the Telecom list of calls from her car phone. I've marked the three that should interest you.'

Malone picked up the list. There were two 047 31 numbers, with the name *Dunne* scribbled beside them; and a 232 number, with *Bodalle* beside it. The first 047 31 call had been made last Thursday, two days before the murder; the second 047 31 call and the 232 call had been made yesterday. He looked across his desk at Clements. 'It doesn't look good for Olive, does it?'

'I think we should pick up Kelpie first before we trouble her. Do I get a warrant to search his house out at Penrith for the gun?'

'Go ahead. But why did she go out of the house to call Angela Bodalle, the friend of the family, as she keeps telling us?'

'Maybe she's already confessed to Bodalle what she did and she wanted to tell her the pressure's on.'

'From us or Kelpie or Mr Jones? It doesn't matter, anyway. Get the warrant, then go out and call on Kelpie. You'll need back-up, just in case. Call Penrith and tell 'em you'd like a coupla men.'

177

'You think Kelpie might start shooting?'

'I don't think so. Kelpie's a mongrel, but he's not a psycho. Until we get the gun, he's still in the clear.'

'You're not coming?'

Malone gestured at the files on his desk. 'Everything's coming to a climax at once. I've got to get the papers on the Lazarus and Paluzzi cases ready for the DPP. Bring Kelpie in and we'll give him some coffee and biscuits.'

'What about Olive?'

'I think I might give her a call, tell her we're bringing in a man for questioning. No names, just a feller we think might give us some information. It might stir her up a bit.'

Clements left and Malone got down to the paperwork on his desk. The big room outside emptied till there were only a couple of detectives at their desks. There was a hush in the high-ceilinged room; the investigation of murder is not all sound and fury. The Hat Factory was a backwater and at times it could have all the silence and tranquillity of a place where the currents were deep and did not cause waves; or so it appeared. Of course the currents *did* cause waves, but the effects were felt elsewhere: this morning, in places as far apart as Penrith and Coogee.

At ten o'clock he rang the Rockne number. Jason answered. 'Hello, Mr Malone. No, Mum's under the shower. The funeral's today, remember?'

'Of course.' He had forgotten; the days had slipped by. He hesitated, prompted for the moment by a reluctance to add to the burden of her day. But she had murdered the husband she was burying, or had had something to do with his killing, and compassion was something she did not deserve and he could not afford. 'Tell her that we are bringing in a man for questioning, we think he can give us some information on your father's death.'

'Mr Jones?'

178

'No, Jay, not Mr Jones. Another man. Just pass it on to your mother.'

He hung up, then rang Ellsworth at Maroubra. 'Are you fellers or someone from Randwick still with Mrs Rockne?'

'Around the clock,' said Ellsworth. 'She had only one visitor last night, Mrs Bodalle, the QC. She's a family friend, I gather.'

'Any more calls on the car phone?'

'None. I'm going over to Coogee now, I'm joining my guys for the funeral, then I'll have to come back here. We've got some break-and-enters we've got to look into. We pick 'em up and four outa five of 'em are kids out of work looking for spending money. My guys are earning more overtime with this recession than they ever did in good times.'

'We're bringing in Kelpie Dunne this morning for questioning. I'll be in touch.'

Kelpie Dunne came in an hour later, making waves, hobbling between crutches, swearing at the top of his voice, dressed in shirt and shorts and a sweater and with his right leg encased in plaster. He was led into the interview room and Malone followed Clements and Kagal in behind the aggressive, abusive suspect.

'Quieten down, Kelpie. What happened to your leg? One of your mates try to kneecap you?'

'Fucking funny! Look, Malone, what is all this shit?'

The interview room had bare walls, a table and three chairs; it was not designed to make the interviewee comfortable. At one end of the table was a tape and video recorder; Clements pushed Dunne into a chair opposite it. The machine was a recent introduction, brought in to counteract charges against the police of 'verballing', the falsifying of written statements, a practice that older police had denied with their hands on their hearts and such looks of innocence that they had usually gone on sick leave a day or two later.

Malone laid the plastic envelope containing the silencer on the table in front of Dunne. 'Seen that before, Kelpie?'

'What is it?' Dunne gazed at it blankly, like a New Guinea highlander presented with a piece of space equipment.

'It's a silencer, Kelpie, a home-made hush puppy. You put it on a gun and it silences the sound of the shot.'

'What'll they think of next!'

Malone had to grin. 'The next bit's not so funny. They found it in your toolbox at Hamill's.'

Malone and Dunne were the only two sitting down; Dunne had commandeered the third chair to support his plastered leg. His sharp-featured face seemed to contract for a moment, everything becoming more pointed. Then he grinned at Malone, looked at Clements and Kagal leaning against the walls, then back to Malone.

'I ain't falling for that. If you found that in my toolbox, you mongrels planted it there.'

Malone's bluff hadn't worked; but he wasn't going to admit that the silencer had been found in another box, a junk box. He looked at Clements. 'Did you find any gun out at Mr Dunne's house?'

Clements had been carrying a black plastic garbage bag. He took out a revolver and four boxes of ammunition. 'This Smith and Wesson Thirty-eight and these three boxes of ammo to fit it. And there's these Twenty-twos, a box of fifty with six bullets missing.'

'Nothing else?' *Like a Ruger .22 with a ten-shot maga-zine?* Clements shook his head and Malone turned back to Dunne. 'Why the gun, Kelpie? You've heard all the public outcry over the past couple of weeks against the use of guns. Or are you part of the gun lobby?'

'I was gunna hand it in,' said Dunne, piety as ugly as a

180

sneer on his thin face, 'but I clean forgot.'

'You have a licence for it?'

'It was a present from the wife. I guess she forgot the licence, you know what women are like.'

'What sort of woman is your wife, she gives you a gun for your birthday or whatever?'

'It was our wedding anniversary.'

'They're not married,' said Clements. 'She's his *de facto*, a nice lady. Too good for him and not the sort to give guns as presents. She's outside with one of the Penrith policewomen.'

'Leave her outa this!' Dunne's plastered leg fell off the chair and he winced with pain and swore again.

'For the time being, we'll do that,' said Malone and pushed forward the box of .22 ammunition. 'What's this ammo for, Kelpie?'

'Ah, that's old stuff. I used it in an old Twenty-two rifle. I used to go rabbit-shooting. The wife cooks it French style, lappin-de-something.'

'Kelpie, that's not old stuff, the box is brand-new. Come on, what did you use it for? Have you ever owned a Ruger handgun?'

'No.' Not a flicker of an eyelid.

'Where's your Twenty-two rifle now?'

'I traded it in on the Smith and Wesson.'

'I thought you said your wife gave that one to you as a present? I think you're getting a bit flummoxed, Kelpie. Where were you last Saturday night between eleven o'clock and twelve?'

'Last Sat'day night?' The face screwed up in an effort to remember; he could have been asked where he was on the night of 12 February, 1968. Then his face opened up: the acting was twice life-sized: 'I was home! We didn't go out last Sat'day. We stayed home and watched TV.'

'What did you watch?'

181

'Oh, I dunno, they all look alike these days, don't they? Some fillum – no. No, it was that thing on Channel Two, the one about the British jacks, *The Bill*. Yeah, that was it.'

'That programme finishes just before nine thirty. We all watch it.'

'You learn anything from it?'

'Only that we're all much nicer fellers than they are. No one ever smiles, not their detectives . . . So where were you between eleven and midnight?'

'I went to bed.'

'Righto, stay there, Kelpie. We'll get you some coffee and biscuits. We won't be long, I just want a word with your wife.'

'Leave her outa this, I told you!' Had he had two good legs, Dunne would have leapt out of his chair at Malone; he was actually snarling like a savage dog. 'I'll fucking have you, Malone!'

'What with, Kelpie? The Smith and Wesson or the Twenty-two? Sit back!' He stood over the smaller man, his own anger apparent but controlled. 'If you've got nothing to worry about, then neither has she.'

Dunne matched Malone's stare; then he slowly sat back, lifted his leg on to the chair in front of him. 'You got nothing on me, you know that. But go easy on her, she's a decent sort.'

'Where'd you meet her?'

'She's the sister of one of the guys I was in Bathurst with. She's decent, okay? Straight.'

Malone left the interview room and had Claudia Dunne brought into his office. With her was the policewoman from Penrith, a small blonde in her mid-twenties named Dickson. 'Take a seat, Mrs Dunne. You too, Constable – I want you here while I talk to Mrs Dunne.'

Claudia Dunne was tall and thin, with a tumble of thick

dark hair, the sort of hairdo that always puzzled Malone as to how its undone look was achieved. Her features were too pointed to be beautiful or even pretty, but somehow she had managed to create the impression that she was good-looking. She was in a flower-patterned dress and had a red cardigan thrown over her narrow shoulders. She was frightened, but worse, she was disillusioned to the point of looking ill.

'He's in trouble again, isn't he? It was bound to happen. But I hoped – I kept telling myself that all he needed was someone like me to straighten him out. Jack, that's my brother, he was in jail with Garry, he was always telling me Garry would never change . . . What's he done?'

'That's what we're trying to find out, Mrs Dunne – '

That was a mistake; she was sharp-witted enough to say, 'Then why's he here? Why all those police searching our house, turning everything over – '

Malone looked at the policewoman. 'Did they make a mess of the house?'

'No, sir. Everything was put back exactly as we found it. I can understand Mrs Dunne's feelings, no woman likes her house invaded, but we did our best to leave it exactly as we found it. I think when she goes home she'll find that's true.'

She was brisk and efficient in a quiet way and she seemed to have established some sort of rapport with Claudia Dunne; she looked at the taller woman and after a moment the latter nodded. 'Yeah, they did put things back. Still, it *was* an invasion, like she says . . . What did they find?'

'They didn't tell you? Garry didn't tell you? They found the gun you gave him as a present.'

'*I* gave him a gun? Did he say *that*?' Then abruptly she looked away, as if from now on she intended to ignore them and Malone's preposterous suggestions.

'What did you watch on television last Saturday night?'

'What?' She looked back at him as if he had asked an obscene question.

'I said, what did you watch on TV last Saturday night?'

She frowned. 'I don't know. I – oh yes. We watched *That's Dancing*. I like it, but Garry thinks it's a comedy show, he says it's funnier than *Home Videos*.'

'That goes from seven thirty till eight thirty. What then?'

Shrewdness suddenly veiled her face. 'I – we watched a movie.'

'What movie?'

'Is this supposed to trick us or something? I've seen the way they do it in the Columbo movies.'

'What movie did you watch, Mrs Dunne?'

'I – I can't remember the title. It was one of those tele-movies, the ones with people you've never heard of in them.'

'Your husband watched it with you?'

'Yes. Why?'

'What time did it finish?'

'I dunno. About ten thirty, I suppose, they always do.'

'What did you do then?'

'Went to bed. Why are you asking these questions? What is Garry supposed to have done?'

'You're sure your husband was home, that he didn't go out and not come back till after midnight?'

'No,' she said, but she had never learned to lie with a straight face. She looked in pain, her large brown eyes suddenly glistened as if she were about to weep.

Malone felt sorry for her; he had seen her kind before. With a relative or friend in jail, they had somehow come to know the hardened criminals like Dunne and, for reasons that Malone could never comprehend, had fallen in love with them. Perhaps, with their own lives deadeningly dull, they had fallen in love with the excitement of

184

knowing a criminal rather than with the man himself; then, to compound their naïveté, they had come to believe they could reform their men. Malone had the common policeman's cynicism, that the villains who saw no difference between right and wrong, who believed the world was theirs to take, were beyond reform.

'That'll be all for now, Mrs Dunne.'

'Are you gunna let Garry go now?'

'Not just yet. You can wait if you like, but he could be here the rest of the day.'

'I'll wait,' she said, setting her jaw. 'You never stop persecuting them, do you?'

'How's that?'

'He's lost his job, you know. You police closed down Hamill's, where he worked.'

'The Motor Squad did that, Hamill's were dealing in stolen cars. Didn't Garry tell you that?'

She opened her mouth, but whatever she was going to say did not come out. She looked away again, ignoring him. He raised his eyebrows at Constable Dickson, who nodded sympathetically at him.

'How will Penrith go in the grand final?' he said.

'We'll win.' She smiled at him, as if grateful for the banal question. She had seemed to grow uncomfortable as he had persisted with his questioning of Claudia Dunne and he wondered if this was her first experience of a murder investigation.

He left them and went back to the interview room, where Dunne, over coffee and biscuits, was abusing Clements and Kagal with a wide selection of obscenities. He twisted his head sharply as Malone came in behind him.

'So what have you done to her, shithead?'

'She's okay, Kelpie. She's waiting patiently till you tell us the truth and then maybe you can go home with her.' Clements stood up and Malone sat down in the vacated

185

chair. 'Why did Mrs Rockne make two phone calls to you at your home? One yesterday week and one yesterday morning?'

Dunne was put on the back foot by the question; the plaster-encased leg seemed to stiffen even more. 'What? What fucking shit are you trying to pull?'

Malone said patiently, 'Kelpie, let's cut out the abuse, it's getting boring. Didn't Sergeant Clements ask you that question?'

'No, he fucking didn't.'

Malone looked at Clements, who said, 'John and I have been at him for his bank, where he keeps his money. All we've got from him is a lot of what used to be called obscene and offensive language, back in the good old days.'

'You'll get a fucking lot more, you keep on with this shit!'

'You're staying here till you answer our questions, Kelpie, so cut it out and let's get down to business!' Malone leaned forward across the table. 'Now, why did Mrs Rockne make those two calls to you?'

'I dunno what the fuck you're talking about.'

'Did she call your wife? You want me to go out and ask her if the calls were to her?'

Dunne sat back in his chair, adjusted his leg, looked at his two crutches leaning against the wall, then looked back at Malone. 'Leave the wife outa this. Waddia wanna know?'

'Mrs Rockne — why did she call you?'

'Business. She wanted me to do some work on her car.'

'What sort of car does she have?'

'A Honda Civic, you know that, I'll bet. I said no, I didn't work on that sorta junk.'

'She rang you a second time, after you'd insulted her like that? Come on, Kelpie, what else did she want? Was

186

it to arrange to pass on some money to you, say five thousand dollars?'

'Why would she wanna do that?'

'Who do you bank with, Kelpie?'

'I told your mates here, that's none of your business.' He looked at Clements and Kagal, gave them an ugly grin. 'There, how's that, no fucking obscene language, okay?'

Malone stood up. 'Well, it looks as if I've got to go back and trouble your wife again – '

'Siddown!' Dunne leaned forward, breathing heavily; he drummed his hand on the plaster cast. 'Okay, it's the Westpac Bank, their head office. The wife dunno about that account, so it's between you and me, okay? It's where I keep my gambling money. She don't like me gambling, but I can't kick the habit, I been a gambler all me life.'

'Righto, I'm warning you, we're going to have a look at your account.'

'You got a warrant to do that?'

'We keep a stock of them, just for occasions like this. Come on, Kelpie, you know the drill.'

'Whatever happened to fucking civil rights?'

'You haven't been civil since you got out of kindergarten,' said Clements. 'Do we let him go, Inspector?'

'Have Constable Dickson take him and Mrs Dunne back home. Don't try doing a moonlight flit, Kelpie – we'll be keeping a twenty-four surveillance on you. You can take it for granted we'll be bringing you in again. Thanks for your time.'

Dunne got awkwardly to his feet, grabbed the crutches as Kagal handed them to him. He had quietened down, there were no more waves. 'You still haven't told me what this is all about.'

'Oh, I thought you'd guessed,' said Malone. 'The murder of Will Rockne.'

Dunne shook his head; his composure was all at once

rock-solid. 'Then I'm safe, ain't I? Why would I wanna waste a guy I hardly knew?'

'For five thousand dollars and anything extra you could screw out of his widow,' said Clements.

'Was that the reason for the phone call yesterday morning?' Kagal, up till now, had said nothing.

Dunne, steady on his crutches now, looked at him, then at Malone. 'So it's his wife who had him bumped off?'

Malone didn't even glance at Kagal, though he was furious at how the younger man had played a card too soon. He was equally angry with Clements: the latter should have known better than to bring Olive into it at this stage.

Dunne grinned at him. 'You guys really dream 'em up, don't you? Fucking theories.'

He shook his head as if at their stupidity, then he went out of the interview room, not hurrying, as sure of himself as if he had no criminal record and had been on the other side of the world last Saturday night when Will Rockne had been murdered.

Malone looked at Clements and Kagal. 'Well, you stuffed that up.'

'Sorry,' said Clements. 'The bastard just got under my skin. But he did it, I'd have an all-up bet on that.'

'I'll go along with that. But it's Olive who has to tell us why. Yes, John?'

Kagal looked chastened, even hesitant; all his quiet cockiness had been punctured. 'There was something I didn't mention. Maybe I should have, instead of mentioning the phone call to Mrs Rockne.'

'What was it?' Malone kept his tone cool.

'The next-door neighbour said they heard his car go out about ten o'clock. It came back some time after they'd gone to bed at eleven thirty. The wife, a Mrs Rostoff, got up to have a look – I'd say she's the sort of neighbour who wouldn't miss anything that goes on in the street. She said the car came in with its lights off, something Dunne usually doesn't do. She complained once that the car lights woke them up and Kelpie evidently told her to get stuffed, though she didn't use those words, and he used to put the lights on high-beam just to annoy her. But last Saturday night he came in with the lights off. She saw him get out of the car, he was on his own, Mrs Dunne wasn't with him.'

'I wonder if Mrs Dunne knew where he'd been? But she's never going to tell us.'

4

Kagal got the warrant and came back from Westpac's head office with a copy of Dunne's bank statement. Nine and a half thousand dollars had been deposited in cash in Dunne's account last Friday, the day before the murder.

'I'll bet that's Mrs Rockne's five thousand, less five hundred he kept in his pocket.' Kagal had regained his cool cockiness, but Malone could sense the underlying eagerness to rush on, to bring the case to a conclusion. There was a coldness about him that Malone had never remarked before and he wondered if Kagal ever looked past the killer to the victim; or to all those on the periphery of a murder, the other, still alive victims. 'But where did the other five thousand come from?'

'Unless Olive, like her husband, also has a little secret account?' said Clements.

'How much is in Kelpie's account altogether?'

'Ten thousand four hundred. Judging by the withdrawals and the few deposits, he hasn't been too lucky lately with his gambling.'

'No wonder he called up Olive again – he was leaning

189

on her for more money. Would he know about the five million?'

'The point is,' said Clements, 'did *she* know about it and she's been bullshitting us that she knew nothing?'

'Well,' said Malone, 'the first thing is to keep Kelpie in place. Tell Penrith we want him kept under strict surveillance, not to let him out of their sight. Second, get on to Immigration and tell them to keep a check on him at all airports. He won't get far if that's all the cash he has, but Olive may come good with some more if he's leaning on her. Then let Sergeant Ellsworth out at Maroubra know what's happening.' He reached for his jacket and hat. 'You do that, John. Russ and I are going out to see Mrs Rockne.'

'Let's have lunch first,' said Clements, always hungry.

'I dunno that I can eat anything.' He was not looking forward to the visit to the Rockne home, not if it should be full of mourners after the funeral.

'Well, try.' Clements, big and rough-edged, had a surprising gentleness about him at times, as some big men do. 'Better now than later. It may be a long day if we're gunna bring her in.'

'She'll just be back from the funeral.'

'So we're gunna look heartless bastards. But that's the picture of us anyway, isn't it? Ask the Abos and the greenies and the gays. Who's ever had a good word for us?'

Chapter Seven

1

They had trouble finding a place to park the unmarked police car; finally, Clements left it in a No Parking zone, standard police practice. Mourners, some of the older women in black, were making their way up the front path of the Rockne home; Malone and Clements went up the side driveway. When they turned the rear corner of the house they came upon a crowd of at least fifty or sixty people standing in tight little groups in the garden. It surprised Malone that the Rocknes should have so many relatives and friends, though he didn't know why he thought that. He had been surprised at funerals before, he should have been prepared for the unexpected here at the Rocknes'.

Jason, dressed in a dark blue suit with a blue shirt and a cerise and blue tie, his school uniform, the same now as Malone had worn twenty-five and thirty years ago, saw the two detectives and came towards them. 'Hello, Jay. Maybe I should've worn my old school tie.'

'You went to Marcellin, Mr Malone?'

'I thought you knew.' The school had produced a deputy prime minister, two or three distinguished judges, several eminent doctors, an international rugby player, a couple of jockeys, an obscure writer and several cops besides himself. Schools, though, rarely boasted that cops were mentionable alumni. 'The funeral go okay?'

The boy nodded. He was sober-faced but relaxed; if

grief was tearing at him, it did not show. 'I guess so. How are they supposed to go?'

Malone accepted the rebuke, if it was meant to be one. He was wishing that he and Clements had delayed their visit, but they were here now, they had been recognized as outsiders and identified as police; he swallowed his discomfort and said, 'Where's your mother?'

'She's inside. I'll go and get her. I told her you'd rung about some guy you'd picked up – '

'Is the house like this – full of friends and relatives?'

'Yeah, this is the spill-over. I'll get Mum – '

Malone suddenly changed his mind. 'No, it doesn't matter – we'll come back later – '

Then Olive came out of the back door, pulling up sharply when she saw the two detectives. She was dressed all in black, even to a small black pillbox hat and a black veil, though the veil was drawn up over the hat. She looked funereally formal, too much so, as if she had dressed for a part in a play and everyone else had turned up in rehearsal clothes. She stared at the two men, then she came, stiff-legged, towards them.

'Surely you're not – what d'you call it, pursuing enquiries? – on an occasion like this?' Even her voice and phrasing were formal.

'I'm afraid so, Olive.'

She flicked a glance at Jason. 'Go inside and take care of Shelley. She's very upset.'

'Mum, I'd rather stay. Mr Malone says they've picked up this guy – '

'Do as you're told!'

The boy reddened, looked rebellious, then spun round and went quickly into the house. As he did so, Angela Bodalle, in a navy-blue suit, came out, looked back at Jason as he pushed past her, then saw Olive with Malone

192

and Clements and came towards them.

'Something wrong?'

'Can you believe it?' Olive was white with anger; or some emotion. 'They've come here – *today*! God, haven't they any sense of decency?'

Angela Bodalle's gaze was direct. 'Have you, Inspector?'

'I think so, Mrs Bodalle. Maybe we could have chosen another time, but our main concern is finding the murderer, not burying the victim.' It was an awkward, crude retort and he knew it. But the two women irritated him beyond measure and the fact that he responded to the irritation also annoyed him.

'And have you found the murderer?'

Malone and the two women had kept their voices low; but the small crowd in the garden beyond them were as still as statues, necks stiff as they strained their ears to catch what was being said. Malone lowered his voice even further: 'We have some information that's helping us.'

'Who from?'

Malone smiled. 'In due course, as you lawyers say. I think it might be easier all round if Mrs Rockne came with us over to Maroubra station.'

'What if I should refuse?' said Olive.

'Why should you, Olive? You're just as keen as we are, aren't you, to find out who killed Will?'

'Go with them, Olive,' said Angela Bodalle. 'I'll come, too.'

'I'll have to thank people for coming.' Olive moved off, threading her way through the crowd which leaned towards her as if waiting for her to whisper in their eager ears what had transpired with the two strangers – police, aren't they? Her back was straight and she walked almost with bounce, as if she had come from some mourners' aerobics class.

193

'She's coping well,' said Clements flatly.

'Women do,' said Angela Bodalle. 'You, of all people, should have noticed that.'

Olive went into the house for a minute or two. When she came out again Jason was standing behind her in the doorway, his young face as gaunt as that of an old man. As Malone and Clements led the two women down the side driveway, Angela paused beside her Ferrari, parked in front of the Honda Civic. 'We'll follow you, Inspector.'

Malone looked at his watch. 'Shouldn't you be getting back to court?'

'Don't you read the papers? The Filbert case finished yesterday — the defence suddenly folded up. We go back on Monday for sentencing. You should be congratulating me, my first prosecution. I got a guilty verdict.'

'Congratulations,' said Malone and tried to keep the sour note out of his voice but didn't succeed.

Driving over to Maroubra Clements said, 'Are we gunna hold Olive?'

'I don't know. Depends how much she gives away.'

'She's not gunna give much away, not with Angela riding herd on her. She's a quick-change artist, that one — prosecution one day, defence the next.'

'They're all actors, even the judges.'

'Meaning we're the only fair dinkum ones on the side of the law?'

'What else?'

Maroubra police station was a modern building, a change from many of the Victorian buildings that still housed suburban police. It stood on a busy road just down from a major shopping centre. Clements pulled the Commodore into the large yard at the rear of the station and the Ferrari followed it. As the two women got out of the red car, half a dozen young policemen suddenly appeared from behind the cars and wagons parked in the yard.

'They think this is a traffic pinch,' said Clements.

Sergeant Ellsworth was in one of the detectives' rooms off a long hallway on the first floor. He looked up in surprise when the two Homicide men and the two women were ushered in by one of the policewomen from the downstairs front desk. But almost at once he covered his surprise and rose from his desk as if he had been expecting them. He was jacketless and his issue Smith & Wesson .38 was plainly evident on his hip. He tightened his loosened tie, but didn't reach for his jacket.

Malone introduced Angela Bodalle, who said, 'I saw you at the funeral, hovering in the background.'

'We're always in the background at funerals, Mrs Bodalle,' said Ellsworth, and Malone gave him top marks.

'Not always. Inspector Malone and Sergeant Clements were very much in the foreground.'

'That was at the wake or whatever you want to call it,' said Malone. 'You should attend an Irish wake some time, Mrs Bodalle. Everyone's in the foreground there. Where's your interview room, Carl?'

'Down the hall, sir. It's going to be a bit crowded – '

'You don't mind, do you?' Olive was ignoring Malone, so he addressed Angela. 'Unless this is going to take all afternoon?'

'No,' she said. 'I shan't let it go on that long. Understood?' She looked hard at him.

He grinned. 'I wouldn't have expected any less of you, Mrs Bodalle.'

They went along the hall to the interview room, which was indeed a bit crowded when they moved into it. Chairs were brought in and everyone sat down in an intimacy that Malone could have done without. But he could not ask Ellsworth to leave: this was his turf, this was, in effect, his *case*.

'Constable Kagal was in touch,' said Ellsworth. 'He said

to tell you that everything's in place on that suspect.'

'Which suspect?' said Angela.

'Not yet, Mrs Bodalle,' said Malone. 'As I said, in due course . . .' He waited for a reaction (a quick glance between the two women?), but neither Olive nor Angela showed any expression. 'We're going to ask some questions, Olive, and there'll be a taped record of this interview. Any objection?' He looked at Angela.

'Are you saying Mrs Rockne is a suspect in the murder of her husband?'

'Yes.'

Olive's hands, on her lap, tightened; against the black of her dress they looked suddenly very white. Angela put a hand on her friend's arm. 'We can refuse to be interviewed, darling.'

Olive shook her head. 'No, let them go ahead.'

Malone waited till Ellsworth had fitted a cassette into the recorder, then he went in boots and all, as in the opening minutes of a grand final: 'Olive, why did you make two phone calls to Kelpie Dunne, one two days before Will was murdered and the other yesterday morning?'

'Kelpie Dunne? Who's he?' She sat in her usual convent girl's pose, knees together, hands in her lap. She had taken off her hat with its veil and left it in the Ferrari. Her hair was drawn back in a chignon and there was a severity to her looks this morning that made her only a distant relation to the frilly woman Malone had known just a week or two ago. 'I don't know what you're talking about.'

'You know who I'm talking about, don't you, Mrs Bodalle?'

'Of course. Olive darling, he's the mechanic who looks after my car and looked after Will's.'

'Oh,' said Olive, as if the information were new to her. 'I've never met him.'

196

'But you called him,' said Clements, taking up the attack. 'Twice. His number's here in the Telecom record of your calls from your car phone.' He held up the sheet of paper. 'Records are kept of all calls on cellular phones. Didn't you know that?'

'Did you know it, Mrs Bodalle?' said Malone.

'Of course.' There was a certain tension to her now.

'I didn't know,' said Olive. 'Will always paid all our bills — he said I had no idea of book-keeping — '

'The fact that the records show there were two calls to Mr Dunne does not prove Olive made them. You say the first was made two days before the murder — it could have been Will himself who made that call.' Angela had taken on a professional lacquer; she was in court. Not flamboyant now, no swirling of the gown, no arranging of the wig: she was businesslike, building a defence. 'That shows only that Mr Dunne got a call from my client's car phone, not that she made the call.'

'There's the second call, yesterday morning — ' Clements checked the records sheet, then took out his notebook and flipped it open. 'This is from your men's report,' he told Ellsworth; then he turned back to Olive and Angela: 'At eleven twenty-three yesterday morning Mrs Rockne was observed to come out of her house, get into her car and use the phone. At the same time, according to this record, the phone was answered at Mr Dunne's number and the call lasted five minutes and twenty seconds.'

'Have you had my client under surveillance?' Angela sounded shocked, though Malone doubted that she had been truly shocked since she was in her teens.

'Just for her protection,' he said. 'She's received threats from a Mr Jones. Or didn't she tell you that?'

Angela for a moment looked uncertain; but Olive didn't even glance at her, just gazed straight at Clements as if she had decided he was the only one she was going to pay

197

attention to. 'What else have you got to say to me, Sergeant?'

'You said you drew five thousand dollars from your joint account to pay for your holiday up on the Reef. You also said you bought clothes for the holiday and you had left them with the shops to be altered. Mrs Rockne, we've checked. You haven't been near the travel agency where you claim you made the bookings, not in three weeks or more. The shops, you gave us their names, they say you've bought nothing from them in the past three months.'

Malone was watching Angela, who was watching Olive; nothing showed in the barrister's face. Then he looked at Olive. 'Why all the lies?'

'You don't have to answer that,' said Angela, putting her hand on Olive's arm.

'Why would she want to avoid answering it?' said Malone.

'My client won't be answering any more questions at all at this stage, Inspector.'

Malone's gaze was steady and direct; hers was the same, but more challenging. The battle of the eyes, he called it; it was a constant in his dealings with criminals and their lawyers. Then he did something that men, in the challenge of battle, too often do, when reason becomes blind. He turned to Clements and Ellsworth.

'We'll charge Mrs Rockne on suspicion of conspiracy to murder her husband.'

Olive drew in her breath sharply and her body swayed; Angela put her arm about her, held her more tightly than Malone had ever seen a lawyer hold a client. But then, come to think of it, he had never been in this situation before, with a woman lawyer defending a woman client on such a serious charge. Olive turned her head towards Angela and for a moment he thought she was going to kiss her; there was a barely perceptible shake of Angela's head, then Olive shut her eyes and sank her chin on her breast. Angela challenged Malone again: 'You don't have a hope in hell of making the charge stick.'

'We'll see, Mrs Bodalle.'

He and Clements left the two women with Ellsworth, went downstairs and out to their car. Clements said nothing till they were in the car and had fastened their seat-belts. Then he looked sideways at Malone: 'Why did you charge her?'

'Because I think she had something to do with the murder.'

'So do I. I'd bet on it. But I wouldn't bet on any magistrate sending her to trial on what we'll give him.'

Malone looked at the red Ferrari parked next to them, then across its low profile to the rear door of the station. 'It's not too late if you think we should withdraw the charge.'

Clements sat very still, his hands on the steering wheel, his teeth chewing his bottom lip. Then: 'No, bugger it! I've backed longer shots than this and won.'

2

Olive was held overnight at Maroubra police station and Saturday morning was taken to Central Court in the heart of the city, where special sittings were held those mornings in front of a magistrate or a justice of the peace.

The courthouse had been built in the last century when courthouses were looked upon as temples of the law. The goddess this morning was a large, untidy woman who looked more like a housewife who had stopped in to check some law item on her weekend shopping list. She sat behind her bench under the big timber canopy with its crest; she had the sort of voice that reverberated in the high-ceilinged room. Malone, from the well of the court, could not tell whether she was sympathetic or hostile to the accused, though she did reply with some asperity to one of Angela Bodalle's pleas. Jason, Shelley and Mrs Carss had come to the court, but Malone, out of cowardice, did not go near the boy or his sister. Mrs Carss had come towards him, battle in her eyes, but he had managed to avoid her and had gone into the sheriff's room until the court was convened.

The magistrate, out of order in her own court, looked at Angela. 'A Queen's Counsel appearing so soon, Mrs Bodalle?'

'I am instructed, your worship – ' Angela, on her feet, looked down at the young solicitor, a blonde girl who looked as if she might have come out of law school only yesterday. Union rules, thought Malone with a cop's contempt for the legal profession: a barrister, even a QC, couldn't appear without being *instructed* by a solicitor. By the time Olive came to trial there would be a solicitor, a junior barrister and Angela, all carrying their invoice book with their law books. The young blonde, however, looked as if she might not bill Olive; she was looking up at Angela with an expression that suggested it was payment enough just to be in the same court as her.

'I am instructed that my client desires bail.'

The magistrate looked at the police prosecutor, a grey-haired sergeant who looked bored with the proceedings and in a hurry to get away. 'Well, Sergeant?'

'It's out of my hands, ma'am, this is a serious murder charge.'

'I know that!' snapped the magistrate, giving him the edge of her tongue as if he were her dumb husband. 'I take it there's someone here from the DPP then? There'd better be.'

'Here, ma'am.' *Another* woman appeared: crumbs,

thought Malone, the bloody law is becoming cluttered with them. She was young, pretty and off-balance: 'Sorry. I fell coming up the steps outside and broke the heel off my shoe. You know what it's like, ma'am.'

'I wear flatties myself,' said the magistrate. 'Get on with it!'

'We oppose bail for the time being, in view of the seriousness of the charge. We'd like it adjourned, with the accused in custody, till Monday morning at Waverley Court.'

The magistrate looked round, then focused on Malone. 'Oh, there you are!' she said, as if he had tried to disappear. 'That all right by you, Inspector?'

Her tone told him and everyone else in the court that she wasn't interested in his opinion; he knew then she had already judged and condemned Olive. 'Yes, ma'am.'

'Right! I would suggest, Mrs Bodalle, that your client look to her finances over the weekend. The bail, I should think, is going to be substantial, if it is granted at all. She will be held in custody. Case adjourned till Monday morning at Waverley Court. Next! Come on, next!'

The young woman from the Director of Public Prosecutions jerked her head at Malone and he followed her out of the courtroom and into a side room. 'I'm Sally Franz. If this case goes ahead, it looks as if I'll be working with you.' She was dark-haired and attractive in a brisk way and, though she was still lopsided from the loss of her heel, she looked calmer and more efficient than she had in his first sight of her. 'Is Angela Bodalle going to be defending Mrs Rockne?' He nodded. 'Damn! She won't make it any easier for me. For us, I mean.'

He grinned at her. 'Miss Franz, Mrs Rockne is guilty as hell. We just have to stick to that thought.'

'Inspector, we'll need more than faith to beat the hell out of Mrs Bodalle. I've seen her in action.'

201

'I'm Irish. We take in faith at our mother's breast.' He didn't believe that, but he liked this girl and he wanted her on his side, though he secretly hoped that by the time Olive Rockne was brought to trial the DPP would have brought in one of its big guns.

'I'm Jewish, Inspector. You don't think Moses accepted the tablets of stone on faith, do you? He negotiated.'

Malone shook his head, no longer smiling. 'No negotiation, Sally.'

Outside the court he hurried down the broad steps towards his own Commodore, where Clements stood waiting for him.

'Scobie, what's the hurry? You look as if *you've* just been let out on bail.'

'I don't want to face the Rockne kids –'

'There's one right behind you,' said Clements.

Malone, about to open the door of his car, turned round. Jason, in jeans, open-necked shirt and blazer, stood there, the morning sun like a cruel spotlight on his puzzled, angry face. 'Jesus, Mr Malone, why did you have to do this to us?'

'I didn't do it, Jay. The law did it. Or, rather, your mother did it to you.'

'She'd never kill Dad – it's unbelievable!' He flailed his arms, as if he were about to strike out at anything, even the sun-filled air about him. On the other side of the street the monorail carriages went silently by; he stared at them high above the street, but his eyes were full of tears and Malone realized the boy had seen nothing. In one of the carriages there was a solitary passenger, a Japanese; he turned round, camera at the ready, recording one of the sights of the tour: captors and captives coming out of a courthouse.

Clements could see the agony in Malone's stiff face; he said gently, 'Jay, wait for your grandmother and then go

202

home with her. She'll need you from now on.'

'What fucking use will I be?' the boy said, more despairingly than angrily, then he turned and shuffled away, as if his large Reebok-shod feet would never again bounce him high towards the basket.

Malone looked up the steps, through the shadows of the big plane trees, saw Mrs Carss and Shelley and Angela Bodalle come out of the courthouse. There were no television crews circling around like metal-headed jackals, but there was a single girl reporter and a photographer. The latter raised his camera and there was a flash. Mrs Carss raised her handbag as if she were going to sling it at him and said something that Malone, too far away, could not hear.

'It'll soon be over,' said Clements.

'Balls. It could drag on for months. You know what I'm talking about?'

'Sure. The Rockne kids, what you feel for them. I'd feel the same way, if I had kids of my own.'

Malone stood leaning on the roof of his car. Across the road was the huge pit of World Square and what was to have been another temple, this time to commerce: the biggest development in the city. But industrial trouble and the recession had put a stop to it. It remained a huge hole with a partially completed lift-shaft rising out of it like the ruins of some memorial to the future, a future that had stopped dead yesterday.

'I'll see you Monday. I'm going home, turn my mind off and enjoy Tom's birthday party. Then tomorrow I'm taking him to the footy.'

'To the grand final? How'd you get tickets this late — you didn't have 'em when I asked you last week?'

'Influence. How'd you get yours?'

'I'm taking Romy. I bought 'em off a scalper.'

'That's against the law.'

'Yeah, terrible, ain't it? Enjoy the game. And Scobie?'

'Yeah?'

'Forget the Rockne kids. They're not your responsibility.'

Malone went home to his son's birthday party, sat with a beer in his hand and looked at the dozen shouting kids who didn't have a care in the world, the ones with safe, law-abiding parents, and saw in the faces of each of the laughing boys another face, that of the anguished, weeping Jason.

Lisa tried to ask him about the court hearing, but he just shook his head and told her he didn't want to discuss it till tonight, when they were in bed. She didn't press the point; she knew that if he promised to talk to her, he would.

When finally, both worn out from the party, they were in bed, he told her about the morning at court, everything, including the encounter with Jason. She said nothing, just held him to her and wept inside with gladness that she had a man who could be so upset by other people's suffering.

Sunday, Malone took Tom to the rugby league grand final. The seats at the Stadium could not have been better, halfway up the western stand and level with the halfway line. Tom, who played soccer and only showed an interest in rugby league for his father's sake, was today wide-eyed with excitement. The big arena, with its swooping roof, like a plastic toilet seat warped by being left too long in the sun but still beautiful in its shape, was packed, every seat filled. Supporters from Penrith and Canberra, the two opposing teams, waved banners and ribbons and scarves: Agincourt had looked no more colourful nor had the passion been greater. Out on the field the pre-game enter-tainment was coming to an end: scantily clad girls danced, two bands played, gymnasts ran around like headless chooks, parachutists floated down, one of them missing the playing area and landing on the roof of the stand, to cheers from the crowd. On the huge replay screen at the northern end of the ground Tina Turner, an old rugby league fan if ever Malone had seen one, did things with a football that would have put her in the sin bin under some of the game's old referees. It was rugby league's circus day and Malone, suddenly feeling old and remembering going to a 1950s' final with his own father, pined for the good old days without the razzamatazz.

'Gee, Dad, ain't it great! I think I'll give up soccer if league is always like this!'

Malone looked at his son, not knowing whether to be pleased or disappointed in him. 'Next year they're putting on lions and tigers eating any player who's a Christian. And there are going to be girls high-diving into pools with no water in them.'

Tom, wise as a nine-year-old can sometimes annoyingly be, said, 'You're old-fashioned, Dad. Anyhow, how did you get the tickets?'

They had arrived by courier at home yesterday morning. There had been no sender's name on the small envelope; just a card inside that said, *Take your son, I'm taking mine.* Malone had made one guess at who had sent him the tickets: Jack Aldwych. His first reaction had been to shove the tickets back into the envelope. An honest cop didn't take presents, no matter how small, from a crime boss, even if the latter was retired (or so he said). Lisa had seen the reaction in his face and said, 'Keep them, take Tom to the match.'

'But I know who they're from.'

'If he asks anything of you in the future, all you have to do is say no. Go, and forget what you've had to do to Olive or are going to do. Go and take Tom and be thankful that this villain, whoever he is, is a man who understands that on certain days a father and son should be together.'

He looked at her, loving her till it hurt, then he kissed

her. 'It's Jack Aldwych, I'm sure. And you've just made him sound like Santa Claus.'

Now, sitting here beside his son in the roaring crush, he said, 'Do they still tell you about manna from heaven at school?'

'Sure. But football tickets are *manna*?'

'They are on grand final day.'

Tom suddenly grinned, the dimple showing in his right cheek, and Malone wanted to hug and kiss him. But real men didn't do that with their sons, at least not the Malone men; that sort of schoolgirl stuff was left to the 100-kilogram mastodons out on the field. Penrith won, 14–12, and Malone and Tom went home satisfied the result was just and right. Any victory over Canberra, the seat of conceit, of Federal government, the cause of the nation's recession, was to be cheered and welcomed.

3

It is history now that that Sunday night Penrith, a town thirty kilometres west of Sydney, called a city but really a distant suburb of Sydney, went wild. The Panthers had never won a grand final; history had to be celebrated. There was another reason: the recession had hit this area as badly as anywhere in the State, hope was dying on the vine, people fought with each other because there was nothing else to fight against. They grasped at the good news, fleeting though it might be, meaningless even, and started a party that lasted for three days.

There was a party going on at the house next door to the Dunnes' and at the house behind it. Kelpie, his plastered leg up on a chair, and Claudia were sitting in their kitchen, both drinking tea and Kelpie eating a slice of Sara Lee's blueberry pie. Claudia was not a good housekeeper and the kitchen resembled a way-station, as if the occupants of the house stopped here only to eat and run. She was a machinist at a clothing factory down by the railway line, lucky still to have a job, and, though she was clean in her personal habits, she preferred factory work to housework. Kelpie, possibly because of his jail training, was, on the other hand, meticulous about keeping the house clean. Except for the kitchen: it was understood between them that that was her turf and he was not to interfere. So he tolerated her untidiness and lack of method and never complained if he had to go looking for a packet of tea or the washing powder or a clean saucepan. He loved her, in a way he didn't understand and had never tried to.

'I won some money on the Panthers today.' They had watched a TV replay of the match and he had sat through it wondering when or whether he should tell her of his good fortune.

'I thought you'd given up gambling,' she said accusingly but without rancour. 'Listen to 'em next door!'

Through the slightly opened kitchen window the music and laughter from next door came in blasts. He grinned. 'If we complained, you think they'd listen to us?'

'So you had a bet?'

'Just this once, for the occasion.' He loved her, but he lied to her regularly; which is not incompatible and not unusual. He had lied to her last Saturday night, yesterday week, when he had told her he had to see the boss at Hamill's about going to the country to do some work on a client's Jaguar.

'How much did you win?' She was practical about money, even though they never seemed to have any to spare.

'Three thousand bucks.'

'Three thousand! Where'd you get . . .?'

'I know a bookie, he gimme good odds early in the piece. He'd of lost a packet today – he'll be quivering like a huge jelly tonight.'

He was smiling at her when, beyond her, he saw the silencer come through the narrow opening at the bottom of the window. Anchored by his leg, he could not move in time: the bullet hit him just below his widow's peak and he died with Claudia just in the corner of his eye, her face half turned to see what had startled him. Then she, too, died, with a bullet in her right temple.

Chapter Eight

1

Clements had never heard Malone so angry. 'Jesus Christ Almighty! Where was the bloody surveillance?' He went on through a stream of obscenities that would have made even a street kid's eyes pop. 'I'll have someone's neck for this – '

'Get off the boil, Inspector,' said Clements, waiting till the fury at the other end of the line had eased a little. 'Scobie, you'll be wasting your time looking for someone's neck over this. It's just been a monumental cock-up and I dunno you could find someone specific to point the finger at. The sergeant in charge of the detail at Penrith had enough on his hands – he needed every man he could muster to handle what's been going on out there, the town's a madhouse. He informed West Region at Parramatta, he comes under them, not us, what he was doing. They were to inform us, which they say they did, but it was lost somewhere in the computer. They couldn't supply anyone to keep watch on Kelpie – they had to send men out to Penrith to help there. Kelpie and his wife would still be alive if the Panthers had lost.'

'Is Olive still in custody?'

'That was the first thing I checked. She's in the cells at Police Centre.'

Malone had simmered down. 'All I need now is for you to tell me you won a bundle on the Panthers.'

Clements grinned to himself. 'Fifteen hundred bucks. I'll

go out to Penrith, see what they've come up with. I'll see you in the office.'

It was seven o'clock on Monday morning. Malone hung up the bedside phone and lay back on his pillow, his thoughts whirling like socks in a washing machine; some thoughts, like some socks, would be missing when his mind settled down. Then he was aware of Lisa, wide awake beside him.

'That was a choice selection of language. Just as well the kids are still asleep. What brought it on? Has Olive tried to escape or something? Oh God, she didn't try to commit suicide, did she?'

'No.' He told her the news. 'We thought we had an open-and-shut case against Olive. We'd have put Kelpie Dunne up against her and one of them would've cracked in the end, trying to save his or her own neck. But now . . .'

'Well, it must prove that this chap Dunne must have had *something* to do with Will's murder. He probably did it and then someone killed him to keep his mouth shut.'

He didn't tell her she was stating the obvious. '*That* we can bet on. But Olive's still in custody, so she couldn't have done it. And if Kelpie Dunne was her paid hitman, how many other hitmen does she know?'

'It could have been that Mr Jones you told me about. Which means Olive could be next on his list.'

2

There was a certain tension to the Monday morning conference. Malone, normally calm, almost placid, was sharp and irritable. Detectives were cut by the edge of his tongue, were told that results were wanted today, not tomorrow or next week. When the conference broke up, the air in the big room at Homicide would have soured milk.

Clements followed Malone into the latter's office. 'You were a bit rough on them, weren't you?'

'Was I?' Malone was arranging papers on his desk, seemed uninterested in Clements's opinion.

'Okay, if that's the way you want it. I'll come back when you've washed the shit off your liver.' Clements, who had been about to sit down, straightened up and turned towards the door.

'Sit down!' Malone sat himself down behind his desk, stared at Clements for a half-minute. Then: 'Wouldn't you have SOL if you'd had a case fold up on you like this Rockne one?'

'I just have.' Clements settled himself in his chair. 'Have you forgotten I've been on this one with you from the beginning? Come *on*, Scobie. This isn't the first time we've had everything bounce back on us. Okay, we picked the wrong suspect, there's another element in it that we hadn't counted on. But the case isn't dead yet.'

'It might be better if it was. Have you seen the *Herald* and the *Tele-Mirror*? Both of them have run stories that we picked up Olive and charged her. We're going to look bloody fools if we have to let her go.'

'If we got upset every time the newspapers and their know-it-all legal columnists got stuck into us, we might as well go outa business. Forget 'em, mate. This case is a long way from over.'

Malone was silent again; then he nodded. 'Righto, cheer me up. What have you got?'

Clements grinned. 'Practically bugger-all. I went out to Penrith. Their Crime Scene team were there – they came up with nothing. There were no footprints – there was a concrete path under the kitchen window, where the killer

211

stood to shoot them. They could pick up nothing distinguishable. No fingerprints on the windowsill – he must of worn gloves. No one next door heard anything or saw anything – there was a party on, but I gather everyone was well away with the grog and they wouldn't have heard the Gulf War if it had happened in Kelpie's back yard. All we came up with was this.' He tossed a small, cheap notebook on Malone's desk. 'It's the record of his bets over the past six months. Last week he bet five hundred dollars at six to one on the Panthers. His bookie has the initials B. B.'

Malone looked at the notebook, then put it down in front of him. 'Why do I get the impression that I'm standing still watching a merry-go-round go past me with all the same people on it?'

'I can't see Bernie Bezrow on a merry-go-round, but I get your picture. There's one guy still missing – Mr Jones.'

'Still nothing on him?'

Clements shook his head. 'I've got out an ASM on his Mercedes, but so far it hasn't been sighted. I've also asked the Queensland cops to keep an eye out for it, just in case he really has gone up to the Gold Coast. But I don't see him turning his back on that five million as easy as all that.'

'His mates in Moscow, or wherever they are, they wouldn't let him do that. I wonder if Will Rockne knew what he was getting into – or what he was putting his family into – when he stole all that cash?'

'If he knew he had the brain tumour and he was going to die anyway, it was never going to be his problem anyway, was it? I never knew the guy, but I don't think I'd of liked him.'

Malone made no comment. The phone rang: it was Clarrie Binyan, dry and matter-of-fact as usual. 'Scobie, Penrith sent in the two bullets they took out of Dunne and his missus. Both bullets came out of the same gun that killed Rockne.'

'We're sure a silencer was used, Clarrie. Any markings from it?'

'No, the bullets are clean of everything but the matching grooves and lands, same's on the Rockne bullet. If a silencer was used, the baffles this time didn't get in the way. Find the gun and the bloke who fired it and I promise you a conviction.'

'Gee, thanks.' Drily.

'Up yours.' Just as drily.

Malone hung up and looked at Clements. 'It was the same gun. I'm willing to bet Kelpie himself made that silencer they found in the junk box at Hamill's. But did he make two silencers? If not, where did the killer pick up the second one to fit the Ruger – if it is a Ruger?'

'You can still buy 'em over the counter in South Australia, but the guys who've been selling them under the counter here in New South have been very shy since the Strathfield massacre. That madman didn't use a silencer, thank Christ – he might of killed even more people before anyone realized what was going on. The hullabaloo since, about guns, has had the gun shops being very cautious about who they sell to. I got that from Clarrie last week. He's got his informers in the trade and they tell him everyone is playing it very quiet. But that's not to say you can't buy what you want if you're prepared to pay for it. Things are nowhere near as bad as they are in the States, but we're heading that way. You know what's happened to Hamill's?'

'The Motor Squad closed it down, at least temporarily, so, put John Kagal on to tracking down Hamill's foreman. Find out who worked beside Kelpie in the workshop. Get John to lean on him, find out if he ever saw Kelpie doing any work for himself — all the equipment would be there for making something like a silencer or cutting down a gun. It's a long shot, but Kelpie may have made a couple of silencers while he was at it. They're always in demand.' He looked at his watch. 'You want to come out to Waverley with me? Olive's case has been put back, she doesn't come before the magistrate till eleven.'

They drove out to Waverley, an inner eastern suburb that had hardly changed in the past half-century; perhaps the faces of the locals had changed, but the landscape of small solid houses had remained much the same. The courthouse, on a main road, was a nondescript modern building that did nothing for the majesty of the law; from the outside it could have been a sex clinic or an annexe of cells to the police station beside it. An overhang of trees took some of the bareness off it.

The two Homicide men were met by Ellsworth and Sally Franz and taken into a side room; both looked even glummer than Malone and Clements. Miss Franz was dressed in a black suit this morning, an appropriate colour. 'I talked with the Director before I came out here this morning. This murder of Mr Dunne rather puts the kybosh on things.'

'What does the Director think?'

'Without Dunne — and we were never sure he was going to say anything — what have we got? We know from that eyewitness, what's-his-name, the actuary, that Mrs Rockne was nowhere near her husband when he was shot. The conspiracy charge is all circumstantial now that Dunne has been eliminated. Angela Bodalle will wipe the floor with us in five minutes if we go into court as we stand now. The DPP suggests we drop the charges.'

'That leaves us with a lot of egg on our faces,' said Ellsworth.

The two senior detectives, those whose faces would

carry the omelette, looked at him and he got the message and had the grace to look embarrassed. Then Malone said, 'Is Angela Bodalle here?'

'She's with Mrs Rockne in the holding cell.' Sally Franz looked at her watch. 'We've got ten minutes to make up our minds.'

'We have no say in it, have we? The DPP's already decided.'

She nodded. 'I'm afraid so.'

'Righto, let's get the case dismissed. Are you disappointed, Sally?'

She shrugged. 'I don't know. Yes and no. It would have been my first murder trial, the Director was going to let me assist whichever QC was appointed. But up against Mrs Bodalle . . .'

'If the DPP had any sense of humour, he'd have appointed her as the Crown Prosecutor. She's just won a prosecution case.'

Outside the court, after the magistrate, a man this time, had made some disparaging remarks about ill-prepared cases and discharged Olive, a small band of media vigilantes fell on Malone and Clements.

'Inspector — ' She was a gangly girl from one of the radio stations who, Malone knew, had once ruined a drug bust by breaking a news embargo. She used her microphone like a gun, thrusting it forward menacingly. Her cynicism was like her make-up, too thick, and Malone had experienced her aggression several times before. 'What happened? Were the police looking for an arrest, come what may?'

'We're always looking for an arrest in a murder. Would you prefer we didn't?' That cheap shot would get him a rebuke from someone higher up.

'There's been a suggestion — '

'Who by? What suggestion?'

'Well, are we talking murder or suicide mode here?'

Malone kept a straight face. 'We're in doubt mode on that.'

'Thanks for nothing,' she said and, in huff mode, backed off.

'Oh, excuse me!' Clements managed to tread on two feet, putting down all his weight, as he pushed a way for himself and Malone through the small crush. He raised a hand and pushed a television cameraman's camera back into his eye. 'Damn, there I go again, using unnecessary force. Don't forget to report that to Civil Liberties.'

Free of the reporters, the two detectives crossed to their car. But one of the reporters, a small blonde woman, followed them. 'Hello, Scobie, Russ. In a bad mood this morning?'

'Hello, Grace. Are you going to make us feel even worse?'

She smiled and shook her head. She was in her thirties, her prettiness baked too hard by too much time on the beach; she could be hard in her reporting, too, but she was always fair. 'I know how it is. I knew Kelpie Dunne.' Her sources were varied and dangerous. 'Was he connected to the Rockne murder?'

'Off the record, yes.'

'Anything I can do to help? You won't be quoted.'

Malone hesitated, looked at Clements, then back at Grace Ditcham. 'There's some money involved – ' He told her about the money in the private bank account. 'You'll have to be careful how you handle the story on that, otherwise you'll have Angela Bodalle on your neck.'

'I can handle Angela. We've known each other off and on for years. I did a couple of stories on her husband before he was killed. Leave the money story with me. I'll handle it as if I stumbled on it all by my little self. Shahriver International? I love asking banks questions they don't

216

want to answer. Smile, Scobie. You look much better. You too, Russ.'

She went off and the two detectives looked at each other. 'It's worth a try,' said Malone. 'It might stir up Mr Jones.'

'I seem to remember you wanted things stirred up for Kelpie. It got him killed.'

As he went to get into the police Commodore Malone saw Angela Bodalle moving towards her red Ferrari parked along the street. He told Clements to wait for him, then headed for the lawyer. She straightened up from unlocking the door of her car and waited for him, her expression giving no hint what her reception of him would be.

'Has Olive gone?'

'Yes, Jason sneaked her away while those reporters were feeding on you and Sergeant Clements.'

'I didn't expect you to be here. I thought you'd be in court for the sentencing on the Filbert case.'

'I've been there, it was all over in fifteen minutes. The judge gave Mr Filbert life. The case was just too easy, Filbert folded up and it was all over before we got into second gear.' She patted the roof of the Ferrari, as if to emphasize the metaphor. 'You must be upset, the way your case has folded up. But the other way round, with Olive just walking away free, as she should.'

'You must be pleased with yourself. A successful prosecution and a successful defence, all in the one week.'

'I didn't have to defend Olive, Inspector. You never had a case against her.'

Despite his dislike of her, Malone found himself admiring her. He was married to a woman who had poise; Angela had it, too. This morning she also had the sweet smell of success about her, like an expensive perfume. She was wearing a beige suit and a cream silk blouse, a tan handbag hung from one shoulder and a heavy gold bracelet glittered like a prize as she lifted her arm. Not a hair on her shining dark brown head was out of place and her make-up, unlike the radio girl's, was just perfect. She was too perfect, he decided, the ultimate successful woman. He just wondered why he didn't feel at ease with her, why he felt he couldn't trust her. He was not a male chauvinist, or at least he told himself he wasn't; and Lisa and Claire saw to it that he should not be. And yet . . .

'Are you going to leave Olive alone now?' she asked.

'The case isn't closed yet. And there's still Mr Jones.'

'Yes.' She considered that, looked troubled. 'Are you now thinking he killed Will and then Mr Dunne? A pity you didn't follow that line before.'

'If all murders went in a straight line, our job would be a breeze. You know things don't work like that. If they did, you barristers wouldn't earn the money you do.'

'Is that what bothers you, Inspector – the money I earn?'

'Not at all. Like all cops, I think I'm underpaid, but I really don't care what other people earn. So long as they make it honestly.'

'Thank you.' She smiled. 'I make mine honestly. Some day you and I may work on the same side in court. Prosecuting Mr Jones, maybe? I'll look forward to that.'

'In the meantime, if you're seeing Olive, tell her we'll be giving her police protection until we bring in Mr Jones for questioning.'

'She won't like it. She's had enough of the police.'

'I think you should advise her to accept the protection. Mr Jones isn't going to let go of that five million dollars without another try for it. If Olive wants a quiet, safe life from now on, she'll have to give up any idea of keeping that money.'

'I've already told her that. But would you turn your back on that much money?'

'I'm a tight man with a dollar, so my wife and kids tell

218

me. I wouldn't know what to do with five million.'

She smiled. 'You'd find a use for it. So will Olive, I suppose. But I'll warn her about Mr Jones.'

She got into her car and drove away, not showing off by burning rubber, the red Ferrari sliding smoothly into the traffic like a salmon into a shoal. Malone walked back to Clements and the Commodore.

'You looked like old mates. What'd she have to say?'

'You're right, she was almost friendly. At least she didn't sneer at me.' He filled Clements in on the brief conversation. 'Maybe she's going to be easier to deal with than Olive. Now let's go and have another talk with Bernie Bezrow.'

It took them only ten minutes to drive from Waverley to Coogee. When they got out of the car and approached the gates of Tiflis Hall, the white bull terriers, pink eyes almost red with anticipation, were waiting for them, fangs exposed and growling in their throats. Clements spoke into the intercom and a moment later there was the piercing whistle from the hidden sound system. The dogs gave a disappointed snarl, like lions who had been told the Christians had just recanted, then turned and went helter-skelter up the garden path and disappeared round the back of the house.

'The neighbours must love that,' said Malone. 'There'd be a lot of headaches in this street from that whistle.'

They made their way up through the garden terraces and were greeted at the front door by the Filipino maid, who still looked apprehensive, still not sure that they were not from Immigration. She ushered them into the same room where they had met Bezrow last Sunday week. He was seated in the same double-chair, as much a fashion-plate as when they had seen him last, but this time looking like a huge blue moon. He didn't rise, but at least greeted them with a smile.

219

'Another visit? What can I contribute this time? From what I read in the papers, you have already arrested Mrs Rockne for the murder of poor Will. It's happening more and more, wives disposing of their spouses. I'm a widower, fortunately.'

'We've just had to let Mrs Rockne go. Not enough evidence.'

'So that's why you're here again? Scraping the bottom of the barrel for any evidence at all? No, I don't mean that, Inspector. Forgive me.'

'There was another murder last night – Kelpie Dunne. It's rather complicated things.'

'Oh yes, I saw that in the papers, too.' He looked at his watch; the gold on his wrist would have cost Malone a month's pay at least. 'Is this going to be a long interview?'

'It could be. Depends on how long or short your answers are.'

Bezrow smiled. 'I can be very terse when it's necessary, Inspector. But I'm about to have lunch – I always eat early. Will you join me or would that be looked upon as consorting?'

'I think we could stretch a point.'

Bezrow rang for the maid, asked for two more places to be set, then led the two detectives through the house and out to a conservatory that looked down over the slope of red-tiled houses and flat-roofed flats to the sea. Out on the horizon alps of clouds were massed and, closer in, a long bulk-carrier crawled north like part of an almost stationary freight train. All that spoiled the view was a security grille that entirely covered the conservatory. Bezrow and his guests were seated at the luncheon table in a glass-lined cage. Bezrow noticed the detectives' quizzical look at what surrounded them.

'Ridiculous, isn't it? This was to be a hothouse where I

could eat among flowers even in winter. Instead it is like eating in one of those new five-star jails. But it's necessary these days, I'm afraid.'

The maid brought them smoked salmon and thin slices of toast and Bezrow poured three glasses of riesling. 'I hope you're not big eaters in the middle of the day?'

'No,' said Clements, avoiding Malone's eye. 'Not before one o'clock, anyway.'

Bezrow smiled, looked at Malone; he seemed entirely at ease, as if he had policemen to lunch every day in the week. 'The sergeant obviously is a trencherman. So am I — or was. Here's to success with your enquiries.' He raised his glass. 'But what are the questions to which you want long answers?'

'Did you know Mr Dunne?'

The fat face had a faint fold in it across the brows; then the frown faded. 'Oh, last night's victim! Yes, I knew him. Slightly.'

'How slightly?' The smoked salmon was good, the best: Lisa would have approved of it.

'He bet with me occasionally.'

'More than occasionally, according to his bets book. Twice a week at least for the past six months.'

'That often?' The surprise was well feigned. 'He was a small punter, Inspector, a hundred here, a couple of hundred there. I don't want to sound like one of our bankrupt entrepreneurs, all of whom seem to have defective memories, but I don't keep track of all those who bet regularly with me. Not unless they are big punters, a thousand, five thousand, ten thousand at a time. My penciller keeps tabs on the others.'

'Charlie Lawson?' said Clements.

'You're well informed, Sergeant. Yes, Charlie Lawson. He'd be the one who would have taken Mr Dunne's bets.'

'These would have been SP bets?'

'Are we men of the world?' Bezrow looked at them both above the rim of his glass.

Malone grinned, sipping his own wine: it, too, was the best. 'We're not from the Gaming Squad. Go ahead, Mr Bezrow, what you tell us about your SP business stays here in this – ' he looked around them ' – glass house.'

Bezrow nodded; they were men after his own heart, pragmatic. 'Starting price betting answers a need. Like prostitution or religion. Yes, I would say that all of Mr Dunne's bets with us were SP bets.'

'There was also a three thousand to five hundred bet on the Panthers in yesterday's grand final,' said Clements.

Bezrow gave a mock grimace of pain. 'Don't mention yesterday. I feel as if I've been hit by the entire pack of Penrith forwards. Mr Dunne's bet, at those odds, wouldn't have been at the starting price.'

'What sort of car do you drive?' Malone had finished the smoked salmon, wondered if that was all that would be served. Especially if the questions got too close to the bone.

'A Rolls. Why?'

'Where do you have it serviced? At the Rolls-Royce dealers?' He looked directly at their host, letting him know that the questioning now was turning sharp.

Bezrow took his time, chewing slowly on the last of his toast and smoked salmon. 'No. It is serviced at a place called Hamill's. They specialize in quality cars.'

'They also specialized in stolen cars. The Motor Squad has closed them down. Did Kelpie Dunne work on your Rolls?'

'I wouldn't know.' The fat man's gaze was as steady as Malone's. 'My chauffeur always takes the car there. I don't drive, Inspector. Was that where Mr Dunne worked? What a coincidence.'

'We find coincidence crops up every day in police work – we'd be surprised if it didn't. Did he do anything else for you besides service your car?'

The maid came in, took away their plates and came back with a crystal salad bowl and a silver tray on which there were three small steaks. Malone wondered if Bezrow ate in such style every day or whether this was to impress a couple of working cops. Bezrow waited till the maid had gone, then said, 'Would you like a claret with the steak or will you stay with the white?'

'Red always makes me sleepy in the middle of the day,' said Malone; and Clements looked disappointed.

'We can't afford that, can we?' said Bezrow. 'None of us . . . Did Mr Dunne do anything else for me? This white is a chardonnay, from the Hunter. I have a half-interest in a small vineyard up there. What else did Mr Dunne do?'

'He had a criminal record, mostly stand-over stuff.'

Bezrow carefully transferred one of the steaks from the tray to his plate. 'Let me ask you something. Am I suspected of being involved in Mr Dunne's murder?'

Malone admired the fat man's footwork. 'In a short answer – maybe.'

Bezrow shook his head. 'The short answer and the true one, Inspector, is no. N-O. I'm no angel, as the saying is, but I'm not, definitely not, a murderer.'

'Did Kelpie do anything for you short of murder, then? Like standing over some punters who were slow to pay up?'

'Do you usually insult people at their own table?'

'Not usually, no. But then we don't usually conduct our investigations over lunch. Not since the government introduced the fringe benefits tax.'

Bezrow smiled. 'What a loss that was!'

Clements had sat silent through most of the meal, concentrating on his eating as if spreading out what was,

223

for him, sparse fare. But now he said, 'Would one of your punters have killed Kelpie?'

Bezrow considered that while he delicately cut his steak. 'Perhaps. It's a thought.'

'If it's a thought,' said Malone, 'have another thought. Why would they have killed him? Because you'd asked Kelpie to lean on them? Can you name a punter who has welshed on you, one who might've killed Kelpie Dunne as a warning to you to back off? Thank you.' He held out his glass as Bezrow offered him more wine.

'Let me put a thought to you, Inspector. If some misguided punter killed Mr Dunne because he wanted to put a warning to me, then what is the connection with Will Rockne's murder? I have a feeling, Inspector, that you are throwing bait into a pond where there is no fish. That's an old Georgian saying. My grandfather was fond of quoting it.'

Malone realized now that he and Clements could sit through an eight-course banquet with Bezrow and they would get nothing from him. 'Every saying or proverb has a saying that contradicts it. But I can't think of one at the moment. Nice salad. What's the dressing?'

'Russian.'

'Which reminds me,' said Clements. 'Do you know a Russian named Jones?'

'Is he one of the St Petersburg Joneses?'

Clements smiled; he was enjoying this lunch, even if the helpings were inadequate. 'Actually, his name is Igor Dostoyevsky.'

'You're still pulling my leg.'

'No, really. He also goes under the name of Boris Collins. He worked for the Soviet embassy in Canberra, but lately he's been selling Mercedes here in Sydney.'

'So why should I know him?'

Malone had been watching Bezrow; the fat man had

thrown up defences with each fencing line in the conversation. Nothing short of torture would ever get an admission from Bezrow. It made Malone wonder if that was why torture featured so prominently in Russian history, or what little he knew of it.

'Russians and Georgians have hated each other since time immemorial, Sergeant. We don't fraternize.'

'Mr Dostoyevsky never came here trying to sell you a Mercedes in preference to a Rolls?' said Malone.

'Dostoyevsky as a car salesman?' Bezrow chortled, in control of the interrogation; torture would, indeed, be needed. But Malone had played the wrong sport, training would be needed. 'The picture is a good one, don't you think? You're wasting bait again, Inspector.'

Bait was never wasted; some ponds were deeper than others, gave up different fish. Later, over cheese and fruit, Malone said, 'Did you lose much on yesterday's grand final?'

'Are we still men of the world or are you now substituting for the Gaming Squad?'

'We never encroach on each other's turf.'

'Not even when there is a murder on their turf?'

'Ah yes, we do then. But they keep the betting franchise on whether we'll solve it or not.'

'Sound policy. Yes, I lost a packet yesterday. The final odds were five to four on, but I'd made the mistake of offering much longer odds than that earlier in the season.'

'Kelpie Dunne must of known something, six to one,' said Clements. 'Who'll get the money, now that him and his missus are both dead?'

'His estate, I suppose. We'll just wait till there's a claim.'

'You won't go looking for the heirs? They might need the money to pay for the funerals. Punters' heirs usually do.'

'Not yours, Sergeant, from what I hear. You're a punter,

you know bookmakers aren't in the Salvation Army game. We're famous for our donations to charity, but not to punters. Be realistic.'

Malone threw more bait: 'Mr Bezrow, your man Charlie Lawson went down to Will Rockne's office last week and asked for your files. The secretary couldn't give them to him because we'd put a seal on the filing cabinets. If you were after your files, that'd suggest Will did some business for you. Yet when we went through the cabinets, there were no files on you. Nor Mr Jones.'

Bezrow was coring an apple; he did it with all the concentration of a surgeon taking out a vital organ. At last he said, 'That's interesting.'

'Yes, isn't it? What would the files on you, if we ever find them, tell us?'

Bezrow looked up, the surgery completed. 'This and that. Bits and pieces. Mr Rockne did some conveyancing for me on some properties I sold.'

'That was all?'

'Yes, nothing more. I was just throwing some business his way because he was a local.'

'So why would the files go missing? And why did Charlie Lawson go asking for them?'

Bezrow ate a thin slice of apple. 'You think your bait has finally got a nibble?'

'I think so. Is there a Georgian saying that covers that?' Bezrow just smiled, and Malone went on. 'The only two files missing were yours and Mr Jones's. Mr Dostoyevsky. There must be some connection.'

Bezrow ate another slice of apple, then said, amiably, 'I don't think I'd better answer any more questions, Inspector, not till I've consulted my lawyer.'

'I thought Will Rockne was your lawyer?'

Bezrow was still seemingly unperturbed. 'Mr Rockne belonged to the lower grades, Inspector. We're coming up to a grand final, aren't we? I'll have to bring in my first team.'

'It wouldn't be Mrs Bodalle, would it?' That was a wild cast into the pond.

Bezrow frowned. 'You have me there, Inspector. I've heard of Mrs Bodalle — who hasn't? — but I've never met her. No, I'm sure you know my lawyer, Caradoc Evans.'

'Oh sure, we know him. A Welshman and a Georgian. We're up against something, don't you think, Russ?'

'I still like our chances,' said Clements. 'You wanna take a bet from me, Mr Bezrow? What odds will you give me?'

'I closed the book a moment ago, Sergeant. Coffee?'

Chapter Nine

1

Jason was in bed with Jill Weigall. It was no dream; yet he couldn't believe it. When she slid off him and lay beside him, he remained flat on his back, every nerve-end wanting to burst out of his skin. He kept his eyes closed, not wanting to wake up. That was what he actually said: 'I don't wanna wake up.'

'I wish you could stay till morning. I'd keep you awake all night. *That*'s unbelievable.'

He was no longer embarrassed by *it*. 'Well, you gotta go with what you've got.'

She just smiled; and he wondered if he was making a fool of himself by trying to sound cool and sophisticated. He would never ask her, but she could not have been to bed with guys as young as himself, at least not since she herself had been his age. She was experienced – God, was she experienced! – and she had spoiled him for any young girls in the future. For a moment he thought of Claire Malone, whom he had never even *touched*, and was instantly ashamed, though he didn't know why. From now on his whole life was going to take a new direction, at least when it came to women.

He had moped around the house all day after he and Mum had come home from the court; he hadn't wanted to go to school and face all the guys with their unspoken questions. Gran had been there, fussing about, picking on him for being in the way, and Shelley, sensibly, had escaped and gone to school in the afternoon. When she came home she had told him she wished she had stayed at home – 'God, you'd of thought I was a *freak* or something! If it hadn't been for Mother Brendan . . . Usually she's a drag, but today she was really nice. I think we should give up school, Jay, move right away. Go somewhere else, up to Queensland maybe, somewhere where nobody will know us. You think Mum might say yes?'

'We can ask her. But not yet . . .' Not till we find out if we can keep that five million dollars. That had been on his mind all day, once they had released his mother from that ridiculous charge of murdering Dad.

Then, almost without thinking, he had rung Jill at the office. Miraculously, she had had no date for tonight, and the invitation had tumbled out of his mouth: would she like to go to a movie with him?

He had had to borrow the money from his mother: 'Fifty dollars? What do you want that much for?'

Just as well he hadn't asked for a hundred, his first thought. 'Mum, I owe the guys a movie and a hamburger. It's my turn to shout.' She would kill him if he told her it was to take out Jill. 'Come on, be a sport. We can afford it.'

She looked at him shrewdly and for a moment he worried that she was going to ask him if he was taking out Jill. But she said, 'You're not thinking of that five million dollars, are you?'

'Yes,' he grinned.

She smiled, too, and gave him the fifty dollars. 'We mustn't, not yet.'

'You're spoiling him,' said Gran Carss, but he felt so good that he even grinned at her.

His mother lent him the Civic, insisting that he put on his P plates – P plates, for God's sake, when taking out a girl like Jill! But as he drove over to pick her up at her flat in Tamarama, he smiled at the thought: he was on a Provisional licence, at least as far as a lover went. But before he went up and knocked on the door, he removed the plates.

He took her to see *City Slickers*, a movie she said she wanted to see – 'I love Billy Crystal.' He was glad she hadn't chosen some R-rated show, all chock-a-block with nudity and sex; that would only have made him uncomfortable. When he came out of the cinema with her he was thrilled and relieved when she suggested they go back to her flat – 'My flatmate is away for the week.' He silently thanked the absent flatmate. The twenty-eight dollars he had left in his wallet wouldn't have bought the supper Jill expected from a guy on his first date with her. They had gone to an early session and there would have been time for him to have had to buy her a proper dinner.

He hardly looked at her flat; all he noted was that it seemed cramped after the rooms in the house at Coogee. He guessed you had to live small when you started out living on your own. She cooked them bacon and eggs and took a Sara Lee apple danish from the fridge for dessert. 'I'm the world's worst cook. Do you want to marry a fabulous cook?'

The question took him by surprise; but it seemed an innocent one. 'I haven't got around yet to thinking about a girl in the, you know, kitchen.'

'Where do you think of them? In the bedroom?'

The apple danish, though oiled with ice cream, went down his throat like a lump of rock. 'Sometimes.'

She smiled. 'I'm teasing you, Jay. Come on, finish that.'

'What about the washing-up?' Why did he ask that, for God's sake? To show he was domesticated or something?

'Leave it. I'm not a good housekeeper, either.' He had noticed that: the kitchen sink was full of last night's dishes.

230

Ten minutes later, he was astonished how quickly it happened, she said, 'Undress me.'

He had lost his virginity twelve months ago to a girl from Ascham at a party in Bellevue Hill, where he had been a virtual stranger. She had been much more experienced than he, though no subtler; it had been like groping a female gorilla. When he first got inside her sweater she told him she had only been screwed (the word had jolted him: he hadn't expected it to come out of Ascham with the la-di-dah Darling Point accent) by Protestant boys from Cranbrook or Scots; she wanted to know if a Catholic boy, with his sense of sin, would be hotter; her mother, it seemed, was a psychologist. The word *sin* had also jolted him; it almost made him go limp. But he had recovered and had sinned, twice, flat out like Lucifer himself.

Now he opened his eyes and turned to look at Jill, at her profile against her tangled hair and at the undulations of her marvellous body. He said, 'I love you.'

She shook her head. 'Not yet, Jay.'

'Why? Because I'm too young for you?'

She put her fingers on his lips. 'No, for other reasons, Jay. Wait till you've known other girls ... I've got something to show you.'

She got out of bed and he shut his mouth tight before he could make some bloody stupid remark about what she was showing him as she went to a dressing table, then turned and came back to him. She sat on the side of the bed and handed him an envelope. He recognized it at once, the sort of legal envelope he had seen many times in his father's office.

'What is it?'

'It's your father's will. I found it today in one of his legal books. Looks like he had hidden it there for some reason.'

231

'I thought Mum had already got a copy of the will?'

'I don't know whether there's another copy of that. After the police released all your father's personal papers, I sent them up to your place in a box. Then I found that copy today when I was going through the books on his shelves. It's one he made three weeks ago.'

'Do you know what's in it?'

She looked at him reproachfully. 'Jay – '

'I'm sorry. I didn't mean had you peeked at it. But why give it to me? Why not to Mum?'

She got back under the sheet, as if the discussion was now too serious for nudity. He eased himself up in the bed, she propped a pillow up behind him, and they lay there like a couple who made a habit of discussions in bed.

'I should give it to her, I suppose. But she turned her back on me at the funeral, did you know that? So deliberate, right there in front of all your relations and friends. But not before she told me I shouldn't even *be* there. God!' He was shocked at the anger in her and didn't even know how to handle it. 'I wasn't there because I was your father's mistress or anything! One weekend, that was all, a bloody miserable failure! I was there, for God's sake, because I worked for him for two years, because he was my boss!'

'I looked for you after the funeral – ' He touched her bare arm.

'I sneaked away. I've never been so humiliated. But it's over now – forget it. Take the will home to your mother.'

'I think I'll open it.' The envelope was only slightly sealed; it was remarkable how easily the flap came unstuck in his hand. 'Is it against the law?'

'What a crazy question! God, your father's been murdered, they arrested your mother, there's millions of dollars that nobody knows where they came from – '

She made him sound really dumb; naked as he was, he

232

seemed to flush all over. 'Yeah, I guess opening your father's will is nothing, then.' He pulled out the single-page document. 'It's not very long. I always thought they ran to pages and pages . . .'

'Maybe it's just a codicil to another will. I didn't see what was in it, he held his hand over it while he got Mrs Rosario the cleaning lady and me to sign it. What's it say?' She didn't appear particularly interested, it could have been just another client's last will and testament.

'. . . I hereby revoke all prior wills and testa – testa – mentary dispositions heretofore made by me and declare this to be my last will and testament . . . Does that mean everything he's written before doesn't mean anything now?'

'Yes. Go on.'

'. . . Blah, blah, blah . . . to divide my entire estate, including the monies in account Number 5104 in the Shahriver Credit International Bank at its Sydney Office, equally between my two children, Jason William Rockne and Shelley Mary Rockne . . . My wife, Olive Mary Rockne, will understand the reasons for my exclusion of her from any benefits from my estate . . .' He turned his head, looked directly at Jill. 'This is gunna floor Mum.'

It was a moment or two before Jill said, 'Did your mother and father hate each other?'

'I dunno. I never thought so. But – there was *something* between them that I never cottoned on to.'

'Jay, I don't think you should let your mother know you know what's in the will. Seal it up and just give it to her without saying anything.'

'I'll have to tell her where I got it.'

'Yes, you'll have to do that. You don't have to tell her where you were when you read it.' She smiled, but tossed back the sheet and got out of bed. 'I'd love some more of what we've just had, a whole night of it, but I think you'd

233

better take the will home to your mother, give it to her tonight and not in the morning. If you get home too late, she might guess we've been to bed. I don't want her thinking that's all I'm intent on, going to bed with the Rockne men.' Then she turned back, leaned across the bed and put her palm against his cheek. 'I'm sorry, Jay. That sounded cruel, mentioning your father.'

He stared at her, wanting to pull her back into bed; she must know how much she was tempting him, yet she was so casual about what she was showing him. God, he was so innocent, he had so much to learn about women!

Somehow he got the thickness out of his throat. 'There's something else in the will.' He read from the page. 'To my secretary, Jill Weigall, I leave the sum of ten thousand dollars, the amount to be found in cash in my office safe . . .'

She sat down heavily on the side of the bed, remained very still. Suddenly he was taking her nudity for granted. When she looked back at him over her shoulder, the lock of hair down over her brow, all he was aware of were her eyes. They were deeply hurt. 'He was paying me off. I feel like a bloody whore!'

'No, Jill. Dad wasn't like that — ' But he wondered. He realized now how little he had known his father. 'He knew he was dying, with that brain tumour, and he just wanted to show how he appreciated you working for him. Don't knock him, Jill. He's dead and can't explain . . .'

'Oh God!' She turned and reached for him, pulled him towards her, held him. It wasn't sexual and he realized it. 'I'm sorry, Jay. I didn't mean to hurt you . . . Forgive me?' She put her hand under his chin, held his face away from her.

'Sure — '

She kissed him softly on the lips. 'Go home, Jay. Call

234

me tomorrow and let me know what your mother says about the will.'

He left her reluctantly, not because he wanted to stay in bed with her, to have that bloody wonderful sex with her, but because he knew now, with utter certainty, that he was in love with her. He didn't have to wait, as she had advised him, till he had known other girls. He *knew*.

He drove home, switched off the Civic's lights so that he wouldn't disturb his mother and Shelley if they had gone to bed, and pulled up sharply as he saw Angela's Ferrari blocking the driveway. He reversed out into the roadway and swung the Civic into the kerb. He got out of the car and instantly a man was standing beside him.

'Oh, it's you – Jason, isn't it? I'm Constable Pilecki, from Randwick police.'

He couldn't believe how rigid he had gone with fright; tonight he was experiencing emotions he had never felt before. 'You scared the hell outa me!'

'Sorry, mate.' He was young and bulky, but a good six inches shorter than Jason. 'We're supposed to be keeping an eye on the family.'

'You weren't following me tonight, were you?'

'Nah. We saw you go out, but our instructions are to stay with your mother. She's been home all night.'

'Why all this security stuff? Because of Mr Jones?'

'Him, and anybody else who might trouble your mother. She has a visitor now, but it's a lady.'

'Sure. That's Mrs Bodalle. She's no trouble.' Just a pain in the arse.

He walked up the side driveway, turned the corner of the house, hearing the rustle of birds in the big camphor laurel, and saw his mother and Angela against the glow of a table lamp in the garden room. They were in each other's arms, mouths swallowing each other's, in a clinch as tight

as he had been with Jill before she had said, *Undress me.*
Angela with her hands up under his mother's skirt, just as
he had put his hands up under Jill's. He stood stock-still,
suddenly feeling sick. He was holding his breath, not
daring to move, not wanting to catch their eye and have
them know he had seen them.

Then his mother and Angela broke apart, holding each
other at arm's length, and both smiled, lovers' smiles: it
was the way he and Jill had looked at each other after
their last kiss tonight at her front door. His mother put up
her hand and stroked Angela's cheek and whispered something. Then they turned slowly and went into the kitchen,
arms round each other. He continued to stand without
moving, still feeling sick and – disgusted? Wondering if he
should just bolt down the driveway, run – but where? And
why? Just because he had found out that his mother was a
– a lesbian, for Chrissake!

He gathered himself together, angry at his shock and
cowardice. He was going to gain nothing by running away,
better to go in now and face them and see what his mother
would say when he told her what he had seen. He almost
marched into the house, found his mother and Angela still
in the kitchen, but with Angela now with her handbag
over her shoulder, ready to say goodnight.

'Oh Jason!' His mother looked surprised; or guilty.
From now on he knew he would be looking at her with a
stranger's eyes. 'You're home early.'

He looked at his watch, calm as you like; even Charlie
Sheen couldn't have acted better. 'It's eleven o'clock. What
time did you expect me home?'

It was Angela who saw the envelope in his hand. 'Have
you got something for your mother?'

'How'd you know?' He was abruptly aggressive, rude.
'Jay!'

'It's all right, darling, don't jump on him . . . It's a legal envelope, Jay, the sort we put wills in. You forget, I've seen hundreds of them.'

'You're pretty sharp.'

'Jay, stop that! Is it a will? Where'd you get it?' His mother snatched it from him and he let her have it.

'Jill gave it to me.'

'You've been with her? You said you were going out with your friends.'

'*She's* a friend . . . She found that today in one of Dad's legal books. He made it out a coupla weeks ago or something.'

'Does she know what's in it?'

'No.' He was surprised at how easy it was to lie to her, how easy it was going to be in the future.

'Do you know?'

'No.'

Olive took out the single sheet, read it, then read it again. He watched the expression on her face; she was stunned, unbelieving. Without a word she handed the will to Angela, who seemed to speed-read it, she was so quick.

Then, unsure now how good his acting was, he said, 'What's it say?'

'Did your father ever say anything to you about making a new will?' said Angela.

What's it got to do with you? he wanted to ask; but, of course, he knew. 'No, never. What's the will say?'

At least Angela left it to his mother to reply this time: 'It leaves everything to you and Shelley, nothing to me. Nothing at all.'

'Everything? To me and Shelley? Why would Dad do something like that?' All at once he was barely holding on, his acting was falling apart.

'I wouldn't know.'

So we're even, he thought: I've lied to you and you've lied to me. But he was certain now that his father must

237

have known that his mother and Angela were — lovers? Was that the word? 'Is there anything else in the will?'

'Yes.'

'What?' Come on, for Chrissake don't lie to me again, Mum!

'Your father has left ten thousand dollars for his girlfriend. Your friend Jill.' The venom in her voice shocked and hurt and disappointed him; the image he had had all his life of his mother was all of a sudden falling apart. Even Angela seemed worried by it: she took his mother's elbow and squeezed it, as if in warning.

'Darling, don't say anything you'll regret in the morning.'

'Jesus, what do you expect me to say!' Olive turned on her. 'What sort of man was I married to?'

Jason felt that at any moment he was going to crumble to the floor. He suddenly felt terribly alone, he wanted someone to lean on; but who was there? From now on there would be only Shelley, and she was too young to be any help. It came to him, even now, that Jill, for all her tenderness towards him, would be no help, either. He had to make this all on his own.

'Mum, he's dead.' His voice was unexpectedly steady; he saw Angela look at him. 'You should have asked him that while he was alive.'

Angela was still looking at him, hard: as if she were seeing him as an adult for the first time. 'You're being rough on your mother, Jay.'

'You mean, like you would be in court?'

He didn't see his mother's hand coming at him, just felt the stinging blow across his cheek. That did it: things he had not meant to say burst out of him like vomit: 'Is that why Dad left you out of his will? Because you and Angela grope each other, because you're a coupla fucking lesbians? You make me sick, Mum!'

He had to push between them to get past them; he did it roughly, only just stopping himself from knocking them both off their feet. He went out of the house, slamming the door behind him. He ran down the driveway, almost falling in his haste; he hit the Ferrari with his fist as he stumbled past it. He came out into the street and stood there, his breath coming in great aching sobs, as if he had just run from Christ knew where. He looked up and down Coogee Bay Road, pained and puzzled, as if he had suddenly found himself in strange territory and had no map, no sense of direction. Then he crossed to the Civic, fumbled at opening the door, got in and started up the engine. Only then did it hit him that he had nowhere to go.

2

Tuesday morning Malone felt no better, but he succeeded in concealing his mood. The report from Ellsworth at Maroubra said that Mrs Rockne was still under surveillance and there had been no apparent interference by Mr Jones or anyone else, unless she had been contacted by phone and had not reported it. The boy Jason had run out of the house at 11.15 P.M. last night, got into the family's Honda Civic obviously distressed and had disappeared and not returned by 7.30 A.M., the time of the report.

'Why didn't they follow Jason?'

Clements tried to soothe him. 'Scobie, that wasn't in the brief. They reported the kid went off, gave a description of the car and its number, but none of the cruising cars was able to pick it up. Not till twenty minutes ago, when Carl Ellsworth phoned in. Waverley police report the Civic's parked outside a block of flats in Tamarama.'

'Who lives in the block of flats?'

'I looked up the running sheet, checked the addresses of everyone we've talked to. Jill Weigall lives there.'

'Well, how about that? What else have we got?'

The report from Penrith contained nothing new, except the preliminary autopsy on Dunne and Claudia. 'Penrith has set up a van outside Kelpie's house and, according to Jim Petrocelli, from West Region Homicide, they've been swamped by people who swear they saw the murderer coming out of Kelpie's front gate. They all have different descriptions – he was six feet six, he was four feet six, he was fat, he was thin, he was Asian, he was a whitey, he was an Abo. The only thing they have in common is that they've all admitted they might have been drunk, celebrating the Panthers' win. Jim says if he gets one piece of concrete evidence out of 'em, he'll be lucky.'

'The public, I love 'em. Always there when you need 'em. What've you got, John?'

John Kagal had sat quietly, immaculate as always, the university tie looking as if it had just been dry-cleaned; or perhaps, Malone thought sourly, he had a dozen of them. 'I have a glimmer of light.'

'At the end of the well-known tunnel? Are we about to stumble into some sort of mode?' Then conscience struck him; Kagal didn't deserve this. 'Sorry, John. I'm still scraping shit off my liver – it's stuck to me like chewy to my boot. I've had at least a dozen calls from the media experts, every one of them fluent in all the buzz phrases. Two of them actually asked me how level was the playing field. Go on, John, what've you got?'

If Kagal had been put out by Malone's sourness, he didn't show it. He said smoothly, 'I tracked down Hamill's foreman at the Newtown shop, a guy named Reevers. He was quite open, said he had a record. Break and entry, possession of an illegal drug. The last time was eight years ago and he swears he's been clean ever since. He also swears he had nothing to do with the stolen car racket at Hamill's — he knew about it, but he had nothing to do with it, he just ran the legitimate front. He's scared he'll be dragged in by the Motor Squad, so he was prepared to be co-operative. Especially now Kelpie is dead and can't stand over him — evidently they didn't get on too well. He said yes, Kelpie was working on things for himself in the workshop. He knows a silencer when he sees one and he says Kelpie made three or four, including one for one of the guys out at Tempe, where the stolen cars were.'

Malone looked at Clements. 'So, whether he knew it or not, he made a silencer for whoever killed him and his missus. Did you get the name of the feller out at Tempe?'

'Yes, I've seen him. His name's Fancett and he has a record, too — Hamill's was a real reunion house for cons. I got a warrant and searched his house out at Bexley. I found the silencer and an unlicensed Colt Forty-five. Ballistics has both the silencer and the gun now and he's been taken into custody for questioning.'

Kagal neither sounded nor looked pleased with himself; but the two senior detectives could feel that he was. He had been detailed to do something and he had done it efficiently and more quickly than Malone had expected. All Malone could say was, 'Nice work, John,' and Kagal nodded, not in acknowledgement but in agreement.

'You think Fancett had anything to do with either Kelpie's or Rockne's murder?'

'Nothing. He's sticking to his story that he kept the Forty-five for protection, though he couldn't explain why he needed a silencer for protection. But I'm sure he had nothing to do with our two killings.'

Andy Graham, one of the other detectives, put his head in the doorway. 'Russ, Liverpool police are on the line for you. They've got some info.'

Clements went out, was back in a couple of minutes.

'Liverpool police have traced Jones's brown Mercedes. It's on a used car lot on the Hume Highway, he sold it yesterday afternoon.'

'Did he trade it in on something else?'

'He was too smart for that. If he'd bought a car from this crowd, he'd know we'd know what to look for. He's gone somewhere else to get himself some wheels.'

Malone stood up. 'Righto, John, that's your job – trace every second-hand car bought yesterday. With the recession, there won't be that many. Russ and I are going out to Tamarama, see what enticed young Jason to spend the night with Miss Weigall, other than the obvious.'

Tamarama was more an enclave than a suburb, a narrow strip of territory running back from a narrow beach. Jill Weigall lived in a modest block of four flats up the hill from the beach; the Honda Civic was no longer parked in front of the flats. Nor was Jill at home. Malone and Clements went back to their car and headed for the Rockne office at Coogee. Jill Weigall was there, but no Jason.

The phone rang as the two detectives entered the front door. Jill answered it, spoke to a client for some minutes, one eye cocked warily at Malone and Clements. As soon as she put the phone down, it rang again and she answered it once more. When she had finished the call Malone said, 'Do you have an answer-phone, Jill? Switch the calls to it for the next half-hour. Lock the front door, Russ. Righto, Jill, can we go into Mr Rockne's office? I think we'll be more comfortable there.'

She stood up, looking decidedly uncomfortable. 'What's the problem, Inspector? I'm not in trouble or anything, am I?'

'What makes you think that? No, I don't think so, Jill. Sit down.' He had taken the chair behind Rockne's desk. The desk top was bare, as if someone had decided that

242

every trace of Will Rockne had to be erased. Malone gestured at the desk. 'Are you closing out the practice?'

Jill nodded. 'Mrs Rockne called me this morning, she gave me two weeks' notice.'

The two men exchanged glances, then Malone said, 'Because of Jason?'

'I don't understand – ' But she did: it was plain on her face.

'Jill, did Jay spend last night with you?'

She hesitated, looking from one man to the other, then she nodded again; the lock of hair fell down over her forehead. 'Yes.'

'Are you two going out together? Has he become your boyfriend?'

'Inspector, is that any of your business?' She showed a spark of anger, but still looked apprehensive.

'No, I guess not. Except it seems to have happened pretty quickly. I really don't care if you are having a romance with him – '

'It's not a *romance* – '

'Is that why Mrs Rockne gave you notice this morning?'

'Probably. She was pretty abrupt. She wasn't on the phone a minute, she didn't mention Jason . . . I – I made a mistake last night. I – *encouraged* him, if you like. I felt sorry for him. But he's *serious* – about me, I mean.'

'And you're not serious about him?'

'God, no. He's only seventeen. I made a mistake – I forgot what I was like at seventeen. He's romantic – '

'Like his father?'

Her look told him that remark was cruel. 'No, Will was anything *but* romantic. What you're really asking me is, did I go to bed with Jason? Yes, I did. And I'm sorry now, dreadfully sorry. Especially for letting it happen the second time.'

'The second time?'

'He took me to a movie, then he took me home and – well, we went to bed. He left my flat about ten thirty, quarter to eleven, somewhere around then, and went home. He was back at a quarter to twelve – I was asleep and he woke me up. He said he'd been driving around, wondering where to go . . . He stayed the night, then I sent him home this morning. He didn't want to go, but I made him. I presume that's where he is now.'

'Why did he come back the second time?' He hoped she would not give him a frank, obvious answer; she seemed free with her favours, but embarrassed to admit it. She might have been less embarrassed with someone younger than himself and Clements; perhaps he should have sent John Kagal.

She hesitated again, then she said, 'He had a terrible row with his mother – '

'Over you?'

She pushed back the lock of hair. 'That was only part of it, I think. No – ' She stopped. 'No, really, I don't think I should tell you what he told me – '

'That's your privilege, Jill. But Sergeant Clements and I are still trying to find out who killed Will Rockne. Sunday night there was another murder that we think was connected to this one – ' He waved a hand around him, as if Rockne had been murdered here in his office. 'There could be another. Mr Jones is still roaming around and we think he could threaten the Rockne family. He already has, in fact. What did Jason tell you?'

She took her time; then at last she shrugged. 'All right, I suppose you're going to hear it all sooner or later. Mr Rockne left a new will – ' She told them the contents of it, as much as she knew. 'Jay said his mother couldn't believe she had been left out of it, that she got nothing. Then when she read the bit about me getting the ten thousand dollars – '

244

'When I counted out that cash last Sunday week,' said Clements, 'did you have any idea it was for you?'

'Not a hint. Why would I expect it? At that time I had no idea that Will was going to die, that he knew he was . . .' Her voice trailed off. She was enmeshed in a drama she didn't quite believe, was slipping deeper and deeper into the net.

'You didn't suspect something when he had you witness the new will?'

'Why would I? Sergeant, we have people coming in here every week changing their wills, every time some man has a row with his wife or they both have a row with their kids. Then they come back the next week and change it back to the original.'

'Was there any reason why Mrs Rockne was left out of the will?'

'There was nothing spelt out. Jay didn't *show* me the will, he just read out parts. There was something about her understanding the reason for leaving her out of it – '

She stopped abruptly and after a moment Malone said, 'Go on, Jill.'

Once more she hesitated; she shook her head, as if in despair, and the hair fell down over her brow again. She's damned attractive, Malone thought, I wonder what she would be like in bed? And felt the thwack of Lisa's hand across the back of his mind.

'God, you'd think I'd be used to it, wouldn't you? People's secrets, I mean, their private feelings. Every day of the week I type them out . . . Jay said his mother and Mrs Bodalle are – *lovers*. They're lesbians, sort of. Bisexual. Double-gaited. But he saw them . . . Will must've known about it and that's the reason he cut Jay's mother out of the will.'

'How did Jay react to what he saw? When was it – when he left you and went home last night?'

245

'Yes. It shattered him. Men – boys – you don't respond to that sort of thing very well, do you?'

Malone looked at Clements, who gave no indication of how he responded; then he looked back at Jill. 'I think it depends on who you find out is a lesbian. A lot of women don't respond too well when they find out their husbands or boyfriends are homosexual. How is Jay? Angry, disgusted, shocked or what?'

'All of those, I think.'

'How do you feel?'

'About Mrs Rockne? I don't feel anything – it's her business. Well, yes, I guess I do feel something. She might've thought about what effect it would have on Jay and Shelley.'

'Are you surprised Mrs Bodalle is that way inclined?'

'No. *You* sound surprised, Inspector.' She was regaining some of her composure.

'I'm not, now I come to think about her. Russ and I are not as innocent as you think, Jill. We're not poofter-bashers and we don't rough up dykes. But every now and again we have to change our views on someone and sometimes it takes a little time. Did you suspect Mrs Bodalle was a lesbian?'

'No. Well, like you, thinking back – maybe yes. I have two friends who are lesbians. I tried to make Jay see that it wasn't the end of the world, his mother being one . . .' She smiled, totally composed now. 'She probably wouldn't thank me for taking her side.'

Clements said, 'Are you going to accept the ten thousand dollars?'

'Mrs Rockne insisted I had to. I think she sees it as another excuse for hating me even more.'

Malone said carefully, 'Do you think she would physically harm you?'

She looked at him just as carefully. 'Do you mean she

might try to kill me? I've thought about it, since this morning. You wouldn't have arrested her, would you, if you hadn't thought her capable of killing Will?'

Then the phone on a side table beside Malone rang. He looked at Jill, who said, 'That's the private line. That's the first time it's rung since – ' She frowned while she tried to remember. 'Since Mr Jones rang last week asking about his files.'

'Answer it. Play it as if you're alone here.'

Jill picked up the phone, cleared the sudden nervousness from her throat and said, 'Hello? Mr Rockne's office.' She looked at Malone and nodded. 'No, Mr Jones, I told you, there are no files here on you ... No, the police found nothing of yours, as far as I know ... No, Mr Jones, I won't – ' She put down the phone. 'He hung up.'

'You won't what?'

'He told me not to tell the police he'd called or I'd regret it.'

3

'The police know about you,' said Bezrow earlier that Tuesday morning. 'They've been to see me, asked me if I knew you. Of course I said no.'

'What do they know me as?'

'All your names. Jones, Collins, Dostoyevsky. Do you have passports in all those names?'

'Yes.'

'You'd better get a new one in a new name. They're on to you, Igor. They didn't tell me what they know about you, but they've already mentioned the Shahriver Bank, so you can have a bet at very short odds that they know about the money you deposited there.'

The Georgian-by-descent and the Russian were at

Randwick racecourse, standing by the rails watching the early morning trackwork. The dawn sun struggled through the spring fog, turning it to pale amber; horses came and went through the mist like mythical beasts in some hugely staged opera. Bezrow came down here one morning a week, the spy in the vicuna trenchcoat coming out into the cold. The true spy beside him, out of a job now, looked around him as if wondering what quirk of events had landed him here in this fog.

'Why did we have to meet here at this hour?' said Dostoyevsky, who still thought in his own name. 'I hate getting up early. It's never been a Russian habit, not in diplomatic circles.'

'Who would think of looking for a Russian fugitive at a racecourse at this hour? Igor, we are safe here.' Two horses galloped past, wide out on the track, the jockeys in the mist looking like nothing more than humps on the horses' backs. The hoofbeats died away like fading heartbeats and Dostoyevsky, a superstitious man, shivered slightly. 'I can understand your concern about that lost money. Five million! T'ch, t'ch.' Bezrow shook his head: even a bookmaker wasn't used to losing so much.

'We haven't lost it! We'll get it back!' Dostoyevsky was suddenly angry and irritable; it was the early rising. 'We don't give up so easily!'

'How? Igor, this country has certain laws. If the money is in an account in Rockne's name, how do you prove it isn't his? By making a statement to the court that it is money stolen by your colleagues in Moscow and sent out here to finance the next revolution? This country is in a mess and getting deeper, but occasionally its laws work. The courts here have become rather accustomed to making judgements about greed, because they'll say that's the main reason, not revolution, why you stole the money.'

'A moralist bookmaker. Isn't that an oxymoron?'

248

'Don't be smart with me, Igor. Your and my arrangement is purely a business deal. I don't have to flatter you or believe in what you're doing.'

'Ten per cent for arranging where I could bank the money.' Dostoyevsky did not sound bitter. Instead he smiled; in the KGB one learned cynicism, it was a necessary quality. 'Come the new revolution, capitalist commission like that will be done away with.'

'Half of the commission went to Rockne. I thought you knew that?'

Despite what he felt towards Rockne, the Russian had to shake his head in admiration. 'He takes five per cent commission, then steals ninety per cent! And he was just a *suburban* solicitor? Those poor fools back home, Yeltsin and the others, who want to join the capitalist system – they don't know what they'll be up against. Wall Street and the City of London must be rubbing their hands. Did you know Rockne was such a thief?'

'Would I have used him for my own dealings if I'd known? He knew nothing about the Shahriver Bank or any bank that took money and hid it the way you wanted yours hidden. But he was shrewd enough to guess that I might know of one. He knew I had my SP business and he guessed not all the money from it went into the reputable banks – which, in these days, is another oxymoron.' Cynicism was a quality necessary, also, to bookmaking. 'What about his father?'

Dostoyevsky shook his head. 'Small-time, an idealist. Too honest for his own good, really. That was why I went to him. I knew he'd keep his mouth shut, even in the Party. We'd had a dossier on him for years.'

Bezrow smiled. 'Did you have one on me?'

'A Georgian bookmaker? You were beyond redemption. I was surprised and a little worried when Rockne told me whom I would have to deal through. Then I checked on you and found you had a reputation for honesty, too. Except as far as the taxman went.'

'Honesty has nothing to do with taxes.'

The Russian nodded in agreement and the two of them stood there in the rising mist while they shared a contempt for taxes that went beyond ideology. More horses went past, less ghostly now.

'There goes — ' Bezrow named one of the horses. 'I've been warned he'll win by the length of the straight on Saturday. His connections are using a new, undetectable dope.'

'I know about it. Our scientists developed it, but now the Cold War is over, what use is there for it? We were going to offer it to Saddam Hussein, but morality prevailed. So now we're offering it to horse trainers and athletics coaches. Science shouldn't be wasted.'

'Of course not. Just don't back that particular horse with me. In the meantime what are you going to do about the five million dollars?'

'I shall have to apply more pressure on Mrs Rockne. My colleagues in Moscow are becoming desperate. After last month's coup failed . . . That comes of relying on stupid old men. All that time in power and they hadn't learned how to hold on to it.'

'You needed a Georgian. Another Stalin.' Bezrow leaned on the rail. He did not marvel at the situation in which he found himself as the business partner of a man whose ideology, even whose nationality, he despised. He was an opportunist and opportunism is an ideology in itself. 'And if Mrs Rockne doesn't give you back the money?'

Dostoyevsky waited till another horse had galloped past, as if afraid that the jockey might hear him: 'Then I shall have to kill her. My masters demand that.'

The sun broke through, but Bezrow felt suddenly chilled.

250

Chapter Ten

1

'Tell me what you know about Angela Bodalle's husband,' said Malone.

He and Clements were leaning on the promenade wall above the beach, each of them eating an ice cream. It was a fine day and there was a sprinkling of people on the beach, though there were few in the still-too-cold water. Half a dozen board-riders, slightly sinister-looking in their wet-suits, sat waiting for waves to roll up out of the flat sea. A wino sat on a bench and gazed with watery eyes, that might have been tears of remembrance, at a young shorts-clad mother and her two small children as they went by. Gulls strutted like grey and white colour gangs protecting their turf and out across the bay a wandering albatross, looking lost, hurried south for its late date with a mate somewhere in the Antarctic. The birds, Malone decided, looked like the only employed in the landscape.

'He would have been older than her,' said Clements. 'I never saw 'em together, but from the way she looks now I'd say he must of been twenty years older than her. I saw him a coupla times in action, but the only time I came up against him in court was when I was with Pillage. We brought in a gang that'd been milking the wharves for quids – we charged 'em with, I dunno, I think it was taking stuff worth a hundred thousand dollars, but they'd got away with much more than that. He got them off, they walked away scot-free and laughing like drains.'

'He and his missus seem experts at getting crims off the hook.'

'He wasn't crooked, nothing like that. He was just like she is, he never missed a detail in a case. He wasn't as — flamboyant, is that the word? — as she is, but you always knew when he was in court, the law students would turn up to watch him. He just had one problem — he liked the grog. Everyone knew about it. He'd never miss a day in court, but I'm told his juniors would sometimes sit two or three feet upwind from him, just so's they wouldn't get drunk on the fumes from him.'

'How'd he die?'

'An accident, somewhere up in the Blue Mountains. I never paid much attention to it, it happened just after I joined Homicide. Why the interest in him?' Clements finished his ice cream, chewing on the last of the cone with all the enjoyment of a child.

'Not him, especially. Her. Who would know all about her, other than Olive Rockne?'

'Grace Ditcham,' said Clements without hesitation. 'She knows more about the court regulars than the Sheriff's office.'

'How's the petty cash? Let's take her to lunch — we'll put her down as a gig on the vouchers. Before we do that, though, we've got to arrange protection for our girl Jill. Pretty soon we're going to have more minders out than President Bush. Greg Random's going to start complaining about the overtime.'

'Our little bit to fight the recession.'

Protection was arranged for Jill Weigall through the Randwick station, where the sergeant in charge complained, not about the overtime, but the stretching of manpower. 'Scobie, we're gunna have to share this around. I can't spare my guys to baby-sit.'

'Dick, she's very pretty.'

'That's different, then. I'll do it m'self. Do I get bed and board?'

Grace Ditcham was available for lunch and Malone and Clements took her to Harpoon Harry's, a seafood restaurant attached to an hotel and just down the road from Homicide. It was not a meeting place for matrons, there were no gloves and flower-bedecked hats here; most of the clients were men and the few women with them looked the sort who could hold their own in a man's world. The food was good, if slightly overpriced according to Malone's antique scale of prices, and the helpings were ample enough to satisfy Clements. Grace Ditcham tucked into her John Dory with all the appetite of a woman who did not have to watch her weight.

'I brought everything I could find on the Bodalles.' She tapped her fork on the manila folder beside her plate. 'She never figured in any stories about her husband, not till Lester was killed. Seems she was the "little woman" . . . Aren't we all?'

'Not you, Grace,' said Clements.

'Only because I go a round or two for a pound or two every Friday night with my husband. Not what your dirty minds think. We go to gym and whoever lasts longest on the equipment, the weights and the rest of it, pays the week's bills. It's called equal opportunity, though Fred calls it extortion, something his mum didn't tell him about when he was growing up . . . Come to think of it, somehow I can't see Angela ever having been the "little woman".'

'Was Lester the domineering type when it came to women?'

'I'd say so, though I don't know what he was like with her. But he was a great one for patting your bum and being condescending about your intellect. Very lovable.' She bit into a piece of John Dory as if biting into a piece of Lester Bodalle.

'What about the accident that killed him?'

She put down her knife and fork, opened the folder. 'I can't give you these tear-sheets, I got them out of the paper's morgue. The stories say he was killed when his car ran off the road on a back road in the Blue Mountains. It was pretty horrific – the car caught fire and he was incinerated.'

'Was he drunk?' said Malone.

'The stories don't say. The fire charred him beyond recognition. But Angela gave evidence and said yes, he was under the influence. They'd had an argument and he rushed out of the house and jumped into his car and took off. They had a holiday home up outside Blackheath.'

'What was the argument about? Did she say in court?'

'About his drinking, funnily enough.'

'What happened then? I mean, after his death?'

'Well, first, she was left well provided for. That's what most women think of first if some prominent man kicks the bucket – what did he leave the widow? It's the battle of the sexes, who gets the spoils.'

Malone looked at Clements. 'Why is it that men are supposed to be the cynical sex?'

'Search me. I put women on a pedestal and they keep stepping down off of it into my face, usually in high heels.'

'Okay, you two, stow your romantic ideas about us – I'm not impressed . . . Angela came out of her shell almost immediately, I gather. I'd only see her off and on, but here are some pix of her in the Sunday social pages. The Freeloaders Parade, we call it.'

Malone looked at the faded clippings. Angela Bodalle was rarely smiling in any of the photos, but her companions flashed the usual display of teeth as if they were posing for some dental competition. The social pages of the Sunday papers were an orthodontist's study chart. 'No men?'

Grace Ditcham took back the clippings. 'You know, I don't think I'd noticed that before. No, not a guy in sight.' She looked at the two men shrewdly. 'Are you telling me she's gay?'

'We're not telling you,' said Malone, 'we're asking you.'

'So that's why you asked me to lunch. And I thought you were after my body.'

'Not if Fred pumps iron.'

'Frankly, I don't know if Angela is a lesbo. If she is, she's never shown it towards me or any of the girls I know in newspapers.' She smiled; she had lively blue eyes, but the squint-lines round them made her sometimes look worried. Or maybe, Malone thought, as a crime reporter she had had to squeeze shut her eyes against too many ghastly sights. 'How come you guys found out she was gay?'

'Accidentally. It's not a crime, so we're not holding it against her —'

'That's big of you.'

' — we were just wondering if she was like it when she was married to Lester.' He picked up the folder again, skimmed through the story on the accident that had killed Lester Bodalle. 'Blackheath police covered the accident. Righto, we'll get in touch with them.'

Grace Ditcham sipped her wine. 'Scobie, this isn't idle stuff. What are you on to? Do you suspect Angela is trying to cover up something on the Rockne murder? Has she got something going with the widow?'

'Maybe.' Malone tried to sound non-committal.

'Has the widow been left well provided for?'

'Not really.' Malone glanced at Clements. They waited while the waiter, middle-aged and brusque, no frills on him, cleared away their plates. He took Clements's order for dessert, the only one, and went away without a word. The waiters here never flattered to deceive one into leaving

255

a large tip. 'How are you going on the tip we gave you on the money in the Shahriver Bank?'

Grace Ditcham knew how to read between the lines; she was not only a reporter, she had a sub-editor's mind. 'So the widow has an interest in that, has she? The bank gave me the bum's rush. In the nicest possible way, of course. Their managing director is so oily, OPEC should keep an eye on him. I've got nothing specific I can turn into a story, not at the moment, but they know I'm getting ready to write one. I let them know — in the nicest possible way, of course — that they were under investigation about the transfer of illegal money out of the country. I think they'll play it safe — for a while, anyway. They'll keep all their money here, no matter what instructions they get from their clients, and try to look respectable. I dropped a hint that our London office was looking into their other branches. Mr Palady, the managing director, looked as if he'd like to cut my throat.'

'Not him,' said Malone. 'He'd get others to do that. When we clear up this Rockne case, we'll give you the lowdown on what's there in the Shahriver Bank. You might even have enough to make a book out of it.'

'I'll follow up the bank story. But Angela's the one who's got me intrigued. I think I might delve a little more into the private life of a female silk.'

'That's what we were hoping you'd say. Two male chauvinists like us would be too obvious.'

2

Once back at Homicide Malone called Blackheath police. A voice that sounded young enough to be a Boy Scout's said, 'I'm sorry, Inspector, there's no one stationed here now who's been here longer than five, maybe six years. How long ago was the accident?'

'Twelve years ago. June, nineteen seventy-nine.'

'I could try, but I don't think there'd be anything still here in the records.'

Malone looked at the notes he had taken from the clippings. 'A Sergeant Reiffel gave evidence at the inquest. Where's he now?'

'Oh, the sarge retired three years ago, just after I came here. He lives up at Colony Bay, on the Central Coast. Hold on a minute, I think we've got a number for him. Here we are, no problem. It's . . .'

Malone put down the phone, looked across his desk at Clements. 'Am I on a wild-goose chase?'

'Every year in police work there's a wild-goose season.'

'A philosopher as well as a punter? Is that Romy's influence?'

'She tells me all German philosophers are pessimists. That doesn't fit a punter's philosophy. Let's be optimistic and assume the goose isn't just flying overhead and shitting on us.'

Malone shook his head. 'Romy's turning you into someone, pretty soon, I won't recognize . . .' He dialled an 043 number on the Central Coast and got an answer at once, as if the man at the other end of the line had been waiting anxiously for a call. 'Mr Reiffel? *Sergeant* Reiffel?'

The voice was an almost ridiculous contrast to that which had been on the line from Blackheath; it was as rough and deep as a coalmine cave-in. 'Yeah, who's this . . . Malone, *Scobie* Malone? Sure, I've heard of you . . . No, I'm not busy.' There was something that sounded like a choked laugh. 'Sure, tomorrow morning'll be fine. You know how to get here?'

Malone hung up, said to Clements, 'I'll go in my own

car. You run the office tomorrow. I'll try and be back by lunchtime.'

'Wasn't there a song once called "Wild Geese"? Didn't Frankie Laine used to sing it?'

'No, it was Tiny Tim. It was called "Wild Canaries".'

It was just chaff tossed between them; they were trying to tell each other, and themselves, that things were not as discouraging as they seemed. It was ever thus: the first grunt ever uttered by man had to be positive. The first curse only came later, when the wild goose shat on him. One had to be in positive mode, Malone thought, as the radio girl could have told him.

He went home, enjoyed dinner and Lisa and the children. When Claire, the last of the children to go to bed, came to kiss him goodnight, he said, 'Have you heard from Jason?'

'He went back to school today. I saw him at Brick's this afternoon.'

'How was he?'

'I dunno – *quiet*. He's never loud, like some of the other boys. But today . . .'

'Did he say anything about how things were at home?'

She drew away from him. 'Dad, are you training me to be an informer or something?'

'Sorry, love. I'd never do that to you.'

'Feel sorry for Jay, Dad. He told me it was awful at school today. Nobody said anything to him, not directly, but he said it was just whispers all around him all day.'

Wait for the whispers when word gets out that his mother is a lesbian.

'That was all he said?'

'Yes. Why, was there something else?'

'No, nothing. Goodnight, love.'

Later he and Lisa watched *In the Heat of the Night* and he wondered what it would be like to be the chief of police

258

in a small town, where the pressures might be even greater because they were more concentrated. Tomorrow he would ask ex-Sergeant Reiffel that question.

In bed, their limbs locked in their usual pretzel of love, Lisa said, 'So what's on your mind now?'

'That obvious again?'

'You told Claire the other night – the night of the murder, God!' She was silent a moment, then she went on. 'You told her you're an open book. You are. Sometimes.'

He told her what he knew of the Olive Rockne–Angela Bodalle relationship. She said nothing, taking her legs out of his and lying on her back looking at the ceiling. The bedside lamps were still on and he could see the frown on her night-creamed face. 'You don't seem surprised.'

'Oh, I'm surprised all right. I don't know why, but I am. I'm not very familiar with lesbians. When I was at boarding school there were one or two girls we suspected. But gay women weren't coming out of the closet, not back then. How do you feel about them, Olive and Angela Bodalle?'

'I've thought about them and I don't really care a damn about what they are to each other. If they're genuinely in love, that's their business. But besides being lesbians, I think they are also murderers.'

She rolled over, raised herself on one elbow. 'They killed Will *together*?'

'I don't know whether they did it together or whether they both paid Kelpie Dunne to kill him. But I think Angela might've killed Kelpie.'

She lay back on her pillow. 'God, what other couples have pillow-talk like this?'

'Righto,' he said huffily and put out his bedside lamp. 'Forget it.'

'Come on, don't get shirty with me. Save that for the office. Why would Angela have killed this man – Kelpie?'

'Kelpie Dunne. *And* his missus. To keep his mouth shut. And his wife's in case he'd talked to her. Kelpie died on Sunday night and yesterday morning Olive walked free. All they have to do now is sit tight and make no mistakes.'

'What happens if they set up house together? Won't that be a mistake?'

'Depends. It'll start gossip, but gossip never convicted anyone in a court of law.'

'They won't *have* to set up house. They can go on living just the way they do. Men keep their mistresses secret — why can't a woman? So what are you going to do?'

'Start finding out what Angela was like before she became Mrs Bodalle, QC.' He kissed her cheek, then grimaced. 'What's that? Dairy Farmers or King Island?'

'Ella Baché,' she said and smeared him with love.

Next morning he left at seven thirty in the family Commodore. It took him forty-five minutes to get over the Harbour Bridge and up Pacific Highway: surely, he thought, one of the slowest exit routes from a major city anywhere in the world. But once on the freeway at Wahroonga he took the Commodore up just above a hundred k's an hour and sat on that till the Gosford turn-off. He drove with his window down and the drive and the wind cleared his mind, so that by the time he got to Colony Bay he felt almost optimistic that something positive would come out of this two-hour trip to see ex-Sergeant Reiffel.

Colony Bay was a small community on Brisbane Water, one of the very good boating stretches behind the headlands of the Central Coast. The entire area had burgeoned since World War Two, had become a mixture of retirement villages, modest weatherboard and fibro cottages that had survived from prewar and expensive would-be mansions that were too big for the plots on which they had been built. Tad Reiffel's house was a modest weatherboard on a waterfront lot that, Malone guessed, was worth three times the value of the house.

'Tad for Thaddeus. Whoever heard of a copper named Thaddeus? My old man was Austrian. I suppose he could of called me Amadeus or Wolfgang. Let's sit outside, the wife'll bring us coffee.' He was bald-headed and red-faced and had a white beard, grown since his retirement; he was also tall and had a beer-belly, another portrait of the Great Australian Profile. He looked more like Malone's image of an Austrian innkeeper than a retired Aussie cop. His voice was just as deep and rough as it had sounded over the phone, the sort of voice that would never have needed a bullhorn. 'Oh thanks, hon. This is Inspector Malone, I told you about him.'

Mrs Reiffel was almost as tall as her husband, built on similar lines; they would have made a formidable pair heading the rush at bargain sales. She was pleasant-looking and her smile was as welcoming as her husband's had been. Malone wondered how happy they were in their retirement, a state of living for which so many were unprepared. Including himself, even though it was twenty years down the track.

Mrs Reiffel left them sitting on the small porch looking out on the broad stretch of water. Reiffel wasted no time: 'The Bodalle accident, right? After you spoke to me yesterday, I spent last night putting my memories in order. I used to drive the blokes who worked under me up the wall, being so methodical. Are you methodical?'

'Yes and no. I'm mostly Irish. Does that answer your question?'

Reiffel laughed, a landslide of mirth. 'It does, my oath it does. Yeah, well, the Bodalle accident. I was the first on the scene, me and one of the junior constables. A bloody

261

mess, in every meaning of the term. A charred wreck, I think they called it in the newspapers. Including Mr Bodalle's body.'

'Did anyone see the accident occur?'

'Not directly, no. I'll tell you about that in a minute.' He had got his memories in order; he wasn't going to have them shuffled around. 'It happened on a back road. The Bodalles owned a holiday place up there, nothing big, but nice and comfortable. They didn't have much to do with the locals, all their entertaining was for friends up from Sydney. A coupla times my blokes pulled him over for driving with too much in his system, but we never charged him, just gave him a warning.'

'How'd he take that? The warning?'

'Oh, he took it okay. He was smart enough to know that if he tried to toss his weight around, he'd of found my blokes sitting on his tail every time he got into his car. A pity they weren't sitting on his tail the night he got killed.'

'What came out at the inquest? You were there?'

'I was the principal witness. Me and Mrs Bodalle. The autopsy found alcohol in his system, despite how badly burnt he was. Evidently it's only high-temperature fires, like a chemical fire, that boils the blood, well, sorta dry. Mrs Bodalle admitted he was probably too drunk to drive, but she couldn't stop him. It looked like an open-and-shut case to the coroner and that was the way he found it. But – ' He looked out at the shining water, where two pelicans planed down like old-time flying-boats. A tourist launch went slowly by and he waved to the passengers, who waved back as if they, like him, were short of company. It was all so peaceful, a long way from the harrowing scene of his memories.

'But?' said Malone.

Reiffel turned away from his contemplation, a scene that, Malone guessed, he looked at every day with the same lost gaze. There was a certain sadness about the big man, for all his cheerful demeanour. 'But? Yes, but . . . The doctor who did the autopsy found that Bodalle's skull had been fractured, right there – ' He put a huge hand on the front of his bald pate. 'He told me he made no emphasis about it, because he couldn't be sure whether it had been done before the crash or when the car crashed and Bodalle was catapulted out of his seat. He wasn't wearing his seat-belt.'

'How did the accident occur? You said it was on the back road.'

'Yeah, it was a gravel road, it didn't get much traffic, except from the few people who lived on the other side of the valley – they'd drive up it to do their shopping in Blackheath. It ran – I suppose it still does – it ran straight down across the face of the escarpment, maybe a third of a mile, maybe a bit more. There was a sharp bend at the bottom – that was where Bodalle's car went off, straight into a tree.'

'You think someone may have clobbered him, then started up the car and let it go?'

'More than that. You want more coffee?' Malone shook his head, waited patiently while Reiffel got up and went into the house taking his empty cup with him. This is what happens to cops when they retire, Malone told himself: they stretch out their memories, rethink their mistakes. He had seen it happen before; it would happen to him some day. He would be sitting in the sun like this, making some young cop wait while he regretted what he might have done in the past: the past which was now the present.

Reiffel came back with a fresh cup of coffee, sat down and said, as if he hadn't moved from his chair, 'A year after the accident we picked up a young bloke from the other side of the valley, a hippy, one of those drop-outs for the alternative lifestyle. He was growing marijuana, acres of it up there in the timber on that side. He told me that a year before, the night of the accident, he saw a car going full pelt down that road, it hit the bend and burst into flames. The only thing was – ' Reiffel paused, took a sip of his coffee. 'The only thing was, he said the car was on fire all the way down the road, right from the top.'

'So why didn't he come forward?'

'The marijuana. He was growing it then, he didn't want us coming across the valley to question him.'

'Did you report what he told you?'

'Not officially. I talked it over with a coupla senior officers and they said they'd look into it. I never heard any more on it, so I let it lay and forgot about it. Except that every now and again I remember it. Like yesterday, when you called up. I didn't sleep last night,' he said and sounded guilty.

'Why do you think nothing was done about investigating it further?'

'I dunno. Scobie, you know how things are. About that time, the Force was having the shit kicked out of it. Senior officers were being investigated, there were corruption charges . . . Things got buried or pushed aside, you know that. Maybe it was just put in the Too Hard basket and nobody's ever bothered to take it out.'

'How did Mrs Bodalle take everything? I mean, when you gave her the bad news about her husband's death? And then at the inquest?'

'You mean did she throw a fit, get hysterical? I'm pushing my memory a bit on this, but no, I can't remember she did anything like that. She was upset, as far's I can remember, but she was always calm. The neighbours, some locals lived on either side of their holiday home, they said she was always like that. Even those mornings after they'd heard her husband belting hell out of her the night before. Bodalle was a very violent man when he was drunk.'

264

It was Malone's turn to stare at the water. Several hundred yards away there was a flat island crowded with villas, miniature mansions that advertised their owners' success. A Hills hoist whirled slowly on one of the front lawns, the laundry on it a mockery of the national flag fluttering from the tall flagpole on the neighbouring lawn. Way beyond the island, high up on the escarpment above Woy Woy, there was a sudden flash. Sun on a windscreen, a car on fire? He waited, but nothing in flames ran down the road that he had come down an hour before.

He told Tad Reiffel everything that had happened so far on the Rockne case. 'It's just between you and me, Tad, okay? Not even a word to your wife, I'm too far yet from winding up the case.'

'Ellie never asks questions, not about police work. All our married life I worked in country stations – Murwillumbah, Dungog, the last twelve years in Blackheath. In a country town, you talk police business to your wife and in no time she's looking at everyone sideways, no matter how good a woman she is. Better she doesn't know. Ellie's not inside now with her ear pinned to the wall. She may ask me a thing or two after you've gone, but she won't be upset if I tell her I can't tell her anything.'

Malone nodded. 'Thanks for that, Tad. I wondered what it would be like working in a country town – I've been to a couple on one or two cases. I was thinking about it last night when I was watching *In the Heat of the Night*. You ever watch it?'

'Never miss it. Life was like that, only we didn't have a major crime every week. And I never managed to be as wise as Chief Gillespie.'

'We're never as wise as the TV cops, none of us. Why did you retire here?'

'I was born here, in this house – my old man was the local plumber, in the days before plumbers became

265

millionaires. I thought we'd come back here and I'd do just what my old man used to do when he retired, sit out there in the boat and fish, read all the books I'd put off, listen to music ... Worst decision we ever made. We should of stayed in Blackheath among all the friends and enemies we'd made in those twelve years. Retirement shouldn't be a matter of running away.'

'I'm going after Angela Bodalle, Tad. If I have to call on you, will you give evidence, tell what you've just told me?'

'A pleasure.' His laugh rumbled through his big body, his red face shone. 'I always hated unfinished business.'

'Me, too.'

3

Picking up a scent is a primitive instinct; the reaction to it is also primitive. Malone knew that Clements, and even Kagal, sensed his excitement, even though he was outwardly his usual laconic self. The scent of Angela Bodalle's evil, criminality, call it what you like, had come on accidental currents, but chance, he had read somewhere, was the nickname of Providence.

'We'll work backwards,' he said. 'I may be way off the mark, but let's assume Angela did in Kelpie and his wife. So how did she get out to Penrith? She wouldn't have used her Ferrari, too conspicuous. So she borrowed a car or rented one. John, get on to all the car rental businesses in Sydney, starting on the North Shore, get someone to help you if you need him. Find out if she rented a car last Sunday.'

'Do I let the car people know I'm looking for a particular client, or do I ask to see all their rentals for the weekend?'

'That might take too long. No, ask if they rented to a Mrs Bodalle — she'd have to show her driving licence and I doubt if she'd have a fake one. If word gets back to her that we're looking into her, what've we got to lose? I don't think she's a panicker, but a little worry might do her some harm. If we're lucky.'

'Do we drop a hint to Olive Rockne that we're investigating her girlfriend?' said Clements.

'It might be an idea. I'll call in there on my way home tonight, pretend I'm checking on their protection, her and the kids.'

'What happens to the kids if and when we bring in Olive and Angela?'

'Don't ask me. I don't think about it.'

'What about a phone tap? Olive and Angela might be dykes, but women love the phone.'

'How does Romy put up with you?'

'I never pass opinions like that in front of her.'

'Righto, apply for a phone tap permit. As soon as you can get it.'

Later, when he was preparing to leave the office, Grace Ditcham rang. 'Can I buy you a drink, Scobie? I have something you might like to hear. The Inter-Continental, in half an hour. Don't keep me waiting, in case they think I'm a hooker looking for trade.'

'I'll slip you fifty as soon as we meet. That should get us both thrown out.'

'Fifty? When did you last see a hooker's price list?'

When he arrived at the Inter-Continental the driveway was busy. He turned the family Commodore, which badly needed a wash and had the back seat full of the children's junk, over to a parking attendant, who looked as if he didn't want to soil his uniform by getting into such a heap; Malone wouldn't have been surprised if he had *pushed* the car down the ramp to the hotel garage. He went into the hotel and Grace Ditcham was waiting for him in the lounge under the towering atrium. They ordered drinks, a vodka and tonic for her and a beer for him, and he waited for her to tell him what she wanted him to hear.

'You'll owe me, Scobie, okay?' He nodded. 'Angela Bodalle, who used to be Angela Arcourt. Her father was a GP and her mother was a psychiatrist. She was an only child. Both parents are dead now.'

The Cortile lounge, as it was called, was filling up, mostly with American and Japanese tourists or business-men. The hotel had been constructed round the old nineteenth-century State Treasury building, the preserved part fitting in well with the new, and this meeting place had a certain charm to it. Malone had been here only once or twice before, always on business, though the atmos-phere was not one that suggested talk of homicide. Although certain Treasurers had died here, politically, and their ghosts still walked.

'Her parents died just after she married Lester Bodalle.'

Malone sipped his beer. 'Grace, you could've told me all this over the phone.'

She ignored that. 'Now comes the interesting bit. When Angela was eighteen, the year she left school and before she could enter university, her mother got another psy-chiatrist to admit Angela to a private clinic out at Castle Hill.'

'How long was she there?'

'Ten months.'

He put down his glass, leaned forward. 'Where'd you get all this?'

'You guys aren't the only ones with informers. I dug up a nurse who worked at the clinic. Angela was one of her patients. No violent behaviour, except for one occasion – she attacked this particular nurse. There's a book that's a sort of psychiatric bible – ' She had taken a notebook from her handbag and now she referred to it. '*Diagnostic and Statistical Manual of Mental Disorders*. There are three major disorders that, according to the nurse, could have applied to Angela. Histrionic, Narcissistic — that's a helluva word to say — and Antisocial. Though not so much of the last, not in her case. The nurse told me that Angela got on well with the other patients, joined in their discussions, though she tended to be a bit intellectually superior, despite being so young. But she was bossy, she liked to run things. The nurse chipped her about it one day and that was when Angela got violent.'

'She went berserk or what?'

'No, that was the most frightening thing, the nurse said. She was cold and calculating — but the nurse is convinced that Angela intended killing her. She had to be rescued by one of the staff and another patient.'

Malone sat silent a moment while around them the chatter seemed as light and inconsequential as the tinkling of glasses on the tables. 'Any other incidents?'

'None violent. When Angela quietened down she apologized to everyone, though the nurse felt she didn't mean a word of it. But from then on she was on her best behaviour, except once she flew into a rage with one of the other patients, though it didn't get physical. Finally, after ten months, she was discharged. There's no record of any further psychiatric treatment, voluntary or otherwise.'

'Do you have any notes on those disorders you mentioned?'

'I have notes on *everything*, Scobie. Including you.'

'I thought you might. Don't let Fred see them. Incidentally, there's a Japanese over there who's looking at your legs — he's the only Jap I've ever seen who's round-eyed.'

Grace looked across at the elderly Japanese businessman, gave him a smile and pulled her short skirt down over her pretty knees. 'Anything to improve foreign relations ... The disorders. The Histrionic Personality can be dramatic and likes to draw attention to itself.

269

That describes Angela in court, if you've ever seen her.'

'That describes half the barristers in town.'

'Agreed. But there's more — there's a craving for excitement, their behaviour in relationships tends to be intense, they become possessive — '

Malone shook his head. 'I've watched her with Olive Rockne — she's always in control of herself.'

'And of Olive, too, I'll bet. Come clean, Inspector — we're friends and I'm buying the drinks. Is Angela a suspect?'

He hesitated, glad of the chatter around them. None of the drinkers looked as if they had a care in the world; but of course they all did. One or two of them may have committed murder; or at least thought of it. 'Yes,' he said. 'I'll give you first break on the story, if and when . . . But till then, nothing, okay? Not a line, not a word.'

She put out her hand. 'A bargain . . . There, that proves to the old Japanese gent and that suspicious waitress over there that I'm not a hooker. Hookers never shake hands, not on a price. So how much do you have on Angela?'

'Nothing much so far, nothing we could take into court. She wouldn't need to hire defence counsel — she could demolish us on her own. But with what you've just told me — ' He finished his beer; he was a slow drinker. 'We can start building a profile. Do me a favour — don't go near her. I want the pressure on her to come from us.'

'Right. What about that other matter, the Shahriver Bank? Incidentally, I looked up Shahriver — I thought it might've been a place name. It's not. He was one of six spirits in Persian mythology, he had another name but I can't remember it, but he made the sun and heavens move and he ruled over metals. Not a bad name for a bank. Has a bit more kick to it than Westpac or ANZ.'

'I'll give you more on the bank when the other story

breaks. You'll have enough to write your own ticket at the *Herald*.'

'The last ones to write their own ticket at the *Herald* were the advisers when the first takeover took place. Millions of dollars to advise someone how to go broke. No wonder the Abos want their land back.' Her newspaper was in the hands of receivers, a 160-year-old institution driven on to the rocks by a young man, a scion of the family that had owned the newspaper all those years, who couldn't have steered his way through a supermarket aisle. Malone felt a certain comfort in belonging to a public service. Corrupt police, certainly, had tried to take it over, but it was in no danger of going bankrupt.

Malone took a ten-dollar note out of his wallet and pressed it into her hand. 'There, now they *know* you're a hooker.'

'At that price, I'll be working here all night, the johns will think it's sale time. I could love you, Scobie, if it weren't for Fred.'

They walked out together, the elderly Japanese staring after them with unabashed Oriental inscrutability.

4

It was midday Thursday when John Kagal came in with the results of his research: one the outcome of his assigned task, the other of something he had attempted on his own initiative. His smug look of satisfaction took the edge off Malone's satisfaction at what Kagal told him.

'Mrs Bodalle rented a car last Sunday afternoon from a small outfit called Luna Rentals, they're in Neutral Bay. She took the car back on Monday morning, first thing. It was a grey Toyota, there must be hundreds, maybe

271

thousands like it around Sydney. She rented it once before, last Saturday week, the same car. I asked the manager how she'd arrived at his place and he said she'd come both times by taxi. So she was keeping the red Ferrari under wraps.'

'Good work, John. We'll have to talk to Mrs Bodalle, but not just yet. You've got something else?'

Kagal had flipped open his notebook to another page. 'I did this off my own bat. Was it okay?'

'Let's hear it first.'

'I went out to Liverpool, to the Hume Highway, and checked with the guy who bought Mr Jones's Merc. Or Mr Collins, as he called himself out there. He said our friend, as far as he could remember, walked off the car lot, said he didn't need a lift. The cheque for the Merc was made out in the name of B. Collins. Twenty thousand dollars for a nineteen eighty-three 280CE. The guy said Jones, or Collins, didn't even quibble, just took the money and walked.'

'You're dying to tell me something.'

Kagal smiled. 'Of course I am. I drove up and down the highway. I figured that if Jones walked, then he wasn't going to walk far — the bus service along there is few and far between. All along that stretch there are used car lots. Sure enough — '

Sure enough, you hit the target, bull's-eye; but Malone had enough grace to keep his mouth shut.

'Sure enough — bull's eye! Five minutes' walk down the road and he bought a blue nineteen eighty-eight Nissan Pulsar. Wrote out a bank cheque for thirteen thousand dollars.'

'Which bank? The Shahriver?'

'No, the Commonwealth.'

'You get the registration number of his new car?'

'Naturally.' Kagal's look was as condescending as a

272

professor's towards a first-year student. 'But I checked with Motor Registry – he hasn't notified them yet that he's the new owner. I'd say he doesn't want the wheels for too long. He's planning to skip as soon as he's done whatever he has to do.'

'Why didn't he rent a car? That's a devil's advocate's question.' Malone sounded defensive and was irritated at himself.

'I guess he figured that would be easier to trace than if he bought one. I had no trouble finding Mrs Bodalle.' Again the self-satisfied look. But Malone had to accept it: Kagal *had* done a good, quick job, more than he'd been asked for.

'Righto, put out an ASM on the Pulsar. As for Mrs Bodalle, we're already working on her.'

'I was hoping – '

'What? That you could work on her? She's too old and experienced for you, John. You can work on the young ones, Russ and I don't have the stamina any more.'

Kagal went away, on an assured road to an assured destination: the Commissionership. And I'll help put him there, thought Malone: despite his dislike of the younger man, his reports on Kagal would always be fair. Sometimes he wished he could be a mean, self-centred sonofabitch.

Chapter Eleven

1

Angela Bodalle knew at four thirty that afternoon that they were closing in on her. The manager of Luna Rentals rang her in her chambers after she had just ushered out two Turkish businessmen who wanted her to defend them against charges of extortion. Sure, the man who was accusing them was a Greek and they hated him, but what fool would think he could get money out of a Greek? Angela had kept a straight face, assured the Turks and their solicitor, a Lebanese, that she would consider their case and had ushered them out. She never enjoyed cases in which there was any ethnic conflict. Prejudice unbalanced too many juries; even some judges. Her own only prejudice was of gender.

'Mrs Bodalle, don't be offended when I ask you this. But did you get into any bother with the police when you had one of our cars out last Sunday? I mean, like speeding or something? In an accident?'

'Mr Foote, there wasn't a scratch on the car I rented, not when I returned it.'

'Don't get me wrong, Mrs Bodalle. I'm not saying there was. It's just that the police have been here asking if you rented a car Sunday night. And the previous Saturday. I had to tell 'em yes – '

She hung up in his ear, suddenly cold: not with fear, but with something she could not immediately define. Anger, hatred? Yes, that was it, hatred: of that man Malone. He had thrown his net and somehow, unbelievably, he had caught her in it. One of her few weaknesses, though she rarely admitted it to herself and certainly not now, was that she would admit to no weakness. That was contradictory, but years ago they had told her in the clinic that people like herself would always suffer from contradictions that she would not recognize. Abruptly she forgot Malone, slamming the door of her mind on him, and was angry at herself. Now wasn't the time to start wondering where she had gone wrong: the past was past and now she had to protect her future. Hers and Olive's.

She rang Olive, felt a certain reassurance in her lover's voice, even though she knew that she herself was the protector. 'Darling, we have to talk. Are those damned police still parked outside your place?'

'Would you believe they are camped in the *garage*? My mother is even *feeding* them!'

'Darling, I think you'd better tell the police you don't want any more protection — tell them it's upsetting the children.'

'Can I do that? Tell them to get lost?'

'Of course. You're not under police *surveillance* — you're under police protection. You'll have to talk to some senior officer — '

'Malone? No, Angela, I can't talk to him.'

Angela smiled to herself; Olive, if she could have seen the smile, wouldn't have liked it. 'Darling, swallow your feelings about the man. He's a shit, but they all are. No, get in touch with him, now, and tell him you want the protection lifted. You'll take responsibility for your own safety and that of Jason and Shelley.'

There was a short silence at the other end of the line. 'I don't know . . . The police are getting on my nerves, but . . . what if Mr Jones comes back?'

'Darling, what's the bigger risk? The police in your back

yard or some mysterious Mr Jones who probably has already been scared off by the police?'

'What risk are you talking about? Are you expecting me to break down or something in front of the police? Sometimes, Angela, you treat me as if I were a child – '

'Olive – ' She was losing her grip, not attending to detail. 'Is there anyone there in the house with you? Your mother? The children?'

'No.' Olive's voice was sharp. 'Do you think I'd be talking like this if there were? God, sometimes you're as bad as Will. I'm not *dumb*, Angela. Unless . . .'

'Unless what?'

'Would they have my phone tapped?'

This time there was silence at her own end of the line. She *was* losing her grip: God, how could she have overlooked such a detail? 'I'll pick you up in half an hour. Tell the police you're going out with me, they can follow us if they like. That's all.' She hung up as abruptly as she had in the ear of the car rental manager. Too much had already been said on the line.

When she arrived outside the Rockne house she didn't get out of the Ferrari but just tooted the horn. Olive came out, crossed the pavement and got into the car. A moment later a white unmarked Commodore reversed down the driveway and swung in behind the Ferrari as Angela pulled it away from the kerb.

Olive reached across and put her hand on Angela's thigh. 'I'm sorry I was so snappy on the phone. God, I want to touch you – '

'Not now, darling. We're supposed to be lawyer and client. Your hair looks better that way. I don't like you with that severe look.'

'It doesn't make me look butch, does it?' She looked relieved when Angela smiled and shook her head. She was wearing her hair loose today; she looked more feminine,

276

almost as frilly as she once used to look. 'I did it this way for you. Where are we going?'

'Out to Maroubra.'

'Oh, for Christ's sake! Why?'

'What happened last Saturday week is still on your mind, right?'

'Of course it is! Isn't it on yours?'

'No.' Which was the truth. Years ago the doctors had remarked upon her ability to shut her mind at will. She had no regrets, no feelings at all at what had been done. 'If ever something traumatic happened to me, my mother would make me go back and face it.'

'She was a psychiatrist? She sounds more like a sadist.'

'It worked – for me, anyway. Darling, the police are going to come back at us. You are going to have to think, and talk, absolutely cold-bloodedly, about last Saturday week. Totally convince yourself and them that you don't know what happened that night. You understand me?'

She had not told Olive that it was she who had had to shoot Will, that Kelpie Dunne, having been driven by her to the car park in the rented Toyota, had refused to go ahead with the hit because there were too many cars in the park and he didn't know how many of them had people in them. There had been a short, fierce argument, then she had got out of the Toyota, gone across to the Volvo and shot Will as he had turned and looked at her in shock in the moment before he died. Olive, some distance away, her back turned, had seen nothing.

'Ye-es, I understand.' Olive said nothing for a while as Angela took the Ferrari up past Randwick cemetery where Will lay buried in the silent village of graves. She didn't look towards the cemetery, but kept her gaze on the road ahead. She still felt fragile, more so beside the composed Angela. She would never describe herself as such to anyone, but she felt like a figurine that had been smashed and then put back together again with glue that had dried too quickly. At last she said, 'Jason hasn't spoken to me since Monday night. He spent the night with that slut Jill, then came home this morning and went straight to school. I hope he showered first,' she said primly.

'Was he home when I picked you up?'

'No. Shelley is — Mum went up to pick her up at school. But Jason . . . What can I do with him?'

'He'll come round. The kids of today are more broad-minded than our generation was. Or is. Does your mother know? I mean, about us?'

Olive shook her head; her hair bounced. 'That's not going to be easy, either. Oh God, why isn't the world more understanding?'

If she were to tell Angela the truth, she had not yet really come to terms with her own lesbianism. She had had crushes on other girls when she was young, but nothing physical had come of them. Sex with Will and the other men, before him, with whom she had gone to bed had been enjoyable, but something had always been missing; she had been, she'd told herself, no more than the means to a man's end. She had said that once to Will, after they had made love, but he hadn't seen the joke. Angela had taught her fulfilment and over the past few months she had been happier, physically and emotionally, than she had ever been in her life before. And yet . . .

'If Will had been more understanding,' said Angela, 'we shouldn't have had to kill him.'

Olive looked sideways at her, said warily, 'That sounds bloody cold-blooded.'

Angela recognized her mistake; she took her hand off the wheel and pressed Olive's knee. 'That was the lawyer in me talking, darling. I love you. That's all you have to remember.'

When she pulled the Ferrari into the car park outside

278

the surf club at Maroubra, the police car followed it and parked facing it, twenty metres away. Angela looked at it and said, 'They probably don't remember, but that's exactly where your Volvo was parked. Have you got it back yet?'

'What?'

'The Volvo – have you got it back yet?'

'No, not yet. The police released it and my brother-in-law took it somewhere to have the blood cleaned out of it. They'll have to put new carpet in the front.' She shuddered, looking at the police car, seeing it turn into the silver Volvo, seeing the bright sunlight fade into the light and shadows of night. She closed her eyes, made a tiny whimpering sound, then opened her eyes; the police car faced her and another Commodore had pulled in beside it. 'Who's that? Oh damn!'

Sergeant Ellsworth, the sun bright on his red head, got out of the second car and came towards them. He squatted down beside the low-slung Ferrari and said, 'What are you doing out here, ladies?'

'Mrs Rockne,' said Angela levelly; she had anticipated such a question, 'is trying to set the scene in her mind again of what happened here last Saturday week. She's trying to recall something, *anything*, she might have seen that would help you trace the man who killed her husband.'

Out of habit Ellsworth had approached the Ferrari on the driver's side; he had to speak across the lawyer to the client. 'And have you recalled anything, Mrs Rockne?'

'No.' Olive was trembling inside; the glue was coming apart. But outwardly she appeared calm; the composure of her lover beside her helped. She thought, incongruously at the moment, that she had never felt any calming presence from Will, not over the past couple of years. She had never thought of herself as timid, but she had always welcomed anyone prepared to make decisions for her; Will had been a natural at that, though in the end he had become too overbearing. Then Angela, strong but calm and loving, had come along. 'No, it's all a jumble in my mind. Have you come up with anything?'

'We were depending on you, Mrs Rockne.'

'What does that mean?' said Angela.

'I thought it was obvious, Mrs Bodalle. Mrs Rockne was the closest witness. We were hoping that her memory might've cleared, that she might've identified Kelpie Dunne.'

'You think he killed Mr Rockne?'

'It's not for us to judge. What do you think?'

'Well, we'll never know, shall we? It's a pity you hadn't given him better protection.'

'That's why we've increased our protection of Mrs Rockne. We're going to increase it even more. We don't think your children, Mrs Rockne, should be unprotected.' He straightened up, leaning down for the last word: 'Don't make our job any harder than it is.'

He walked away and Angela said, 'They *know*.'

'Know what?'

'That we did it.'

'They don't know *we* did it. They think Mr Dunne did it. But who killed him?'

'I did,' said Angela.

And instantly was furious with herself. Her boastfulness was part of her flamboyance, there had always been the urge to be noticed. There was, however, a difference between being noticed for her successful defence of criminals and her own defence. She had murdered Lester to gain her freedom, she had murdered Will to possess Olive and she had murdered Kelpie Dunne because he had threatened to betray her. She must not be trapped into boasting of any of those crimes.

'No,' she said, 'I mustn't joke. I don't know, darling, who killed him. I'm beginning to think it might have been our Mr Jones.'

'I hope so.' But Olive really wasn't thinking about Mr Jones: 'Darling, no more jokes, okay? Killing Will – that was enough.'

Angela pressed her lover's hand. 'No more jokes. All we have to do is keep our nerve.'

2

Jason, guiltily, held Claire's hand. 'It's just, hon, that, you know, I've been – well, I dunno, *elsewhere*. In my head, I mean. Today, in class, Brother Aidan twice asked me if I'd like to leave and go home. Not sarcastic – I mean, he was *understanding*. But I wasn't *there*, in the classroom, you know what I mean?'

He was glad that Claire was not dumb enough to ask exactly where he had been. In his mind he had been *everywhere*: with Jill; watching his mother and Angela again; even with his father when Dad had been alive. But he couldn't tell Claire any of that. She was his friend (which was all she was, he realized now) and he wanted her to remain so. When Jill had sent him home on Tuesday morning he had known she was telling him, without saying it, not to knock on her door again. Not in any cruel, callous way; she was telling him, again without saying it, that he had no right to hang his problems about her neck. And he had suddenly become adult enough to recognize it.

The coffee lounge's sound system was playing 'Calling Elvis': Dire Straits were reviving memories for near-oldies like Brick. Brick himself lounged behind the counter, not really hearing the music of the present but that of the past, of the King Himself.

'What are the guys like now?' said Claire.

'They don't look at me like I'm a freak any more. It's weird, you know. Your father is murdered and some guys, they look at you like you had something to do with it. I don't mean that's what they really think, but that's the way they *act*. One thing, I'm really learning about *people*.'

'Are you learning anything about yourself?'

She's smart, he thought: the best sort of friend to have. Dumb friends were no use, you finished up helping *them*. 'A lot. But I dunno whether it's gunna do me any good. You want another Coke?'

'No, thanks. I've gotta go. I've got so much study – I'm like you, I think my mind's elsewhere.' She put her hand on his. 'You'll be okay, Jay. Really. I wish I could kiss you.'

He lifted her hand, kissed her knuckles, a real Continental, Marcello Mastroianni from Coogee; he saw Brick, one eye on them, raise an eyebrow, then nod approvingly. Impulsively he said, 'You wanna go to a movie Saturday night?'

'Sure. How about *City Slickers*? I'd like to see that. You seen it?'

'No,' he lied gallantly.

Once outside Brick's they held hands a moment while they said goodbye. Then Claire turned and walked away, pausing in her stride to glance back over her shoulder at him. He was smiling after her when someone beside him said, 'Come with me, Jason. Don't act foolish, just do as you are told and you won't get hurt.'

He turned and saw Mr Jones, one hand in a pocket of his jacket as if he were holding a gun. Then Claire came running back: 'Jay, I forgot! Saturday night – '

There was no one on the pavement near them; no one had followed them out of Brick's. Two old women stood at a bus stop on the opposite side of the road, complaining to each other that buses, *nothing*, ever ran on time these days. Traffic went by, but the cars and trucks might just as well have had no drivers or passengers. A long-haired youth zoomed by on a skateboard lost in his own imagination. Jason, later, would not believe that one could be so alone in a busy suburban street.

'This way, both of you,' said Mr Jones. 'No fuss, please. No foolishness.'

'What?' said Claire, then saw the stranger's hand come halfway out of his pocket; a policeman's daughter, she recognized the butt of a gun when she saw it. She was suddenly terrified. 'Jay?'

'Let her go! She's got nothing to do with this!'

'Shut up! I said, no foolishness. Just walk quietly, both of you. There, to that car there, the blue Pulsar.'

The car was parked just round a corner in a side street. Jason and Claire, each carrying their schoolbags, walked with the tall man to the car, stood like obedient pupils while he opened the doors; he could have been a teacher who had picked up a couple of wayward students on their way home. 'In the back, miss. You drive, Jason.'

'I – I don't drive – '

'I told you, boy, no foolishness. I've seen you drive your mother's car – I've followed you. Monday night when you drove over to Tamarama. Get in!'

Jason glanced up and down the narrow street, for one moment wanting to dash somewhere for help, to yell so loudly that someone would come out of the shut-faced houses to see what was wrong. But his legs were too weak to run, his mouth too dry to shout. Obediently he got into the front seat of the car, shifted across behind the wheel and waited for Jones to follow him. Instead the tall man got into the back seat beside Claire. 'I'll ride here with your friend. What's your name, miss?'

'Claire.' In the driver's mirror Jason could see how

283

scared she was; but she wasn't about to become hysterical. 'Claire Malone.'

'Fasten your seat-belt, Claire. You too, Jason. We don't want the police pulling us up, otherwise there might be some gunfire and who knows who'd get hurt? Claire Malone? You wouldn't be some relation of Inspector Malone, would you?'

Oh shit, thought Jason, this is where he's going to do his block!

'Yes. He's my father.'

Jones's smile was no more than a thin grimace. 'I hope you're not going to threaten me with him?' Claire said nothing; and Jones tapped Jason on the shoulder. 'Let's go, boy. Turn right at the bottom of the street and I'll give you more directions as we go along.' He sat back, took out the gun and held it in his lap. 'Any foolishness and you will be shot. Take my word for it.'

It was a slow drive to wherever they were going; Jones at times seemed unsure of his directions. It was forty minutes before Jason turned the car into a street and Jones said, 'That's it. Pull up there,' and Jason recognized territory that he dimly remembered from the one visit he had made here with his father. He had been ten years old and it had been the first time he had met his grandfather's new wife Sugar. Since then there had been outings to the movies and lunches in the city with the oldies, but he had never been back here again till now.

He pulled the car into the kerb, switched off the engine and, sick with dread, said, 'Does my grandfather know about this?'

'No,' said Jones, putting the gun back in his pocket and getting out of the car. 'But I'm hoping he will co-operate. So far you two have been very sensible. I hope your grandfather will be the same.'

On the other side of the road and further down the

street Jason saw three Asian youths watching them. He wanted to yell at them, *Get the police!* But something about them told him they would take no notice: *he* was the alien out here.

He and Claire walked ahead of Jones up the short path to the front door; Claire was unsteady on her feet and Jason took her arm. The metal butterflies on the security door looked dead, their wings still spread; the ceramic kookaburra had had its beak broken off by vandals, the white beak still undiscoloured. The front door was opened almost at once, as if Sugar had been waiting behind some window-curtain for visitors.

'Jay, what are you doing out here? What's wrong?' Then she looked in puzzlement at Claire and Jones.

Jones said, 'May we come in, Mrs Rockne? You remember me?'

Sugar blinked; the puzzlement still veiled her face, but she said, 'Oh yes. Mr – Jones? Yes, yes, come in. George, we've got visitors!'

Jason's hand was still on Claire's elbow as they entered the house ahead of Jones; he could feel the nervousness in her and he hoped he was not communicating any of his own fear and sickness to her. Jesus, surely Pa was not involved in any of this, whatever it was!

The old man, in T-shirt, shorts and thongs, came in from the back of the house. He pulled up sharply in the living-room doorway when he saw who the visitors were. 'For Chrissake, what's going on? Jay, what're you doing here? And who's this?'

'My friend Claire, Pa. Inspector Malone's daughter.'

George Rockne nodded at Claire, then looked at Jones. 'What's the joke, Igor? What're you up to now?'

'Don't you think we should sit down?' said Sugar, ever the hostess. She was wearing a short housecoat, but her hair was done and she was wearing earrings; she would

285

never be caught with her face down. 'How about some tea? A cool drink, Jay? Dear?'

'No, love,' said George, skinny in the T-shirt and shorts but still determined-looking, a bantam who would take on any heavyweight, 'not till Igor tells me what's going on.'

'I think it should be obvious, George,' said the Russian and took the gun from his pocket. 'I've kidnapped these two young people. The girl was an accident – she shouldn't be here. The boy is the one I wanted. I want your help, willingly or unwillingly, I don't care which.' He jerked the gun, and Sugar twitched as if he had prodded her with it. George Rockne stood unmoved. 'If you act sensibly, all of you, no one will be hurt. If the boy's mother acts sensibly, I shouldn't be here longer than tomorrow midday at the latest. I hope to be gone sooner.'

'Has this something to do with the money?'

'It has everything to do with the money. We no longer kidnap for political reasons, George. That's all in the past. May we have tea, Mrs Rockne? Black, weak, with lemon. Russian style.' His smile was unexpectedly charming, took the edge off what had sounded like a rude order.

Sugar had recovered from the shock of seeing the gun; ten years in the clubs around Kings Cross had coated her with some armour-plating. She looked at Claire. 'Would you like to help me, dear?'

'I'm afraid she stays in here,' said the Russian. 'And Mrs Rockne – don't attempt to call anyone. The police, for instance.'

'Don't tell me what to do in my own home!' She abruptly turned from being puzzled to being angry. 'And put that bloody gun away! There's no need for that!'

'Better do what she says, Igor,' said George and looked with admiring eyes after his wife as she went out to the kitchen. Then he looked at his grandson, smiled encouragingly. 'Siddown, Jay. You too, Claire. Don't be scared.

I'm not gunna let Mr Dostoyevsky hurt you.'

'Who?' said Jason.

'Oh, what's he told you to call him? Mr Jones? Mr Collins? No, his name's Dostoyevsky. Written any good books lately?'

'That joke was stale before I was ten years old,' said Dostoyevsky/Jones/Collins. 'Let's be friends, George — at least for the next twelve hours or so.'

'Why me? Why come here? Christ Almighty, Igor, how do you expect me to be your friend when you kidnap my grandson?'

'For that very reason, George. You will help me, let me hide here, because more than anything else you will want to help Jason. And his young friend.' He smiled at Claire; his charm seemed genuine. 'I am truly sorry, young lady, that you had to be involved.'

'It was stupid — ' Claire, seated now, no longer dependent on unsteady legs, looked composed; but she held tightly to the hand of Jason, seated on the couch beside her. 'My father will have all the police force out looking for me.'

'You are threatening me — ' Dostoyevsky's smile faded, but he continued to look at her, the charm no longer working. Then he turned to Rockne. 'I want to use your phone.'

'It's there.' George Rockne nodded to the phone on a small table in the hallway just by the living-room doorway. 'You want us to go outside?'

'Not at all. I don't mind if the young people's education is broadened.' He moved to the phone, stood in the doorway so that he covered them all with the gun. He dialled a number and waited. Then: 'Mrs Rockne? This is Mr Jones — no, don't hang up! I have your son here with me. And for good measure, his young friend, Claire Malone . . . Listen to me — you hear me, listen! . . .'

Malone was just leaving the office when the call came.

'Inspector Malone? This is Sergeant Kisbee, I'm in charge of the phone tap on the Rockne home. I – I've got some bad news.'

'Go ahead.' Bad news had become a joke; he actually smiled at the thought. 'Keep me awake tonight.'

'I'm afraid it will, Inspector. There's just been a phone call from the Russian, Jones, to Mrs Rockne. He's kidnapped her son and – '

'And who else?' Malone filled in the pause.

Something like a deep-drawn breath came over the line: 'Your daughter Claire.'

Malone sat down heavily. 'Christ, no!'

'Something wrong?' Clements, jacket on, ready to go home, stood in the doorway.

Malone stared at him; the voice on the phone said, 'Inspector, you okay? I'm sorry I had to spring it on you like that – '

'I'm okay.' But he wasn't, he was sick and weak. 'Fill me in. What's he want, what's he threatening to do?'

'He's told Mrs Rockne he wants the money – he didn't say what money, but she seemed to know – '

'We know about it, too. Go on.' He was having trouble keeping his voice under control; he was shocked that he actually wanted to scream. 'Go on – '

'He wants the money transferred at once – *tonight*, he said – from the bank, I dunno which bank, he didn't mention the name – he wants the money transferred overseas. He said a Mr Palady – I dunno how it's spelt – he knows what's to be done as soon as Mrs Rockne gets in touch with him. He gave her Palady's home phone number – '

'What about my daughter and the Rockne boy?'

'He said they'd be okay if Mrs Rockne did what she was told.'

'Did you get a trace on the call?'

'No, I'm sorry. We didn't catch on what was going on till too late . . . He said he'd call back in an hour to see if she'd contacted Palady. He said he'd be contacting Palady, too. Your daughter and the boy will be released tomorrow morning if the money goes off tonight. We can trace him when he calls back in an hour. I'm sorry, Inspector – I mean the news about your daughter – '

'Thanks. I'm going out to the Rockne home now – you can contact me there.' He hung up, looked at Clements. 'The Russian has kidnapped Claire. And Jason,' he added.

Clements nodded. 'I got that. Why Claire? Jesus!' He beat a fist against the door jamb as if against the kidnapper's head. 'They're okay so far, the kids?'

'I dunno. I guess so. You coming with me?'

'Of course. Gimme a minute, I've gotta call Romy. We were going out to dinner.'

He went out to his desk and Malone stared at the phone on his own desk: should he call Lisa? But he knew at once that he shouldn't. You didn't use the phone to hit your wife with the biggest crisis of their married life; even Telecom wouldn't recommend that. He stood up again, his body as heavy as iron, his legs hollow, and waited, actually afraid to move, while Clements, beyond the glass wall, talked on the phone. He had been in physical danger more times than he cared to remember, but his body had never gone dead on him, it had always responded. But on those occasions, of course, *he* had been in danger, not his daughter.

When he saw Clements put down the phone he willed himself to walk, got himself moving. Clements said, 'Romy will go out and keep Lisa company. I think she knows how to handle situations like this better than most. Come on, we'll go in a police car.'

'No, I'll drive my own car home – '

'Leave it where it is. You look like shit, mate. You wouldn't know a red light from a sunset – we don't want you driving through an intersection, not in peak hour. Leave it, I'll get one of the fellers to take it home for you.'

Once in the police car Malone had recovered; or his body had. He hardly spoke on the way out of Randwick; Clements did what little talking there was: 'We'll let him have the money, right? Christ, it was never the Rocknes' money anyway. We'll get Claire and the boy back first, then we'll nail him. We'll get him eventually, my oath we will. The thing right now is, we've gotta stop Lisa from expecting the worst.'

'She's not like that.'

Clements looked sideways at him. 'No, she's not. I didn't mean she was gunna go to pieces, you know that. But – ' Whatever he was going to say, he decided against it and said no more till they drew up outside the Malone house.

Lisa was in the front garden, hose in hand, when the two men came in the gate. One look told her something was wrong; she dropped the hose and it writhed like a berserk snake, water spraying wildly. 'What's wrong? It's something to do with Claire, isn't it? It's six o'clock and she's not home – '

Clements turned off the hose. Malone didn't put his arms round Lisa; something told him that was for tragedy and the situation wasn't yet tragic. He took her by her elbows, held her: 'Claire has been kidnapped. She and Jason Rockne – ' He told her as economically and quietly

290

as he could all that they knew: 'We've got very little to go on at the moment, except that he doesn't know the Rockne line is tapped. When he calls again . . .'

He could feel the anguish in her body; but all she said was, 'Why Claire? What has she got to do with all this?' She looked at Clements. 'I've always been afraid of this. That some psycho would take it out on the kids because of something Scobie had done to him.'

'This man's no psycho,' Malone said. 'And I've done nothing to him − not so far. I don't know why he's snatched Claire. We don't even know yet where she and Jason were taken. Russ and I are going down to the Rockne place now −'

'I'll come with you −'

'No, stay here with Tom and Maureen. Romy's on her way, she'll be here any minute. Get your mother and father over − ' His mind was clearing, was working again; he even thought of the family jealousies: 'You'd better call Mum and Dad, too. They'll want to be here.'

She didn't argue. She knew that what he was suggesting was right, but her instinct was to go with him because she knew that he, as well as Tom and Maureen, would need her presence. 'All right. But call me every half-hour − '

'We may know nothing till morning − ' He didn't tell her that once the call had been traced the State Protection Group would be called in and the Russian, wherever he was, would be surrounded and a siege might have to be set up. He hoped, almost hopelessly, that Claire and Jason would be released before it came to that. He did not want a dozen high-powered guns pointed in the direction of his daughter, even in her support.

Maureen and Tom came to the front door. 'What's happening? Dad . . . Hi, Uncle Russ! You coming for dinner?'

'Tell them,' Malone said to Lisa, released her and went

291

to the front gate. 'I'll see you later, you two. Look after Mum — '

Once in the car he said, 'I'm ready to bust.'

Clements took the car quickly away from the kerb, but without burning rubber. He refrained from switching on the siren; it was as if he thought this crisis too personal to be broadcast. 'Go ahead. I've never thought tears made a wimp of a man.'

'No, I'm all right. It's just — ' He let anger push out fear. 'I'll kill the bastard if he hurts Claire.'

'I'll help,' said Clements. 'I mean that.'

There was still only the one police car on duty at the Rockne house, an unmarked white Commodore parked in front of the garage at the back of the house. The Honda Civic was parked at the top of the driveway and in front of it was the red Ferrari. Malone and Clements hurried up the driveway and the two young detectives, sitting in garden chairs, each with a beer in his hand, jumped to their feet as the two senior men came round the corner of the house.

'Oh! Sorry, sir — ' Tilleman, the burly one, looked at his hand, as if it had been caught holding a girl's breast instead of a beer glass. 'We were just — '

'Forget it,' said Malone. 'Hasn't Mrs Rockne told you anything about a phone call she received? About forty-five minutes ago?'

'No, sir.' Tilleman was puzzled. 'Her friend, Mrs Bodalle, brought us these beers — ' He looked at the glass again, not knowing what to do with it; Clements wouldn't have been surprised if he had tossed it over his shoulder into the gardenia bush behind him. 'She didn't say anything — '

'Sergeant Clements will fill you in. Russ, get on to Sergeant Ellsworth, get him over here right away . . .'

Then he went to the screen door of the garden room,

knocked and opened the door as Olive came out from the inner part of the house. She was white and strained and as soon as she saw Malone she pulled up and he thought she was going to collapse.

'Why didn't you call me, for Chrissake!' He was so angry that, if she had collapsed, he would have stood over her, not helped her to her feet. 'Jesus, woman, my daughter's being held by that bastard!'

'How do you know?' Angela Bodalle appeared behind Olive, put her arm round her and supported her. 'Did Mr Jones phone you, too?'

'We've got her phone tapped – ' He nodded at Olive, hating her; he had forgotten he was a policeman, he was a father and nothing else. Then Clements came in behind him, he felt the big man's restraining hand on his arm and he knew he had almost gone too far. Because he was so angry at Olive, he had missed the flash of concern on Angela's face. 'Has he called back yet?'

Olive shook her head; her voice was faint, a little girl's voice: 'Not yet, no. I'm sorry, I should've called you about Claire, but – '

Malone, mind and sight clearer now, saw Angela squeeze Olive's shoulder. But all he said was, 'Have you been in touch with Palady yet, at the Shahriver Bank?'

Angela answered, her arm still round Olive's shoulders: 'He's not home. We left a message with his wife to call as soon as he gets in. How long have you had Olive's phone tapped? You have a permit?'

Malone nodded. 'You can check, if you wish.'

'You still haven't told us how long her phone has been tapped.'

'Why are you so concerned about that, Mrs Bodalle? Civil liberties mean more to you than a couple of innocent kids being kidnapped?'

He had never expected Angela to flush; that reaction

293

seemed totally foreign to her. But she did; and for a moment was lost for words. He waited, but she said nothing. Then he said, knowing he had won a point, 'It's been tapped long enough for us to pick up a few other things besides the call from Mr Jones. What's Palady's number?'

Olive waited for Angela to answer; she even turned and looked at the other woman. But Angela was still silent and it was Olive who gave Malone an eastern suburbs number. Malone said, 'Russ, get someone over to Palady's place — if his number's unlisted — '

'It is.' Angela had evidently decided she had to regain control, of herself if not of the situation. 'I checked.'

She doesn't miss a trick, Malone thought: attention to every little detail. Except that she hated being caught on the hop. 'Righto, Russ, get Tilleman to call Telecom, get the address. Then have someone pick up Palady, bring him here.' He looked at Olive, ignoring Angela. 'We're taking over, Olive. This is going to be our command post till Claire and Jason are safe.' Angela went to say something and he looked at her: 'I wasn't talking to you, Mrs Bodalle. Okay, Olive?'

She nodded weakly. He felt that, if the circumstances were different, he could get her to confess to the murders; but, of course, it was the circumstances that had made her so defenceless. And he knew that the iron woman beside her would protect her.

'Right,' he said and wished he felt as strong as his voice suggested. 'Now we sit and wait.'

4

'Now we sit and wait,' said Dostoyevsky.

Jason and Claire were still sitting on the couch, still

holding hands. He was less scared now than he had been on the drive out here; perhaps it was the presence of his grandfather and Sugar. He could see that they were both worried, but there was a certain down-to-earth matter-of-factness about them that was comforting.

'I want to go to the bathroom,' said Claire.

'Come with me, dear.' Sugar rose, took Claire's hand. She glared at Dostoyevsky when he, too, rose, gun in hand. 'Give us some privacy, Mr Whatever-your-name-is. We're not gunna try anything foolish. I don't want you hurting my hubby or Jason. Come on, Claire.'

They went out of the small living room and Dostoyevsky looked at George Rockne. 'Is she a believer, George?'

'Sugar?' He shook his head. 'Nah. And I never tried to convert her. Live and let live, that's always been the politics in this house.' Then he said, 'You're not gunna get away with this, Igor.'

'I think I shall.' Jason, watching him closely, wondered how truly relaxed the Russian was. But he appeared really at ease, as if he were used to this sort of situation. As if the question had been aired, Dostoyevsky said, 'Twice before I got out by the skin of my teeth, as they say. Once in Iran, once in France. You don't know what I've been through, George, for the sake of communism. You've had a picnic in a country like this. You've achieved nothing, so perhaps that explains it. Do you have any politics, son?'

'Me?' Jason swallowed; he hadn't spoken for so long his throat had gone dry. 'Not yet. But I don't think I'll ever be a communist. Sorry, Pa.'

George Rockne, sitting in a chair close by, leaned across and patted his grandson's knee. 'It's all right, Jay. I give up trying to recruit any new believers.' He turned back to Dostoyevsky. 'It's all over, Igor, finished. You've been in Australia long enough – you know you can't surf the same wave twice. I wish you'd get that into your thick Russian head. There's nothing more to believe in.'

There was a sadness to the old man's voice that touched Jason. In turn he put his own hand on his grandfather's knee and the old man looked at him gratefully. 'There are other things to believe in, Pa.'

'Such as?' George Rockne's smile was not sarcastic, but almost whimsical.

'I dunno for sure. But there are,' Jason said doggedly.

Then Claire and Sugar came back and Sugar, practical as ever, said, 'Well, do we sit and starve or do we eat? I've got enough spaghetti and home-made sauce out there for all of us. Come on, Claire, you can help me.'

'We'll all come,' said Dostoyevsky, getting to his feet again. 'Just in case.'

'Please yourself,' said Sugar. 'Just don't get under my feet in *my* kitchen. That's my Kremlin, as George calls it.'

As they moved out into the narrow hallway, George turned left and walked towards the front door. Dostoyevsky said nothing, but watched him with his gun raised. George peered out through the narrow glass window beside the front door, then came back down the hallway. 'What sorta car did you come in?'

'A blue Pulsar. That's it parked right in front of your gate.'

'Not any more it ain't. It's been pinched, Igor. The hoons around here do it all the time, especially the Asians if you're a whitey and own a car. They'll probably strip it to the bone if they find out you're a commo.' He laughed without merriment. 'You're not gunna get away with this, Igor. The omens don't look good.'

'I don't believe in omens.'

'Come off it, mate. You Russians are more superstitious than the Irish.'

They went on into the kitchen. George, Dostoyevsky and Jason sat round the formica-topped table while Sugar and Claire prepared the evening meal. Jason couldn't believe the situation; it was weird, like a gentle sort of nightmare. If he lived through this, the guys at school were never going to believe his story. Only Claire, as scared as himself, seemed real. But even she was working as practically as Sugar, pushing the males aside as she set the table.

They were halfway through the spaghetti bolognese, much better than Jason's mother made, when Dostoyevsky looked at his watch. 'Time for my call. Come, Jason.' The boy put down his fork and stood up, glancing at his grandfather. Dostoyevsky saw the look and said, 'I've already told you, there's nothing to be afraid of if there's no foolishness. Go on eating, George. But if you or your good wife or the young lady try anything . . .' He raised the gun, which, till he had picked it up, had been lying in front of his plate like a dessert utensil.

'You wouldn't do that, Igor,' said George quietly.

'I would, George,' said the Russian just as quietly.

'Did you kill my son?'

'No, I didn't. I know who did, but I don't think now is the time to talk about it. You don't seem to get it into your thick Australian head, my life is on the line, too. Come with me, Jason. This won't take long. Warm up his spaghetti, Mrs Rockne.'

Jason noticed that he dialled the Coogee number without hesitation, as if he had memorized it to perfection; but maybe that was how you were taught in the KGB, or whatever he belonged to. There was an immediate answer from the other end; his mother must have been sitting right beside the phone. 'Mrs Rockne, I promised to call back. Have you been in touch with Mr Palady?' He frowned, his eyes darkening till Jason thought they had turned black; but maybe it was the dim light in the hallway. 'Mrs Rockne, don't fool with me! He was supposed to be at home waiting for your call . . . His car was in an accident? Mrs Rockne — all right, all right. Don't get hysterical. All right, his car was in an accident — was he hurt? . . . No? . . . How do you know all this if you haven't been able to contact him? . . . When did his wife say he would be home? . . . All right, I'll phone in half an hour. And, Mrs Rockne — I have your son right here beside me. I have a gun at his head — ' He raised the gun and put the barrel against Jason's temple; Jason closed his eyes, said Oh Jesus! and waited to die. Then the gun was taken away. 'Half an hour, Mrs Rockne. The money has to be transferred tonight . . . No, you cannot speak to him. You can do that when you tell me you have contacted Mr Palady. Half an hour, Mrs Rockne.'

He put down the phone, motioned for Jason to go ahead of him back to the kitchen. He sat down at the table, put the gun back in front of his plate, picked up his fork and began to eat the spaghetti.

'Well?' said George Rockne.

'Another half-hour. Our banker's car was involved in an accident.'

'Another omen, Igor. Give up.'

Dostoyevsky shook his head. 'That's why they failed in Moscow, George. They gave up.'

5

There had been controlled bedlam in and around the Rockne house for the past hour. There were four police cars out in the street; another four were on call at Randwick police station a kilometre up the road. There were four TV vans and half a dozen other media vehicles in the side street off Coogee Bay Road; they had been marshalled there by three motorcycle cops, who were also holding back the small crowd that had gathered. Drinkers from the hotel down on the promenade had come up the road, bringing their beers with them; this promised to be more entertaining than watching *Home and Away* or some other soap opera on television.

Chief Superintendent Greg Random arrived to take charge; with him was a thickset man with close-cropped hair and a face that could have been used as a bulldozer. 'This is Mr Salkov, from the Soviet consulate. He's representing the embassy in Canberra.'

'Would you excuse us, Mr Salkov?' said Malone and led Random aside. 'What's going on? Why's he here?'

'Because of that five million. Fred Falkender — ' Falkender was the Assistant Commissioner, Crime ' — he read the running sheets and he decided that the Russians down in Canberra had to be told about the money. After all, it belongs to them — or anyway, Moscow — and not to Mr Jones and his mates. They want it back.'

'Jesus, Greg! Don't you see how that complicates things? What sort of leverage have we got now to make Jones release Claire and the Rockne boy? He's demanding the five million. Are Mr Salkov and *his* mates going to hand it over for us?'

'I don't know, Scobie. I think you'd better go home, be with Lisa and your other kids.'

Malone was torn; but: 'No, I can't. I couldn't sit still there, I'd be back in ten minutes, probably with Lisa. I've talked to her since I got here, she and Maureen and Tom are okay. The grandparents are with them.' He looked around him, at the dozen or more police officers standing around with that stiff impatience of men and women who know they can do nothing till their quarry makes the next move. 'I'm feeling bloody murderous, Greg. If that bastard harms Claire . . .'

'Quit thinking like that. How's Mrs Rockne?'

'Fragile. It's going to be bloody cruel, but if I can get to her right after this is over — assuming we get the kids back safely — ' He stopped, his mind going black at what he had just said. Then he went on. 'If I can get to her, I think she'll tell us everything we want to know about the murders.'

'Do you like irony?'

'I don't know that I *like* it, but I put up with it. If I couldn't I might as well give up police work.'

'I wonder if Mrs Rockne appreciates it? A murder suspect and the cop who's after her, both waiting for their kidnapped kids to come home safe and sound. How's her friend, Mrs Bodalle?'

'In command of their side of the fence. But I think she's a bit like Olive, worried.'

'About the kids?'

'I hope so. I don't think she's entirely heartless . . . I haven't seen you for a couple of days and I didn't put it on the running sheets. Olive and Mrs Bodalle are lesbians. They're lovers.'

They were standing in the garden beside the pool fence and apart from the uniformed police. There was still some light in the sky, the last of what had been a bright red sunset; dust drifting east from the drought-stricken bush had turned on an Outback sunset for the urban voters. Random's sallow face had turned bronze and the lines in it were black, like tribal markings. His expression didn't alter at Malone's news.

'So you think Mrs Bodalle really did have something to do with the murder?'

'Both murders. I think she might've done in Kelpie Dunne and his missus on her own.'

'You have imagination, mate.' The light suddenly lost its colour; his hair turned grey again. 'I'm glad there's only one like you. Who's this?'

Russ Clements came round the corner of the house with

300

the managing director of the Shahriver Credit International Bank. Palady looked less than comfortable. It was not just the strand of hair falling down over his forehead and the unloosened tie, but the look of mental pain on the face that had become so practised at being a mask. The sight of so many police seemed to have unnerved him. He could only have felt worse if an avalanche of auditors had fallen on his bank.

'His car was in an accident,' said Clements. 'Someone shunted him from the back.'

Malone introduced Palady to Random. 'You know what this is all about, Mr Palady?'

The banker was trying to put himself together again. He smoothed down his hair, tightened his tie. 'Yes, Sergeant Clements explained. But it is not going to be easy – there are certain rules – '

'Stuff the rules! Break them!' Malone's voice was soft but fierce; he saw Random give him a warning look and he simmered down. 'Getting my daughter and the boy back is what's important, not bloody rules.'

'There's something else, Mr Palady,' said Random. 'That gentleman over there is from the Soviet consulate. The money in your bank doesn't belong to Mr Jones or the Rockne family. It was stolen twice, by Jones and then by Mr Rockne. It belongs to the government in Moscow.'

Palady looked even more pained. 'Will they release the money as ransom?'

'I don't know,' said Malone, and didn't look at Random. 'I'm not going to even ask Mr Salkov, not at this stage. Come inside, Mr Palady. We'll talk this over with Mrs Rockne.'

As they went into the house Clements said, 'Grace Ditcham is outside, she grabbed me as I came in. She said to remind you, you owe her.'

'I know. But she'll have to wait.'

'The other vultures were yelling, when are we gunna throw 'em something?'

'Stuff 'em, they'll have to wait, too. If word gets out what Jones is demanding, where the money actually came from, Christ knows what he'd do. We don't want him knowing that that bloke from the consulate is here demanding the money.'

There were police in the kitchen, one of them manning the emergency phone that the Telecom men had run in from the nearest link in order to keep the Rockne line free for the call from the kidnapper. Malone led the way into the living room where the three Carss women sat with Angela Bodalle.

'Mrs Carss,' he said, 'would you mind taking Shelley into her bedroom? We have some business we have to discuss.'

'Yes, I do mind!' Mrs Carss was all belligerence; if the Russian were here, she'd have shown him how the Cold War was won. 'Our place is here beside my daughter, Shelley's mother — '

Malone waited for Olive to back him up, but she sat silent. Then he said, 'Mrs Carss, go into the other room — *please*. I don't want to have to call on one of our men to escort you in there — '

'Come on, Gran.' Shelley stood up, pulled on her grandmother's arm. 'I don't like you, Mr Malone. You're a real pain in the bum.'

'I know, Shelley. I'm also Claire's father.'

She stared at him; then her eyes glistened and she nodded. 'I know. I'm sorry. Come on, Gran.'

The old woman and the young girl went out. Malone shut the living-room door, introduced Random and Palady and explained why the latter had been delayed. Then the four men sat down facing Olive and Angela, who sat hand in hand on a couch.

302

'Olive, there's a complication. There's a man from the Soviet consulate outside demanding the money in the bank – he says it belongs to the Soviet government and it does. But we're keeping him out of this for the moment – ' He looked at Random.

The senior man ran a hand slowly over his shock of hair. 'Jesus, Scobie . . . okay, go ahead. But if this gets out of this room – ' He looked at the two women. 'You understand me, ladies?'

'Yes,' said Angela and squeezed Olive's hand. 'We understand.'

'Right,' said Malone. 'Forget the rules, Mr Palady. Jones has been in touch with you, is that right?'

'This morning, early. He came to see me at my home – I don't know how he learned where I live – '

'What do you have to do?' Now that Random had committed himself, he was once again his calm, decisive self. Malone was glad to have him here in the room.

'He gave me an account number in our branch in Bangkok – '

'Bangkok?' said Clements. 'You're all over, it seems. That branch isn't mentioned on your letterheads.'

'You have a very good memory, Sergeant. We have quite a few branches that are not listed . . . Mr Jones – is that his real name?'

'It's Dostoyevsky,' said Malone.

Palady looked at him, smiled as if sharing a joke he didn't quite understand; then saw it wasn't a joke. 'Really? Well. Well, he said I was to transfer the five and a quarter million, in round figures – ' he added with a banker's precision; or what used to be a banker's precision, thought Malone, before bankers started their juggling acts ' – as soon as Mrs Rockne gave me the word. Of course, that was before the other Russian appeared on the scene – '

'Forget the other Russian, we told you!' Malone looked

303

at Olive. 'Give him the word, Olive. *Now!*'

'Yes,' said Olive, her voice dry and small. 'Transfer the money, Mr Palady. At once.'

Palady twisted his hands together; he looked nothing like the man Malone had accosted at their first meeting. Indeed, he looked as if he would have preferred to be back in Kuwait. In the chaos there bankers had had to make no decisions that kept them within the law. 'The account is frozen. I did it on police instructions, there is a court order – '

'If we're going to be so legalistic,' said Angela, 'there is another point. The money doesn't belong to Mrs Rockne – forgetting the Russian claim to it, for the moment. It was left by Mr Rockne to Jason and his sister. They are both minors.'

'Holy Jesus!' Malone wanted to lash out at something, anything; but he had the distinct feeling that he was standing in a vacuum.

Clements said, 'If that's the case, then Mrs Rockne is their legal guardian. Can't she agree for the children?'

'No,' said Angela. 'Only after the children themselves have agreed.'

'Let's cut out the bullshit – excuse me, ladies.' Random was working towards a cold temper; Malone had seen it in action and knew it could be as devastating as any wild fury. 'What we are doing is illegal, anyway – the money belongs to the Moscow government. Now, we either ask Salkov outside to sign over the money or we go ahead and bullshit to Dostoyevsky that the money has been transferred.'

Palady shook his head. 'It won't work, sir. He knows the phone number of our Bangkok branch. All he has to do is call them and ask if the money has arrived.'

'All we have to do,' said Malone, 'is call Bangkok and tell them what they have to say.'

Then the phone on a nearby table rang. Clements reached for it, but said nothing, just held it out to Olive. She stood up; for a moment it looked as if her legs might fold beneath her; then she took the phone and looked at Malone. He nodded, then whispered, 'Keep him talking.'

Olive cleared her throat: 'Mr Jones? . . . Yes – ' She glanced at Palady, but Malone leaned forward and vigorously shook his head. 'Yes, I've called his home, but – but he's not there. He – he's been in an accident . . . Mr Jones, it's the truth!' Her voice cracked, a spasm of terrible fear passed over her face. 'All right, half an hour – I'll hear from you in half an hour. No, I'll give you the money . . . But please, Mr Jones – please don't hurt my son. And Claire.' She put down the phone, stood leaning with both hands on the small table. 'He'll call back in half an hour. He said he had a gun to Jason's head.'

'And Claire?' said Malone.

'He didn't mention her.' Then she looked at Angela, ignoring the men. 'He'll kill them, I know it! What have we got ourselves into?'

It was a cry of anguish, of surrender, but Malone couldn't take advantage of it. The murders of Will Rockne and Kelpie Dunne and his wife had, for the moment, become unimportant.

Then Clements, who had gone out to the kitchen, came back to the living-room door. 'They got a trace! He's out at Cabramatta – the number is – ' He gave the number.

Olive said, 'That's my father-in-law's number!'

6

Dostoyevsky looked at his watch: the half-hour was up. He pushed back his chair. 'I must make another phone call.'

'I think what Pa says is right, Mr Dostoyevsky,' said Jason. 'I think you should give up, let me and Claire go.'

He was scared stiff, he couldn't believe he was speaking so calmly. He saw his grandfather and Sugar stare at him as if they didn't believe what he was saying; Claire blinked, looked sort of stupid. But the Russian believed what he was saying: 'Why is that, Jason? You've been very quiet up till now – as young people should be. I was brought up in a very strict household,' he explained to George Rockne. 'You've kept your mouth shut, but now you think you know more than your grandfather, is that it?'

'Yes, I think I do – sir.' He added the *sir* as if he were speaking to one of the masters at school. If the bastard had been brought up in a very strict household, give him the respect he thought he deserved; it cost nothing. 'My mother can't authorize the transfer of the money.'

'No? Why is that?' Dostoyevsky had sat down again at the kitchen table. Jason had risen when the Russian had gestured, with the gun, for him to follow him into the hallway. 'Sit down, boy. Sit down, I said!'

Jason slid into a chair beside Claire. 'My father taught me a bit about the law, sir. You see, the money is mine, mine and my sister's. My father left a will that said we were to get it all, my mother was to get nothing.'

'Well!' Sugar let out a long hissing gasp. 'That must of put the cat among the pigeons.'

Jason glanced at her, smiled weakly. 'Mum didn't like it – she blew her top – '

Dostoyevsky swore in Russian; then: 'Damn your mother! Why didn't she tell me that?'

'Give him the money, Jason,' said George Rockne.

'I can't, Pa. Not just like that. Shelley and I are minors. I'm not sure what the legal thing is, but I think Shelley and I have to say okay and then Mum authorizes it. I dunno, but I think that's the drill.'

306

'You'll make a good lawyer, dear,' said Sugar.

'If I live,' he said and looked warily at Dostoyevsky.

George sat relaxed in his chair at the head of the table, tapping the table with the tines of a fork. 'Somehow, Igor, I think you're getting further and further up that well-known creek, without a paddle.'

'What?' The Russian's cold, calm exterior was beginning to crack like ice under shifting pressures. 'Don't talk in fucking riddles, George!'

'Stop that!' Sugar's voice was as harsh as Dostoyevsky's. 'There's a young girl here. Watch your language in my house, you hear!'

He glared at her; then he composed his face again, gave a little nod to both Sugar and Claire. 'I apologize.'

'Good,' said Sugar; she would have made a superior mother superior, except for the striptease past. 'Forget you heard what you did, Claire.'

Claire managed a smile, patted Sugar's hand. 'I've heard worse, Mrs Rockne.'

'Not in my house, dear.'

George Rockne had watched this exchange with wry amusement; his old lady was a wonder, but so was the Malone kid. The Party, maybe, could have done better with more women in it. 'I don't think you're winning any friends in this house, Igor. But then it was never the KGB's job to win friends, was it, not unless you wanted to recruit them as agents?'

'He's with the KGB?' said Jason. 'This is getting bloody unbelievable!'

'Watch your language.' George grinned and winked at Sugar. He was the only one at the table who seemed unperturbed; Jason wondered if it was an act his grandfather was putting on. 'Igor, think about it. If you get outa here, where are you gunna go? Once, when the heat was on me, before I met Sugar – ' He smiled along the table at

307

her; she reached out a hand, but he was too far away. 'I once looked up all the countries that don't have extradition treaties with Australia. There's sixty-three of 'em, I think, from Afghanistan to Zaire. But I dunno if any of 'em would appeal to you. Vatican City, for example. You think a commo, a KGB bloke to boot, would be welcome there? Of course they took in Nazis, so maybe they're not choosy. Togo or Bhutan? The trouble, Igor, would be getting there, they're all thousands of bloody miles away. You think the authorities here would let you get far without someone along the way stopping you? This isn't like hijacking a plane somewhere in the US and flying to Cuba. If the people here don't catch up with you, your hard-line mates in Moscow are gunna be chasing you. Or Gorbachev and Yeltsin, they'll be after you, too. Give up, Igor, and maybe Jason and Claire will put in a good word for you, say that you never tried to hurt them.'

'He put the gun to my head,' said Jason.

His grandfather looked at him: it was a schoolmaster's look. 'What sorta lawyer are you gunna be, Jay? This is a bargain plea. Isn't your life and Claire's worth a white lie? Or anyway, a greyish white one? Grow up, Jay.' For a moment the old communist surfaced: 'That's the way the system works, on lies and deals and bargain pleas.'

'Sweetheart,' said Sugar, 'I don't think you should be preaching propaganda, not to youngsters like Jay and Claire. Do you know what he's talking about, dear?'

'I think so,' said Claire, like Jason, still unbelieving of half of what she had heard and experienced in the past two hours. 'But we don't get it in social studies at school.'

Dostoyevsky looked at the gun he had placed again in front of his plate. The plate was now empty of spaghetti and Claire, as if wanting something to do, stood up and reached for it. The Russian grabbed her wrist and she winced and gasped.

'Let her go!' George Rockne half rose out of his chair, looked for a moment as if he would hurl himself at Dostoyevsky.

The Russian and the young girl stared at each other; then Claire said, 'I was only going to take away your plate – '

He glared at her a moment longer, then he let go her wrist. 'I'm sorry. I thought – ' He picked up the gun, but didn't put it away in his pocket. 'Sit down, George. I'm not going to hurt any of you.'

George sank back. 'You're hopeless and helpless, Igor. Both. And you know it.'

Dostoyevsky pushed the plate towards Claire, who went to the sink with it and began to rinse it, watched with smiling approval by Sugar. Jason watched this with detached bemusement; he would never understand women, they were a foreign species. He realized now he hadn't a clue how Jill really thought or what she thought of him; as for his mother and Angela, that was territory where he was completely lost. As he looked at Claire, she glanced at him over her shoulder and he saw how afraid she really was. She had been scared stiff when the bloody Russian had grabbed her wrist; and he couldn't blame her, Dostoyevsky for a moment had looked as if he might kill her. He turned to the Russian and said, 'Let me phone my mother, sir. I'll tell her I agree to transferring the money, wherever it has to go. I know my sister will agree, too. Then Mum can sign for us minors.'

'There you are, Igor. You've got your five million or whatever it is.'

'Yes?'

'Yes what?'

'You were going to say something else, George.'

George Rockne paused a moment. 'Yeah. Yeah, I was gunna say you've got your money, that should satisfy your

309

mates. That only leaves you, Igor. How do you manage *your* transfer?'

'I don't think you should of brought that up, sweetheart.' Sugar had begun collecting the rest of the plates, was piling them up on the draining board while Claire continued to rinse them.

'Love, Igor and me, we once believed in the same thing. I can't not point out some things to him. He's forgotten the money now, haven't you, mate? It's self-preservation now, isn't it? It usually is, in the end. Take my advice, Igor. Cut your losses – I know what I'm talking about, that's the story of my life. Go now, Igor, walk outa here and disappear. Change your name, call yourself Gogol or Pushkin or something. I'll see that Jason's offer is honoured, the money'll be transferred to wherever you've named. But leave the kids and me and my wife alone and walk outa here and, like I said, disappear. There's still time, Igor. Go somewhere and write your memoirs. Everyone else does when the dream folds up.'

'You're very free with advice, George.'

'That's all I have left, mate.' He saw Sugar turn away from the sink, look hard at him, and he grinned. 'Except you, love. And I'm never gunna give you away.'

Jesus, thought Jason, now I know what love really is! He couldn't believe oldies could feel that way about each other. But there it was, right before his eyes. Something welled up inside him and he wanted to reach out to both of them. Instead he turned his gaze on the Russian.

Dostoyevsky sat very still, one hand on the table still clutching the gun. Jason, watching him closely, would have been shocked, but not surprised, if he had lifted the gun to his head and fired it. The thick eyebrows were drawn down over the sombre eyes, the thick lips were turned inwards so that the wide mouth was just a slit. Jason would not have attempted to guess what was going on behind the stern face; the Russian might have been reviewing his whole life. Jason was too young even to guess at what went on in your mind when your life suddenly seemed to be over. When Dostoyevsky had put the gun to his head while they had stood by the phone, his mind had gone utterly blank.

Then Dostoyevsky got slowly to his feet. Claire, at the sink, had turned off the tap; she and Sugar stood waiting. Jason and his grandfather sat still, looking up at the tall man. No one said anything, as if they all knew that any word from them might make the Russian change his mind.

'Goodbye, George.' He put out his hand and Rockne shook it; then he nodded at Sugar and Claire and Jason. 'Goodbye. Just make sure the money is sent where it is supposed to go. I'm trusting you, George. The dream isn't dead, we can still do what they set out to do all those years ago.'

'Sure,' said George Rockne, but his voice was as dead as the dream. 'Take care of yourself, Igor.'

Dostoyevsky turned abruptly, went out of the kitchen and down the narrow hallway. They heard him open the front door, waited for the security door to slam behind him. But there was nothing. Jason, nearest to the kitchen doorway, moved into the hallway. Dostoyevsky stood outlined against the street-light shining through the open front doorway, one of the metal butterflies seemingly perched on his shoulder like a carrion bird.

'Something the matter, sir?'

Dostoyevsky closed the door. 'Yes. The street is full of police.'

The street was indeed full of police.

The State Protection Group had been on stand-by within minutes of the first phone call from Dostoyevsky. Within five minutes of the tracing of the kidnapper's second call, the group was on its way to Cabramatta. So were Malone and Clements in their own unmarked car; Random followed with his driver and Olive and Angela Bodalle. A call had been put ahead to the local area police to warn them what was coming. Trailing the police cars as they sped south-west were the media vehicles, some of their occupants still unsure what story they were actually following. Palady and Salkov, unwanted spectators, indeed forgotten in the rush to depart, were left behind.

The peak hour was over, but there was still a lot of traffic on the roads. Malone tried to contain his impatience as, several times, they were hindered; but he said nothing, knowing that Clements, behind the wheel, was doing his best. They made the trip in a continuous wail of urgency, Clements keeping the siren going all the way.

When they pulled into the street where the Rocknes lived, the local police were already there, cordoning it off and moving neighbours out of their houses and down to the far end of the street. As Malone and Clements got out of their car, Random's car drew in behind it. The Chief Superintendent got out, said something to the women in the back seat, then came towards Malone.

'Okay, Scobie. I'll run this. You get in my car with the women.'

'Greg – '

'That's an order, Scobie. In my car. I don't want any interference.' Malone hesitated, looked as if he were going to argue; and Random said, 'Come on, mate, you know you'll only be in the way. You're not thinking straight. Just stay out of it. We'll get Claire out of there, her and the boy. Go and sit with the women. Here come the cavalry.'

The Protection Group's two wagons had arrived, its men, in their body armour and with their weapons at the ready, piling out and deploying themselves along the garden fences on the Rocknes' side of the street. Malone, seeing the firepower, was suddenly sick at the thought that there might be a siege. He hoped the Russian had no thoughts of turning this quiet suburban street into a small Stalingrad.

'Go on,' said Random, more gently this time. 'Get into my car. You come with me, Russ — I want to talk to the SPG commander. We don't want this to get out of hand. I'll talk to Dostoyevsky on the phone from one of the neighbours' houses.'

Malone looked towards the Rockne house, neat and peaceful, spotlighted by the street-light outside its front gate, a target waiting to be blasted. Then he turned quickly and went along to Random's car. He slid into the front seat, said to the driver, 'Could you leave us alone for a while?'

The driver nodded, got out, and Angela Bodalle, in the back seat, leaned forward. 'Who's going to negotiate with Mr Jones? Why not you?'

'My boss thinks I'm too involved.' He was sitting sideways in the front seat, not looking at the two women but at the house down the street. 'He'll handle it. You all right, Olive?'

'Just. God, how did it come to this?'

Out of the corner of his eye he saw Angela press Olive's hand warningly. That started him: 'It came to this, Olive, because Will got greedy and it's gone on from there. If you

313

and Angela hadn't had him killed, he might've given back that money before our kids had to be kidnapped.'

He turned then and faced them. Both women stared at him: Olive was afraid, but Angela's look was one of hatred. 'You're not going to let up on her, are you, not even at a time like this!'

'I'm not accusing just her, Mrs Bodalle. I'm accusing you. Did you kill Kelpie Dunne and his wife, too?'

Down the street the SPG men were moving closer to the Rockne house, shadows running through shadows. Random was with them, then suddenly he left them and ran up into a house where the front door was wide open. Clements stayed with the SPG men, curling his bulk into a big ball as he huddled down behind a garden fence. The purple Fairlane was parked on the opposite side of the road and one of the Andrews Sisters impersonators was yelling as he was held back by two uniformed officers, 'Don't let him shoot at you behind my car! I'll sue you bastards if it's damaged!' Two other young officers came out of the house into which Random had disappeared, almost carrying an elderly woman who was complaining in a loud voice that she was going to miss tonight's episode of her favourite soap opera; she wasn't interested in the opera going on in her street. At the end of the street, beyond the police barricades and the TV vans and cars, a crowd had gathered. Most of the faces were Asians, blank at this distance of excitement or curiosity, and Malone had a bizarre image of watching an old Saigon newsreel.

He had looked away from Angela as he put the question of the Dunnes' killing to her, his eye caught by Random's running up into the house two doors from the Rocknes'. Now he turned back to her in time to catch the stiffening of her neck, the raising of her chin. He had seen enough body language over the years to be a fluent interpreter of

314

it. He knew now that he had nailed her against the wall. But:

'You have no evidence at all, Mr Malone, to support either of those charges.' Her smile was ugly, like that of a comedian who knew her jokes were awful but who had to keep trying. 'Prove what you're saying.'

'You'll back me up, won't you, Olive?' He said it with confidence, if false; he wasn't going to plead with her. 'She killed her own husband, too, did you know that?'

At that Angela leaned forward. There was spittle at the corners of her mouth, she was at the extreme limits of her control. 'When this is over, Malone, I'll have you! You'll be finished, you hear? Finished!'

Malone had drawn back, but he hadn't faltered in his stare. He had gone beyond the bounds of what he could have said in a taped official interview; but here in the car there was no recorder, no witness, no lawyer other than the accused. He stared Angela down; she eased herself back in the seat. He turned his head towards Olive, who seemed bone-rigid with shock.

'You could be next, Olive.' He made no attempt to dampen the malice in his voice. These two women had helped towards putting his daughter in danger; it was stretching the connection, but he was in no frame of mind to be fair. 'She's your lover, but that doesn't make you safe from her. She spent ten months in a psychiatric clinic when she was young, did she ever tell you that? How did she get you to agree to killing Will? Was she the one who hired Kelpie Dunne to do it?'

Olive said dully, 'I don't care, Scobie. I love her. But all I want right now is for Jason to come out of that house safely.'

It was a slap in the face for him. He turned round, wondering at himself: how could he have forgotten Claire?

315

The policeman in him had run amok, taken over from the father. His shame and anguish blinded him for a moment; he stared down the street, seeing nothing. Then his gaze cleared, he saw Random hurrying towards them. He got out of the car, disgracefully glad that he had been alone in it with the two women; he would have hated Clements to have heard him. He went towards Random with hands outstretched, like a man seeking forgiveness rather than news.

'He wants to see you and Mrs Rockne.' Random was showing no agitation; one could imagine his calm approach to the kidnapper. 'He wants to make a deal.'

'What sort of deal?'

'He wouldn't say, he said it had to be with you and Mrs Rockne. You want to go in there?'

'Of course!'

'Okay, give me your gun. Come on!' Random held out his hand demandingly as Malone hesitated. 'He insisted on that and so do I. I'm not going to have you doing your block in there.'

Malone handed over his gun. 'Put two fellers on to Mrs Bodalle – I'm going to charge her when this is over. I'll get Olive.'

He went back to the two women who had got out of the police car. Olive was holding on to the door, her legs still weak; but Angela was all arrogance, defiance in every line of her body. Malone ignored her, spoke directly to Olive: 'The Russian wants to see you and me. Are you game?'

She nodded. Angela put out a hand, either to restrain her or to comfort her: it didn't matter, because Olive just stepped away from her, saying nothing, and followed Malone across the road and down towards the Rockne house.

They passed the SPG men crouched behind fences and between parked cars; Malone saw Clements give him the thumbs-up sign, heard him say, 'Take care, mate.' He pushed back the Rockne front gate, took Olive's arm as they walked up the short path between the marigolds which, colourless in the street-lights, looked like white fists. He could feel the tension in her, her arm was like a vibrating iron rod.

'Let me do the talking, Olive. We give him the money like we agreed, okay?'

'Yes.' It came out of a dry throat.

The beakless, mirthless kookaburra stared with stony eyes at them; the butterflies were dead specimens against the security door. As they stepped up from the path, the front door was opened by Jason. He pushed open the security door and Olive fell up the last step and into his arms. Malone waited while they embraced, then he heard a voice back in the hallway say, 'Come in, please. Shut the door behind them, Jason.'

There was no light on in the hallway; when the front door was shut behind them, Malone at first could see nothing. Then he made out the shape of a tall man against the light coming from the back of the house. Jason was still supporting his mother, his arm round her waist; Malone moved past them and down towards the kidnapper. 'I'm Inspector Malone. Where is my daughter?'

'Here, Daddy!' Claire came round the Russian, flung herself at Malone. He wrapped his arms round her, felt the tears start in his eyes; love and relief choked him. Then he saw the gun in the Russian's hand and he straightened up, holding Claire tightly against him.

'This way, Inspector. You too, Mrs Rockne.'

He led the way into the kitchen, where George Rockne and Sugar stood, she clutching his thin arm. The blinds were down at the windows over the sink; Dostoyevsky gestured at them. 'I don't want your snipers trying to pick me off while we talk, Inspector. I know you have the house surrounded.'

'That's why he decided to talk to you,' said George. 'Listen to him. You too, Olive.'

'Put your hands against the refrigerator, Inspector.'

Malone released Claire, leaned against the refrigerator; right in front of his face were reminder notes in a neat hand: *Defrost Monday: Call Electrician.* The refrigerator's motor started up and Malone started. 'Keep your hands where they are,' said Dostoyevsky and proceeded to frisk him. Then he stepped back. 'Very sensible, Inspector. No tricks, no hidden gun. Turn round and we'll talk.'

'What have you got to say?' Malone face to face at last with the kidnapper, with the ex-KGB man, felt now that he could handle him. He was angry and frustrated when he had to deal with shadows.

'Not in front of the young people. Take them into the living room, Mrs Rockne. *Both* Mrs Rocknes,' Dostoyevsky said as Sugar remained by George's side. 'Don't attempt anything foolish, ladies. Or you, Jason.' He lifted the gun, pointed it negligently at Malone and George Rockne. 'You understand what I'm saying?'

'You hurt my hubby,' said Sugar, 'and I promise you, you won't leave this house alive. You understand what I'm saying?'

'Better listen to her, Igor,' said George; then he patted his wife's arm. 'Go on, love, take Olive and the youngsters inside. Inspector Malone and I'll be okay.'

The two women and Jason and Claire went out of the kitchen, Claire looking back at her father as she went. 'Be careful, Daddy. Give him everything he wants.'

When the three men were alone, Dostoyevsky motioned for them all to sit down at the table, which was now clear of the evening meal. 'Has Mrs Rockne agreed to transfer the money?'

'Yes,' said Malone. 'She has seen Mr Palady, from the

318

Shahriver Bank. My boss, Chief Superintendent Random, said you wanted to make a deal?'

'I have been listening to my friend here – ' He nodded at George, who sat at the end of the table picking at a loose thread in his T-shirt. 'I am going to have difficulty in getting out of this country. Unless – '

'Unless what?'

'You bring no charges against me for taking your daughter and Jason, and I'll be a sworn witness to who killed Will Rockne.'

Malone held on to the sudden surge of excitement. 'You saw the actual murder?'

'Yes.'

'Who did it?'

The Russian shook his head. 'No, not till you make the deal.'

'And if we won't agree to the deal?'

'Then I'll shoot someone, then kill myself.' He tapped the gun on the table.

The thread snapped as George's hand jerked. 'Igor, kill yourself if you want to, but why kill someone else? Who? Me? Inspector Malone?'

'Not you, George. You're my friend – or almost. A lapsed believer, but once you were on our side. No, it would probably be Mrs Rockne – no, not your wife,' as George suddenly looked as if, regardless of the threat of the gun, he would hurl himself along the table. 'The boy's mother. Of everyone in this house, she is the most expendable.'

'Is she the one who killed my son?' George's skinny arms, beneath the short sleeves of the T-shirt, were like tensioned hawsers; cords stood out on his thin neck. 'Is she?'

'No names, George, not yet.' The Russian looked at

319

Malone. There was a tiredness about him that Malone had missed when first coming into the kitchen; it gave Malone hope. Tired men, unless they are psychotic, are easier to deal with. 'Well, Inspector, do we discuss the deal? I'll be your witness and you lay no charges against me and give me free passage out of Australia.'

'To Bangkok? To pick up the money and take it somewhere else?' Malone had no interest in what happened to the money, other than its use as a bargaining point. He was working for time, for the shaping in his mind of all the ramifications of a deal. The Rockne and Dunne murders were important, but he had come into this house to rescue his daughter and the Rockne boy and that was the paramount point: 'Let my daughter and Jason go now and then I'll talk.'

'No.'

'You have the rest of us as hostages. How many do you want?'

'I want you all in here till you agree to the deal.'

Malone hesitated, then spread his hands. 'I can't agree to it, Igor.'

'For Chrissakes!' George thumped the table with his fist. 'Jesus, man, what's the problem? Is it the fucking money? Is it because you won't make deals with crims? Christ, you coppers do it all the time – '

'Shut up, George. No, it's not the money and it's not because we don't make deals. But I can't make the decision on this. My boss is outside – he's running the show. I could say okay to whatever Igor's got in mind and my boss could veto it – '

'He wouldn't do it! Jesus, the kids are still in here – '

Malone looked at Dostoyevsky. 'Can I go and talk to him?'

The Russian bit his thick lips, then nodded. 'There's always someone higher up, isn't there? No, you can't go

320

out. Bring him in here. He gave me a phone number when I talked to him before.' He took a piece of paper from his shirt pocket and pushed it across the table. 'Tell him to come in as you did, no gun.'

Malone rose and went out of the kitchen when George told him where the phone was. Dostoyevsky also rose and stood in the kitchen doorway watching Malone as he dialled and waited.

'This is Inspector Malone. Is Chief Super – oh, it's you, Greg . . . No, everything's okay so far. But we have a problem. I think you'd better come in here . . . Mr Dostoyevsky insists, no gun . . . Yes, my daughter and the boy are okay.' Standing in the hallway he could just see into the living room; he caught a glimpse of Olive leaning forward intently. He put his hand over the mouthpiece and looked down the hallway at the Russian. 'I want him to bring someone else in here.'

'Who?'

'Mrs Bodalle.' He couldn't see Dostoyevsky's face against the light from the kitchen, but there was a certain stillness to the tall man's silhouette that told him all he wanted to know. 'I think she might be part of the deal.'

'No!' Olive suddenly appeared in the living-room doorway.

Malone ignored her. 'Well, Igor?'

'Yes. Bring her in.'

Malone took his hand from the mouthpiece. 'Greg, bring Mrs Bodalle with you.'

Random didn't query why: 'We're on our way, Scobie.'

Malone put down the phone. 'Why don't you want Angela here, Olive?'

She shook her head helplessly; he had the feeling that right now she could give him no answers to anything he asked her, even though she had surrendered. She had given up; or almost: 'Forget it, Scobie. Only – '

'Only what?' He was gentle with her.

She half turned her head, but didn't look over her shoulder at Jason and Claire and Sugar in the living room behind her; Malone saw Jason leaning forward, straining to hear what was being said. 'Nothing,' said Olive and went back and sat down beside her son and took his hand.

'Is everything going to be all right, Dad?' Claire sat primly on the edge of her chair, knees together, hands in lap, as she might sit waiting for an interview with Mother Brendan.

'Everything's gonna be all right.' He grinned at her. It was an old joke between them, the quoting of the cliché from every second movie one saw on television. Then he looked along the hallway at Dostoyevsky. 'Chief Superintendent Random is coming. Will I open the front door?'

'Do that, Inspector. But remember, no tricks.'

Malone was suddenly tetchy: 'For Chrissakes, stop harping on that! I want this to go as smoothly as you do!'

He went along the hallway, opened the front door and pushed open the security door as Random and Angela Bodalle came up the front path. He stood aside for them to go in past him; Angela gave him a hard look. He looked out at the lighted street, saw the SPG men still in place, guns at the ready. He raised a hand, gave the thumbs-up sign and closed the door. He would make any deal, give away the whole country if it meant no shots were fired at this house while his daughter was in it.

Random and Angela had stood waiting for him. As he stepped past Angela he caught a strong whiff of expensive perfume; she might not be sweating, but her body heat had risen. He led them into the kitchen, introduced them to Dostoyevsky and George Rockne.

'Are you carrying a gun, Superintendent?' said the Russian.

'No.' Random flipped open his coat. 'Do you want to frisk me?'

'No, I think we can take it that we are men of honour.'

Random looked sceptical, but said nothing, just glanced at Malone, who said, 'Mr Dostoyevsky has a proposition, Chief.'

'Before we get to that,' said Angela, still arrogant, or making a good pretence of it, 'why am I here?'

'That was my suggestion,' said Malone. 'I think when Mr Dostoyevsky tells us his side of the deal, you'll understand. Have I guessed right, Igor?'

'You have, Inspector. Chief Superintendent – ' The Russian, it seemed, was meticulous about rank. 'The deal I want is this. I am not to be charged with bringing the young people here – '

'Kidnapping would be the charge,' said Random coldly and flatly. 'Don't start by watering it down, Mr Dostoyevsky.'

The Russian gave a small acknowledging bow of his head. 'Kidnapping. In return for not charging me, I'll swear that I was a witness to the murder of Will Rockne and I'll identify who did it.'

He flicked a quick glance at Angela, but said nothing. She gazed steadily back at him, as if whatever he had hinted or would have to say meant nothing to her. She's as good as I've ever come up against, Malone thought. She made any so-called Iron Lady look like plastic.

'What else are you demanding?' said Random.

'Not *demanding*. Asking. You're not really interested in me and the money I want back – that's something between me and the impostors in Moscow.'

Random glanced at Malone, but said nothing about Salkov, the representative of the impostors in Moscow. It struck Malone all at once that five and a quarter million dollars could sometimes have no value at all.

'Go on,' said Random. 'What else are you — asking?'

'Free passage to a destination I'll name. I'll give you a sworn statement — '

'That won't be enough, I'm afraid. You'll have to stay here in this country until the murder trial comes to court. Isn't that right, Mrs Bodalle?'

'Thank you for asking me.' She had adopted the defence of being wryly detached. She was totally composed, as if giving advice to a client. Except, Malone thought, that she was her own client and she knew it now. 'A good defence counsel would challenge the statement, would demand the right to cross-examine the witness. Juries like to *see* witnesses, not be shown pieces of paper in lieu of.'

Random was silent a moment. He raised an eyebrow at Malone, who nodded pleadingly. Then: 'All right, Mr Dostoyevsky. If you are prepared to stay in this country till the trial comes up, we'll give you protection and then free passage to wherever you want to go.'

'What about the money?'

This time Random didn't look at Malone. 'We'll draw up a release of the money, whatever the bank demands, signed by Mrs Rockne and her son. I think it will also need to be signed by the daughter.'

'Are you a man of honour, Chief Superintendent?'

'Up to a point,' said Random honestly.

Dostoyevsky smiled, glanced at George Rockne. 'One can't ask for much more than that, can one, George? Not in a capitalist society.'

'Don't push your luck, Igor.'

The Russian nodded, then abruptly sat down heavily, as if he had lost all strength in his legs. 'I'll take your word, sir.' He looked up at Angela, standing with her back to the kitchen stove. 'Mrs Bodalle killed your son, George. I saw it from no more than twenty metres away.'

The two detectives and George Rockne looked at

324

Angela. Her expression had not changed, except that she glanced rather pityingly at Dostoyevsky. 'He's insane,' she said coolly.

'No.' George was more than merely cool; there was a chill to him. 'I've spent the last two hours listening to him. He may be crazy about what he expects to happen in Russia, but he's a long way from being insane. Did you kill my son?'

'Easy, George.' Malone moved towards the older man's end of the table, but he kept his eyes on both Dostoyevsky and Angela. He noticed that Random had moved to stand with his back to the draining board under the windows, where the supper cutlery, knives among it, lay like a small heap of shining steel guts. 'Could you get us a writing pad?'

'No,' said Dostoyevsky. 'Don't write anything down yet. I'll give it all to you on tape, when Mrs Bodalle isn't present. All I'll say in front of her is that I saw her kill Will Rockne.'

Random said, 'You know the drill, Mrs Bodalle. Anything you may say, et cetera, et cetera . . .'

'You're wasting your time and the taxpayers' money,' she said.

Random shrugged. 'You lawyers would know all about that.'

George Rockne had not taken his eyes off Angela from the moment Dostoyevsky had named her as the killer. At first he seemed more puzzled than angry, but now his face had settled into a mask, cracked by the lines in his leathery skin.

'Why?' he said quietly. 'Why, for Chrissake?'

She stared at him as if he were a stranger who had no right to ask such a question. Then she turned her back on him and took a step towards the doorway. Random stepped quickly in front of her.

'Stay here, Mrs Bodalle . . . Scobie, do you want to bring Olive in here now? But not her son – keep him inside.'

Malone went into the living room, brushing by Angela again; the smell of her perfume had thickened, was almost overpowering, like a woman in the heat of love-making. He stood at the living-room door and said, 'Olive, would you come out to the kitchen? No, not you, Jay,' as the boy rose. 'Just your mother.'

'I have to sign the release of the money – '

'Later, Jay. Come on, Olive.'

She stood up reluctantly, stiffly, like a much older woman, arthritic with dread. Malone ushered her out to the kitchen. She paused as she came into the room, looked at Angela but made no attempt to move towards her. Instead she looked back at Malone, as if he had suddenly become a friend. In that instant he saw that she was terrified, that she had come to the end of a road that she had not bothered to explore beforehand.

'We are arresting Mrs Bodalle for the murder of your husband,' said Random. 'We are also arresting you, Mrs Rockne, with conspiracy to the same murder. If you have anything to say – '

'Keep your mouth shut!' Angela's threat was unmistakable; Malone felt Olive back into him. 'I'll handle these fools!'

Chapter Twelve

1

Statement by Igor Sergeyvich Dostoyevsky, taken at Maroubra police station. Present: Det-Inspector S. Malone, Det-Sergeant R. Clements, Det-Sergeant C. Ellsworth.

'I followed Will Rockne and his wife in their car out to the car park at Maroubra Surf Club on the Saturday night in question . . .'

Inspector Malone: 'Why were you following them?'

Dostoyevsky: 'Late on the Friday I had found out by accident that Rockne had transferred the money I had given him, the five and a quarter million dollars, from a trust account into his own name. I wanted to know why. I tried to contact him all day on the Saturday, but he seemed to be avoiding me – he would never come to the phone, his wife or his daughter would say he was out. I saw him and his wife go out on the Saturday night, up to the school further up Coogee Bay Road. I was going to wait for him outside the school, but it is right opposite the Randwick police station and I didn't know how he was going to react when I met him. So I drove back and waited outside their house. They came back at, I think, around ten fifteen or so, but after pulling up, he drove on. I followed them out to Maroubra.

'They pulled into the car park outside the surf club. There were a lot of other cars parked there. I stopped my car in the street, got out and walked towards them – I went towards them from the rear, walking between the other cars. Then I saw Mrs Rockne get out of the car, they sounded as if they were arguing, and she walked away from the car, their Volvo, and just stood. Rockne didn't follow her, he stayed in the car with the driver's door open.'

Malone: 'Were the lights on? The car's headlights?'

Dostoyevsky: 'No, he had turned them off. I walked towards him, but stopped again. I was beside a van, I can't remember what sort except it had lots of graffiti on it, when I heard voices arguing in a car on the other side of the van. I couldn't hear what they were saying, they kept their voices low. Then I saw a woman come out from the other side of the van and go towards the Rockne car.'

Malone: 'Do you know now who the woman was?'

Dostoyevsky: 'Yes, it was Mrs Bodalle, Angela Bodalle. She went up to the car and Rockne turned towards her, went to get out. I couldn't see whether he was surprised or not. Mrs Bodalle had a gun, it had a long barrel. She fired the one shot and from the muffled sound I knew the long barrel was really a silencer.'

Malone: 'What did she do then?'

Dostoyevsky: 'She came back to the car on the other side of the van, the other side from where I stood. I saw her face and I know now who she was.'

Malone: 'She didn't approach or call out to Mrs Rockne?'

Dostoyevsky: 'No. As far as I could tell, Mrs Rockne had her back turned to the shooting – I don't know, perhaps she didn't want to see it. The car on the other side of the van then drove away – as it did so, I saw Mrs Bodalle in the driver's seat and a man was sitting beside her. As soon as it had gone, Mrs Rockne came back to their car, the Volvo. Then she screamed.'

Malone: 'What then?'

Dostoyevsky: 'I thought it best that I leave. I went back

to my car, out in the street, and drove away.'

Malone: 'The man who was with the woman – did you recognize him?'

Dostoyevsky: 'No. I'd never seen him before nor since.'

Malone: 'Would that be him?' (*Photo of Garry Dunne shown*)

Dostoyevsky: 'It could be. I wouldn't swear to it.'

Malone: 'What sort of car were they in?'

Dostoyevsky: 'I'm not sure. It looked like a small Japanese car, but I couldn't be sure. It was grey, I think.'

Malone: 'But you have no doubt that the person you saw shoot Mr Rockne was Angela Bodalle?'

Dostoyevsky: 'None at all. It was Angela Bodalle.'

Statement by Olive Mary Rockne:

'Is this going to be made public? Are my children going to read it? . . . Oh God! (*Breaks down. Tape disconnected for three minutes*) . . . I'm sorry . . . Well, I can't say when it was actually agreed we had to kill Will – my husband. Yes, I did agree, I admit to that. It was because – well, mainly, I suppose, because my husband wouldn't give me a divorce. I used to love him, our marriage was reasonably happy up till, I dunno, I suppose about three years ago. We managed to conceal it from the children that we weren't getting on – at least, I think we did. We still slept together, but sex isn't love, is it?

'Will was always putting me down. I don't mean he ever laid a hand on me, he never did that, but he could hurt me in other ways. Then I met Angela – do I have to say her full name? Angela Bodalle. I was fascinated by her at first – she was everything I wasn't. Or so I thought. Then I fell in love with her, really and truly in love. More in love, I think, than I'd ever been with Will. It's a shock, or it was to me, when you find out you are as much a lesbian as a heterosexual. Maybe it isn't to some women, but it was to

329

me. But I didn't fight it, not when I fell in love with Angela. I hate her now, now I've found out so many things about her. But I did love her. You men probably won't understand that. I wish you had a woman in here, a woman police officer . . . No, it doesn't matter now. You all seem sympathetic enough. A bloody sight more sympathetic than Will was! . . . Maybe you'll all learn something from women about this . . . Where was I? Oh yes, Angela. No, I didn't know she was the one who actually shot my husband. Not till, well, after you'd arrested me . . .

'We had paid Mr Dunne to do it and Angela drove him out to Maroubra that night. But he wouldn't do it, he said there were too many cars in the car park, there might be people in them. There were, weren't there? That man, the actuary you told me about who saw me that night, him and his girlfriend . . . Anyway, we had paid Mr Dunne, I gave him five thousand dollars and Angela gave him five thousand. When he refused to do it, we asked for our money back. But you don't ask a hitman for your money back, did you know that? It's a non-refundable down payment, like schools ask you for now when you register your child. Why am I laughing? (*Breaks down. Tape disconnected for four minutes*) . . . Afterwards, he phoned me and tried to blackmail me – he wanted more money, even though he hadn't done the actual killing. That's a hard word to say when you're talking about your husband – *killing* . . . No, I'm okay, Scobie. I'll be all right, don't turn it off . . . Mr Dunne said he had lost his job through us . . .

'Angela did tell me that she had kept the gun and one of the silencers – Mr Dunne had made two silencers. She said she kept the gun in case he tried any funny business with us – like he did, with the blackmail. She also said she had taken the original silencer – I never saw any of this, the gun or the silencers – she took it back to Hamill's and dumped it in a box there. She did that on the Monday morning, when she took her car, the Ferrari, there for servicing – that was her excuse for turning up there on the Monday. She thinks of everything – but then you probably have seen that. When she told me she'd killed Mr Dunne – and his wife, too, poor woman . . . I, I dunno, I began to see another side to her. I still loved her, but . . . Women can love men who do terrible things – it happens all the time. Women can love women who do the same terrible things. But then . . . Well, then, things started to get out of hand immediately after the – the killing of my husband. The Russian money, for instance. That was a shock – at first I thought it was God playing an ironic joke. I believe in God. I'm not a *good* Catholic, I suppose I'm what you'd call a convenient Catholic. A lot of people use religion as a convenience, don't you think? It helps them convince themselves they're truly sorry for whatever they've done wrong. I *think* I'm sorry I killed Will. I *know* I am, if only for the children's sake. But if everything had gone right, if we'd got away with it and I hadn't found out about that dark side to Angela and had been happy with her – I don't know, maybe I wouldn't be sorry . . .

'All I ask now is that they don't put me in the same prison as her – I don't think I could bear that . . . As for Jason and Shelley – I just hope I haven't lost them. Not for ever . . .'

Statement by Angela Bodalle:
'Whatever they have said, I refuse to answer any questions on the fantasies of those two liars.'

Summer had come and almost gone, lingering on with high temperatures and high humidity into March. The football season had started again and players were collapsing from heat exhaustion while administrators sat in air-conditioned committee rooms and planned more ways of making more dollars. The USSR had gone the way of a dozen other empires and various peoples in its republics had discovered there were long-buried hatreds of each other that were far more virulent than any hatred they had felt for those in the West. The recession worldwide had got deeper and old men came out of the closets of history to tell how tough life had been in the Great Depression and that the spoiled generations of the postwar years 'ain't seen nothin' yet'. From one end of Africa to the other, if people were not dying of starvation they were dying of AIDS or from the guns of rival tribes. Americans were finding that their President spent most of his time looking outwards instead of inwards, where their problems lay, and for the first time in years the White House went a paler shade of white at the possibility that the President might not be re-elected. Australia had a new Prime Minister, an abrasive man who rubbed voters up the wrong way but at least stirred them out of the smug apathy they had long thought was the true way to happiness. History stumbled on through its accidents, while in the news, which may or may not be history, men and women passed judgement on the criminals among them.

Igor Dostoyevsky, having given damning evidence, was given free passage out of Australia and disappeared into Oblivion, with which there are no treaties of extradition. Olive Rockne received a life sentence for conspiracy to murder her husband and Angela Bodalle received a double life sentence, her papers marked never to be released, for the murders of Will Rockne, Garry Dunne and Claudia Dunne.

Malone walked out of the Central Criminal Court, blinking for a moment in the bright sunlight. After a lifetime of going without them, he had started wearing dark glasses last summer; but he never wore them on duty. He knew from the experience of questioning crims who wore dark glasses that hidden eyes concealed hidden answers. This afternoon he wanted to wear an open face, no matter how difficult it might be.

He saw the Rockne family standing in a group, doing their best to turn their backs on the photographers snapping at them. Jason detached himself from the small group and for a moment it looked as if he was going to hit the photographers nearest him, but he walked right through them and came towards Malone. The latter braced himself.

Jason pulled up, said nothing, just stared at Malone. He was dressed in blazer, slacks, a blue shirt and a plain tie; not his school tie, Malone remarked. In the background two photographers and a TV cameraman came forward, but Clements suddenly appeared in front of them and said something. Whatever he said, threatening or appealing, had its effect: the men with their cameras turned back.

At last Malone said, 'I'm sorry, Jay. It had to happen.'

The boy nodded. 'I know, Mr Malone. Shelley and I don't blame you. Life, that's a bloody long time when you actually *say* it. How long will Mum have to serve?'

Malone shrugged, not wanting to give the boy too much hope. 'Depends. I think it usually works out they serve only about eleven years.'

'Only? Jesus! I'll be twenty-nine, going on. Probably married, with kids. No, not with kids,' he said almost savagely.

'Jay — ' He hesitated; it wasn't his place to tell someone else's son what to do with his life. And yet: 'Jay, don't start now planning the rest of your life. What's happened to you and Shelley won't necessarily happen to your kids.'

'Do any of us know what we'll do or be doing ten or twenty years from now? I'll bet when Mum married Dad — she wasn't much older than me — she never dreamed she'd . . .' A big hand gestured.

'What's happening to you and Shelley? I mean, where are you going to live?'

'It hasn't been easy. Deciding, I mean. Gran Carss wanted to look after us, but I couldn't stand that. Neither could Shelley, she told me. So we're gunna live with Pa and Sugar. Or they're gunna live with us — they've sold their house out at Cabramatta and they're coming to live with us in Coogee. Gran didn't like it, but she's accepted it. It would never have worked out, she knows that. She still thinks Mum should've got off, that Mrs Bodalle was the real murderer.'

He had been looking down at his shoe scratching the ground; but now he looked up at Malone. The latter dodged the unspoken question: what do you think? He said, 'You should be okay with your grandfather and Mrs Rockne. Sugar.'

'Yeah. Well — well, I can't say thanks, can I? But I meant what I said — we don't blame you. Oh, give my regards to Claire. Tell her I'll call her. If that's okay with you?' he added dubiously.

'Come around any time, Jay. You'll be welcome.'

'Thanks. You wanna come over and speak to Pa?'

Malone looked across to where George Rockne, the porter of broken dreams, stood slightly apart from Mrs Carss, Olive's sister, Shelley and Sugar. Even though he stood only a few feet from the women, he looked a lonely figure, like a man in a landscape where all familiar features had been obliterated.

'No, Jay. Maybe I'll drop in to see him when he moves to Coogee. Take care.'

He walked away and in a moment Clements caught up with him. 'You going home or coming back to the office?'

Malone looked at his watch. 'I think I'll go home. School will be out pretty soon — I think I'll collect Claire and Maureen from Holy Spirit, then go and get Tom at Marcellin. I'll buy 'em all a drink at Brick's.'

Clements looked sideways at him. 'Family's great, isn't it?'

'Sometimes,' said Malone, but didn't look back.

Kirribilli
August 1991–March 1992

☐	REBEL Bernard Cornwell	0-00-617920-7	£4.99
☐	THE DARK SIDE OF THE HILL Rodney Stone	0-586-21738-X	£4.99
☐	ALPHA 7 Mark Joseph	0-00-647260-5	£4.99
☐	HIGH HUNT David Eddings	0-00-647593-0	£4.99
☐	CORMORANT Douglas Terman	0-00-647309-1	£5.99
☐	DUE NORTH Mitchell Smith	0-00-647642-2	£4.99
☐	NIGHTWING Martin Cruz Smith	0-00-647908-1	£4.99
☐	ALONG CAME A SPIDER James Patterson	0-00-647615-5	£4.99

All these books are available from your local bookseller or can be ordered direct from the publishers.

To order direct just tick the titles you want and fill in the form below:

Name: _____

Address: _____

_____

Postcode: _____

Send to: HarperCollins Mail Order, Dept 8, HarperCollins *Publishers*, Westerhill Road, Bishopbriggs, Glasgow G64 2QT.

Please enclose a cheque or postal order or your authority to debit your Visa/Access account –

Credit card no: _____

Expiry date: _____

Signature: _____

– to the value of the cover price plus:

UK & BFPO: Add £1.00 for the first and 25p for each additional book ordered.

Overseas orders including Eire, please add £2.95 service charge.

Books will be sent by surface mail but quotes for airmail despatches will be given on request.

24 HOUR TELEPHONE ORDERING SERVICE FOR ACCESS/VISA CARDHOLDERS –

TEL: GLASGOW 041-772 2281 or LONDON 081-307 4052